RANSOM for a Song

Also by Phyllis Clark Nichols

THE FAMILY PORTRAIT
The Christmas Portrait – Book One
The Birthday Portrait – Book Two

THE ROCKWATER SUITE
Return of the Song – Book One
Freedom of the Song – Book Two

Christmas at Grey Sage
Silent Days, Holy Night

RANSOM for a Song

The ROCKWATER Suite

—

Book Three

Phyllis Clark Nichols

Ransom for a Song: Book #3 in The Rockwater Suite

Published by Southern Stories Publishing

ISBN: 978-1-7344522-3-5 (paperback)
ISBN: 978-1-7344522-4-2 (ebook)
Print Edition

Cover art and design by Jeff Gifford

Dedication

For all my Friends who have journeyed with me
to Guatemala through the years,
compassionate, selfless, tireless men and women and youth
who worked among "the least of these"
to bring help to the helpless and hope to the hopeless, and
who left their beautiful soulprints on other souls
in the Highlands of Guatemala.

Prelude

Thursday night, February 12, 2009

Caroline grasped the low-hanging limb to keep her face above the rushing, muddy water of the swollen Guatemalan river. Clinging for her life and his, she clenched David's arm, her nails sinking into his muscular flesh, but he was slipping as the current and debris pulled his inert body from her.

The water was too powerful.

He was gone.

The scream echoed inside her as if in a hollow chamber and was the loudest sound she ever heard, but the wind and the torrent muted her wailing. She wanted to let go of the limb and follow David, wherever that might be. Miles of raging river or maybe heaven. Nothing could be worse than this hell of hanging on, just waiting for the flood to overcome her. But she instinctively held on, gasping to breathe as time lost meaning.

"Caroline."

She thought she heard her name but did not respond.

"Caroline. Caroline, look at me."

His voice. Caroline felt the sun on her face as she lifted her head. Her eyes opened mechanically, like her childhood baby doll whose lids shut when she was laid down and opened when she was picked up. A scant look showed calm, clear water reflecting a blue sky. Green branches had sprouted from the dead limb that had been her lifeline. Butterflies, thousands of blue ones, swirled around her, almost lifting her from the water. She listened for his voice again and strained to see.

"CC? It's me, love." He paused. "Storm's over. You must let go." He was on the riverbank, in clean jeans and his favorite University of Georgia T-shirt, motioning for her to get out of the water.

"David, you're here? You're okay?" She let go of the limb and climbed ashore.

"That's right, my love. I'm fine. Storm's over, and you're alive." He stood in the sunlight, as winsome as ever.

She had never been able to resist touching the soft brown curl at his temple, but when she stepped toward him and reached for his hair, he backed farther into sunlight so bright she could no longer see him.

"David. David?" She inched closer to the memory of where he was, the light moving as she moved, but always the same distance from her. "David, where are you?" She twirled around, her eyes gleaning the green hills for a glimpse of him. He wasn't there. "David? Don't leave me," she whispered.

A familiar melody emanated from the stream as if to summon her. She turned to hear. "Where are you? I know you're here, but I can't see you." She dropped to her knees at the water's edge and closed her eyes. The music was distracting and so enchanting. She breathed deeply to inhale its beauty and then opened her eyes. She stared into the still surface of the water, now a liquid mirror reflecting her square jaw, her blue eyes, and hair like her father's, near-black and wavy.

The water also reflected his image behind her. "Go ahead. Step into the water, my love. It's time."

"But I can't. Not without you."

"Yes, yes, you can. You must cross the stream, and I must go my way. I'm where I am supposed to be, Caroline, and soon you will be too."

A single, silent tear fell from her eye into the water, causing a ripple that moved in slow motion to the rhythm of the music. When the surface lay as smooth as glass again, David's likeness was gone. In its place was the reflection of another man across the stream. He was older and taller, with dark hair graying at the temples, and dressed in a business suit. "Come, Caroline."

Not David's voice, but familiar. It was that edgy baritone she'd first heard on the telephone. "Roderick?"

"Yes. I'm here." He pointed to the pool. "See the stones? Remember? That's why we call it 'Rockwater.' Just one step at a time, and come to me." He extended his arm. "I'm waiting for you."

"Roderick?"

Chapter 1

Concert and Cab Ride

The sound of Caroline's own voice woke her. She lay still until her racing heart slowed and synchronized with the ticking clock on her bedside table and the tea olive branches brushing the window ushered her back into reality. She was in the bedroom of her studio apartment at Twin Oaks. Tomorrow she would drive an hour to the University of Georgia to perform a recital, where she would see Roderick.

That was real.

She raised herself up on her elbows and looked at the clock. Four thirty-three. She removed the layers of blankets and sat on the side of the bed, feet fumbling for her slippers. More reality. David had been killed in floodwaters in Guatemala seven years ago, but a dream about him could still wash her down in sweat even on the coldest night in February.

The clock was set for six, and she was about as likely to go back to sleep as David was to walk through the terrace door, so she grabbed her robe and headed to the kitchen. It was so cold she thought she might see her breath if the light was on, but she was comfortable in the darkness. She put on the teakettle and walked back down the hallway to return the thermostat to its daytime setting. Since childhood, she'd hated sleeping with the heat on.

So, what would she do with an hour and a half? It was too early for any real news, and infomercials didn't interest her, so she punched the button for instant Mendelssohn. His hypnotic melodies would calm her. Maybe she'd turn on a light and read or go over her checklist again. What a perfect time for a fire, but no firewood.

Her last student had left the studio at six thirty the night before, and she had run up to the main house for a quick dinner with Sam and Angel, lingering longer than intended over a cup of hot chocolate and a slice of Hattie's Italian Cream cake. The temperature had dropped another eight degrees before she got back to the studio. Two hours of piano practice and one steaming, hot shower later, she had turned off the heat and gone to bed. But the dreams . . .

She steeped the tea an extra minute. On her way to her favorite chair, she balanced her teacup and picked up the journal from her desk. The worn velveteen-covered swivel rocker had belonged to Grand Ma'am, and its once-firm cushions—now soft—hugged her, almost like her grandmother had.

She sipped her tea and read the first paragraph of her notes . . . twice. Reading wasn't working. Neither was Mendelssohn. The dream had been too graphic and too real, almost as if David had actually appeared to her. And then Roderick.

Caroline put down the journal, picked up her cup, and walked to the large windows next to the piano. Dark sky provided no light to see the wind's effect, but she could hear it and feel it. The night's chill seeped in around the shriveling window frame like an old man's breath.

Stetson. She smelled Stetson. That's what David had worn. His bottle of cologne had had its own place on her dresser until Betsy, her best friend, had coaxed her into getting rid of it after five years. Betsy said she needed to let go of the past.

The whiff of Stetson. The dream, too vivid. His voice. Roderick's reflection. Guatemala. Rockwater. Why now? Why, after all this time, just when she was beginning to let go?

Morning light would bring new energy, but for now she stood at this familiar window and imagined Roderick sleeping again under Kentucky skies after his trip to New York. Acer would be flying him to Athens this afternoon. Down in Ferngrove, her parents and brothers would rise early to get ready for the day's drive to the university.

She walked into the kitchen and put down her teacup. Through the window over the sink, she saw the lights were already on at the main house up the hill. Angel would be in the kitchen, and that thick Louisiana brew Sam labeled coffee would be percolating soon as it did every morning about this time, and Sam would be starting a fire in the library. The Meadow's ante-bellum home was beautiful and relatively cool in the Georgia summers but virtually impossible to heat.

Sam and Angel would be riding to Athens with Gretchen and Bella, who were most likely still burrowed under homemade quilts until Bella's internal, never-faltering alarm clock woke her. Gretchen had told Caroline how her granddaughter rose every morning, made exactly thirty-two barefooted steps from her bedroom to the upright piano, and began to play. The instrument was Bella's link from her autistic world to the world around her.

All the important people in Caroline's life were moving

their own lives around today so they could attend her performance, and she was determined not to disappoint them. She took the last sip of tea, sat down at the piano, and played intensely for the next hour as though her playing would coax the sun from its hiding spot below the horizon.

Daylight, another cup of tea with a day-old cinnamon bun from Bobbie's Bakery, a shower to warm her bones, a check of her packed bag, bundling up to stay warm, and Caroline was in the car. She removed the thick glove from her hand in order to put the key in the ignition and to insert the practice CD.

The car was slower getting started than usual. She pressed the accelerator, careful not to flood it. The engine sputtered, and the smoke from the exhaust pipe would have killed mosquitoes had there been any on this cold morning. She needed a new car, but her earnings as a piano and voice teacher in Moss Point provided only a living, with a designated monthly sum going into a retirement account. Single and twenty-nine, she had to think ahead. She didn't want to add a car payment to her list of expenses, in spite of her father's advice. There was hardly any place in Moss Point that she couldn't walk to, and she drove to Athens only a couple of times a month and down to Ferngrove to visit her parents a few times a year. That kind of driving was no justification for the purchase of a new car.

She drove carefully as always. It was her nature to be cautious about everything, but especially this morning since the news reported possible patches of ice on the road. She hummed along with the lyrical melody. The music had lived in her head—she had played it, recorded it, and listened to it so many times—but it still amazed her that it was her composition, her creation from its first simple, one-fingered phrase to three movements for solo piano with expansive orchestration.

More than a trickle of water had gone under the bridge—a covered bridge outside of Lexington, Kentucky—since the original melodic line took shape on her first visit to Rockwater. Her quest to find her childhood 1902 Hazelton Brothers piano had led her to Roderick Adair and to his family's estate in the Bluegrass region of Kentucky last summer.

Since last April, she had discovered her piano and Roderick. Or, as things were turning out, perhaps they'd discovered each other. Since David's death, Roderick had been the first and only man who entered her morning thoughts and her last thoughts before going to sleep at night. Her stale, quiet life was beginning to hold music—real music—again, and color, like the new growth on the dead limb she had clung to in last night's dream.

Her fingers rhythmically tapped the steering wheel, and she hummed with the violin as it introduced the second theme. Hearing the rise in that melodic phrase brought thoughts of Bella, the platinum-haired, green-eyed adolescent musical savant who'd had the whole town of Moss Point on edge this time last year. The police department and all her neighbors had been on the lookout for the intruder who had broken into Caroline's studio and who was creeping at night through holes in the fence surrounding the Twin Oaks property. When the young Bella was discovered as the mysterious snooper, the excitement abated, but not for long.

Caroline's fingers pounded harder on the steering wheel as she thought of Ernesto Silva, Bella's abusive grandfather, who had beaten her and her grandmother almost to death last October. He was in prison now, and Gretchen and Bella were free. Big changes in their lives too.

She wondered how Bella would react to being back on campus and in the recital hall for the first time since her introduction to the American public at a press conference there last November. Since that time, specialists from multiple disciplines had vied for access to Bella. The University of Georgia's offer to provide housing and an education for her had been matched by an offer from Duke University, where Roderick's sister, Dr. Sarah McCollum taught.

Caroline had spent many nights thinking of all the broken pieces of lives that had come together over the last few months, just when each needed the other. She couldn't imagine how different Bella's discovery would have been if she hadn't met Roderick and Sarah.

Caroline slowed the car and reached for the volume knob. The strident cymbal and bellowing bass announced the sound-painted storm of the third movement. The humming stopped. No lyrical line, yet music. She knew the storm would subside in roughly one hundred twenty-eight measures, and the melody of peaceful waters would return with the entwining of the musical themes of the first two movements.

The suite finished, and the recording of Mendelssohn replaced the rehearsal CD. Its normal hypnotic effect had not worked at four forty-five this morning, but maybe it would work in the daylight. Caroline drove the last half hour, her fingers playing the steering wheel along with Horowitz.

Pulling into the parking space in front of the library and switching off the car, she looked at her watch. Eight fifteen. The library was open. She needed to return a couple of books and search for two journal articles. She buttoned her coat and reached for the scarf and hat Angel had knitted for her. Drawing the hat over her ears, she covered as much of her dark shoulder-length hair as she could. The damp air had made her curls more unruly than usual. She locked the car and hurried down the sidewalk, which was lined with trees, their limbs now naked from winter's abduction of their leaves.

———•———

Late Friday afternoon, February 13, 2009

The cab driver slammed on brakes and blew his horn as the blue truck swerved around him, picked up speed, and changed lanes again. "Everybody's going somewhere, and they're all in a big hurry. Now tell me again where you're going."

Roderick repeated, "University campus, Hodgson Hall, please." He pulled the Italian-leather wallet from his tuxedo pocket. "And I hate to ask it of you, but could you hurry?"

The driver looked at Roderick in his rear-view mirror. "Guess I could. You running late or something?" The driver's dark eyes shifted back to the road.

"Yes, and late will not do this evening." Weather conditions had caused a flight delay. No time to wait for Acer to secure the plane and rent a car. Acer would have to take care of things and join him at the concert. Roderick had taken the first cab he saw.

"Well, mister, sometimes you're late. Sometimes you're early, and sometimes you just don't get there at all." He paused. "Yeah, life's a real struggle, ain't it?"

"It certainly can be." In a designer suit, just having stepped off his private plane, Roderick thought his struggles might be different from the cabby's, but nonetheless his privileged life had not been without sorrows. He hoped that was about to change. The piece of folded parchment he had carried in his wallet since Christmas felt smooth and familiar in his hands. He unfolded it and read it as he had many times in the last six weeks.

You are invited as the honored guest for the debut performance of

Rockwater Suite

. . . A moment in time where life, spirit, and music flow freely . . .

Composed and performed by Caroline Carlyle, pianist

Hodgson Hall on the University of Georgia campus

February 13, 2009, at 8:00 p.m.

Life, spirit, and music had stopped abruptly more than once in his lifetime, but they flowed freely again every moment he was in her presence.

The driver whined when he spoke and snatched Roderick from his thoughts. "If I say so myself, you don't look like a man who knows much about problems."

"You can be quite certain no man has ever lived without problems."

Right turn onto East Campus Drive. Almost there. He folded the parchment, returned it to its place behind his favorite snapshot of Caroline, and took out a bill before putting his wallet back in his inside coat pocket next to the sealed envelope. Stretching out his right leg, he checked his pants pocket for the red velvet bag and fingered its contents.

From the looks of the fog and plunging temperatures, Lilah, his housekeeper, had been right again. She had insisted on his wool trench coat when he left Rockwater. He took it from the seat next to him as they pulled in front of the performing arts center where streams of people shedding overcoats filed in through all the doors.

The cab stopped, and the driver punched the meter. "Well, looks like if you're late, you're not by yourself. Must be something big going on tonight. That'll be twenty-three fifty, mister."

"I'm on time, and you're right. Something big is happening tonight. Thanks for getting me here." Roderick shoved the fifty-dollar bill into the cabby's hand and got out of the car. "Keep the change."

He stood on the sidewalk, putting on his overcoat and gloves and watching the driver kiss the bill and smile, then walked briskly to the concert hall. Caroline would be backstage while the front-row seats were being filled with her parents and her brothers and their families coming in from Ferngrove. Sam and Angel and Gretchen and Bella would already be seated. Angel had phoned him earlier in the day with the news that a half dozen mothers of Caroline's piano students were surprising her by bringing an entourage of about thirty.

Dr. Annabelle Martin, professor and Caroline's teacher, greeted Roderick in the lobby. Dr. Martin was Caroline's connection to the university community and was trying to persuade her to return to the university as a piano teacher and begin her doctoral studies in the fall. Roderick had hopes of changing those plans, but he wasn't quite ready to reveal them yet.

"Hello, Mr. Adair. How very nice to see you again."

He took her fragile hand that had played the piano for close to seventy years. "Why, thank you, Dr. Martin. It is indeed my pleasure to be here and to see you, and I assume it gives you greater pleasure to hear your protégé perform this evening."

"You are correct, and I suppose correctness is a necessity in my line of work and yours. It will be a glorious evening." She took his arm, worked her way through the crowd, and showed him to his front-and-center reserved seat between Angel and Martha Carlyle, Caroline's mother.

Caroline's father introduced him to her brothers, James and Thomas, and their families. Roderick shook their hands and kissed the cheek of Caroline's mother, Martha. Sam remained seated and extended the hand that wasn't propped on his walking cane. Roderick leaned to kiss Angel on the cheek as well. Next to Sam stood Gretchen and Bella. Reserved but with warmth, Gretchen hugged him before Roderick cautiously approached Bella, took her hand, and awaited her response. Her arms went around his waist, and she squeezed him hard. He winked at his sister, Sarah, and her husband, George, who were seated behind him on the second row amid Caroline's students and their parents from Moss Point.

Bella backed away and gave him the thumbs-up sign. "Bel Canto sings a new song. Bel Canto sings a new song." Bella started to sing syllables in a very high-pitched voice. Gretchen immediately stood to silence her.

"So did you teach Bel Canto the new song?" Roderick whispered in Bella's ear.

Bella continued to stand and rocked back and forth, never looking at Roderick when she replied with a whisper, "Bel Canto teach me the new song. Bel Canto teach me."

Roderick smiled and winked at Sarah again. Bel Canto, a yellow canary, had been his Christmas present to Bella. She had enjoyed the canaries in the aviary at Emory Hospital last fall when she and her grandmother were recovering from their injuries after Ernesto's beating and had learned to imitate their songs just as she could reproduce anything Caroline played on the piano. He had no doubt Bella was playing the *Rockwater Suite* by now, even though she could not read.

No time to see Caroline before the performance, but he had the weekend in Moss Point to look forward to. He folded his coat over the back of his chair and took his seat to wait her stage entrance.

The applause started when Caroline was two steps onto the stage but quieted when she sat at the piano. She was stunning in a simple black gown. Not the pink cloud of a dress from her first parlor concert at Rockwater last July nor the indigo velvet she had worn there at Christmas, just a black, lace-sleeved gown tailored for the moment. Her petite frame was dwarfed at the concert grand, surrounded by the empty orchestra chairs.

The first half of her program was from her piano repertoire—Mendelssohn, Bach, Chopin, and Debussy. He thought he'd never heard her play so well, not even in Kentucky when he was completely captivated by her and her music.

Roderick's eyes never left her. He memorized the wisps of misbehaving curls at her temple and the nape of her neck. He felt the music's cadence and observed the rhythm of the muscles in her arms—tense and relax and tense again—as she became one with the instrument. He watched the slight rise of her body from the bench with the dynamic crescendos and increased intensity of the music. She was exquisite.

After the first half and a brief intermission, the orchestra members took their seats and began their ritual of tuning, all becoming quiet when Caroline and the conductor walked onto the stage. Roderick had anxiously awaited the debut of the *Rockwater Suite* since December when Caroline gave him the invitation as his Christmas gift.

The music began, and Caroline struck the chords that needed to be struck and caressed the clean, tender melodies that called for caressing. He listened and relived their walk to the trout stream, their picnic in the garden, and the dramatic thunderstorm that had served as a backdrop for her parlor concert. Each scene had been preserved with a melody and painted with the harmonies of the strings and woodwinds. It truly was as her invitation read: "a moment in time where life, spirit, and music flow freely." Rockwater was his home, and if the weekend went as Roderick planned, it would be Caroline's home before next Christmas.

Chapter 2

Homecoming Surprise

Saturday in Moss Point

The back-porch door slammed, and Hattie, apron blowing in the wind, was halfway down the pebbled drive before the two cars came to a stop. She bypassed Sam and Angel and headed for the second car. Roderick got out on the driver's side.

"Good mornin', Mr. Adair." She tackled him with a hug and whispered in his left ear, "Everything's fine—just like you wanted." She turned to Caroline. "And who's that you got in the back seat?"

Caroline opened the car door and motioned for Bella to get out. "Bella just couldn't part with Roderick this morning. She's been his shadow since before breakfast."

"Smart girl, she is. It'd be a dumb, numb gal who'd let this man out of her sight." Hattie put her arm around Caroline as they walked up the drive to the house. "I want to hear all about it—the concert, the party afterward, and the hotel. So tell me, Miss Blue Eyes, how was the concert?"

"Maybe you should ask someone else."

"I know that's right. You'd just start picking it apart like I plucked that chicken this mornin'." She raised her voice so that Angel could her. "Miss Angel, how was the concert?"

Angel was almost to the back-porch steps, holding on to Sam's arm and walking slower than usual. She turned, "Perfection, absolute perfection, and so was the party at the hotel afterward."

"Uh-huh. Just like that lunch that's almost ready to jump on the table." She hugged Caroline to her, as though shielding her from a fierce north wind, and stopped on the steps to hold the door for them. "Come on inside, everybody. There's a fire crackling in the library, and Mr. Adair, your room's ready, and I'm gonna ring the lunch bell before you can get all these jackets off."

After nearly forty-five years, Hattie still took great pleasure in putting together a meal at Twin Oaks for Sam and Angel. Seeing how short of breath Angel was while walking up the driveway this morning reminded her that every day and every meal they shared was a gift.

Hattie circled them in the kitchen and sputtered directions. "Okay, Mr. Sam, you show Mr. Adair to his room, and Miss Angel, you sit down right here at the breakfast table. Gretchen, you and Caroline can help me. Bella, you just sing me a song. A pretty one."

Gretchen waited at the sink for Caroline to wash her hands. "Oh, Hattie, she hardly needs encouragement to sing. Did she sing all the way home, Caroline?"

Caroline dried her hands. "We all sang on the way home. Nothing much sweeter than Bella's voice."

"Oh, that's sweet all right, but I can think of one or two things sweeter." Hattie laughed her raucous, I-know-something-you-don't-know laugh and gently pinched Caroline's cheek.

In the time it took for the butter to melt on the cornbread, Hattie corralled everyone to the table. Sam said grace like he had pronounced verdicts in his courtroom for over forty years, loud and distinct. When the "n" on "amen" had resonated, Hattie stood and with great pride recited the menu. "Today, we're dining on chicken and dumplings, turnip greens, garden pea salad, baked sweet potatoes, homemade pickles, cornbread with Ned and Fred's honey, and . . ." She turned to the breakfront behind her and reached for something covered with a tea towel. "And for you, Mr. Adair, a platter of fried chicken." Hattie's smile was wide and bright against her coffee-colored skin, with teeth straighter than those in the short comb Sam carried in his pocket.

"Why, Hattie, you remembered how much I enjoyed your chicken last summer!" He took the platter from her and set it on the table in the spot she had obviously reserved near his plate. What are we waiting for?" He stuck his fork in the largest piece on top.

Hattie took her seat. "And Mr. Sam, when your plate's clean, there's something sweet in the kitchen just for you."

"Oh, the Valentine's Special, is it?"

"That's right. Eight inches of red-velvet cake with cream-cheese frosting. Measured it with Miss Angel's yard stick."

"It took my yardstick?" Angel took the platter of chicken from Roderick and nodded at him. "You certainly know when to show up. Hattie makes red-velvet cake only on Valentine's Day. I can't even persuade her to make it on my birthday, even when I beg."

"Oh, it's Valentine's Day, is it?" Roderick winked at Hattie. "Glad someone around here reminded me."

Bella strummed on the table and began to sing. "Happy Valentine's Day to you. Happy Valentine's Day to you. Happy—"

"Shh, not at the table, my sweet." Gretchen covered Bella's hand with hers.

Comments about the concert and the plans for the weekend were passed around the table like the bowl of turnip greens. When the cake had been served and the kitchen cleaned, Gretchen and Bella went home, and Caroline thought it time to head for her studio to unpack.

Hattie stood at the kitchen sink and watched Roderick and Caroline walk the stone path through the garden and down the hill. Roderick opened the gate in the picket fence, and they disappeared through the shrubbery to the back door of Caroline's studio apartment.

Hattie turned to Sam and Angel. "Hmmph, some girls get roses on Valentine's Day. Miss Blue Eyes is in for a surprise, a big surprise."

Caroline fumbled with the key at the backdoor. Her nimble fingers, nearly numb from the cold, couldn't insert the key into the lock.

"Here, allow me." Roderick stepped closer, took the key from her, and opened the back door. "Home again."

"Yes, indeed." She stepped inside and began to remove her jacket. "Oh . . . oh my!" She looked around the great room—a vase filled with white irises on the kitchen counter, another on her drop-leaf dining table, another on her desk, and another on the table next to her favorite chair. "They're so beautiful. You didn't forget." She turned to him as he closed the door and faced her.

"Forget what? That it's Valentine's Day or that you love white irises?" He removed his coat and followed her into the room.

"Both." She looked around the room again and then back at him.

"Can't give a girl red roses when her favorite is something else, even on Valentine's Day." He took her hands and pulled her closer to him. "I don't know why it is that we always seem to be surrounded by a crowd, but finally we're alone, and I've been waiting to do this since last evening." He lifted her chin with his right hand and kissed her on both cheeks before his arm slipped around her, drawing her to him for the kiss he'd been waiting for.

When he finally relaxed his arms, Caroline did not move away. She laid her head on his chest.

"Umm, I do believe that was worth . . ."

"Shhh." Without moving her head, she raised her left hand to his lips to quiet him.

He didn't finish his sentence. He just stood silently and held her until she stirred. She rose on her tiptoes and kissed him gently again, and then backed away from him.

Puzzled, he asked, "And what was that all about?"

"Just listening to the rhythm of your generous heart to see if it was different."

"Well, was it?"

"I'm not sure since I've never listened to anyone's heart before, but it's strong and steady, just like you." She walked to the counter for a closer look at the irises. "You do realize that in spoiling me you've added a touch of romance to Polly's life and a new *ching-ching* in her cash drawer, don't you?"

He joined her at the counter. "And how is that?"

"Polly's been Moss Point's florist for longer than I've been alive." She ran her finger across a velvety white petal. "Funeral sprays keep her doors open, with an occasional wedding. And prom comes once a year. But not too many men around here order flowers and special deliveries. She enjoys telling the town matrons about her new regular client."

"Umm."

"You must know she really gets into this."

"I suppose that's why she said I couldn't let Valentine's Day roll by without at least one red rose—" He paused. "—which is somewhere around here, and I suppose you'll have to look for it."

Her eyes moved around the room. No rose in sight. Her thoughts moved down the hall to her bedroom, but her feet wouldn't carry her there. Her feelings for Roderick were real and deep, but she still lived behind a white picket fence, and she wasn't ready for a rose on her pillow. They had made their feelings for each other very clear at Christmas and had decided to move slowly. Perhaps his tempo was changing.

"A rose, you say? One rose?"

"One very red rose."

She walked around the counter, her eyes still surveying the room. There on the piano, lying on the keyboard in utter simplicity against the black-and-white keys, was one long-stemmed red rose—no ribbon, no lace, no box, but one envelope with her name on the front. His tempo had not changed, and her relief was like hearing the town siren and realizing it was only their weekly, Thursday noon test—no danger. She turned where he still waited at the counter. "Seems its fragrance has given away its hiding place." She didn't disturb the rose but picked up the envelope. "The card. Polly's idea too?"

"Can't say."

"Well, then, I think I'll see for myself." She opened the envelope and there penned in Roderick's handwriting, she read,

> *Would you join me for dinner this evening at seven o'clock? It will be served here in your studio.*

"Dinner served here? Did you bring Lilah with you, or should I prepare myself for your cooking?"

He chuckled. "No, she'd love to be here, but it's all taken care of."

"All taken care of." Hattie was right. A woman would have to be numb and dumb to let this man out of her sight. "You truly are amazing, and it would be my pleasure to have dinner right here with you, Mr. Adair."

"That's lovely." Roderick came around the counter to join her, kissed her on the cheek and took her hand. "Let's sit down. I have something for you." They sat in the chairs facing the tall windows surrounding the piano as he reached inside his sweater to retrieve the envelope from his shirt pocket. "I so wanted to give this to you last night, but time and circumstances didn't allow it." He unfolded the letter-size envelope and handed it to Caroline.

"This isn't your handwriting."

"No, it's from someone else. I'm just a delivery boy."

Caroline laughed out loud and turned the envelope over.

"What's so funny?"

"'Just a delivery boy.'" She glanced sideways at him. "Not many delivery boys fly in on private planes. And besides, if what you tell me is true, most of your deliveries come in the form of new business plans or takeover bids."

He tapped the envelope in her hand. "This is neither, and I think you'll be happily surprised."

When Caroline opened the envelope, a check gently floated to the floor. Roderick leaned out of his chair to pick it up. "May I hold this while you read the letter inside?"

Not with the hesitation that comes with dread, but with the hesitation that comes with I-can't-believe-this-is-happening, she said, "Certainly."

He settled back into his chair while Caroline unfolded the letter. She rubbed her left thumb over the gold-embossed letterhead and began to read.

Dear Miss Carlyle,

It is with great pleasure and with as much expectation that I present you with this check. A nonprofit organization has been established for your dream of starting a Guatemalan children's choir. A bank account has also been set up in Lexington, and this check will be your first deposit. Gladly I offer the services of those who manage our family foundation to oversee the financial and business side of the Guatemalan Children's Choir until such time you desire to make a change.

Your passion was evident in our conversation about this project last summer. So evident, I've not forgotten it. My family has been involved in many projects in Appalachia working with those living in poverty, so I understand the needs of the poor. I appreciate your incredible talents and your desire to use them to make the world a better place for the disenfranchised children of Guatemala.

Perhaps we can have a personal visit during your next trip to Rockwater.

Until then, I am satisfied you will be busy making plans. My only request is that the Guatemalan Children's Choir's debut performance in the States be in Lexington. What a joy to make plans for that!

Sincerely,
Lorraine Evers Carson

"Lorraine Evers Carson? The tiny, elderly lady dressed in white with large rubies dangling from everywhere? The one seated beside me at the recital dinner last July?" Her face showed her disbelief.

"The very one. Apparently, you impressed her. I can assure you, she's not usually that easily won over, even when the cause is worthy, and she's rarely so generous with the first gift."

"I don't know what to think." She stared at the letter.

He twirled the check between his slender fingers and rattled it to get her attention. "Oh, perhaps you'd want to know how much money you can deposit."

"But this is just a dream I've had. I've heard these children sing, and they sing with such vitality, even the sad ones. Roderick, I have no idea how much money it would take to do this."

"Neither did Mrs. Carson, but she thought this would get you started." He leaned across the marble-topped table separating their chairs and handed her the check.

Her eyes blared as she sat up straighter in her chair, her elbows pressing into its cushioned arms. She was silent.

He sat relaxed, legs crossed and with a satisfied look on his face. "Well, now what do you think?"

She didn't take her eyes off the check. "Two hundred fifty thousand dollars? But she doesn't even know me." She swallowed. "How does she know that I just won't take the money and, and . . ."

"Oh, she knows, and besides there are laws to govern how the money in a nonprofit organization is spent. I can assure you she didn't do this on a whim."

She looked at him through the lamplight. "I've spent hours dreaming about how a traveling choir could change the lives of those orphans and how they could raise money to help house and educate other orphans, and I've even thought about music curriculum and how to choose the children. But money? I only know how much an airline ticket to Guatemala City costs and that a dollar is worth about seven and a half quetzals."

"Then I'd say you have some groundwork to do. And . . . I do know someone who has some sketchy experience in designing a business plan, which seems to be what you need most at the moment."

Caroline sprang from her seat and knelt on the floor in front of him. Holding the check in one hand and the letter in the other, her arms went around his neck. "You'll help me? You know I can't do this alone."

"I'm here, and I'll help." He held her, glad for her excitement and determined to keep his secret.

She rose from her kneeling position. "I should call Mrs. Carson right now. Would she take a call from me? I just have to tell her how surprised and grateful I am." Her eyes sought his approval.

"Of course you should call her, and she'll be happy to take your call. Why don't you go over and sit at your desk and take a deep breath before you do? Her number should be on the letterhead."

Sitting comfortably in his chair and observing her in the quiet moments before she made the call, he studied the arch of her wrist and her tapered fingers, longer than usual for such a diminutive hand. The hands that had played flawlessly last evening and held an audience of hundreds now held the futures of countless children from another land. What man would not be proud of her?

He held his breath during the conversation. Mrs. Carson's memory was somewhat unpredictable, but he prayed she'd remember to keep his confidence.

Caroline finished the call. Her eyes were bright and the muscles in her face tensed with excitement. She swiveled in her chair to face Roderick. "Oh, she's such a gracious lady. And now there's so much to do I don't even know where to start."

"Just one step at a time."

"Just one step at a time." Her demeanor changed, her facial muscles still tense but void of the excitement. Suddenly, she was back on the Guatemala riverbank staring at Roderick's reflection in the glassy pool. "What did you say?"

"I said, 'Just one step at a time.' That's all it takes, and I'll be there to help you."

She responded quickly and under her breath. "That's exactly what you said the other night."

"What? The other night? I think I've lost you."

She waggled her head as though her disturbing thoughts would disappear with the shaking. "Oh, I'm just addled. Don't mind me." She was not ready to tell him about her dream. That was behind her picket fence too. Her dimples returned. "I'm so glad you're here and we have time to talk about this project and Gretchen and Bella's plans, and then we have tonight."

"Yes, we have tonight."

A few hours later, Roderick stood in front of the bathroom mirror, brushed his hair and straightened his paisley tie against the crisp white shirt. He wore only white dress shirts, and he wore paisley ties even when stripes were in. His mother had been fond of the design and had a tailor make his father a wardrobe of paisley ties, all colors and sizes of print. Roderick kept them after his father died. Lilah had tried to talk him into getting rid of them, but nearly twenty years later, he was still wearing his dad's ties, now tailored for the current style. He leaned into the mirror for a closer look.

Well, John Roderick Adair, not very imaginative proposing to the woman you love on Valentine's Day, but you can't wait any longer, can you?

He walked back into the bedroom, turned on the bed-side-table lamp, picked up the small red velvet bag from the dresser, and checked its contents one last time. Sam and Angel were at the breakfast table sharing a slice of red-velvet cake when he walked through the kitchen. He dangled the red bag in front of them before putting it in his pants pocket. "Well, if she says no, then I'll return before long."

He saw the way Sam and Angel looked at each other and smiled before Angel said, "Oh, she'll be surprised, real surprised. She's always surprised when good things come her way."

"But, will she be too surprised to say yes?"

Angel shook her head and wiped red cake crumbs from her bottom lip. "Heavens, no. The chance that she'll say no is about the same as my finding a beehive in an igloo."

"Oh, she'll say yes. Who says no to good things?" Sam responded.

Roderick stepped closer to the table. "You don't know how pleased I am that you think this is a good thing. I have the blessing of her parents, but is this your blessing?"

"Oh, you have our blessing. You know we love that girl like our own. We've watched her grow up, we've watched her grieve, and we've watched her slowly come back to life. Nothing in this world could make us happier than to see her happy." Angel pointed her finger at him. "And, you've done that for her, Roderick."

"Angel's right. And we'll be around to make sure you keep putting a smile on our girl's face. And I'm here to tell you after sixty-five years with this woman, that's not always an easy task, but it surely makes life interesting."

Roderick observed the familiarity of Sam's arm around Angel. He desired that now and for the next forty years. "I promise you, just like I promised her parents. I'll take care of Caroline, and I'll work to make her smile every day."

"Enough said, now get to it." Sam picked up his cane and pointed it toward the door. "Get your coat; it's icy cold out there. And don't come back for a long time."

Roderick quietly closed the kitchen door and began his walk down the stone path. Putting his gloves over his sweaty palms took longer than his brisk walk to her studio. He gave up and put them in his overcoat pocket and knocked on her back door. The sight of her always brought a smile to his face, even through the windowpane. She wore winter white—wool slacks with a matching sweater, a stark contrast to her shoulder-length sable hair.

She opened the door. "You're finally back. I've been waiting."

He checked his watch. "I'm right on time, but I'm glad you were waiting." He kissed her sweetly. "You're really beautiful tonight. But you're beautiful every time I see you." He watched her face warm with color as she lowered her head. He liked that about her.

"Why thank you, Mr. Adair. So now, you can wait with me." She closed the door and helped him with his coat.

"Wait?"

"Um-huh. For dinner to arrive."

"No dinner yet? Not to worry about that." He followed her through the kitchen into the great room. "Glad to see you kept the fire going. I don't think it would be any colder at Rockwater, and that's several hours north." Taking her hand, he led her to stand with him in front of the fireplace. He leaned over, rubbing his hands together in front of the fire, but before they were warm, there came a knock at the terrace door.

"Dinner, do you suppose?" Her bright eyes flashed.

He straightened and turned toward the door. "Could be." He thought her form perfect as she walked across the room.

When she opened the door, Ned and Fred were standing there, gray hair plastered to their heads. It was the first time she'd ever seen them without their John Deere ball caps, except at church. Their plaid shirts and overalls had been discarded for Sunday clothes and heavy jackets. Ned carried a rather large box, and Fred gripped a folded card table. Ned was the one who always spoke for the both of them. "Evening, Miss Caroline."

"Well, good evening, Ned, and to you, too, Fred."

"Ah, we're here to set up for your supper." Ned extended his arms, holding the box.

"Oh, then please come in."

Fred followed without uttering a sound and stopped next to the piano, where he began unfolding the table. Ned put the box on the counter. "Yes, ma'am. It's all right here. Why, when Hattie and Miss Angel, the chatelaine, asked us to do this, we didn't have no argy-bargy, and we sure couldn't show up looking frowsy."

Caroline turned away from them, quite puzzled, and raised her eyebrows at Roderick. She closed the door behind them. "Well, you certainly don't look frowsy."

"Now you just go back over there next to Mr. Adair, and we'll get this done quicker than old Fopaw could corner a jackrabbit." Ned opened the box. "I miss that old hound.

He was a good one, and we ain't had one since that was worth a durn."

In no time, the table was set up and covered in a white linen cloth. Fred stood guard next to the terrace door while Ned took dishes, glasses, flatware, and a rose bowl of blossoms from the box and set them out on the counter. When Fred opened the door, Hattie came in with another box. Fred resumed his position at the door while Ned handed items to Hattie like a surgical nurse passing instruments to the surgeon. In a few short minutes all was set, and Hattie spread her mommy arms to present the table. "Your dinner is served."

Caroline and Roderick walked to the table. Ned joined his twin at the door. "Yessir, and we hope your supper is real auspicious. I'm sorry for going on about ol' Fopaw. Don't know how he came to my mind like that." Fred jerked on his twin's sleeve, and they disappeared through the door before anything else was said.

Caroline looked at Hattie and then again at Roderick. "Chatelaine? Argy-bargy? Didn't want to look frowsy? And now we're supposed to have an auspicious dinner?"

Hattie laughed as Roderick pulled out the chair for Caroline. "Oh, Ned calls it self-improvement. He's learning a new word every day. Since Fred don't talk, I just imagine old Ned's tired of listening to himself." She laughed again and walked toward the kitchen door. "Well I do hope your dinner is . . . is that word that Ned said." She was still laughing when she closed the door behind herself.

Roderick took his seat. "I believe the word was 'auspicious,' and may it be so."

Chapter 3

Pink Profession

Caroline's apartment

The crackling sound of the fire became the percussion section to the lyrical piano melodies playing softly in the background. Seated across from her, Roderick noticed the firelight behind Caroline was near perfect backlighting. He reached across the table and lifted the cover from her plate. "Now, my lady, your dinner."

From the look on her face, whatever she expected, this wasn't it. It pleased him. He had surprised her.

"A grilled cheese sandwich? Well, that's comfort food on such a cold night."

"Not just any grilled cheese sandwich—a grilled three-cheese sandwich and barbeque potato chips just like . . ."

She interrupted him before he could finish. "Just like the late-night dinner at the hotel in Atlanta—the day you flew me home for little David's birth and then flew me back to Atlanta that night to take care of Bella and Gretchen last October."

"The very night. And that's how you remember it?" He

lifted the cover from his plate and picked up his sandwich and then put it down. "I vaguely remember the grilled cheese sandwich and keeping the chef after the restaurant was closed, but what I remember every detail about is being with you out on the terrace after we ate." He watched her as she dropped her head slightly, her sapphire blue eyes still looking intently at him.

He leaned forward. "I remember the crunch of the leaves as we walked across to sit and drink our tea. I remember holding you in the light of that full moon as we stood to say goodnight. You said the moon looked like one of your grand ma'am's crackled china plates pasted against the dark sky. I remember the shower of leaves when the wind blew. But most of all, I remember that was the night I knew, I absolutely knew, I no longer wanted to walk around on this planet without you. Caroline."

She lifted her head as he reached into his coat pocket and pulled out the red velvet bag.

"Caroline, this isn't exactly how I had planned it, but I cannot wait any longer." He pulled the ring from the bag and held it out to her across the table. "Caroline, I want to look at every full moon in my lifetime with you beside me. Will you marry me?"

He watched, almost without breathing, as her eyes filled with tears, but not one rolled down her cheek, and not one muscle in her body moved. The clock her father had made chimed the half hour, so loud as though ringing from a bell tower. Her silence was even louder. Roderick rose from his chair, walked around the table, and knelt in front of her and held out the ring. "Caroline, will you marry me and allow me to do the one thing I want to do most with my life, and that is to spend it with you?"

She was stone-chiseled still and had not even turned to face him or to see the ring. "Caroline?"

Turning in her chair to face him, she looked past the

ring and into his eyes. "I'm sorry, Roderick."

"Sorry?" The lump in his throat was like the day he'd held his dying mother as she lay in the wet grass.

"You want to marry me? I've only dreamed of this . . ."

He took her left hand. "Does that mean yes or no?"

"Of course it means yes." She rose and pushed her chair away and knelt on the floor in front of him. "Yes. How many times have I wanted to say it? Yes, yes, yes."

Her arms went around his neck, and he sensed more passion in her kiss than ever before. In this moment, he sensed her release from her past, that she clung to him and the present. He took her face in his hands and kissed her cheeks and her forehead and her lips once again. "Oh, Caroline, you have made me the happiest man who ever walked this earth. Now I can live and breathe. And I can look at a full moon again."

"Roderick, are you sure? I mean, are you absolutely certain you want to marry me?" They sat facing each other on the floor in the firelight.

"Surer than I've ever been of anything." He handed her the ring. "Let me explain about this. This ring may not be your choice, and it's very important to me that you have exactly what you want. Sarah wanted me to give you my mother's diamond."

"Sarah knows?"

He chuckled. "Yeah, she knows, and your mom and dad, Sam and Angel, Gretchen, and Hattie and Lilah, and Ned and Fred. They all knew this was the night. I'd say they're great secret-keepers."

"Seems I'm the last one to know." She blinked the tears from her eyes. "Just tell me that Polly doesn't know."

He laughed. "No, Polly doesn't know. But I had to get the blessing of those who love you most, and I needed help to make this happen. Someone had to make the grilled cheese sandwiches, Miss Blue Eyes." He brushed the strands of hair from her cheek and then took her left hand from her lap. "Now, about the ring." He slid it onto her ring finger, a perfect fit. "I had the ring made for you. Somehow a diamond didn't suit you. Every woman has a diamond. But I chose a Caribbean pink pearl, rare, like you, and if you look at it under the light, it produces flame-like shimmers. The way you looked the night last July when you played your first recital at Rockwater. I'll never forget the sight of you in that pink dress." He paused. "But if you don't like it, I'll get you anything you want."

She extended her hand into the light made by the fire. "It's perfect. How could I want anything else?"

He was convinced the ring had pleased her, but he sensed he could have given her his mother's diamond or his grandmother's emerald or a ring from a Cracker Jack box, and she would have been pleased. She was unlike the other women he had known, women who had certain expectations because of his wealth. Her values were different, and that was one of the reasons he cherished her so.

"Understand, I had it set in yellow gold because it's warm like you. And the small diamonds surrounding the pearl . . . You'll notice that every other one is a pink diamond. They're also rare, and the designer didn't have enough to go all the way around. When he's collected the rest of the matching stones, he'll call me, and the regular diamonds will be replaced with pink ones. But I don't know when that will be."

She smiled broadly. "That means more than you know."

"Oh, do you like the pink diamonds?"

"Yes, but more than that, it means you didn't want to wait on the arrival of pink diamonds to propose." Her arms went around him again.

That was his Caroline. He rose from the floor and helped her stand. "Maybe now we can eat our dinner before it gets too cold, and then we have a really special dessert."

"But we have so much to talk about."

"That we do, but we have all evening, and all day tomorrow and forever." They embraced and kissed before taking their seats at the table again. In between bites, they decided it wasn't fair to leave their family and friends in suspense and came up with the list of phone calls they'd make this evening.

When they had finished their sandwiches, Caroline reached for the cover on the dessert plate. "So let's see what's for dessert." She lifted the lid. There, in its white wrapper with blue-and-red lettering, sat a Baby Ruth candy bar. "My special dessert?"

Roderick nodded. "Isn't it your favorite?"

"It most certainly is." She removed the wrapper and took the first bite. "This will be some story to tell our children. Your father proposed to me over a Valentine's Day dinner at a folding table, dining on a grilled cheese sandwich and a Baby Ruth." She held her hand out and looked at the ring again.

They had never spoken of children, but she added to his happiness by speaking of them so naturally. Perhaps there would be a next generation of Adairs after all.

Laughing and crying, they made their phone calls to all those on their list. She even called Ned and Fred and told them the results of the auspicious dinner Ned had wished for them.

Angel hung up the phone and put her book on the bedside table. She curled into Sam's arms the way she had every night for the last sixty-five years. "Caroline said yes, Sam. Our girl's getting married."

"We already knew that, didn't we?" He brushed her

white, fuzzy hair with his fingers as she lay against his shoulder. "You never really thought she'd say no, did you?"

"Heavens, no. But now we have to get busy. Martha and I have a wedding to plan. There hasn't been a wedding at Twin Oaks since your parents were married here, Sam, and that was in the last century." She rose up and turned off the lamp. "A wedding at Twin Oaks . . ."

Martha Carlyle put down the phone and returned to the game table. "Well, the boys are happy. James is a bit cautious, but he's a lawyer and he's always cautious."

J. fiddled with the wooden tiles on the Scrabble board. "That's just James. He's the oldest, and he's always looked out for his little sister." J. looked up at his wife. "Our girl's finally getting married, Martha. Did you get a hold of Thomas? What'd he say?"

"Oh, he's happy, too, but he was more interested to know if Roderick likes to hunt or fish and if we have to call him Roderick for the rest of our lives." Martha began to clear the Scrabble board.

"What are you doing? We didn't finish the game?"

"I don't have time to play games. I have a wedding to plan."

"Well, you don't have to do it tonight. They haven't even set a date, and besides I was winning."

"J., you just said it yourself, our daughter's getting married, and I need to start making a list of all the things I need to do. You know Caroline won't have time for that, and besides, this wedding has to be perfect for these two, and a wedding the likes of which Ferngrove hasn't seen in a very long time." She poured in the last of the tiles, folded and secured the board, and put the lid on the game box.

J. rose from the table. "Well, Caroline might have a thing or two to say about this."

"Oh, I don't want to her to bother about wedding plans. I had just about given up hopes of her ever getting married, and I can't wait to get started. I'll need you to get the trunk out of the attic tomorrow. My wedding dress is in a sealed box. I know she'll want to wear it."

He left her standing at the game table. "I think I'm going to bed." He kissed her on the cheek and started his shuffle down the hall. *Caroline getting married in Ferngrove in her mama's forty-year-old wedding dress. Business is about to pick up.*

Roderick and Caroline cuddled on the sofa near the fireplace, finishing their cups of tea after talking for the last two hours. "I have only Sarah, my sister to consider. I told you, I'd get married tomorrow if we could. Being married to you is what's important to me, not the ceremony, but I want you to have the kind of wedding that would make you and your family happy. I certainly don't want to disappoint them or Sam and Angel."

The room became quiet with only the whistling wind and the crackling fire invading the peaceful silence. Caroline sat up on the edge of the sofa and put her teacup on the table. "I've seen Rockwater in July and December, but I've never seen it in the springtime."

"Next to December, April's the most beautiful month of the year."

"And what's your schedule like in December?"

"Are we about to set a date here?"

"I'm game if you are. And the place too." She walked across the room to pick up her calendar from her desk and returned to cuddle next to him under the afghan. She flipped through a few pages until she reached December. "What about a Christmas wedding?"

"If we can't get married tomorrow or in April, then a Christmas wedding will do." He pulled her to him and kissed her temple. "That's ten months I have to wait."

She leaned against his shoulder. "Oooh, that does sound like a long time. But it's a reasonable and respectable time to be engaged before we get married."

Roderick laughed. "Reasonable and respectable, and that's better than spontaneous and spectacular?"

"Sounds like fun, what did you have in mind?"

"Making love to you under a full moon in Curaçao." He pulled her closer to him.

"Hmm, not that something so sensual doesn't sound splendid, but perhaps we should get back to reality and 'reasonable and respectable.'" She nuzzled her head gently into the crook of his neck and kissed him. "December would allow me to finish the year with my students and help Gretchen and Bella get settled, and I could go to Guatemala to get things started this summer. Besides, Sam and Angel and my parents will have to get used to the idea that I'm getting married."

"That's a deal. Christmas it is, and I'll just make certain Acer keeps the jet fueled up and ready to go, and I'll spend as much time with you as I possibly can until then."

"I'd like for us to get married where all of this started."

"You mean you want to get married at Rockwater? But what will your mother say? And Sam and Angel? You're their darling, and you're not getting married in the church?"

"Didn't say I wasn't getting married in the church. I want to stand beside you in front of the huge window at

Rockwater, and I want it just to be immediate family or those who are like family. That's the most beautiful cathedral I know. And besides, that's where I knew I loved you." She paused. "That's not true. I think I knew I loved you the day we walked down to the stream and climbed up the rocks."

"I remember. You sat on the boulder with your legs dangling over the water and you prayed with your eyes open. Never heard anybody pray you like you did."

She pulled away from him, crisscrossed her legs on the sofa, and faced him. "And I remember sitting there, and you told me the story of how your father taught you to swim. He didn't throw you into the water to sink or swim like your grandfather had thrown him in, but your dad got in the water first and told you to jump to him. And he told you that the most important thing in life was to make certain when you jump in, someone was there who wants to help keep your head above water." Her eyes filled with tears, and she took his hand and held it to her cheek. "Roderick, in lots of ways we're jumping into a large pool of life's uncertainties, but I'm certain you won't let me sink." She kissed the palm of his hand. "And I promise to always be there to love and support you and keep your head above the water. That will make me so very happy."

She felt Roderick's arms slip around her and turn her body so that she lay against him as he sat and held her. "I've done nothing to deserve you, Caroline, but I do love you, and I'm so grateful you love me."

They kissed long, in a rhythm of warm passion and a sweet gentleness. She lay in his arms looking up at him. "And there's no more perfect place than Rockwater to say these things to each other in the presence of those we love."

"So, Rockwater it is, my love."

Chapter 4

Eavesdropping

Late March in Moss Point

Fred moved the paint bucket, almost empty of its white paint, picked up the broom, and began sweeping the last bits of sawdust from the floor of the gazebo. Ned took the plastic tarp and the paint bucket and started down the steps. "You be careful, Fred. Use that dustpan, you hear? Don't you even think about sweeping that pine sawdust off this floor into that flower bed. I just put out that dark compost Miss Angel wanted around them azaleas, and she didn't say nothing about wanting no sawdust on top of it."

Fred kept sweeping.

Ned stopped in his tracks and turned around. "Did you hear what I said, brother?"

Fred grunted.

"Then you'd better act like it. I'm getting ready to load this stuff up."

Fred grunted again.

The cell phone lying on the gazebo steps rang as Ned

started to the truck. "Get that phone, would you, Fred?"

Fred kept sweeping. The phone kept ringing.

"I said, would you get the phone?" Ned realized it was hopeless, dropped the tarp and paint bucket, and ran back to answer the phone.

He heard Angel's voice. "I'm just checking to see how things are going and to let you know the roses have come in."

"Yes, ma'am. We done planted the azaleas, but if the roses came in, we'll get to it."

"I'm glad for that, Ned. Sam and I will be coming in a little while to bring them. Would you two like a slice of Hattie's cake? I'll bring it to you."

"Yes, ma'am, Miss Angel. We'd sure like a slice of cake if it ain't too much trouble." Pause. "Yes, ma'am. Good-bye."

He put the phone down. "Fred, dadburnit, I told you to get the phone."

"No, you didn't."

"Yes, I did."

"No, you didn't. You said, 'Get that phone, would you, Fred?'"

"That's right. So why didn't you answer it?"

"Well, you asked if I would, and I wouldn't. It was your turn."

"Fred Pendergrass, if Miss Angel wasn't on her way down here with two rose bushes, me and you'd get tangled up about this. You knew what I meant."

Fred kept sweeping. "You know what Pa said. He always said, 'Say what you mean and mean what you say.'"

"So why is it you don't say nothing? Buying this dad-burn cell phone was all your idea, but there ain't no need in taking turns answering it. You ain't never going to use it 'cause it means you got to say something. I'm just putting it in my pocket, and don't be surprised if it winds up in the same place as my fishing rod the catfish jerked out of the boat at the river last summer." He put the cell phone in the bib pocket of his overalls and started to the truck again.

By the time he reached his truck—the only pea-green one in town with picket-fence side bodies—Angel and Sam were driving up. The canes from two rose bushes protruded from the open, back-seat windows. Ned secured the paint bucket and tarp in the back of the pickup before getting the wheelbarrow.

Sam was already out of the car and opening the back door.

"Mr. Sam, don't you pick up them ponderous roses. I'm coming. I'll get them."

"And I'll let you get these roses." While Ned loaded the five-gallon containers onto the wheelbarrow, Sam walked around the car to open the door for Angel. Ned tried not to notice as Sam mouthed *ponderous roses* inaudibly and shook his head.

Her mouth twitching, Angel asked, "Okay, Ned, where's Fred? It's time you fellows took an afternoon break. I brought you a thermos of coffee and some cake." She handed the thermos to Sam as she got out of the car.

"You truly are an angel, Miss Angel. But me and Fred don't take breaks. Maybe we could just take the cake home with us. And besides, Mama always said we had to wash our hands before we eat, and there ain't nowhere around here for hand washing." Ned parked the wheelbarrow right in front of her but held on to the handles.

"Ned, I have two things to say about that. Children will be playing in this park and eating ice cream and skinning their knees, and who knows what else, so we must do something about this water situation. And second, do you see your Mama anywhere around here?"

Ned was taken aback. "Ma'am? Miss Angel, you know my mama's done dead and gone a long time ago."

"Yes, I do. So, who says you can't take off your gloves and have dessert in the middle of the afternoon? Your mama's not here and I brought cake, so I'm going to find Fred." Angel waddled off with the thermos and cake, obviously having noticed Fred standing with the broom in his hand. "Just bring those Bella roses, and we'll have the first picnic in the gazebo."

"Now, Miss Angel, you don't need to be . . ."

"Let her go, Ned. I need to talk with you about something else anyway." Sam leaned against the car.

"Yes sir. Something else you need us to do before Saturday's ribbon cutting?"

"No. Don't know of a thing. Of course, that's Angel's department. Just get these two rose bushes planted like she wants them." He motioned for Ned to come nearer and lowered his voice. "You know it's about that time when you and Fred need to be thinking about who's receiving your scholarships this year. Graduation's just a few weeks away, and the principal needs to make the announcement."

"Yes sir, we sure do. You know of some kids who could use the help?"

"Principal's checking on it. But something else is on my mind. Ned, I think it's time the town knows where the scholarships are coming from. You and your brother have educated lots of Moss Point's kids for the last twenty years, and most of them have made something of themselves all because of you. Don't you think they'd like to thank the men who gave them a good start?"

Ned released the handles of the wheelbarrow, stood up straight, and put his hands in his overall pockets. "No, sir, Mr. Sam. It's got to be a secret. Me and Fred like it that way. We didn't get no education. We just went to work, and we been toiling ever since. And we didn't know nothing about no stock 'til Pa died. By then it was too late for us to go to school. We got everything we need—a house, a truck, plenty of something to eat. What else we going to do with that money?"

Sam tapped the toe of Ned's work boot with his cane. "You're doing good deeds with those dividends, Ned. Your daddy would be proud."

"So how much we got to give away this year?"

"I don't know. I'll check with Brooks down at the bank and let you know." He moved from leaning against the car to face Ned. "You sure we can't announce it this year?"

"Just as sure as I am Mrs. Melton's got a house full of cats. And this is one cat we don't want out of the bag. If that cat gets out, there ain't no putting it back in. Me and Fred likes things like they are. And you make sure Mr. Brooks at the bank knows that too. I don't trust nobody but you and him."

"I'll remind him. Don't you worry about a thing."

Ned picked up the wheelbarrow handles and followed Sam down the straw path to the gazebo. He was glad the Bella roses had come in. Miss Angel had just lit up when she told him she ordered some Bella roses from a catalog. She'd been watching for them every day for the last two weeks. She said it wouldn't be right to name the gazebo for Bella if there weren't some Bella roses next to the steps. Miss Angel was always right.

The twins removed their gloves, enjoyed the cake and coffee, and quickly went back to work transplanting the azaleas, filling the spots where Angel wanted the roses planted. After sitting on the steps and watching the brothers work until the dark compost now covered the ground around the roses, Angel got up, walked a few steps away to look at the Victorian work of art Ned and Fred had created, and leaned over to check the rose buds.

Ned looked over her shoulder. "Think they'll be open by Saturday?"

"Of course, they'll be open. They'd be afraid not to. You gentlemen have done a magnificent job with everything, and the daffodils and azaleas and irises and these roses right here will be showing off at the opening. They're not about to disappoint us. And that guy from Atlanta wouldn't disappoint us either. He's bringing the swans Thursday afternoon." She patted Ned on the back, waved at Fred, who had picked up his broom again, and picked up the thermos. "Come on, Sam, we need to get home."

Ned watched them walk away holding hands, their heads swiveling from side to side to take in all the views of the park and the straw-covered paths snaking through the garden patches.

When Sam and Angel had driven away, Ned loaded up the wheelbarrow with most of their tools and took them to the truck. He came back for the last load and stood in front of the gazebo steps and admired their work, from the hand-carved step railings to the gingerbread facing under the eaves. Ned pulled the wadded-up handkerchief from the back pocket of his overalls, wrapped a layer of it around his index finger, and began to wipe the smudges off the brass plaque nailed at eye level to the right front post of the gazebo. "Well, this don't look nothing like that old shack we tore down right here on this spot, now does it, brother?"

"Nope." Fred was on the bottom step watching his twin.

Ned continued to put a spit shine on the brass plaque. "We had to tear down that pretty little Bella's safe place, but we sure did build her a mighty beautiful place to come and sit and look at the pond and all the flowers, didn't we?"

"Yep."

"I hope it makes her forget that old shack where her and

her grandma had to come when her grandpa was drunk. Maybe one day we'll tell her we used the wood from that old shack to build this one."

"Maybe."

"Yeah, Pa always said ever'thing and ever'body' s redeemable. Had to turn that trash into treasure." Ned ran his hands down the post. "I'd say we redeemed them old splintered boards. They as smooth as the doors on Ma's old chifforobe now."

Ned froze in his tracks and got quiet.

Fred waited before speaking. "Yep, no more splinters."

Ned put his handkerchief back into his pocket and got out his glasses. "Would you listen to this?"

"Yep," Fred said quietly.

Ned put on his glasses and stepped closer to the plaque. "'Bella's Porch designed and built by Fred and Ned Pendergrass.'" He stepped back and turned to look at his brother. "Now would you please tell me why it says Fred and Ned Pendergrass? Why does your name get to be first?"

"'Cause Ma didn't name you Ed. If she named you Ed, then you wouldn't be Ned and Fred wouldn't come before Ed." He took his broom and headed to the truck.

The sun rose to reveal clear blue skies on Saturday morning. Caroline's parents and Roderick had arrived in Moss Point the night before. Perfect timing for discussing wedding plans and for celebrating the opening of the park, endearingly referred to now as the "Meadows" by the town's grateful citizens.

"Where's my bride?" Sam, dressed in his seersucker suit, red tie, white loafers, and his favorite straw hat, stood at the back-porch door with the others.

"Just give her a minute." Caroline came through the kitchen door and joined Roderick standing next to the wicker table. "She's checking her lipstick."

"Bella and Gretchen planning to meet us there?"

"No, Sam. They're sitting in my studio. They'll join us when they see us coming through the garden. You know it's just a few steps from the studio terrace to the back entrance of the park."

"Good, I want them to be front and center today." Sam spied Angel coming through the kitchen toward the porch. "Why, there's that blue-eyed beauty that chased me 'til I caught her sixty-six years ago!"

Angel, dressed in a sky-blue muumuu she had made for the occasion, waltzed across the back porch, took Sam's arm, and led him out the screen door without even slowing down. "Sam Meadows, you're retired. You're not running for office, and that kind of flattery won't earn you one vote." She looked back at the entourage and winked.

They walked the path to the studio where Gretchen and Bella joined them. The latch on the back gate had been there for three generations of Meadows, and Sam refused to replace it. But Fred's polishing worked. Even with Sam's knotty fingers, the lock slid with ease, and the gate, without even a hint of a creak, opened to reveal the back path to the gazebo. "If God ever made a finer day, I'd say he kept it all for himself."

The high school band was playing, children were laughing, swans were swimming, and flowers of all colors were smiling at the sunshine. The mayor and the city council members worked the crowd, grateful for the opportunity to glad-hand. Brother Andy was there to thank God for his creation and ask his blessings on all who would enjoy the park.

Delia Mullins had traded in her steno pad and pencil for a palm-sized tape recorder for notetaking and interviewing for the *Moss Point Messenger.* Folks might have stayed put as long as the camera was in her hand, but they scampered like the fox squirrels that once thought they owned this plot of ground when they saw Delia approaching with the tape recorder. Moss Point dignitaries knew there was such a thing as a dumb question.

If Sam had been wearing suspenders, they would have popped when he and Angel cut the yellow ribbon at the top of the steps to Bella's Porch. Sam kept his remarks short but loud. No using a microphone for the judge. It was worth every penny he had paid the Pendergrass twins just to see them all dressed up and to watch their faces when he called them up the steps to give them the credit he had paid for.

Once the ceremony was over, the band started up again, and so did the volume of the many conversations around the grounds. Sam enjoyed watching Angel hold court with Caroline and Bella and Gretchen beside her. He took his opportunity to slip away to speak with Ned and Fred. "Well, gentlemen, could you have imagined this park when you were sitting in wait at midnight for the Peeping Tom who kept coming through that old fence a year ago, and that you would have built a gazebo named for the intruder?"

Ned hung his head and rubbed his chin. "No, sir, Mr. Sam. I'd have to sit down and have me a long think before I could come up with a tale like that. A pure vagary, that's what it is. Just don't seem likely that pretty little Bella and Miss Caroline would meet like that."

About as likely, Sam thought, as old Walter Pendergrass buying stock in Coca-Cola right after the Great Depression. From then on, any time he'd had extra money, Walter had put two-thirds of it into Coca-Cola stock and one-third into the bank while his wife wore dresses made out of flour sacks.

And now no one in town but Sam and Fred Brooks down at Moss Point Banking Company had any idea that the Pendergrass twins were worth a fortune. Ned and Fred had inherited sixty years' worth of stock growth and splits and considerable cash when their pa passed away, but it made little difference to them. They lived simply like their parents, knowing the difference between their needs and their wants. And lucky for about forty Moss Point graduates through the years that the Pendergrass twins didn't want much.

"You're right. Doesn't seem likely, and that's what six Moss Point High graduates are going to be saying when they get full scholarships to the university this year."

Ned grinned. "We got that much money to give away?"

Fred stepped a little closer to his brother when GiGi Nelson walked by with her pumpkin-colored hair, in a white sweater showing cleavage that had obviously been on display too long and Levi's that would have looked better if GiGi had been preshrunk.

Sam, engrossed in his conversation, continued in his do-not-need-a microphone voice even when the band had stopped playing. "Yes, your dividends were enough to add six more scholarships this year." When he realized that someone might have overheard what he said, he stepped closer to Ned and continued to explain more quietly their income from the stock dividends.

Fred, standing with his hands in his pockets and arms akimbo, nudged his brother with his right elbow.

"I didn't forget." Ned gave his twin the same look his pa always gave his ma when she reminded him to zip his trousers. "Me and Fred want to know if we have enough money to help Mrs. Silva and little Bella too?"

Sam rubbed his brow. "Well, the answer to your question is yes. You have the money, but Mrs. Silva's doing just fine financially, and she has offers from Duke and the University of Georgia to provide a place for them to live and to educate Bella."

Ned rocked back and forth as he spoke. "That's mighty fine, but you didn't have to tell me all that today. That means Caroline's getting married and little Bella's leaving. No more real music in this old town." Sam noticed Ned's eyes following GiGi when she passed by again and waved at Fred, whose teeth were peeking through a tight-lipped grin. "You don't suppose Caroline and that fellow of hers would give a think about staying in Moss Point."

"No need supposing about that. Makes no sense when Roderick owns two estates in Kentucky."

"No need in spoiling today's sunshine with tomorrow's clouds neither. We'd appreciate it if you'd just take care of the scholarships, Mr. Sam." He shook Sam's hand and tugged at Fred's shirtsleeve. "Come on, me and you are going to get a funnel cake, Brother."

Sam was looking for Angel when GiGi ambled by a third time. He tipped his hat as she stopped in front of him.

"Well, Judge Meadows, you and Angel just outdid yourselves with this park." She pointed toward the food booths with orange claws painted the same color as her hair. "And those Pendergrass boys did too. Why, the gingerbread on that gazebo will make Tandy Yarbrough turn green! It's just a shame that neither one of those fine men ever got married. Either one of them would've made a fine husband."

Before Sam could respond, GiGi strutted off toward the funnel cake tent.

Chapter 5

Travel Plans

Mid-April in Moss Point

Blustery breezes had blown March right off the calendar, and it was well into April. Caroline had spent Easter weekend visiting her parents and Betsy down in Ferngrove. But it was Monday morning in Moss Point, and she had a full day and an afternoon of piano students.

Angel had called her early to come up for pancakes. She ambled through the garden on her way back to her studio after breakfast. The azaleas and dogwoods in full bloom and the smell of honeysuckle drifting through the air caused her to second-guess herself. The park Sam and Angel had given to the community was open, and the gazebo would be ideal for a spring wedding. But she knew it was too soon. Too many plans and too many things to wrap up neatly before a wedding, and she needed the eight months until December.

She was careful opening the kitchen door. Wrens were constructing their nest in the basket of Swedish ivy next to the door, and she didn't want to alarm them. Unlike the wrens, Caroline's nesting instinct began at the first sign of fall, not spring. When she sensed the shadows changing as the sun moseyed south, she began readying her house for the winter months. As much as she enjoyed the spring mornings and nights, she knew a winter wedding was perfect timing in every way. She sat at her desk and opened her calendar.

Mimicking the mockingbird perched in the tea olives, Bella's whistling alerted Caroline before the knock on the door. She glanced at her to-do list and rose from her chair. Today was decision day to pencil in dates for travel and moving schedules with Gretchen.

She opened the door and spied the small basket, its contents covered with a blue-checkered napkin, swinging back and forth in Bella's hands. Before she motioned for them to come in, she said, "Please tell me that's not pastry in the basket."

"You ask me to tell you an untruth? I must not. It is indeed a new recipe with Bavarian cream and almonds, not pecans. Real almonds." Gretchen retrieved the basket from Bella. "And I believe the buns might still be warm."

Bella hugged Caroline quickly and darted for the piano. "I play the piano. Mamá. I play Caroline's piano." She sat down on the bench but never raised her hands to play until Caroline gave permission. The smile on Bella's face was almost as sweet as the birdsong she'd whistled earlier.

Caroline followed Gretchen around the counter into the kitchen, reached for the teakettle, and headed to the sink. "Would you get us a couple of plates?"

"Certainly. Tell me, how was your visit with your parents?"

"Fine. Just so much talking. Mama finally accepted the fact I'm not getting married in my home church, but having a Sunday afternoon reception in Ferngrove was my concession."

Gretchen gently set the plates down on the counter as

Caroline thumbed through the box of foil-covered tea bags. "'Concession'?"

Caroline laughed. "My mother and I both gave in a bit and came to an agreement about the wedding plans. I conceded to have a reception in Ferngrove to introduce Roderick to my hometown friends."

"Yes, I understand now. Concession. I suppose that is what I have done in choosing to move to North Carolina rather than Athens. I know what I have chosen, but now I have a new word to describe it."

Caroline put the teakettle on the stove and turned the knob to High. "Try hanging around Ned if you want to learn new words. He's had me running to the dictionary for the last two months. Seems like a part of his daily routine when they work around here is to come over and use his new Word for the Day in a sentence. Gets right funny sometimes."

"The Pendergrass gentlemen are very unusual, are they not?"

"That they are." Caroline got the teacups from the cupboard. "You know, they're in their sixties, never married, and I could probably count on my two hands the number of times they've been out of this county. Think I should invite them to the wedding?"

"I think I should like to hear what concessions you must make with your mother about that." As Gretchen removed the warm pastry from the basket and put them on the plates, a slight giggle slipped from her lips, a rare event for her. "Would you like to take our tea here at the breakfast table or out on the terrace?"

"Let's sit on the terrace like old times. Go ahead and I'll bring the tea. Be sure to get your notebook."

She grabbed her calendar and stuck it under her arm, careful not to spill a drop of tea as she exited the studio for the terrace. She left the door slightly ajar so the music could be heard. The wrought-iron table had supported hundreds of cups of tea over the last seven years. She put down the teacups and her calendar and reached for a pastry before she sat down. "Glad we're taking advantage of having tea on the terrace. Not many more April mornings to do that. Do you ever think about what we might be doing this time next April?"

"Ah, I do, but those thoughts are too much for my thinking. I do believe this is where our friendship began about this time last year at this very table over a cup of tea. And just think of all that has changed since that morning! You have fallen in love and introduced my Bella to the world."

"And you are free of Ernesto, and Karina has returned to you."

The delight on Gretchen's face was as sweet as the almond cream drizzled on top of the pastry. "Yes, my friend. And I have news about my Karina."

"From the look on your face, it must be good news."

"It is wonderful news that pleases me beyond the words I have to tell you. Now that I have decided to accept Sarah's offer for Duke University, Karina has decided to come with us. Sarah has offered to help Karina get into a local community college until she can build up her grades and credits. And . . . if she does well, Sarah will help her get into Duke along with Bella."

"That's wonderful news, Gretchen."

"But there is more."

"Oh, please don't tell me that Skipper or whatever his name is has decided to come too?"

Another of Gretchen's giggles escaped. "His name is Skeeter, and Karina has decided for herself that she would be better off without him. She is leaving him and will make the move to Durham with us in early June."

"Wonderful she's moving and even more wonderful she's getting rid of Skeeter. 'Skeeters' seem to be only a nuisance." She remembered the deep sadness in Gretchen's eyes months ago when she'd talked about Karina running away from home after giving birth to Bella. "I feel so good about this. Sarah will be there to look out for you, and Karina will be there to help with Bella. And Roderick and I will see you often."

"Karina is helping me with some other things." She sipped her tea.

"My, you're really full of news this morning."

"We talked about this before, but now I have decided. When I move to Durham, I will be using some of my savings to open a bakery. I must earn a living, and I must have something to do while my beautiful and talented daughters are in school. Karina has offered to help me since she has experience working in a bakery. And . . . Karina is going to Austria with me next year to find my sister, Elfi."

"But you haven't seen or heard from your sister in nearly thirty years. How do you expect to find her?" Caroline took the last bite of her pastry and dabbed her mouth with her napkin. "By the way, if you're offering these in your new bakery—" She pointed to her empty plate. "—I'll take the first ten dozen."

"Oh, thank you, my friend. I am creating new recipes, and I plan to serve only authentic Bavarian pastries. That is another reason to return to my homeland. I will visit bakeries and get fresh and delicious ideas."

"Don't forget, Roderick said he wants to invest in any business that involves your cooking." She smiled and squeezed Gretchen's hand before settling back into her wrought-iron chair. "So tell me, what is this about Elfi? Do you really expect to find her there after all these years?"

"I have only my hopes and prayers. My prayer that Karina would go with me has already been answered."

After the beating last fall, Gretchen had told her the story of how she abandoned her home and family when she found herself pregnant at eighteen. "Karina knows about Peter and Nicolai? And the reason you ran away?"

"Yes. The only thing more difficult than leaving my family years ago was telling Karina the truth: that Ernesto was not her father." Gretchen stared at the rim of her plate. "She surprised me by saying that she always knew he could not be her father. It seemed to satisfy her wondering when I explained my betrothal to Peter, and how Peter's brother, Nicolai, accosted me, and I became pregnant. I believe she really understood my shame and why I chose to leave."

Caroline saw a return of the sorrow in Gretchen's eyes when she talked about her past and when she talked about her life with Ernesto, the man who had kept her a virtual prisoner and who was now serving time for beating her. "Do you plan to try to find Peter, or do you think Karina wants to see her biological father?"

Gretchen swirled the last bit of tea in her cup and stared into the golden drops of Darjeeling. "Oh, no, no. I think not. On her last visit here, we talked about how much pain we have endured and how grateful we are that order is replacing the chaos in our lives. Karina and I understand the results of making choices—not the best choices, but the least of the worst choices—and neither of us will choose to disrupt someone else's life."

Caroline was about to respond when the phone rang. She hurried inside with Gretchen right behind her, coaxing Bella to stop playing the piano so that Caroline could hear. This was the call she'd been waiting for, a call from Dr. Lydia Pipkin, the founding director of the Ugandan Children's Touring Choir.

The polite hello and introductory conversation quickly turned to business, and Caroline listened, writing hastily, almost snatching her calendar off the desk when she turned the page abruptly in order to keep writing. The conversation lasted only about ten minutes, but Caroline had what she needed. Dr. Pipkin agreed to accompany her on a preliminary trip to Guatemala to explore the beginnings of the Guatemala Children's Choir. Dates were firm, and now she could make travel arrangements and help Gretchen choose moving dates.

She put the phone down and headed for the terrace. "Bella, want to play the piano some more?"

Chopin emanated through the cracks around the plate-glass windows as Caroline sat again at the terrace table. "You're not the only one this morning with good news." She paused, watching the sorrow in Gretchen's eyes vanish. "That was Lydia Pipkin, the woman I've told you about—the one who started the Ugandan Children's Touring Choir."

"Oh? Will she help you?"

"Yes. Even better than that. She's agreed to go with me to Guatemala this summer, and we've set the travel dates. So, get your list out, my friend. You and I are about to make big plans."

Over a second cup of tea and accompanied by Bella's renditions of Chopin, the two friends penciled in a move to North Carolina and Caroline's trip to Guatemala on their calendars.

Roderick pulled his tie from around his neck, threw it and his suit coat on the bed, and opened the sliding doors. The corals in the sunset sky over the harbor in San Diego were the same color of the pink jade Fu dogs on his mother's writing desk. Travel had become laborious over the last few years, but somehow, he knew a sunset's colors would be more enjoyable when Caroline could travel with him. He reached into his pocket for his phone and dialed her number. Her voice was like music to him; even a simple "hello" was melodic.

"I'd like to enroll as a piano student. Is Miss Carlyle home?"

"Oh, I'm so sorry. You just missed her. She's somewhere over the Gulf of Mexico on her way to Guatemala City. Could I take your name and number?"

"Not necessary. Would you please tell her I'll meet her there?"

"I certainly will. I know she'll be so happy to hear that. Oh, and could you tell me who you are?"

He heard her muffled giggle and lowered his baritone voice almost to a raspy whisper. "I'm the man who'd fly anywhere anytime to meet her. Tell her that, would you?"

She broke the spell. "Hi, Roderick. How's San Diego?"

"Beautiful at sunset." He felt the sea breeze against his face. "And if you want to know how I am, I am lonely and crazy in love with you."

"That's good since you and I are jumping off the boulder at Rockwater together in a few months."

He laughed. "Not soon enough, but I'll warn you, the water will produce golf-ball sized goose pimples in December. What about if we opt for July? It's just a few weeks away and considerably warmer."

"Don't tempt me. Too many more conversations with my mother and Angel, and a private ceremony with a justice of the peace this weekend might be preferable."

"Whatever pleases you, my love. How was your day?"

"Productive. Had a steady stream of students coming and going this afternoon, and I spent a good portion of the morning with Gretchen and Bella. Now we have a moving date for Gretchen and talked about her travel plans to Austria next year. And guess what else?"

"Ned taught you another new word today?"

"No. I haven't seen those two today, but I did get a call from Dr. Lydia Pipkin."

"Oh, I know you've been anxious to talk with her."

"I did more listening than talking, but she's not only agreed to help, she's going to Guatemala with me in June. And I think she's rather excited about it."

Leaning on the balcony railing, he watched a sailboat pull into its slot in the marina across the street. "That's wonderful. Sounds like from what you've told me, she wrote the book on how to navigate a project like this."

"She's the expert all right. Her African children's choir is world renowned, and she's raised millions of dollars for the orphans in Uganda. I was checking flight schedules when you called. She'll be in the States in June. With her schedule, I think it best to fly her from Miami, and I'll just meet her in Guatemala City."

"You know my plane can't fly out of the country, so I'll get Liz to book our flights and I'll go with you." He walked back into the hotel suite to get his calendar from his coat pocket.

"I'm afraid you'd get bored, and can you really spare two weeks?"

"Two weeks? When are you going?" He thumbed through his calendar for June.

"Okay, here's the plan. Gretchen's moving on June fourth. I'll ride to Durham with her and stay a couple of days to help her get settled. Oh, and Karina is moving with her. Duke's providing a spacious apartment for them. I'm feeling so much better about Gretchen's decision, especially since your sister's there."

"I'll warn you. Sarah tends to take charge, but that might be what's needed for a few weeks." He scanned a full calendar of appointments in June, including another trip to London. "Now, when are you leaving for Guatemala?" Upon hearing the dates, he realized his London trip fell right in the middle, and these were plans he really shouldn't change. An important board meeting to finalize the merger he'd been working on for months. "Hmm . . . I really don't like this."

"What's not to like?"

"For starters, I'll be in London those dates, and I don't like the idea of your traveling around Guatemala with just another female."

"Would that be a bit of male chauvinism I hear?"

"Probably. But learn to live with it, and besides I really don't want to be away from you that long."

"Somehow, I don't think Dr. Lydia Pipkin is just another female. I've read about her, and the stories about her paint her as fearless. The woman has managed to stay alive and well in Africa for nearly twenty years." She paused. "But so you won't miss me so much, what if I come to Rockwater from Durham for a few days before I leave for Guatemala?"

"Perfect. Bring your swimsuit, and we can practice jumping off the boulder."

"Is that all you intend to rehearse, Mr. Adair?"

He was enchanted by her innocence but intrigued by her playfulness. "Why, Miss Blue Eyes, is this the voice of the beguiling woman who can make Liz Blevins turn green in less than three seconds?" He laughed at the thought.

"Me? 'Beguiling'?"

"Oh, for certain. By the way, I'm using a promotion to move Liz to the Lexington headquarters. Although, Lilah may poison her first. But if not, she'll make the move in early July. If you and I need an assistant, we'll hire someone else."

He heard Caroline's whispered sigh. "Lovely. And the new assistant will not have red nails, wear six pounds of gold jewelry, and carry a lifetime spa membership card."

"Your choice, my love. But let's allow Liz to book your Guatemala reservations for you and Dr. Pipkin. Just email the dates and a general itinerary, and I'll get her to take care of the details. I'll instruct her to get you a phone that'll work internationally too. If I can't see you every day, at least I'll get to hear your voice."

"Thank you, Roderick. I wish you were going with me, but there'll be other trips."

The sun had completely set over the harbor by the time they finished their conversation. He came in from the balcony but left the glass doors open to allow the sea breeze to freshen the room. After a call for room service, he opened his computer, checked his email, and sent Liz instructions to make Caroline's reservations when she received the details of the trip and to book a driver, a car service, and a satellite phone for the length of her visit.

A knock at the door, a generous tip, and he uncovered his favorite room-service comfort meal: a grilled cheese sandwich, tomato soup, and a bowl of melon. Since his boyhood, he rarely ate a grilled cheese sandwich without thoughts of his mother and now Caroline. He missed them both. Death had cheated him of his mother, but he'd protect Caroline.

He ate, showered and crawled into bed to look over his notes for tomorrow's meeting and to check the news. The lead article in his online news service immediately caught his eye: "Femicide in Guatemala: 4,000 Women Murdered or Missing Since 2001." The comfort food that normally cajoled him into a restful night's sleep slowly churned in his stomach.

Chapter 6

Last Things

Saturday afternoon in late May

Caroline leaned against the closed terrace door, the last guest and all her students gone. Her studio was quiet again, no more music or excited conversation, only the low-pitched humming of the refrigerator punctuated by the rhythmic ticking of her desk clock. Today marked her seventh and final student recital in her Twin Oaks studio. A mingling of sweet sadness and a sense of completion had come over her as she sat on the front row, listening and fingering every piece played by every student. She had deliberately programmed Bella to play last and prepped her to play the *Rockwater Suite*, after which Caroline said her final words as Moss Point's piano teacher. It was hard enough to say goodbye to her students and to watch Sam and Angel in their reserved seats, knowing this kind of afternoon wouldn't happen again. But the afternoon was easier without the presence of her mother and Roderick.

Keeping them away had not been easy. Martha Carlyle had never missed a recital. Over the years, she had taken great pride in creating the refreshment table, from arranging fresh flowers to preparing every morsel and delicacy served. Caroline had convinced her to save her creative energies for the reception in Ferngrove in December. Martha agreed when she learned that Gretchen would do the baking for the recital. Caroline convinced her that Gretchen was creating recipes for the opening of her new bakery in Raleigh-Durham and needed a venue to try them out.

Yes, her last Moss Point recital had been something she needed to do without her mother and future husband. And it was done.

Gretchen and Bella were the last to leave. They'd offered to stay and help clear the table and clean up, but this was something else Caroline needed to do alone. She changed her clothes and trudged to the refreshment table now covered in wadded paper napkins, silver trays offering only sparse crumbs, and a few more strawberry stains on the white linen tablecloth. For her, this last cleaning-up was like putting the copyright sign and date on a musical manuscript, which she never did until she was absolutely certain the work was completed to her satisfaction.

With the kitchen clean and silver trays stacked and ready to be taken up to the big house for their return to Angel's butler's pantry, Caroline was on her way down the hall to put the table linens in the laundry. A knock at the door summoned her to look at the wall clock. Six fifteen. She dumped her armload on top of the washing machine that was slightly older than the humming refrigerator and headed for the terrace door.

As predictable as a metronome, Ned and Fred had arrived to pick up the borrowed folding chairs and return them to the church. "Why, good evening, Miss Caroline. We're here to pick up the chairs," Ned said. The twins stood side by side, John Deere caps in hand.

"Right on time, gentlemen. I can always count on you."

"Yes, ma'am. You'd be right about that. It's a sorry somebody you can't count on, and our ma and pa didn't raise us to be no sorry somebodies."

"Would that the world was full of somebodies like the two of you. I'm going to miss you, you know." She opened the door wide and motioned for them to come in.

As though choreographed, they removed their caps and twisted and stuffed them into the hip pockets of their overalls. "Now, you don't go talking like that." Ned looked at his brother. "We don't want to hear no talking like that do we, Fred?"

Fred shook his head, never making an audible sound.

Ned stood up straight and looked Caroline in the eye. "You're autochthonous around here, Miss Caroline, and we just ain't ready to think about you leaving. We think you belong right here, don't we, Fred?"

Fred shook his head again.

"Autochthonous"? Caroline made a mental note of the new word. She'd look it up later. What Ned lacked in verbal skills he made up for in his use of new words. "I'm all done with the cleaning up. Let me get my gloves, and I'll help you load the chairs."

"I know you're a smart girl, Miss Caroline, but seems like you forget this ever' year. My pa would rise up from his grave and start singing 'Mine Eyes Have Seen the Glory' if we let you pick up one of these chairs. You're just too twee to be doing such a ponderous task. Ain't she, Fred?"

Fred nodded in agreement, and Caroline made note of another unfamiliar word. *"Twee."*

"Okay. I'll finish my job while you do yours." She started back down the hall to the washer but turned around. "Oh, and I fixed you a box of goodies to take home with you. Gretchen made most of them, except for the few cookies I made."

"Whew-ee, Fred. The only thing better than back to back episodes of "Hawaii Five-O" is to snack on Miss Gretchen's and Miss Caroline's sweet treats while we's a-watching them. Ain't it so, Fred?"

Caroline thought she saw the hint of a grin on the silent twin's face. "I still have a few things to put away, but let me know before you leave, okay?"

"Yes, ma'am." Ned and Fred worked methodically, folding and stacking all the chairs before loading them into their truck. The Pendergrass twins finished within half an hour and called for Caroline.

She headed for the basket in the kitchen, checked underneath the striped napkin to make certain their pay envelopes were tucked away, and deliberately handed the basket to Fred at the terrace door. He uttered a muffled thank you before Ned could say a word. Ned was generous with his gratitude before they removed their caps from their hip pockets, turned toward one another in synch, and walked away. Caroline closed the door behind them, slid the café curtain to one side, and watched them walk slowly in step until they disappeared around the corner and behind the hedge. She was beginning to savor moments like these, moments with the characters who were a part of her life. After a seven-year intermission, Act Two of her life was beginning, and with it would be a novel set and a new cast of characters.

For months since Roderick's proposal, Caroline had known that change was coming, but her days had clicked off the same—morning workouts, practice and paperwork, afternoon teaching sessions, nightly reading or rehearsals sprinkled with evening meals with Sam and Angel. Saturdays for catching up, Sunday church responsibilities, and then Monday would come again. But this week would be different. No teaching. Monday, she'd get out the last invoices for piano lessons. Tuesday, she'd drive to Athens for her final piano lesson with Dr. Martin. Wednesday and Thursday, she'd help Gretchen prepare for the move.

Still, when she'd talked to Reverend Bixley last week about her need to resign her piano responsibilities at the church due to her sporadic travel schedule this summer and her impending move, he had persuaded her to stay on and play when she was in town.

Sam and Angel had gently told her that the studio would not be available for a renter after she moved. Without explanation, Caroline sensed Sam was keeping the studio available in case they needed a caregiver on the property for more daily assistance. Angel had grown steadily weaker since her heart attack almost a year ago. Sam and Angel were both in their mid-eighties, and with Caroline moving, they would need someone around and close by.

This time last year, she had assumed the change she'd been preparing for would take her to the university to begin her doctorate as a teaching assistant and even told her piano teacher to count on it. She'd thought Gretchen and Bella would move to Athens with her and take Dr. Spencer up on his offer to provide an education for Bella in exchange for access to observing, testing, and studying her.

But after meeting Roderick last summer, her daydreams about a future with him would creep into her mind and then vanish like the steam from her cup of tea. No more evaporating fantasies now. Twisting the pink pearl ring around her finger several times a day reminded her that in a few months, her home would be in the Bluegrass region of Kentucky and she'd be Mrs. Roderick Adair. She loved him more than she thought she could ever love again, and the only thing that deprived her of uncontainable joy was her fear—her fear of losing him like she lost David.

A Tuesday in early June

Listening to the last movement of the Beethoven sonata with Caroline at the piano, Dr. Annabelle Martin stood at the window, feeling the weight of her years and looking out over the university campus. Caroline, her finest student who truly understood the piano, how to finesse a melody from its keys and how to coax the music in the silence between the notes, was here for her final lesson.

When the last phrase came to its cadence and with its major chord still resounding, Dr. Martin turned from the window and began her walk across the aged wood floor, scarred by the brass casters from moving the piano around her studio over the years. "Well, I guess this is it."

Caroline, still lingering in the nether region between Beethoven and the piano, removed her hands from the keyboard and pivoted to face Dr. Martin. "Does that mean you're resigning as my teacher?"

Dr. Martin, tall and lean and now almost frail, approached the piano, but didn't answer the question. Her back, which had always remained perfectly straight as she sat on the piano bench, now bent slightly as she lowered herself into the chair next to the Steinway. The lacy edging of the handkerchief she had tucked predictably underneath her watchband, peeked from under the cuff of her blouse as she moved her hands across her lap, smoothing the folds in her purple skirt. "You know I had always counted on your becoming the teacher. That's why I've stayed at the university, just waiting for the time you were ready to make the move here and to prepare to assume my position."

"Oh, Dr. Martin, I could never, not in a hundred lifetimes, be ready to fill your position. I'm so very sorry to disappoint you by not coming to the university, but I know in my heart I've made the right decision."

Annabelle cleared her throat. "Yes, I trust you have. Is it ever wrong to choose love, real love?" She paused. "The good thing about marrying Roderick is that you won't have to choose between your passion for the piano and your love for him." She paused again. Keeping her head erect and allowing her wrinkled eyelids to veil her eyes, she no longer looked at Caroline. "I did, you know. I chose. Nearly fifty years ago, I had to make a choice because the young man who said he loved me forced me to choose."

Caroline leaned forward. "You never told me that."

"No, I never did. That is another choice I made. And now you want to ask me if I regret my decision." She raised her eyelids slowly as if the weight of the wrinkles made it difficult. "I only regret that I am a childless, old lady who never found love again, but I do not regret choosing the piano over someone who never understood my needs. His ultimatum was selfish and unfair, and I'm certain our union would have ended sadly. I would have lost both the piano and him."

"He wanted you to give up the piano entirely?"

"Oh, I'm not quite certain what he expected other than he didn't want me to play publicly anymore or to continue my studies. Even that was too much to give up, so I gave up on him." Her gaze was transfixed not on Caroline but on something or someone in her remembering. "What kind of love requires such an unnecessary sacrifice?"

"Perhaps it wasn't love at all."

She focused again on Caroline. "Perhaps you are right." The aging professor pulled at the linen handkerchief underneath the cuff of her blouse. "Since this is our last lesson, I have something to say to you, Caroline."

Caroline sat resolute as if not to miss a single syllable.

"You are marrying a wealthy man. Because you are his wife, certain people—his family, his friends, the community, his business associates—they will all have expectations of you. I know you, Caroline, and you are a pleaser. You'll want to fulfill all those expectations so they'll be happy with you, but be chary about anyone who wants you to renounce who you are. Do not allow them to suffocate you with so many other activities that the music in your soul cannot breathe." She delicately touched the corner of her eye with the handkerchief. "You have a gift, little one, a rare and divine gift. You must not forsake it, because it is a part of who you are. Do not deprive us of Caroline Carlyle. Will you promise me that?"

Caroline slid to the end of the piano bench and took her teacher's slender hands in hers. "Thank you, Dr. Martin. No words have ever meant more to me, and I'll do my best never to disappoint you."

"Caroline, I'm never troubled about your disappointing me. It's just that the piano has been your hiding place when your reality was too hard. The piano has always responded to you and has been something you could control, and you have poured every ounce of your passion into bringing music from the instrument. But things will be different now. With so much love and joy in your life, the piano will no longer be the buffer between you and living. You're free." She paused and wiped her eye again. "I just know that your very best days of playing and composing are ahead of you." She squeezed Caroline's hands, and they both stood up. "Be who you are, and don't deprive us of that." She embraced her favorite student as ripe tears traced the wrinkles in her cheeks.

Caroline pushed open the hallway doors and stepped into the rotunda, where she saw Dr. Wyatt Spencer sitting on the stairs.

Clipboard and pen in hand, he rose and approached her. "So you've had your last lesson? It doesn't have to be. There's still a spot for you here, and my offer's still good for Bella and Gretchen. Need my handkerchief?"

"That's kind of you on both offers, Wyatt. But no thank you. Gretchen's satisfied with her decision. She's actually moving to North Carolina the end of this week."

"Dr. Martin tells me you've made another decision too." He clicked his pen.

Caroline froze, worked at a smile, but gave no answer.

"So you're really going to marry the lucky lad from Lexington?" He walked around her as though examining her while he spoke. "You know, you and I could have had something, Caroline Carlyle."

She remained silent.

"All these months, I never hid my interest in you. Yeah, I was interested in Bella. The research I did with her will advance my career. But you . . . you were the sweet icing on the cake." He clicked his pen continually. "If you'd just given me a chance, I think I could have made you a happy woman." He stepped closer. "It's not too late. You haven't said 'I do.'"

Never quick with appropriate retorts, Caroline panicked for something clever to say. "You're a highly trained professional, Dr. Spencer. And I'll be forever grateful for all you've done for Bella and Gretchen. But that's as far as it has ever gone or will go."

Wyatt crossed his arms in front of him. "It's his money, isn't it?"

That did it. Her insides quivered, adrenalin pumped, and butterflies soared in her stomach just like before a concert. If she'd had the can of wasp spray she kept under the head of her bed in case of an intruder, she would have doused him. If her right hand had been free, she would have planted its imprint on his left cheek. But it held an umbrella.

Picking up her bag with her left hand, she took the umbrella with her right and ground its metal tip into the soft leather of the top of his left loafer as she took a step to walk away.

"Oowww!" He hopped until he dropped to his knee to check out the injury to his toes.

"Oh, I'm so sorry, Dr. Spencer. How utterly careless of me! I'm sure it will heal in time." She paused to watch him hobble. *Sweet icing on the cake.* "Have a wonderful life."

Caroline walked briskly down the hall, tapping her umbrella rhythmically with every step. How unlike her! Houseflies were the only living things she'd ever hurt deliberately. Unfortunate for Dr. Wyatt Spencer that she found him just as annoying.

Chapter 7

Advice for Roderick

Wednesday afternoon at Rockwater

Lilah's sprained ankle and limping around the kitchen didn't keep her from her usual humming. The coffee was brewing, and her thoughts were stewing. Mothering Roderick and taking care of Rockwater since Angeleah's death had earned her the right to say some things he needed to hear, and he would hear them this afternoon. She wiped the granite counter and slid the coffee mug in front of the sugar bowl.

"Do I smell coffee?"

The sound of that whiny voice from the office down the hallway was enough to make Lilah break out in hives. She grumbled quietly to herself as she continued to sponge down the countertops. "She says 'Do I smell coffee?' How am I supposed to know what that woman smells? I don't know how she could smell anything but that loud perfume she wears. The thing that woman doesn't know yet is that she's so out of here." Catching herself grinning, Lilah didn't bother to answer the whiny voice but turned to look out the large kitchen window to see Roderick strolling from his quarters across the courtyard.

He stepped into the kitchen, quietly closed the door and was headed to the cookie jar when Liz whined again from the hallway. "Lilah, did you hear me? I asked if I smelled coffee."

"I have no idea what you smell, but coffee's brewing in the kitchen." Lilah gave Roderick her that-woman's-worse-than-having-the-measles face. Roderick snickered and kissed her brown cheek before he bit into her famous teacake—the ones that had kept the cookie jar filled since he was a child.

"Then I'll have a cup." The annoying whine approached.

Lilah handed Roderick his cup of coffee and whispered, "That woman never misses an opportunity to be in the room with you. Why, she knows you're marrying Caroline and that doesn't slow her down one bit."

Even in the midafternoon, Liz's perfume entered the kitchen before she did. "Who's not slowing down one bit?"

"Oh, I was just telling Roderick I'm trying not to let my ankle slow me down."

Lilah was certain Liz was a closet contortionist. That hot-pink dress required it. Liz wore nothing that wasn't form-fitting, thigh-revealing, and cleavage-exposing and left Lilah wondering how she ever got into the garments she chose. Her white stiletto sandals clopped as she walked across the Brazilian cherry flooring and showed off perfectly pedicured pink toenails. Her every sensual move was deliberately designed to attract attention, from the slight swaying of her hips to the way she flexed the muscles in her calf when she leaned to get the coffee mug to the way her fingers played with the gold chains around her neck and strayed slightly south to supple flesh that rose and fell with every breath.

Liz poured her coffee and perched on the barstool next to Roderick. "All the arrangements for your meetings in London have been made. I faxed the final business plan to Deirdre this afternoon. She'll get it printed and bound and sent ahead of you."

"No, I don't want it sent ahead of me."

"But you always—"

"Not this time. I have a lot riding on this deal, so make certain Deirdre understands."

Lilah shuffled back to the refrigerator with the cream but did not miss the way Liz swiveled on the stool, her thigh so close to Roderick that the side of his trousers would probably have a hot-pink streak from his hip to his knee. Neither did she miss Roderick as he pivoted in the opposite direction and moved to the end of the counter.

He brushed the last of the teacake crumbs from his shirt. "Have you made the reservations for Caroline's trip to Guatemala yet?"

"Working on them. I'll need copies of her passport and also Ms. Pipkin's. I would imagine that Ms. Pipkin is well traveled, but does Caroline even have a passport?" She tapped her long pink claws on her coffee cup as she held it in both hands.

Lilah could no longer contain herself. "Why, if she doesn't, that beautiful woman will need one. I know Roderick has plans to take her to every romantic city in this world. He's just dying to show her off."

Roderick made her day. One more dig at Liz. "Lilah, you've been reading my mind, or have you been looking at my calendar?"

"I just know how head-over-heels in love you are with Miss Caroline Carlyle soon-to-be Mrs. John Roderick Adair."

He turned to Liz. "That I am, and yes, she has a passport, and I've asked her to bring it with her this weekend. And for the record, she's already made a number of trips to Guatemala."

"She's coming this weekend?"

"Yes, Acer and I are flying over to Raleigh-Durham Friday afternoon, and she's coming back with us on Sunday morning and will be here for a few days before she leaves for Guatemala."

Noting Liz's glare and the air turning green around her, Lilah chimed in again. "Why, yes! We have big plans to make. Never had a wedding at Rockwater before. And Roderick, we need to talk about a couple of things." She headed toward the kitchen door. "Help me totter over to the library. I can prop my foot up, and we can sit a spell."

She led the way through the morning room and took the right turn down the loggia to the library. "Hmm, looks like an afternoon shower's on the way." She stopped to look out the twenty-foot-high windows behind the grand piano. "April showers have already brought May flowers, but the rain keeps coming, and here it is June. Mind you, I'm not complaining. Something about a gentle, summer afternoon shower to clear the air." Hoping to clear the air about a few things with Roderick, she gestured. "Come on and let me sit down. My ankle starts to swell about this time every day."

Roderick fluffed the pillow-topped ottoman and positioned it for her to prop up her leg and then took the armchair next to her. "So tell me, Miss Lilah, what's on your mind?"

"Don't you give me that 'Miss Lilah' attitude, John Roderick Adair. You know what's on my mind, but I'm going to say it anyway." She adjusted the pillow under her knee. "What's first on my mind is—have you told Liz you're moving her to Lexington?"

"No, I haven't told her yet. I'm lining some things up,

and I need to inform her new boss, and then I'll bring her in and give her the news."

"God bless the poor man that takes that woman on. Or maybe her new boss will be a woman."

Roderick laughed. "Oh no. Liz working for another woman? I don't think so. I know she's a pain to you, but with her education and corporate knowledge, Liz is an asset to the company. Besides, it's smarter to promote her and keep her than it is to make her angry. Best to keep her until we can get a noncompete signed."

Lilah shook her head. "'Noncompete'? Oh, I get it. You're scared of her."

"No, but there's no reason to deliberately upset her right now."

"Well, I can't wait to see how you make her think she's being promoted. She's been working for you for four years, and you own the company. So tell me, how's working for somebody else going to be a promotion."

"Easy, Lilah, easy. Working here, she's basically been my administrative assistant, no authority, no decisions . . ."

"Is that so? Then you need to come and hear some of the phone conversations I hear." She crossed her arms and perched them on her abdomen as though resting her case.

"I don't doubt what you hear. But in her new position, she'll actually head up some projects and some small acquisitions. She's learned well, she's shrewd, and she's capable of the job."

"So, when does she become a bee in someone else's bonnet, and when is she out of here?"

"I think things will be lined up in a couple of weeks, and then I'll tell her. After that, she'll be working in Lexington within ten days to two weeks."

"Okay, I'm satisfied with that. I just don't want to spend the rest of my life in jail for doing something awful to that woman, so maybe I can control myself for a few more weeks. And if I can't, I'll try to make it look like an accident." She knew how to make Roderick laugh, and she needed to lighten the moment because her next questions would be like poking into a tender wound. Lilah relaxed her arms on the rounded leather arms of the chair. "Well, that's out of the way, now I want to know: have you told Caroline about your mother? I mean, about how she died?"

The muscles in Roderick's face tensed, and he paused before he answered. "You never have a problem getting to the point, do you, Lilah?"

"No time to waste pussyfooting around. There's no gentle way to ask that question. So did you tell her?"

"No, I haven't told her yet." He looked away from Lilah and out the window to see a delivery truck winding up the road to the house. "UPS is making a delivery. Something for you?"

"I haven't ordered a thing, and don't you change the subject, John Roderick Adair the third."

"That's twice in this conversation you've called me by my full name."

"That's because this is twice serious business. I already told you what I think about this, and you agreed. Now why haven't you had your talk with Caroline?"

He got out of his chair and walked over to the window. "I guess I just haven't found the right time."

"I think it's high time you make time. Caroline's going to be your wife. She'll live right here under this roof, and she'll be hobnobbing with your friends. Do you want her to hear the story from Rosemary Crooms or Lorna Carson?" She stopped, prepared to wait out his silence, but couldn't. "Do you want to start a marriage with your wife thinking you're hiding something?"

"You're right, Lilah. I need to tell her. Maybe this weekend while she's here would be a good time." He remained at the window.

Lilah imagined he was most likely thinking of his mother as he looked onto the terraced garden Angeleah had created. After her death twenty-eight years ago, his father had instructed the gardener to keep the garden, with its prize-winning roses and rare daylilies, just as she had designed it. Roderick's gardener followed the same instructions.

"I think this weekend would be the perfect time. And there's one other thing. You know how much I loved your parents, and you know how I feel about Rockwater. But this is going to be Caroline's home with you now. This house and those gardens you're looking at are a beautiful shrine to your parents. But you couldn't even live in this house yourself, so you built an apartment across the courtyard. And Caroline's not going to like living in that apartment when there's a magnificent old house thirty yards away."

Roderick turned from the window to look at Lilah. "I know. I really wasn't planning to live in the apartment."

"Fine, so if living in the apartment isn't in your plans, what is?"

"Interesting that we haven't talked seriously about where we'd live, but I've always assumed we'd live here at Rockwater."

"Careful, that road of assumption might just lead to the same place as the road of good intentions."

"Don't want to go there, but I can't imagine Caroline wanting to live anywhere else. She's not even seen the manor house in Lexington. Besides, I've turned that house over to Sarah and George." He walked across the room and sat on the edge of the ottoman where Lilah's foot rested. "I guess I haven't thought about the possibility that Caroline would not want to live here."

"Well, there's only one way to find out, and that's to ask her." Lilah shifted her swollen foot from the ottoman to the floor and sat up on the edge of her chair. "And one more thing, and then I'm finished. A woman's got to make her own nest, Roderick. And moving into a house that hasn't seen one change in the last thirty years just may not be her idea of a nest. You need to think about that and decide if you want a shrine or if you're going to let Caroline bring some life back into this house." She attempted to lift herself from the chair.

Roderick stood, took her left hand, and assisted. "Guess I should look at this like a merger of sorts and deal with the compromises accordingly."

Lilah stabilized herself on her feet and looked directly up into his eyes. "You're right. It is a merger, but the likes of which you've never negotiated. And I don't know about that 'dealing accordingly' part. My advice is to forget your wheeling and dealing; we're talking about matters of the heart. You put Caroline's needs and desires first, and you'll be one happy man." She held his face in both her hands and asked him the same question she'd been asking him after every serious conversation they'd had since he was a small lad. "Roderick, do you get what I'm telling you?"

"Yes, ma'am. I get it."

She dropped her hands from his face and turned to walk away. "Good. And you'd be wise not to forget it."

Saturday afternoon in Durham

"Hi, sis. Just landed."

"Hi, Rod! We've had a light lunch and a nap. Your timing's perfect."

"Acer's securing the plane, and someone called a cab for me. Shouldn't take more than a half an hour to get downtown. Did you decide where to meet for a cup of coffee?" Roderick took out his pen and calendar from his shirt pocket.

"Yes, you have a pencil?"

"Certainly."

"Remember, we had a light lunch just so we could meet you at the Amélia Café. It's at 905 West Main. Just tell the driver it's on Brightleaf Square. He'll know. They serve Guatemalan coffee and fabulous pastries. Oh, and they have lunch fare if you like. We'll be there in half an hour."

"Great! Just need your thoughts on a couple of things. I told Caroline I'd meet them on campus at three o'clock. And according to our flight plan, we need to take off at four thirty." He closed his calendar, clicked his pen, and put them back in his pocket.

"That'll give us around an hour to talk and another hour on campus with the girls, and then we'll get you and Caroline back to the airport."

"Thanks, sis. See you in half an hour."

The cab ride was relaxing—almost no traffic, the last sprinkling of rhododendron blooms along the roadside, and a Brahms string quartet resonating from the radio. Spring was almost over, and the heat of summer approached like a slow-moving grass fire in a pine forest. More than seasons were changing.

Sarah's car was parked right in front of the café. He paid the driver and got out. Sarah met him at the door with open arms.

"Hi, little brother." She hugged him and led him to the booth where George was already stirring honey into his tea. "Haven't seen you since Easter. Seems we've been too busy."

After shaking, George's hand, Roderick sat down across

the table from them. He ordered coffee for himself and Sarah and a plate of pastries for sampling before beginning their conversation. "Caroline tells me Gretchen's already settling in and getting to know the area."

"They are, and Bella's done amazingly well. I worried about her being overly stimulated with all the new surroundings, and especially having Karina around." Sarah sprinkled cinnamon on the cloud of whipped cream floating atop her coffee.

"Caroline was worried too. Glad it's working out. Karina's the wildcard here, but I guess time will tell." He sipped his coffee before sinking his fork into the classic éclair filled with Tahitian vanilla cream. "Glad I could speak with the two of you before I see Caroline."

"What's on your mind, little brother?"

"Had a talk with Lilah earlier this week, and as usual, she brought up something I needed to hear." He put down his fork and took another sip of coffee. "You know Caroline and I have set the date and made plans for the wedding, but I think I might have been assuming too much about where we're going to live."

"You haven't talked with Caroline about where you're going to live?" Sarah's dropped jaw showed her surprise.

"No. I just assumed since she doesn't own a home that she would join me at Rockwater. But Lilah's not certain." He stirred the Tahitian cream on his plate. "I haven't asked her if she wants to live in Georgia or in Lexington. Again, I just thought she'd want to live at Rockwater."

"Do you think she'd prefer living in the Lexington manor house? That's no problem with George and me if you want to live there."

"Thanks, sis, but that English Tudor is yours. You and Dad were the Anglophiles in this family. So, if Caroline wants to live in town, we'll buy or build a place."

"But you love Rockwater."

"That I do. But I love her more, and I want her to be happy. Rockwater's so remote, and she might not want to be so isolated." He wiped his mouth with the stiff paper napkin.

"Don't jump ahead, Rod. Just talk to her. Ask her where she wants to live."

"I'm planning to this weekend. But how would you feel if Caroline wanted to make some changes at Rockwater, maybe do some renovating?" He watched her expression closely, always able to read the lines in his sister's face before the words came out of her mouth.

"Rod, Rockwater's your home to do with as you please. You and Mother were the Francophiles and loved the countryside."

"But think about it. It's where we grew up. And in a way, it's still home for you. How would you feel about the changes?"

Sarah turned to George, who was pushing his empty plate of sparse chocolate crumbs toward the end of the table. Then she looked back at Rod but sat silently.

George finally spoke. "Just tell him, Sarah."

"Tell me what?" Roderick put down his fork.

"Roderick, you're right, we grew up there. The house is full of memories, some sweet and some not so sweet. I've wanted to say this to you for several years, but there's been no real reason until now." She cleared her throat. "Look, you're not preserving anything by keeping marble floors and thirty-year-old heavy drapes and the furniture our parents bought when they built the house. Our parents are dead, buried side by side with a sculpted work of art as their headstone. Do you really think Mother would want you to live out back in an apartment just so the house could stay the same?"

"I guess—" Roderick attempted to speak.

Sarah interrupted him. "Mother was the most—"

George placed his hand over Sarah's hand on the table. "Let your brother answer the question, Sarah."

Rod stammered. "I guess I built my quarters because I didn't know what else to do."

"I can tell you what to do. Mother was more vibrant and alive than anyone I've ever known. She's probably rearranging heaven right now, and I can almost guarantee if she were still alive, that house would have gone through several changes to keep it from becoming a museum—or worse, a mausoleum. She gave her money to support the museum, but somehow I can't imagine her wanting to live in one, or for you to live in a shrine. Now, don't you wait for Caroline to ask. Talk to her about what she wants, and ask her to help you make Rockwater a real home again, whatever it takes."

"Well, that's fairly clear and simple."

"The only thing sacred in that house is the portrait of mother in the garden and maybe the old swing in the oak tree out back. If Caroline doesn't want the portrait, then I'd like it for the manor house."

Roderick tensed. The thought of not having his mother's portrait in the master suite was like not wearing his father's paisley ties or not having the rose garden to walk through in the early mornings. Occasionally, late at night, he would leave his quarters and go over to the house, walk down its corridors and through the loggia to his parents' bedroom. He would turn on the lamp highlighting his mother's portrait above the fireplace and stand in the darkness, trying to remember how she sounded when she laughed or how her hair would trail in the wind when she galloped across the pasture, or how the grass would smell when they rode together in the freshly mown meadow.

"Rod. Rod, where'd you go?"

"Nowhere. Just thinking about what you said. You're right, and I'll do it." He looked at his watch and then back at the platter of pastries they hadn't touched. "Anything else for you? Want your coffee warmed, sis, or another cup of tea, George?" They nodded. "If you're certain you want nothing else, I think I'll ask for a to-go box for Gretchen and Bella and order another assortment to take home."

Sarah smiled. "I'm sure they'd all appreciate having the best pastries in Durham at their fingertips."

George added, "The best pastries until Gretchen opens her bakery." He reported that he'd found a small shop not far from the Duke campus and that he was checking into the purchase of the equipment she'd need. They small-talked until the waiter brought the boxes of goodies and George excused himself to the restroom.

Sarah took Rod's arm as they walked toward the front door. "Since you haven't talked to Caroline yet about where you're going to live, I'm assuming you probably haven't told her about Mother either."

"No. Something else I'm planning to do while she's with me this weekend. Lilah reminded me that it's better if she hears it from me." He looked straight ahead through the glass door, never turning toward his sister.

"Lilah's right. I know it won't be easy for you, but you've never been one to run away from difficult tasks, not even the most difficult one with Mother."

He might as well have been a time traveler. Sarah's words catapulted his soul, his memory, and the essence of who he was back in time nearly thirty years ago, leaving only his well-dressed flesh standing at the entrance to Amelia's Café. He stood on the pebbled bank of the stream near the covered bridge at Rockwater, listening to his mother begging him not to leave her . . .

"Rod, Rod?" Sarah shook his arm. "You're gone again."

He returned. "No, no, I'm here. I was just thinking of what you said about running away from troubles."

"You're not going to be a runaway groom are you? Getting cold feet about getting married, little brother?"

"No, not about my running away. But what if Caroline runs after I tell her?"

Chapter 8

Confessions

Sunday morning at Rockwater

Would daylight ever come? Last night before turning in, they had agreed on breakfast at six thirty and an early-morning walk down to Blue Hole, but he'd been awake since before four. Conversation sitting on a boulder with their legs dangling above a deep pool would be different than last night's exchange over his grilled steak and baked potato.

Dinner conversation had provided him all the details about how Gretchen and Bella and Karina had moved into their town home, chosen rooms, and put out their personal things. Roderick had strained to feign as much interest in Bella and Gretchen as Caroline had exuded, but his mind was on other things—things like why they'd be sleeping in separate quarters tonight when they'd be married in December and how Caroline would respond to his questions about where they'd live and how she would react to hearing about his mother.

That kind of thinking made him sweat. He turned over

again, kicked the sheet off his legs, and lay on his back, arms folded under his pillow, and thought of Caroline lying in his parent's bed in the main house. The house was large and hollow, dark and still like a tomb, but she was warm and alive and alone. He should have slept in his old room, but he had kissed her good night and sprinted across the courtyard in the rain to his own quarters. Thoughts of sliding into bed beside her and the sound of rain on his tin roof had lulled him to sleep, but other thoughts had awakened him.

Another punch of his pillow, and he rolled over to see the clock—four fifty-three. An hour and a half before breakfast.

He got up, stumbled over his boots left too close to the closet door, grabbed his running clothes and shoes and headed to the bathroom. He turned on the light and looked in the mirror. Splashing cold water in his face and running his wet fingers through his dark hair was his routine but would do nothing for red, sleep-deprived eyes. He brushed his teeth, buzzed off his beard, dressed, and headed to the kitchen to make coffee and check the news. Through the kitchen window he could see the draperies, normally drawn to cover the large window, were open, giving him a full view of the house. Lights were on in the loggia and the kitchen. Forget the news and coffee, Caroline was up.

It was nearly an hour before sunup. He glanced at the fluorescent sliver of a new moon and the morning star across the horizon as he crossed the courtyard. *Should be a postcard sunrise this morning.* He warned Caroline with a knock on the door before he entered the kitchen. "Just didn't want to frighten you."

Caroline pulled her terrycloth bathrobe tighter around herself and brushed the wisps of hair escaping from her ponytail away from her face. "You're an hour early, and I'm not dressed."

He walked over to her where she was measuring coffee and slipped his arms around her waist. "So this is how you look early in the morning?"

She frowned. "Yeah, it is," she said hesitantly. "Is it a deal breaker?"

Stepping back to look at her, he saw her bare feet. "Not sure yet . . . Could be."

"You're such a shallow man, Roderick. I have hidden qualities, you know." She started to swipe him with the dishtowel, but he caught it in midair.

"Yes, and I'm dying to find out what they are." They embraced for a long kiss.

She pulled away. "Enough, sir. I'm hungry, and if you'd been here on time rather than an hour early, a ham-and-cheese omelet with the last croissant from the bakery in Durham would have met you at the door."

"Well, if you hadn't turned on the lights, then I wouldn't have known you were up, and I wouldn't have been an hour early."

"Speaking of the lights, you must teach me about all these light switches. I've never seen so many."

He went to the fridge for milk and eggs. *She wants to know about light switches. That's positive.* "I know it looks complicated, but it's really simple once I explain the system to you. My father had this engineering mind, and he designed the electrical around here and the security system."

"Security system? I wasn't aware of that. Glad I didn't flip too many switches." She reached for the box of pastries.

"We're rather secluded out here. No neighbors in sight, and my father wanted my mother to feel safe." He cracked the fourth egg into a mixing bowl. "Actually, I think my mother loved this place so much that being afraid never entered her thoughts. Maybe all this security business was more for my father's peace of mind."

"I'm with your mother. Oh, the privacy and looking out on rolling hills to see only what God made. It's like a head start on heaven."

"You like it out here?" He began whisking the eggs.

"Like it? It's like my dream is suddenly going to become my address."

She has no intention of living anywhere else. But if I don't ask her, I'll never hear the last of it from Lilah. He put down the bowl and whisk and walked to the counter where she was putting croissants and muffins on a baking sheet. "Caroline, if I don't ask you this, Lilah will most likely chain me to that big oak tree out back and feed me only oatmeal and buttermilk for the next month."

"Oh, Lilah couldn't do that. She might want to, but I don't think it's in her to do it." She closed the box and licked the crumbs from her finger. "Ask me what?"

"Lilah called me into the library Wednesday afternoon for a talk. Around here, when Lilah takes you to the library, it's serious." He saw the look of concern on Caroline's face. "In this case, not that serious. She just wanted to be certain that you and I talked about where we will live."

Her look of concern melted into one of bewilderment. "Interesting. We've talked about wedding plans, honeymoon plans, all kinds of plans. But you're right, we've never actually talked about where we would live. I think I just always assumed it would be Rockwater. This is your home, and I can't imagine living anywhere else."

He picked her up off the floor and twirled her around, smiling more broadly with every circle.

"Roderick, put me down please. I'm getting dizzy."

He gently touched her feet to the floor and held her until she was steady. "Oh, I'm so glad to hear you say that out loud." He kissed her and pulled away. "Are you certain you don't want to live somewhere else or maybe in

Lexington? There are no shops and no city lights for miles out here."

"I'm absolutely certain, but is Rockwater where you want to live?"

"I want to live where you'll be happy, but if it's here at Rockwater, then I'll be doubly happy." He walked back over to the counter to the bowl of eggs. "One other thing, though. This place hasn't seen any changes in nearly thirty years. I want you to make this place our home. If it means tearing down walls or ripping up floors or buying new furniture . . ."

"Or putting just one light switch in each room?"

"Or putting just one light switch per room. Whatever you want, it's yours."

"So that means we'll live in the house and not in your apartment out back?"

No other woman he knew would have ever considered living in his apartment when an estate home sat ninety paces across a well-groomed courtyard. But that was Caroline. Simple. Humble. And unassuming. "Yes, we'll live right here, and Lilah will be here to take care of everything. I want you to make glorious music and do whatever makes you happy. But we do have my apartment in case the renovations get messy." He poured the eggs into the hot, oiled skillet.

"Oh, I think we should live here a while before we make decisions about changes. This is the home where you and Sarah grew up."

"Don't you worry about Sarah. She's already given me the heretofores about this house. She reminded me that my parents wanted this house to be a home and not a shrine to their memories. She'll be happy with whatever you choose to do except . . ."

"Except?"

"Yeah, she's got this thing about that old rope swing in the oak tree out back."

"Tell your sister not to worry. I wouldn't think of removing it. After all, I was planning to use it to tie you to the tree when you need flogging."

Her playful nature made him eager.

She grinned and raised her right eyebrow. "Pay attention, Roderick, you're burning the eggs."

Caroline stood at the front door waiting for Roderick. "What's the hold up? We'll be late for church."

"Coming, and what's this about church?" He came through the morning room into the hallway.

"This is just shy of fabulous. It's Sunday morning, and we're headed to church dressed in shorts and T-shirts, and there'll be no sermon, only contemplation."

Roderick took her hand and pressed it to his lips. "Guess we're headed to Rockwater's sanctuary. The first time I took you there, you prayed out loud, but not like any prayers I ever heard in church."

"Would you prefer I pray like people pray in church?"

"No, but I had just never heard anyone talk to God like He's sitting on the boulder next to you."

"He was, you know."

Roderick never tired of her blue eyes looking through him. "I suppose He was. What do you say to a walk through the front gardens and then circling around to the path to Blue Hole, or will that make us too late for the contemplating part?" He closed the curved front door and led her down the stone steps.

"Sounds wonderful! I need to walk until lunchtime after

the breakfast you fed me."

He squeezed her hand. "You've never seen the roses in the late spring. The blossoms have been stunning this year. Some of them have been almost the size of a dinner plate."

"Who around here has such a green thumb?"

"I have a man who takes care of the horses, and he has a son who takes care of the property."

"You hire someone just to take care of the horses, and then someone else to take care of the garden?"

"You don't know much about running a horse farm, do you? Rafe, like his father before him, does more than just take care of the horses. He's in charge of the breeding, the training, and anything else to do with the horses. It's like running a business."

"You have this farm, hire a man to take care of the horses, and you don't even ride?"

"Not anymore, but could we talk about that later?" They descended stone steps to the bottom of the trilevel terraced garden where a clean path lay covered in tiny pebbles and raised beds, edged with river rock gathered from the property, lined the walkway.

"So Rafe's son takes care of the gardens?" She stopped to peer into the throat of a daylily the creamy color of well-beaten egg yolks.

"Fletcher's like his father. He does much more than take care of the gardens. He grew up here, went away to study forestry and thought he wanted to be a park ranger, but when I offered him this job, he took a few horticulture classes and moved back home."

"Is anybody else employed around here that I need to know about?"

"One or two, but that'll come later. Fletcher takes care of all this property. Keeps the forest floors clean, the meadows fertilized and mowed, the timber select cut, and all the gardens growing. You just missed the daffodils. Acres of them." He pointed out to the hills in the distance. "A few weeks ago, that whole meadow just before the hills was yellow and surrounded by blue grass."

She squeezed his arm as they climbed the steps to the next terrace. "But I won't miss them next April. And before that, I won't miss the October sycamore leaves or the December snow on the cedars."

He stopped to hug her. "I can hardly wait to experience it all again through your eyes. All you'll miss is the heat of the summer."

"But I'll have a couple of weeks in the Guatemalan Highlands. It'll be cool up there."

"Wish I could go with you. Been lots of places, but never to Guatemala."

She stopped in her tracks and faced him. "Terrific. So there's one place in the world that I can show you. Next trip, Mr. Adair, and I promise it will be memorable."

They strolled the upper terrace and crossed the stream over the south bridge before taking the lane down to Blue Hole. The grass bordering the dirt ruts was lush and green, and an occasional canopy of tree limbs shaded them as they walked.

"I've been thinking about the wedding, Roderick. If we hadn't settled on December, we could have had the ceremony underneath the pergola just beyond the south bridge. It would be a shaded, lovely walk from the house for our guests, and then we could have our own private ceremony at Blue Hole after everyone was gone."

"You mean tying the knot and jumping in?" He raised his hands in the air. "Then we don't have to wait until December?"

"Yes, we must wait, and we'll wait until next summer for our private ceremony downstream. Just thinking we'll keep Blue Hole as our place—a place for our private memories."

"I like that thought." He wondered if she'd still feel the same way after the conversation he was about to have with her. They walked the last quarter of a mile quietly except for Caroline's humming. He recognized "Plaisir D'Amour."

Early-morning mist still hovered over the serene water as they climbed the boulder to their favorite perch. "Heard you humming 'The Pleasure of Love' while we walked. I still see you surrounded in pink and sitting at the piano playing and singing that."

"If I remember correctly, after you found out that Rachmaninoff and Liszt were not options, that was the only request you made for my first recital. Wasn't it your mother's favorite?"

"I rather think it was. She sang it often for her soirees, and she hummed it when she worked in the garden. I wish you could have seen the way she looked at my father when she sang it." He paused and tried to stare through the mist to see the clear pool beneath it. "I wish you could have known my mother, and I wish she could have known you."

Taking his hand, she held it in her palm and traced the length of his fingers. "It's interesting. In many ways, I feel that I do know her. She left her fingerprints all around us, and she made you for me."

"You remember how I told you Lilah took me to the library for a talk?" He turned his hand over in hers and held her fingers tightly. "Caroline, I need to tell you something. You've been open with me about your deepest hurt when David was killed, and how it nearly destroyed you. It's time I was straight with you about something."

She nodded her head but remained quiet.

"This won't be as easy as talking to you about where you want to live." He paused, cleared his throat, and waited for her to say something.

She didn't.

"Caroline, you need to hear from me how my mother died." Pausing again, he looked at her face, her expression as still and serene as the deep waters beneath their feet. "Mother was passionate about everything—my father, Sarah and me, her music, her gardens, and riding. Neither Sarah nor my father took to riding, but my mother and I rode together over every inch of this land. Mother said riding made her feel free, and she rode most every day. You've seen the covered bridge my father had built over the stream so she'd have a place to cool off or to wait out a rain shower when she was out riding."

He realized the tight squeeze he had on Caroline's hand, let go, and rubbed his sweaty palms together.

"Mother died the summer I was nine. Sarah was away at camp. Father was in Lexington on business, and my mother had a group of her friends over for lunch. They were planning some charity event, and Mother promised me that morning if I would read or entertain myself while her guests were there, then we'd go for a long ride that afternoon. She always kept her promises, and not even the threat of rain kept us from riding. Morrell—that's Rafe's father—tried to talk us out of going, but Mother asked him to saddle the horses anyway and assured him we'd be back before the rain set in.

"We hadn't been riding long when the sky began to darken, just a typical July afternoon thunderstorm, we thought. But we were closer to the covered bridge than we were to the stable when the rain started. It was just a sprinkle at first, but then it started coming down in sheets. I remember Mother turning around to me and saying, 'Let's ride, John Roderick.' Starlight, her horse, took off in a gallop toward the bridge, and I followed. My hat blew off and the rain was leaving welts on my face. We made it through the pine grove and were headed toward the turn in the stream where we could cross and then make a straight shot for the bridge. We had reached the edge of the stream when a flash of lightning struck one of the tall pines. The lightning strike was so close that we heard the thunder at the same time we saw the streak. I can remember the ground trembled, and my hair, even wet, felt like it was standing on end." Roderick's voice broke, and he stopped to swallow.

Caroline still said nothing.

He tried to start again. "The lightning . . . the lightning spooked Starlight, and in the chaos, Mother was thrown hard and landed in the bed of rock at the edge of the stream." He released his hands that were laced together and nervously rubbed the boulder on each side of where he sat. There had been no reason for him to tell this story in years, but the scene was so present to him, he could feel the rain in his face as he ran to his mother. "I was able to stop my horse and get off and run to Mother. Her . . . her body was twisted among the rocks. She was face down, and I maneuvered to turn her over. The blood . . . there was so much blood. And the rain. She moaned when I turned her, but I had to see her face. She had to tell me what to do. There was a big gash in her temple and blood oozed from her mouth and nose. Then I saw her leg, the outline of the bone protruding through her riding pants, and more blood. I knelt on the rocks and held her as best I could and tried to shield her face from the rain. I begged her to open her eyes. 'Mother,' I said, 'Look at me. Look at me, Mother. I don't know what to do.' I said it over and over and over." He turned to Caroline. Her blues eyes, like his mother's, brimmed with tears.

He stared back into the pool, almost void now of the mist that had covered it earlier. "It seemed so long that she didn't respond, but then she opened her eyes, and in this garbled voice, she said, 'I'm almost there, Roderick. It's so beautiful.' Her eyes were open, but I don't think she was looking at me. Somehow, even then, I knew she was leaving me.

"I asked her where was so beautiful, but she didn't seem to hear me. I just looked at her and kissed the wet curls that looked like someone had painted them on her forehead. I kept calling her and asking her what to do. I looked around for my horse. I called for him. I had to go and get help. When I tried to lay Mother's head down and get up, she looked at me. She was really looking at me then, and she said, 'My little gentleman, you stay right here with your mother. That's what you must do. Don't leave me, son.' Those were her exact words: 'Don't leave me, son,' and the last ones she spoke." He felt Caroline's hand rubbing the back of his neck gently just the way his mother use to do, but she remained quiet, never interrupting his story.

"I don't remember much after that. I remember lying down beside Mother and holding her and watching the rain wash the blood from her face, leaving red trails down the rocks and into the stream until there was no more blood. Morrell had been on the west side of the farm and waited until the storm blew over before driving home. He discovered Starlight and my horse around the stable. He knew something was wrong and rode in the late-afternoon mist until he found us at dusk.

"I didn't speak until Father got home. I was able to tell him what happened, and I can still hear my father wailing as though he had been gravely wounded. He had been. We both had been. For the next few weeks, I moved in and out of uncontrollable crying and total silence. I was afraid to go to sleep because of the nightmares. I knew it was my fault she was gone. If I just hadn't made her promise to go riding.

If we had just waited to see what the storm was going to do like Morrell told us to do. If I had just found my horse and gotten help.

The doctor told my father her injuries were so extensive and severe that little could have been done even if they had gotten her to the hospital within minutes. I learned later that he found it miraculous that she ever regained consciousness enough to speak to me. But none of them were there, and what does a nine-year-old boy understand about blame?"

"Lilah took care of us. I was so traumatized that I rarely spoke for the next year, so my father hired a tutor to work with me. I saw doctors, counselors, psychologists, psychiatrists, but no one could pull me from the place I had retreated to. Truth be known, I think that's largely why Sarah became a child psychologist. She became my protector and my voice. She stayed with me every night until I went to sleep. She would stand quietly beside me and hold my hand while I stared at Mother's portrait. Somehow, she understood. I owe so much to Sarah."

Caroline broke her silence. "Is Sarah the one who convinced you it was an accident and it wasn't your fault?"

Roderick, stunned that she had broken her silence with such an insightful question, turned to her. "No, it wasn't Sarah. It was Mother." He waited for Caroline's next question, but it didn't come. She was patient like Sarah had been, not pushing him or putting words in his mouth. "A little more than a year after the accident, I dreamed of Mother one night. It was a vivid dream. She was so beautiful, sitting in the daffodils under an oak tree singing one of the lullabies she sang to me as a child. I was running around her, singing along, and picking daffodils one at the time until I had a handful. When I handed her the flowers, she took them and smiled at me. Then she said, 'Why thank you, my little gentleman!' She always called me that. Then she said, 'And thank you for doing as I asked and for staying with me until I found this beautiful place. You were a good boy, John Roderick. We had fun, didn't we?' And then she started singing again."

"What a gift that dream was!" Caroline moved closer to kiss his cheek.

"It truly was. It turned things around for me. When I woke from the dream, I ran to my father's room, and I remember telling him 'Mother said I was a good boy.' I said it over and over until I could tell him about my dream. It was a slow process, but I've healed, like you have. But I think the scar deep inside will always be tender." He rubbed his shoulder across his cheek to catch his tears.

"I cannot believe how much I love you, Roderick. I know it was like opening a fresh wound to tell me this, but I'm glad you did. I want to know absolutely everything about you." She rose on her knees and turned to him and kissed his tears, then gently pressed her hand against his chest, guiding him to lie on the sun-warmed boulder. Like a soft blanket, she covered him with her body and kissed him long. Finally, she moved to lie beside him and held her hand to his cheek. "Let's just lie still and quiet for a while."

"Yes, my love. But I must say something: you must always be safe. I'll do my best to take care of you. I don't want to walk around on this planet if you're not on it." He held her close, closed his eyes to the midmorning sunshine, and breathed deeply.

They lay serenely, she stroking his face occasionally, and he squeezing her arm. After a while, Caroline raised herself to her elbows and began to sing softly, again "Plaisir D'Amour."

Roderick rose to his feet and pulled Caroline to him. "Shall we go home?"

"Hmm, let's do. Let's go home."

Chapter 9

Foreboding

Thursday, June 10, late afternoon in Moss Point

Caroline fumbled to answer the phone before it woke Little David. "Oh, hi, Roderick. Already in London?"

"Just landed in the rain and catching a cab to the hotel for a little shut-eye before the meeting in the morning. You sound sleepy yourself."

"Actually, you caught me napping. My parents came up yesterday to see me before I leave for Guatemala. Brought Betsy and the kids, and we stayed up late talking after we put the little ones to bed. Then this afternoon, we took David and Josefina to the park to feed the ducks and went for a swim. You should see him in the water. He's not quite nine months old, and I think he might just grow fins and scales."

"Took to the water, did he?"

"He did indeed, but right now, he's lying beside me sound asleep on the sofa, and Betsy and Josefina are in my bedroom napping as well."

"I wish I was there. I want to get to know Betsy. She's

been your best friend since before kindergarten, and she's probably wondering about me, if I measure up and if she can trust me to take care of you like she has."

"You got that one right. Betsy thinks she's taken care of me my whole life." Caroline pushed herself into a sitting position, careful not to rouse the baby. "But I don't know about the two of you getting together. Betsy knows too much."

"That's another reason to get to know her."

Caroline could hear the traffic in the background. "What time is it in London?"

"It's around ten o'clock."

"But I can hear the traffic over the phone even this late."

"Well, it's a large, busy city. You'd really like it here. There's a certain castle that I . . ."

David stirred and called for his mother. Caroline attempted to lift him with her free hand. "Oops, just the mention of castles, and the baby's awake."

"Does that mean the conversation's over?"

"Getting close. I did want to tell you that Mason's driving up this evening. We'll leave for Atlanta very early in the morning. Betsy and I will go for our fittings at the dress shop before noon, then they'll drop me off at the airport. They're spending the weekend in Atlanta."

"I still can't believe you're traveling to Guatemala while I'm halfway around the world. Got your satellite phone and all the information for the driver?"

"Yes. Liz sent everything just as you instructed, although I doubt she did it with a smile on her face."

"Well, you won't be dealing with her much longer. She'll be moving on to Lexington after I get this merger done. This trip to London should take care of that."

"Sounds lovely. My bags are packed, and frankly, I'm looking forward to being in Guatemala again. I want to take you there some day—no castles, but magnificent volcanoes and clouds like you've never seen before, and then there's Antigua and Lake Atitlán. Haven't been back since I went with Betsy and Mason for Josefina's adoption nearly four years ago. It'll be good to see Reyna and the sisters."

"No misgivings about going alone back to the country where David was killed."

She paused before replying. "Oh, I expect some of those memories to enter my mind while I'm there, but I just know thoughts of coming home to you and my enthusiasm for starting this children's choir will chase them away." She wrestled with the toddler climbing over her to get to the floor. "David's little namesake is anxious to find his mother. I need to go. I hear Betsy coming down the hall. I'll call you tomorrow before I board the plane."

"I'll expect to hear your voice. Love you, Miss Blue Eyes."

"Me too. Don't know if I love you or miss you more. Bye for now." Caroline hung up the phone, stood and stretched, and looked down the hall to see David crawling toward Betsy.

Betsy picked David up and sat down in the chair next to the piano. "So who had the gall to call during our nap, not that it bothered Josefina?"

"It was Roderick. He just landed in London."

"Wow, Caroline. He just landed in London, and you're flying off to Guatemala with a quarter of a million dollars to start a choir of orphans. This is some kind of life you're going to have." She stroked her baby's hair. "You won't forget about me, will you?"

"Hmm. I might forget the girl who wouldn't walk down the hall with me in eighth grade because I was too short, but I won't forget the friend who's seen me through every season of my life, even the dark, cold ones."

"Speaking of that. I heard what you said to Roderick about your memories of Guatemala? I know you're all excited about starting this children's choir. But what are you really thinking?"

Caroline sat back down on the sofa, curling her legs up under her and grabbing the chenille pillow to hold close. "Why don't you ask me what you really want to ask me?"

"Okay, I will. How are you going to handle this continual relationship with Guatemala and your memories of David's death? How's that going to color your relationship with Roderick?"

"Apparently he was wondering, too, because he just asked me practically the same question. Answer to question number one: I'm not sure how I'll handle my memories, but you know how I've talked about starting this choir for years. Somehow I think it'll provide meaning to David's death and all that he tried to do there." She paused and looked down as she twisted the fringe on the pillow. "I know I'll be thinking of him while I'm there. I'll think of him when the rains come and when I'm riding through the mountains. I'll think of him when I'm sitting across the table from Reyna. But if she can remain in Guatemala and work among the poor when her husband was washed down the mountain with David, then surely I can make a few trips to Guatemala to begin a new work." She hugged the pillow closer and continued. "And as far as what it will do to my feelings about Roderick, I can't wait to get back home to him."

"Good, so all of this change because of a dream you had a few months ago where you were with David in a Guatemalan flood, hanging onto a tree for dear life, and he told you to cross the stream to Roderick?"

"No, not just because of the dream, but because of seven years of grieving and you telling me it was time to toss out David's cologne and time to buy some new clothes and time to take a chance on a man from Kentucky."

"That's better. No more hopes of David's return and no more investigation about his death while you're there?"

"No. I've accepted his death even though there was no body to bury, and no more investigation into the accident while I'm there. I'll get my work done, and then I'm coming home to Roderick."

Caroline's expression and the glassy look of her eyes did not go unnoticed. Betsy rose and joined Caroline on the sofa and hugged her. "CC, we've honored David by naming that little guy over there after him, and you will honor him with the building of this choir. We'll never forget him, but I'm so glad you're finally letting go." They embraced in silence.

"David will always be my first love, and no one knows of the nights I've spent hoping he'd coming walking across the terrace or dreaming about what might have been if he had lived. But he didn't, and I'm at peace with my love for Roderick. It isn't the same, but I'm not the same person either. My love for Roderick is real and deep and true, and I have no thoughts that my love for Roderick dishonors my love for David."

"You're short on legs, but you're tall in brains and heart, girl." Betsy grabbed the pillow from Caroline, threw it to the other end of the sofa, and stood up. "I know it's Thursday and it's usually a Friday-night thing when we're here, but what do you say to calling Mabel and seeing if she'll fix us a bag of greasy cheeseburgers and onion rings? We can call Sam and Angel and see if they want to join us. I know they'll want to see you before you leave."

"Sounds fabulous. I'll be eating eggs, rice, and beans for

the next couple of weeks, so a cheeseburger sounds great. And maybe a chocolate malt."

Sam opened the door to the back porch with one hand and held his cane with the other. "I smell onion rings. Smelled them when you opened the gate coming from the park." He tapped his cane in front of Josefina. "Come in, my little lady. You're just growing like trumpet vine, only prettier."

"Hi, Mr. Meadows." Betsy guided Josefina in ahead of her. "Go ahead, Josefina, tell him how much you enjoyed the park today and feeding the ducks. It's not everyone who owns a park next door with only a wooden gate to walk through."

Josefina wrapped her brown arms around Sam's knees. "I fed the ducks two bagsful. They quacked and chased me for the peanuts."

Sam stumbled a bit, steadied himself with his cane, and took Josefina's hand to lead her into the kitchen. "Not one, but two whole bags, you say? So now they'll be chasing me for peanuts."

Josefina giggled. "No they won't. They can't run good. They just waddle."

Inside, tales of waddling ducks and Guatemalan volcanoes passed around the table until the last onion ring was consumed and David got fussy. "Okay, okay, I know. You're sleepy." Betsy looked at Caroline. "I think I'd better get him down to the studio and to bed before he spoils the party. Besides, Mason should be driving in before long."

"Oh, we all need to go." Caroline started clearing the table. "It's been a long day for all of us, and we have another one tomorrow." She put the glasses in the sink. "Why don't you just walk on ahead of me? I'll help Angel clean up, and I'll be right there."

Betsy said her goodbyes and instructed Josefina to give her goodbye hugs. Caroline ushered them out the back porch door and returned to the kitchen.

"Oh, I can do the cleaning up. You just come sit for a minute." Angel pointed to Caroline's chair at the table.

"Yeah, we won't see you for a spell," Sam chimed in. Since Caroline moved to Twin Oaks nearly eight years ago, she'd never been away for more than a week at a time, and that was rare. As much as Sam wanted Caroline's happiness, the reality of her marrying Roderick and moving to Rockwater caused him to grieve a bit every day. No more Mendelssohn floating up the garden path like a southern breeze. No more student recitals. No more snickerdoodles to eat with his ice cream. No more need to look after her, and no one close to call if he needed her. Caroline's presence on the property had brought activity and life, and her absence would create a void.

"A spell is only a couple of weeks, though."

Sam fingered the mustard stain on the embroidered tablecloth. "Only a couple of weeks this trip. But I suppose it's time we get used to your being gone. A few more months, and you'll be taking a life-long trip."

Angel took his hand in that familiar way that comes from decades of handholding. "Why, Judge Meadows, you sound like you just pronounced a life sentence. I rather think her life with Roderick will be an adventure. And they'll probably be visiting here before I can get that mustard stain out of this tablecloth."

Caroline told them of her plans—Mason's arrival later tonight and an early-morning drive to Atlanta with a wedding-dress fitting before being dropped off at Hartsfield International Airport for a midafternoon flight. "You sure I can't do the cleaning up for you?"

Angel stood up from the table. "I'm absolutely positive. No shilly-shallying around here."

"Another one of Ned's new words?" Caroline giggled.

"Yep. But thank goodness this one sounds just like what it means. I'm keeping the dictionary on the table beside my recliner in the library these days. Who would have dreamed that Ned Pendergrass would have been the reason for that?"

They followed her to the back-porch door and embraced for their goodbyes. Sam kissed her on the forehead. "You promise old Sam you'll be extra careful, little one, you hear me?"

"I will. I have a driver, Dr. Lydia Pipkin with me, and a satellite phone. I'll call you along the way, and I'll see you as soon as I get back." She was almost to the bed of daylilies on the stone path to the studio when she turned to wave.

Sam studied Angel's face under the yellow porch light. "Call it old school or whatever you want to, I just don't like it that she's headed off to that drug-infested, volcano-spewing, disease-riddled country where women are treated worse than the family mule. I don't like it one bit."

"Sam, what in the world's gotten into you? Hush that kind of talk. Guatemala's the land of eternal spring. Think about that, would you?"

"I know what I'm talking about. I read the newspapers. I know what's going on down there, and I don't like Caroline going off to that hotbed of criminals all by herself. I just don't have a good feeling about this."

Angel walked back into the kitchen. Sam stood at the porch door and watched Caroline's image fade in the graying distance until he could see her no more.

Chapter 10

Bella's Obsession

Friday morning in Atlanta

Mason wiped strawberry ice cream from little David's mouth and looked at Betsy. "It's about time you got finished. The food court at the mall is not an ideal place to leave your husband and two kids while you're trying on a dress." He handed David to Caroline as she sat down beside him. "And CC, would you please explain to me why you need to get fitted if you're wearing your mother's old wedding dress?" He removed the napkin he had tucked into the neck of Josefina's T-shirt and wiped her mouth as he spoke.

"The dress shop has a fine alterations lady who's done work for me before, and the dress had to be altered to fit me, plus I needed a veil. She's making it to match the dress."

Betsy was still wiping ice cream from David's face and shirt. "Did you have to get him strawberry, Mason? Or do you think these pink stains look good on his new white polo shirt that you insisted he needed?"

Caroline grinned. "Score one for the little wifey."

"Yeah, everyone knows a nine-month-old should have a fifty-six dollar white polo shirt hanging in his closet. Okay, let's get out of here and go get some lunch. Mason, where's the diaper bag?"

They drove to Mason's favorite Italian place, a quiet restaurant where business executives gathered for lunch. Betsy didn't think it a good idea, but he convinced her it was time the kids learned how to dine in fine city style. Mason and Caroline scrapped over who would pay the bill after they finished off one serving of tiramisu being passed around. "Okay, I give in," he finally acquiesced, "but only because you're marrying a man who just took his private jet to London."

David and Josefina were asleep in their car seats before they reached I-85. Mason drove while Betsy and Caroline conversed softly on the drive to the airport. As they approached the airport exit, Mason asked, "You want me to park?"

"No. Don't park. There's really no need. Just drop me off at United."

Betsy turned around to look at Caroline in the back seat, wedged between her two godchildren asleep in their car seats. "Are you sure, CC? We can go in with you."

"No. Really. There's no need for the hassle. You can't do a thing inside. Not like it used to be when you could go to the gate with me and watch the plane take off."

Betsy recalled Caroline's repeated story of bringing David to the airport eight years ago and watching his plane take off to Guatemala. That had been her last sight of him. Betsy was relieved not to have to go inside. "Okay, so what time do you land?"

"I fly through Houston and I'll arrive in Guatemala City around nine thirty. Lydia's coming in from Miami, and she'll be waiting for me at the airport. She gets there about a half an hour before I do."

"And then you're staying in Guatemala City for the night?"

"Yes. Tonight, we're staying in Guate, as the natives call it. The shuttle service from the hotel is picking us up. We just have to call them when we get there."

"Reyna's not picking you up? I thought she was meeting you in the city." Betsy squirmed in her front seat.

"She is. She'll already be at the hotel, but there's no need for her to be driving around alone at night in the city. The shuttle will be fine and easier for everyone. I'll give her a call when I get in, and then I'll see her for breakfast. We have a few things to do in Guate before we leave for the Highlands."

Betsy nodded. "But what about your driver? I thought Roderick's assistant was getting you a driver. What's her name, that secretary of his?"

"Oh, you mean the one with cleavage, a perky butt, and her claws into Roderick and her evil eye out for you?" Mason jeered.

Caroline caught his eye in the rearview mirror. "Yeah, that one. Her name's Liz. But she won't be around much after July."

"Uh-oh. I can see the claw marks now." His gaze turned thoughtful. "I'd let her put claw marks down my . . ."

"Shut up, Mason." Betsy turned back around to face Caroline. "He's firing her?"

"No, he's not firing her. He's moving her out of his home office and over to the company headquarters in Lexington. Some kind of change in title as a guise, I think. It was either that or Lilah was moving to Lexington, and Roderick's committed to Lilah. After all she raised him."

"And this Liz made your arrangements for Guatemala and got you a driver? I'd be extra careful if I were you."

Mason snickered again as he parked the vehicle at the United entrance.

Caroline turned to kiss the sleeping baby's cheek before crawling over Josefina to get out of the car curbside. She leaned back in and lifted Josefina's hand to her cheek and pressed it to her own.

Sleepily, Josefina said, "You're flying away, CC? Are you ever coming back?"

"Of course I'm coming back. Got to be around for a wedding. Remember, you're my flower girl. Now that you're awake, one butterfly kiss before I fly away." Her long, dark eyelashes brushed Josefina's brown cheek. "And guess what! A surprise just for you. If you look in the bottom of your travel bag, I left you a bag of candy kisses until I get back from Guatemala." Leaving a bag of candy kisses when they said goodbye had been a tradition since Josefina was old enough to eat chocolate.

In her groggy voice she asked, "You're going to Guatemala, CC?"

Caroline nodded her head.

"That's where Mom and Dad chose me?"

Caroline nodded her head again. "It is, and maybe your mom and I will take you there very soon. And I'll bring you a big surprise when I come back, okay?"

"It doesn't have to be a big one. It might not fit in your suitcase."

Caroline kissed her again and shut the door. She joined Mason as he lifted her large, hard-sided bag out of the vehicle and put it on the sidewalk.

"Gee, Caroline. What you got in this bag? Are you carrying all two hundred and fifty thousand in gold bars to Guatemala to start this choir?"

Betsy came from around the car. "Don't be talking like that in front of an airport. You want to be hauled off to security for interrogation, or do you want some low-life grabbing Caroline's bag? Here, let me help. I'll roll it to the desk for you." She took the heavy bag. "Mason, just get back in and stay with the kids. I'll only be a minute. If you wake the baby, he's yours."

Mason hugged Caroline and kissed her on both cheeks. "Come on, CC, let me see it. Just one more time. Raise that right eyebrow for me."

She had been raising her right eyebrow at Mason's shenanigans for twenty-five years. She wasn't about to disappoint him this time and gave him the look.

"That's it. Just like I remember. I hope Roderick understands what that means."

She pulled his ear, another old habit, and walked off with her backpack slung over her shoulder, dragging her carryon behind her.

Betsy rolled the large bag up to the desk, helped Caroline lift it to the weigh station, and turned to hug her. She waited until Caroline had her boarding pass and was ready to go to her gate before she said anything else. "Look, I'd really like it if you called me or emailed me along the way. I worry about you, you know."

"Not to worry. I'll stay in touch, and thanks for bringing me to Atlanta. Anything you want me to bring you back from Guatemala? Coffee, chocolate, fabric, anything?"

A head taller, Betsy put both her hands on Caroline's shoulders and looked her straight in the eye. "Just you, my friend. Just you. You know God kissed me on both cheeks with our friendship. I just want you to go, get your work done, enjoy it, and come home safely. That's all." They hugged.

"I love you, too, Betsy." Caroline adjusted her backpack and grabbed the handle of her rollaboard. "See you in a few weeks." She walked toward the line at security.

"Yeah, we have a wedding to get ready for." Betsy waved and watched Caroline hand the TSA agent her boarding pass and passport. She wished Caroline had not planned this trip. A trip to Guatemala had already swallowed up one wedding.

Friday morning in Raleigh-Durham

Gretchen sat at her writing desk making changes to a new recipe. She had spent the morning in her new kitchen, baking and listening to sublime music. Caroline would call this a bright-yellow morning, and it was. Only a week after their move, she, Bella, and Karina were settling into an untried way of living in an unfamiliar city. Neither she nor Karina had ever even visited a university campus, and now they lived in the middle of one, thanks to Bella.

The sound of the doorbell brought a smile to her face. "Oh, good morning, Sarah. Please come in."

"Thank you, Gretchen. Something smells absolutely wonderful and cinnamony."

"You just sit right here, and I will bring you a taste with a cup of tea." Gretchen led Sarah to the sofa. She'd never thought she would own a sofa covered in her favorite lavender chintz pattern that she'd picked out herself. And she certainly never dreamed that she would have a Friday-morning visit from a college professor who came to have a cup of tea with her.

"Where are your girls?"

Gretchen returned from the kitchen with two cups of tea and a plate-sized cinnamon roll. "'My girls.' Those are beautiful words. My girl Karina took my girl Bella to her appointment this morning with the music professor. She thought it would be a good time for her to learn her way around the music department. They will be home for a late lunch."

Sarah pinched off the corner of the bun and took a small bite. "Karina assuming some responsibility is really wonderful, Gretchen, but not as wonderful as this." She held the piece of cinnamon roll up high as though she were making a toast.

"Too much cinnamon, I think."

"I think it's perfect."

"Oh, thank you, Sarah." Color came to Gretchen's face. She was still unaccustomed to so much attention and compliments. "I will send home a box for you and George."

"Just one, please. It will last the weekend. We'll share."

"In my home country, one would never see a sweet bun so large. But here, customers think they must have more—more butter, more sugar, more spice, and more sweet bun. I must make changes to my thinking if my bakery will be successful."

Sarah chuckled. "Perhaps we gluttonous Americans should change our way of thinking, but meantime, I'll enjoy every morsel." She sipped her tea. "Tell me, how are things going around here?"

"Oh, Sarah, I have never been so happy. Remember, my heart was so heavy and my mind was so busy worrying about how Karina would like her new life? No more. My fears have faded in just a few days. How can I ever thank you enough?"

"Thank me? You must be doing something right if things are going so well."

"If I do them right, it is because you told me how. I am learning how to live with Karina as an adult young woman. It is not easy. In my heart, I want to grab her and hold her and make up for the twelve years that were snatched from us. But I listened to you, and I am giving her room. No not 'room,' space. I am giving her space just like you said."

"What about Bella? Are you jealous that Karina is spending time with Bella?"

"No, no, never. I want her to love Bella as I do, and I want Bella to love Karina. I want us both to learn everything we can about Bella and her rare gift."

"You're in the right place to do that, you know?"

"Oh yes, I know, and never has there been a more grateful heart than mine. We are free, and I can afford to give my daughters a very good life."

"Gretchen, I think you have the purest heart of anyone I know. I'm so happy for you, and I'm very proud of Karina. I know she was anxious to start class, but I really think taking the summer to get acclimated to her new life was a wise decision. Plus, I know she'll be a great help to you in starting the bakery."

"Yes, but I do not wish to burden Karina with my dreams. She has been working in a bakery for many years, and now she has a chance for her own dreams."

"Dreams. Your dreams are coming true. Roderick's and Caroline's too. I am so happy to see so many people's dreams come true."

Gretchen did not miss the sadness in Sarah's eyes. "I know you have dreams, too, Sarah. They will come true. Just when you think they are so far and so faint, the color will return to them, and they will become flesh. You will have a child, Sarah, and you will be the best of all mothers."

Sarah's only response was the hint of a smile as she pulled papers from her briefcase and finished her business with Gretchen's signature on several documents before saying her goodbye.

Gretchen watched her from the window as she balanced the box of baked goods while she opened her car door.

Karina and Bella walked toward the car hand in hand. Karina approached with a hint of caution, but Bella dropped Karina's hand and rushed to wrap both her arms around Sarah and hug her long and hard.

In a moment of silence, Gretchen prayed that Sarah would one day know the joy of being hugged with such sweet abandon by her own child.

A ringing phone broke the silence and the sacredness of the moment. Gretchen answered. "Oh, good morning, Caroline. Where are you?"

"I'm in the airport in Atlanta about to board my flight to Guatemala, but I didn't want to leave without saying goodbye."

"What an adventure you will have! You will return to a country that captured your heart and to some children who need you. You will see old friends, and you will make a new friend."

"You make it sound so much fun. Talk to me some more. I think I am just frightened."

Gretchen sat down at her desk. "Tell me, friend, what about this frightens you?"

There was a moment of silence. "Oh, I don't know, maybe just returning to Guatemala after a few years, or maybe it's traveling alone or thinking this project is so much bigger than I am."

"I understand about being afraid of new things, but my little friend, you were made for this project. It is just your size. It is in your heart and in your thinking. God will give you the hands to do the work, and He will take away your fears and give you faith."

"You're right, Gretchen. I needed to hear those words. Maybe I'm just afraid of Dr. Pipkin and what she will think of me?"

Gretchen heard the door. "Oh, Caroline, the girls just

got home. They have been at the music school. I know hearing your voice would put a smile on Bella's face this morning."

"Great. Maybe she could sing me a song."

Gretchen turned to Bella. "Guess who is on the phone, Bella. Someone needs you to sing a song." Gretchen held out the receiver and hit the speakerphone button so they all could hear.

Without a word, Bella began singing, "Tomorrow, tomorrow, I love you tomorrow. Tomorrow's just a day away."

As Bella finished the phrase, Gretchen put her hand on Bella's shoulder to quiet her. "Don't you want to know who is on the phone?"

"Caroline, my Caroline. My Caroline is on the phone." Bella stopped.

"Hi, Bella. You are a great guesser. How did you know it was me?"

"Caroline. You come home tomorrow, Caroline."

"No, I won't be home tomorrow. I'm going to Guatemala. I showed you on the map where it is. Remember? I'm going to start the children's choir."

"No, Caroline, you come home tomorrow, just a day away." Bella walked away to the piano.

Gretchen picked up the phone. "I'm sorry, Caroline, she just walked away. We will pray for safe travel for you."

Bella began to play the piano. Gretchen waved her arm to shush her, but Bella continued to play. "Can you hear her, Caroline? She's playing your music."

"Oh, yes, she's playing the storm scene from the *Rockwater Suite*. Bye, Gretchen, they are calling me to board. Love you."

Chapter 11

Where There's A Will

Friday morning at Cuttin' Loose in Moss Point

Gracie continued to spray Edna's hair the same way she had for the last twenty-eight years. Every Friday morning at nine thirty—shampoo; rollup; dryer; the teasing, fluffing, and spraying that would last until the next Friday. Gracie had lived in Moss Point all her life, and that was long enough to know some things just don't ever change.

She twirled Edna around in the chair. "Look okay to you?"

"Why, it looks lovely, just like always, Gracie." She handed Gracie a ten-dollar bill. "Oh, and here's your tip." She handed her another buck just like she'd always done.

Edna was on her way out the door when GiGi Nelson swished in and nearly knocked her down. Gracie imagined Edna would look at GiGi just like any southern, upstanding, church-going woman would—amazed that a woman GiGi's age would pair short shorts and stilettos together, exposing far too much broomstick leg. Gracie wondered if Edna's eyes ever made it north of the rhinestone belt buckle.

GiGi stormed in, not with her usual strut, but more like a woman headed to the bathroom after a long drive. She grabbed Gracie's arm on the way to the shampooing station. "Come on, Gracie, hurry up. You gotta work your magic this morning. Today is the day. No, today is my day, and I need to look beyond fabulous."

Gracie followed GiGi and mumbled under her breath. "Yeah, like fabulous on your way to ridiculous." In the last fifteen years alone, she had seen GiGi through three husbands, a dozen lovers, more than ten shades of red to nearly purple hair, and through weekly fad diets that only made her legs skinny but left the barrel around her middle. GiGi alone had more than paid for the tanning bed in the back room. When she left the salon after a tanning session, the girls took bets as to which one of the neighborhood dogs would mistake her for a chunk of beef jerky on her walk home.

Gracie felt guilty at times for taking so much of one client's money, but she took it anyway, knowing that whatever money GiGi had left after a day at Cuttin' Loose she spent on push-up bras and gold jewelry from the cable shopping channel. Hair color and weight fluctuated, and her dreams of being a movie star were packed away in the trunk with her prom dress, but one thing would never change: GiGi's man-chasing ways.

On the way from the shampoo bowl to Gracie's station, GiGi instructed, "Hand me the color samples. I want something different and smashing—something that'll make him take notice."

"But you just got color two weeks ago, and besides, I thought you and Carl called it quits." Gracie handed her the color chart.

"Yeah, Carl's history." GiGi ran her glued-on, neon-orange fingernail down the chart, tapping on a few colors until one caught her eye. "Here, I like this one." She pointed to number 817, which was somewhere between the color of an overripe tomato and the rust behind the lavatory that Gracie had had to clean and paint over when she bought the salon.

"Are you sure that's what you want?"

"Are talking about me wanting Carl back or my hair this color? If you're talking about Carl, like I said, he's history. And if you're talking about this color, yep. This is the one."

"But it may not look like that over the color you have now."

GiGi took hold of the counter and twirled the chair around to face Gracie. "Then we'll keep coloring it until it does. That's your job, and that's what I pay you for. It's got to be this color. Put that plastic cape on me and let's get started."

"Must be somebody special."

"It is. Somebody that's going to put me on Knob Hill if there was a Knob Hill in this town."

Gracie mixed the color in the plastic bowl while mentally flipping through the files stored in her brain, quickly concluding there wasn't a man in Moss Point fitting that description who would even slow down if GiGi had four flat tires in front of the Methodist church. *Either this one's from out of town, or all this hair color has really seeped into her brain and she's completely delusional.* "So, pray tell, who's the mystery man?"

"You wouldn't believe me if I told you."

Gracie stayed quiet. She knew that GiGi couldn't hold that information for more than about . . .

"You gotta swear on your mama's tombstone you won't tell a soul. I mean not a living soul. I don't want some money-hungry woman stealing him right out from under me."

"Well, Mama's alive and walking around, so I can't swear on her tombstone. Anything else you want me to swear on?"

"No, but if anybody finds out, I mean if anybody in this town finds out, then I'll know where it came from, and that's from you, Gracie." GiGi paused, curled up her finger, motioning for Gracie to come closer, and whispered, "It's Fred Pendergrass."

Gracie laughed out loud. "You think that's a secret? Well, if you do, don't offer your thoughts to anyone for a penny. They're not worth it. I've already had three clients in just the last week talking about seeing you hanging around the park where the Pendergrass twins were working."

"Who was it? Who said that?" GiGi's eyes were so wide the shiny lavender eye shadow on her lids disappeared.

"Oh, nobody that matters. Just making conversation, mostly wondering why in the world you'd be after the Pendergrass twins. Everybody in town knows they're good, honest, hardworking men, but neither one of them's ever had a date. Nobody can figure what would interest you about Ned or Fred." Gracie slathered the brownish, purple goop on GiGi's hair, saying a silent prayer that in thirty minutes it would be red. "Wait a minute. You said your mystery man was going to put you on Knob Hill. It's a long way from the Pendergrass farm to Knob Hill. Have you seen their place?"

"Yeah, I've seen it. Looks like it's about to fall down. In fact, from the road, the barn looks better than the house. But that's not what I'm talking about."

"Then what in the crappola are you talking about, Gi-gi?"

"You gotta swear on something that you won't tell."

"Okay, okay." Gracie thought for a few seconds while she wiped goop off GiGi's neck. "Okay, I'll swear on the

Bible my daughter got when she was baptized. Is that good enough?"

"Yeah, that'll do. And she'll be going to hell if you tell a soul. Okay, here it is. The Pendergrass boys are rich. I mean filthy rich."

"What? No way."

"Yep. They are. I mean they got lots of money."

Gracie put the bowl of hair dye on the counter and took her gloves off to set the timer. "So how do you know this?"

"I heard it with my own ears the day of the ribbon cutting at the park. Ned was talking to Sam Meadows about giving out the scholarships this year. Them twins are the ones who've been giving out these scholarships every year all this time. They're the ones nobody knows about but me and now you."

"You cannot be telling the truth. For real, they're the ones?"

"Yep, the very ones. I heard them say something about some dividends from the Coca-Cola stock their daddy left them. Can you just imagine those two having money and driving around in that old truck and living and working like they do? Sounds like something you'd see on Saturday-afternoon television movies, don't it?"

"Rich, you say?"

"Well, maybe not rich like that Kentucky man Caroline Carlyle snagged for herself, but richer than most folks around here. Do you know of anybody educating our young people and giving away that kind of money? Judge Meadows doesn't even do that."

"That's true."

"By the way, I heard Caroline left town."

"Yes. Angel said she was going to Atlanta then flying to Guatemala."

"Isn't that where her first boyfriend got killed?"

Gracie nodded.

"What in God's name would she want to go to that place for?"

"Angel says she's starting a Guatemalan children's choir to help the orphans of Guatemala. She's making a trip to get it all started. She'll be back in a couple of weeks."

"Um-huh. Got into all that money. Now she's figuring a way to give it away. See I would do something like that too. Why if I could put up a new Civil War monument or build a new library, Tandy Yarbrough would be peeing green 'til Christmas."

Gracie grinned and nodded her head. "And you think making your hair a new color is going to land you some of that money?"

"A new hairdo and a few other tricks I got down my cleavage."

Gracie was thinking it would take more than that.

Kneeling on the soft dirt, Ned checked the water pipe, wiped the sweat from his forehead, and tucked his white handkerchief into his overalls pocket. Job done, with practically no help from his twin. He methodically returned the wrench to the same toolbox his father had used for decades and snapped it closed. The sight of his brother sitting in the gazebo with that floozy still perplexed him. In his nearly sixty-two years, Fred had rarely spoken, but the past few days, he had been all eyes and teeth smiling back at GiGi when she just happened by the park where they were working.

GiGi Nelson didn't know that body parts that had been around as long as hers would be better off covered up, and she had smoked so many long cigarettes that her hair and her fingers had turned orange. Since the day of the Twin Oaks Park opening, she had been on Fred's trail like Uncle Henry's old hound dog after a possum.

Ned picked up his hat and toolbox and walked toward the truck. Not even when he deliberately threw his shovel into the truck bed did Fred even once glance that way. "No fool like an old fool," his mama would say if she could see Fred right now. Something had to be done.

He walked the pine-straw covered pathway toward the gate to the Twin Oaks property. Just weeks ago, he and his brother had worked side by side, raking that straw, hauling it in a wheelbarrow, and creating that path. He unlocked the gate from the park into Twin Oaks, entered, and cautiously locked it again. The giggling made him turn around and look one more time. Fred must be protected, and only Mr. Sam could help him do that.

Ned walked past the studio apartment and beyond the shade garden where the hostas hugged the earth and allowed only the impatiens to peek through. He fiddled with the keys in his overall pockets as he walked and thought. Miss Caroline was gone to Guatemala, and there was no piano playing today. Mrs. Silva and that pretty little Bella were gone, too, and they weren't coming back. In a few months when Caroline gets married, the music would really stop. And what in the world if his brother took up with that woman?

Ned could hear Mr. Sam and Miss Angel in the kitchen, and the back-porch door was probably unlocked, but he wasn't about to touch the door handle. His knuckles would be bruised and bloody from knocking first.

"I see you out there, Ned, and I'm coming, just slow."

Ned accepted Sam's offer to sit a spell and to sip a glass of Angel's fresh lemonade. He was glad to report that the park's sprinkler system was installed and working and the three water fountains were producing cool water.

"You didn't need to walk all the way up here to tell me that. Besides, you left your brother down there working by himself."

"No, sir, my brother's not working. Hadn't hardly put in a lick o' work in the last few days."

"Fred's not sick, is he?"

"Sick in the head," Ned mumbled.

Sam put his lemonade down on the wicker table. "What did you really come for, Ned?"

Ned pulled his handkerchief out again. The ceiling fans kept the air cool in the shade of the porch, but he was sweating like he had been shoveling dirt in the noonday sun. "I been thinking, Mr. Sam. You know, when my daddy died, he left Fred and me a place to live and plenty of money to live on. He took care of everything, and I'm just thinking maybe it's time me and Fred do the same thing."

"You mean like your daddy did in his will?"

"If that's the way you do it, then yes, sir. I think that's what we oughta do."

"You're not planning on dying anytime soon, are you?"

"No, sir, don't have any plans of getting on that heaven-bound bus just yet, but you know, dying's just plain *ineluctable*. Now, we don't have no family to speak of, just a cousin or two, but they never had a thing to do with us, thinking we were poor. So I'm thinking we better come up with what happens to all this stuff when we're dead and gone on to Glory."

"That sounds reasonable to me. Is this your way of asking me to draw up your will and file it?"

"Yes, sir, it is. Don't nobody but you and Mr. Brooks down at the bank know anything about our business. I got some ideas about what ought to happen to our money once we're gone, but I sure would like to hear what you have to say about it."

"Now, Ned. You know I've never been one to back up when it comes to expressing my opinions, but in this case, I think I'd like to hear your ideas first."

"Well, if I go first and Fred's left by himself, I want him to be taken care of good. You know the two of us ain't ever spent one night in different places, not even when he was eight years old and had his tonsils out. Me and Mama spent the night in the hospital and stayed right next to him. Fred don't know nothing about handling no money. That's always been my responsibility since Pa up and died. So I got to make sure Fred's going to be taken care of and nobody can get to his money that ain't supposed to."

"A good trust will take care of that."

"And if there's anything left after Fred goes, too, then I'd like to leave some money to Mrs. Silva and her little girl, and to Hattie, and some for Miss Caroline."

"But Gretchen has money to take care of herself and Bella. And besides, Caroline thinks that Bella will be able to earn a fortune if someone writes a book about her and more money than that from all her public appearances and concerts."

Ned rubbed his forehead again with his handkerchief.

"And Caroline, she's marrying into a family that's got more money than your hound dog's got ticks."

"But I want to give them both some money to say thank you for being nice to me and Fred, and for making all that pretty music we enjoy. Ain't Miss Caroline starting some kind of choir to help some orphans?"

Sam shook his head in agreement.

"Then we'll give it to her to help the orphans. That'll be a good thing to do, won't it?"

"That will be a good thing. And as far as Hattie, Angel

and I are taking care of Hattie because she's taken such good care of us all these years. But if you wanted to leave her a little something, I know she'd appreciate it. You know, Ned, if we set up a trust, and then you appoint some trustees to manage the money, you and Fred could keep on giving scholarships even after you're dead and gone. You'd just need to appoint somebody that you trust to carry out your wishes."

"Would you be willin', Mr. Sam?"

Sam chuckled. "Ned, I'm eighty-six years old, and you just told me you're not planning on catching the bus to heaven anytime soon, so with all probability, you're going to outlive me by about twenty years. You need to get somebody young. Now, Mr. Brooks down at the bank, you can trust him. And you need one more."

"What about Miss Caroline? She's good all the way down to the bone. I would trust her with anything." Ned sipped the last drop of his lemonade.

"That's a good choice too. I think we can get her to do that, and that would mean she'd have to come back to Moss Point to see us every now and then." Sam sat silently waiting for Ned to respond. Finally, he gave in and said, "Ned, I've known you since you were born. What's eating at your craw today?"

"It's that perfidious woman down there in the gazebo, canoodling with my brother." He wiped his brow again and let out a sigh like a man who'd just laid a full house down on the poker table.

"You're not jealous, now are you, Ned?"

"No, sir, Mr. Sam. I am not jealous, not of that woman or nobody else. It's just that my brother is into big-time woolgathering if he thinks GiGi Nelson's really interested in him. Why she's never so much as looked our way or said one word to us until after the opening of the park. I think she knows something, Mr. Sam. I truly do."

"Knows something. Like what?"

"I think she heard us talking about the stock and the scholarships the day of the park opening, and I think she's after Fred's money. She knows not to come toward me. I'm too smart for that. But Fred? Fred's different, and women like her can just smell it when a man's dumb and he's got money."

"Now that I recall, we were having a conversation about the scholarships that afternoon, weren't we?" Sam sat up on the edge of his wicker rocker. "You may be right on this one, Ned. And on the chance that you are, we need to take care of things pretty quickly. I'll get in touch with Ed Brooks down at the bank, and I'd like to give Tom Ellison a call if you give me permission. Tom's a good attorney, and he knows about financial planning. I've used him myself, and he got things done for Gretchen Silva too."

"Yes, sir. If you trust him, ain't no better recommendation than that in my book." Ned stood up and stuck his handkerchief in his pocket.

Sam used his cane to steady himself as he got out of his rocker. He followed Ned to the back door. "Don't you worry one bit. We'll get something drawn up so you don't have to give this another thought. GiGi Nelson won't be strutting around Moss Point spending one dime of your money. You can rest assured of that."

"Thank you, Mr. Sam. I knew I could count on you, and I'd just as soon me and you keep this to ourselves, if you know what I mean."

Sam extended his right hand to shake Ned's. "I do understand, and by the way, you need to send me a bill on this last work over at the park."

"No need for a bill. You just paid it." Ned walked down the path and fiddled with his keys until he opened the gate and walked into the park. There they were in plain sight—GiGi and Fred, sitting far too close together. *You can sit as close as you want to, Miss Whistle Britches, but that's as close as you'll ever get to Pendergrass money.* He walked past the gazebo and climbed into the passenger's side of the truck. Without a word, he honked the horn.

Fred came reluctantly with GiGi hanging on.

"Come on, Fred, get in this truck. It's time to go home."

Chapter 12

Guatemala Arrival

Friday night in Guatemala City

The La Aurora International Airport was quiet, most travelers having arrived earlier in the day and already engaged in Guate's nightlife. Caroline retrieved her large bag and stood in a line of three Guatemala-looking travelers before approaching the custom agent's desk.

The agent took her customs form and passport. "Do you speak Spanish?"

Caroline could get by in Spanish and had limited understanding but was not fluent in the language. "No." Previous international travel and Roderick's schooling prepared her to answer succinctly and politely.

The brown-skinned agent flipped the pages of her passport. "I see you come to Guatemala before. Yes?"

"Yes."

"Why did you come to Guatemala before?"

"Humanitarian aid, and I was here to be with some friends who were adopting a baby."

"Your friends rich Americans?

"No, just Americans."

"Are you here to adopt another child?"

"No."

"Then why are you here?"

"To visit some friends who are helping me start a Guatemalan children's choir."

"Does that take much money?" He looked back at her customs form.

Caroline sensed his curious brown eyes perusing her and her bags, and she realized that possibly he had been given more information than he needed. "I don't think so."

"Do you have more than ten thousand dollars in US money with you?" He motioned for another agent who joined him.

"No." She had already indicated a negative response on her customs form and was perplexed why he was asking.

"Please go with this officer. She will check your bags."

Caroline knew not to ask questions and followed the young woman, who took her to a small glassed-in room with a metal table and two folding chairs. The female officer lifted the large suitcase onto the table and began removing its contents. She shuffled through Caroline's clothes, searched the zippered pockets of the luggage, and checked for hidden compartments or anything stashed underneath the lining. Clothes, once neatly folded and packed in gallon plastic bags, were now crammed loosely back into the suitcase. Without any conversation, the agent searched the carry-on bag and her backpack in the same fashion, closely examining her phone.

The officer led her back to the customs agent's counter when the bags had been thoroughly searched and mostly trashed. The two agents conversed quietly in a language that was not Spanish but a Guatemalan dialect Caroline had heard before in the Highlands.

"How long will you stay here?" The agent stared at the paper.

"Two weeks."

"And your address here is the Quinta Real?" He wrote something on the pad next to the phone.

Knowing it was the most luxurious hotel in the city, she was reluctant to reply, but it was already on her customs form. No need to dispute it now. "Yes, that's my hotel while I'm in the city."

"You stay in the city all the days you are here?"

"No, I plan to spend a few days in Xela."

He wrote something else on the pad. "You may go. Enjoy your visit in our country."

A bit uneasy but relieved, Caroline returned her passport to the zippered wallet hanging from her neck, repositioned her backpack on her shoulder, and pulled her bags through the narrow passageway and then into the airport's main lobby. This airport had been modernized and cleaned up over the last eight years and was not nearly so frightening. No more machine-gun-carrying adolescents dressed in well-worn, outdated camouflage, and no more eight-year-olds selling beaded bracelets or wanting to shine your shoes. But Caroline found this unusual scrutiny intimidating.

Lydia Pipkin's plane from Miami had arrived ahead of schedule, according to the overhead screens. Caroline surveyed the lobby. Surely there could be no more than one very tall, sixty-ish-year-old woman with blue eyes and platinum hair dressed in African garb in the airport terminal entrance. There she was, not in native African clothing as Caroline expected, but in khaki cargo shorts, a long-sleeved white shirt, a khaki travel vest with bulging pockets, and a safari hat that barely covered a crimped mop of thick, wavy hair the color of Gulf Coast sand. Lydia leaned against the wall, reading a paperback and guarding her duffle bag with tanned legs that could have belonged to a high jumper. She was striking, but not what Caroline expected.

She approached confidently. "Lydia."

The woman closed her paperback and turned. "Caroline?"

"Yes, how wonderful to finally meet you, and I'm so grateful you'd join me on this exploratory trip." She stretched out her hand to Lydia.

Ignoring Caroline's extended hand, Lydia put her book in her bag and zipped it. "My God, I have nine-year-old children in my choir bigger than you. But you're beautiful. My hair used to be dark like yours, but I grayed early. Still got the waves, though." She effortlessly picked up her oversized duffle bag and tossed it over her shoulder. "Let's get going. I already called the hotel shuttle when I saw that your plane had landed. If they're not here, they shouldn't be long."

Having only seen snapshots where Lydia was always in the background, Caroline wasn't certain what she expected, but this wasn't exactly it. No handshake. No hug. Nothing of the politeness and gentility she'd assumed about a woman who worked with African orphans, but she liked Lydia immediately.

They walked curbside where Lydia, head and shoulders above the Guatemalans, spied the hotel van immediately and began waving her arm and trudging toward it as though she were on a mountain hike. It was all Caroline could do to pull her bags and keep up. Once their luggage was loaded, they took their seats near the front across the aisle from each other and began the fifteen-minute drive to the hotel.

Lydia took off her hat and ran her long fingers through her hair, brushing it back from her weather-wrinkled face. "Rather humid here in the night air."

"It gets worse. It's the rainy season."

"Rainy season, you say. Never been to Guatemala before. I've trekked all over Africa and the Mideast, but never to Central America. I'm rather looking forward to this."

"I'm so glad. Did you get my suggested itinerary, and is there anything you'd like to add to the trip while you're here?"

"Your itinerary looked fine. I'd like to visit some ruins and at least see the lake while I'm here, as long as we keep the same return flight schedule. I only have two days in Miami before I return home."

"But I thought Miami *was* your home."

Lydia cleared her throat and pushed hard on the van window to close it. "They don't think too much about fuel emissions down here, do they? Can't imagine what it must be like in heavy traffic. And to answer your question, no, Uganda's my home now. Miami's where I used to live."

"I see." Caroline wondered if Lydia's move to Uganda had insured the success of her work there. What did that mean for running a successful Guatemala operation from Kentucky?

"I was in Miami raising money." She looked toward Caroline in the darkness of the van. "I need to tell you up front, you got a really good start with a quarter-million-dollar gift, but the fundraising never ends. I hope you like dressing up and going to fancy dinners, because you'll be doing a lot of that. Me? I like my khakis, and I use more DEET than I do perfume. I brought a can with me to ward off mosquitoes. They find me, even in a crowd."

Caroline chuckled. "Oh, you won't be needing DEET where we're going."

"I thought you said we'd be seeing some jungle."

"I did. We'll be passing through some mountainous jungle, but once we get to our destination, we'll be at an elevation of about six thousand feet, and you'll not see or hear a mosquito. The air will be crisp and cool, just right for the enjoyment of the finest cup of coffee you've ever tasted."

Lydia fanned herself with her hat. "Then you've not had Ethiopian coffee, but I'll take a cup of anything about six a.m. every morning."

Guate was alive on Friday evening, pulsating with bright and unusually colorful lights and honking horns. Billboards infiltrated the cityscape like a bad rash. Caroline marveled at the changes in the last four years and pointed out places of interest to Lydia as they rode. After they decided on seven for breakfast in the dining room, Lydia said, "Now tell me about this Dr. Reyna Morris. You said she'd be traveling with us. What does she do, and how can she help you?" She cleared her throat and started again before Caroline could answer. "And another thing I need to tell you. Time's money, and there'll be well-meaning persons who will eat up your time, never give you a dime, and never do anything to really help. You need to learn the difference up front."

"Well, Reyna can and will help us. It's a long story, but perhaps you should hear an abbreviated version before you meet her in the morning. Reyna's a pediatrician and lives about an hour outside the city. Her mother is Guatemalan and married an American. Her father wanted Reyna to get her education in the States. So she went to boarding school in San Antonio, Texas, and then to college and medical school at Emory University in Atlanta. That's where she met her husband, also a medical student."

"They both practice here in Guatemala City?"

"Reyna does, but her husband is now deceased."

"Deceased? Sounds rather young to be deceased."

"That's why this story's long. You see, Josh Morris, her husband, and David Summers, my fiancé, met at a global health conference about ten years ago. Josh had already married Reyna, and this was about the time they were finishing medical school and getting ready to move to Guatemala to start their medical practice. David was in graduate school and very interested in global health and humanitarian aid projects. Once he met Josh, they collaborated on several missions over the next couple years. These projects took them to some of the remote villages up in the Highlands west of here."

"Now, you said David Summers is your fiancé?"

"He was, but he and Josh were killed almost eight years ago in a mudslide up near where we are going."

Lydia gave her a startled look then reached across the aisle, took Caroline's hand, and squeezed it. She held it gently. "I wish I had known before."

"There was no reason to tell you before. I figured I'd tell you the story once we got here. David and Josh had been delivering medical supplies to some remote villages up in the mountains, and they got caught in a sudden storm. Apparently the rains came so heavily and quickly that it caused a massive mudslide that took their lives. Their bodies were never recovered. As they say, out doing good one minute, and the next they're gone."

"Oh, I hate to hear that, especially when they were trying to make a difference. What a waste of two good men with fine educations and hearts for helping. A senseless episode like that always begs the question, 'Where was God it happened?'"

"I've asked myself that question more than a few times over the last eight years."

"Suffering always asks the hard questions." Lydia stopped. There was only the humming of the motor. "I found some answers in a village in Uganda. I'll tell you when the time is right, but not right now."

"I'll look forward to that conversation."

"So will I, but I'm glad you told me these things before I

meet Reyna." She removed her hat and fanned her face. "So you never married?"

"No. David was killed six weeks before we were to be married. I was devastated and just couldn't imagine my life without him. It's taken a long time to accept his death and try to make some sense of my life." She paused. "Starting this children's choir is something I've wanted to do for years. Somehow, I'm hoping it will bring honor to his life and work here."

Lydia's thumb traced the outline of the pink pearl on Caroline's finger before releasing her hand. "But now, there's someone new in your life?"

Caroline's resolute expression broke into a smile. "Yes, there is. After all the sadness, there is joy in my life again, and his name is Roderick Adair. We're to be married in December. And that's another whole story we'll get to later." She shifted her weight in the seat as they approached the arches of the hotel entrance.

"Well, that's worth beating the drums and doing a ceremonial dance for." Lydia looked out the window. "We're here?"

"Yes, we are. Right here in one of the most beautiful residential areas of Guatemala City, and the Quinta Real is perched above it all." The driver parked at the hotel entrance, and Caroline and Lydia stepped out of the van. "Would you look at that city?" Caroline swept her arm across the horizon of light-speckled hills as though she were presenting it as a gift to Lydia.

"Not like the plains of Uganda, but truly beautiful." Lydia swept her unruly hair from her face and put her hat on. "Probably as beautiful as that ring on your finger that you should remove while you're here."

Caroline twisted the ring on her finger to where only the gold band would be visible. "Enjoy your whirlpool tub and the sumptuous, Egyptian cotton linens. It'll be downhill from here."

"You mean I won't be sharing my bath in a river with a hippo or sleeping on the floor of a mud-packed hut tonight?"

"Not tonight. That'll come later." Caroline smiled secretly and followed Lydia through the open doors of the Quinta Real. Somehow she knew everyone followed Lydia, hoping to keep up, and that Lydia was at home wherever she was.

Caroline called Reyna's room within the same minute she closed and locked the door to her hotel suite. They chatted briefly and decided to meet in Las Ventanas restaurant at six thirty, thirty minutes before Lydia was scheduled to join them for breakfast.

The bedside clock read quarter after eleven by the time Caroline had settled into her room and showered. She pulled the phone from her backpack and crawled into bed, trying to calculate the six- or seven-hour time difference in London. Either way, she figured Roderick was awake, and she had promised to call him when she arrived. Sitting with only the sheet covering her feet, she dialed his number then pulled the scrunchie from her ponytail and started to brush her hair while she waited for him to answer.

"Hello, my sweet. I was lying here waiting for your call."

Hearing his voice reminded her of the first time she spoke with him on the phone over a year ago. She hoped his voice would always be as titillating. "So I didn't wake you?"

"Only my heart, but my head's been awake for more than an hour. So how was your flight? And tell me about Lydia."

"Flight went smoothly. Coming through customs at the airport took a while since they questioned me and searched my bags. Now I have to repack everything before we head out Sunday. Everything was emptied and gone through. Haven't had that experience before. So it took me longer to get to the hotel."

"Hmm, that's interesting. I mean you really do look very suspicious." He chuckled. "Maybe they just wanted to spend more time with you. I know I would."

"Yes, but you know I make good snickerdoodles."

She heard him almost hum. "That you do. And Lydia? Tell me about her."

"Lydia." She paused and laid the brush down. "Well, she's not at all what I expected, but I like her. I really like her."

"What do you mean? I thought you had a fairly good idea about her from your phone conversation and your research."

"I did, too, but one conversation and reading a few articles couldn't have prepared me for Dr. Lydia Pipkin. She's no fairy godmother. She was dressed like she was on safari, hiking boots and hat included. I think she's sixty-ish, at least six feet tall, unruly hair like mine, only sandy gray, and she's direct. I mean extremely direct."

"Direct in a rude way?"

"Oh no. Direct in a I-have-no-time-for-nonsense way. No nonsense and no pretense. I think that's why children love her. Children have an extra sense about pretense, you know."

"I suppose that's why you're a kid magnet too. No pretense and just enough nonsense to make you fun. Sounds like you two are a match made for a job like this. Ying and yang. Salt and pepper."

"We'll get a test run tomorrow. Reyna's lined up an

appointment with some music faculty members at the university here in the city, and then lunch with a senator who could be very helpful to us. Sounds like I'll be playing an unrehearsed mini recital at the university for a few of the faculty. Reyna promised them I'd play if they'd give up their Saturday morning to accommodate our travel schedule. Then we're off to a couple of music stores to look for instruments and equipment. We'll stay one more night here and then head to Xela on Sunday morning."

"Sounds like a plan, and I'm not surprised. It's already Saturday morning here, and my day's a bit more relaxed than yours. Morning brunch with a board member, and I'm taking Acer to the theater tonight. Tomorrow's a free day, and I'm planning to sleep in. One more board meeting early Monday morning, and Acer's to have the plane ready at noon so we can fly out of here before the ink's dry on the merger documents. Don't want them changing their minds."

"You'll be at Rockwater Monday evening?"

"That's my plan."

"Good. At least we'll be on the same side of the Atlantic."

"I have hours to talk, but you've had a long day. You'd better shut those big blue eyes and dream of me and the surprise I have for you when you get home."

"That's not the way to get me to sleep—and by the way, no surprise could make me love you more."

"Maybe not, but when I saw this, it had your name on it. Good night and sleep well, my love."

With its Mexican neocolonial architecture and décor, Las

Ventanas was about as far from Moss Point as Miami was from Uganda. Ten-foot-high windows and French doors framed a tropical garden in the foreground and a panoramic view of the city with Pacaya, an active volcano, in its backdrop. Reyna was drinking coffee at the table with the best view when Caroline entered the restaurant. Her tanned skin and athletic build had gone unchanged since Caroline last saw her four years ago when she was here with Betsy and Mason to adopt Josefina, but Reyna's long brown tresses were gone and replaced with a short pixie cut.

The half hour before Lydia came in was filled with conversation that only two women with a shared past could have. Reyna told of her loneliness without Josh and how her sole reason for living had been her work until she had adopted a five-year-old girl with scoliosis and a three-year-old boy with congenital deformities. The state had practically given Reyna the children, circumventing the normal paperwork and exorbitant fees. Anna and Enrique had brought new life into an otherwise stagnant home.

Reyna's news gave Caroline permission to share her own good news without restraint. She had deliberately kept her left hand resting in her lap, sliding a picture of Josefina across the table with her right. Reyna toyed with the photo and smiled as she heard about Betsy's miraculous pregnancy and the birth of David's namesake. Then Caroline stretched her left arm above the table, nearly sending a vase of hibiscus flowers to the stone floor. A pink pearl surrounded by pink diamonds told her story.

Reyna grabbed Caroline's hand. "*Hijole*! Caroline, what is this?"

Caroline told how Roderick had come into her life as a result of her search for her childhood piano and how their relationship had developed over the last year. She couldn't help but notice how Reyna's face brightened when she heard

Bella's story and how this young, musical savant had plucked Caroline from a deep rut and had restored purpose in her life just as her own adopted children had done for her. Caroline was in the middle of telling Reyna about composing the *Rockwater Suite* and how Bella could play it perfectly when Lydia, wearing the same clothes she'd had on the previous night, approached the table.

"Good morning, Caroline, and you must be Reyna." Lydia sat abruptly as Caroline and Reyna stood to greet her and before either of them could speak.

Caroline eased back into her chair and caught the surprised look on Reyna's face. "Good morning, Dr. Pipkin. Yes, this is Reyna, Dr. Reyna Perez-Morris."

Lydia took the napkin from beside her plate and shook it before putting it in her lap. "I'm glad to know that, and now we'll just dispense with the doctor stuff. I'm Lydia, and I'll just call you Reyna." She picked up her coffee cup. "What does a woman have to do to get a cup of this coffee you were bragging about last night?" She looked at Caroline.

Reyna waved her hand, and the waiter appeared with two silver pots. "*Café?*"

"*Sí, gracias. Con leche, por favor.*" Lydia held up her cup and watched the waiter pour in the coffee and warm milk together.

"You didn't tell me you spoke Spanish, Lydia."

"You didn't ask, and you can't very well live in Miami without knowing how to order coffee in Spanish. Don't use it much anymore, though."

They chatted and drank a cup of coffee before approaching the buffet and filling their plates with fresh pineapple and papaya, fried plantains, black beans, eggs, and corn tortillas—not a typical Saturday morning breakfast in Moss Point, where grits and bacon reigned. Lydia wanted to know the exact plans for the day, and then they passed around the conversation like it was on a lazy Susan in the middle of the table, each telling brief stories and making inquiries of each other.

Finally, Lydia folded her napkin and put it beside her plate. "So I get to hear you play this morning? That'll be a treat. Use that to your advantage in this endeavor. Make them think you're a rock star. It'll get you places."

"I hardly think Chopin and Mendelssohn classify me as a rock star." Caroline joined Reyna's laughter.

"Look, I'm an anthropologist who happened to fall in love with some orphans in Africa, but don't think I didn't use my credentials when it was convenient or necessary. Being an eccentric old lady doesn't get you in the same doors as being a published anthropologist will."

"I get it. Today, I'm a composer and concert pianist." She nodded with certainty.

Lydia looked down at her travel vest and shorts. "Guess that means I'd better change my clothes after breakfast."

Neither Caroline nor Reyna discouraged that idea.

Lydia pointed with her fork toward the window. "Tell me about that volcano and how I might go about climbing it."

"Well, that's Pacaya. Hikers climb it even though it's above eight thousand feet, but I do not recommend it, especially not for you."

"And why is that? You think I'm too old? You think I can't do it? My footprints are atop Kilimanjaro."

Reyna stammered. "Oh no, *señora*, I'm most certain you could, but it is not safe. It is a two-hour climb up an active volcano, complete with boiling lava and an occasional spewing of steam and ash. But armed robbers are the most serious danger, and they prey on tourists."

"Armed robbers, you say?"

"Yes, they steal your money and anything you have on

you they could sell, but they usually do not hurt you unless you put up a fight."

"So what you're really saying is that the people are poor, and they make their living stealing. And if they started hurting or killing people, then tourists would dwindle along with the thieves' income."

"You are insightful, Lydia. Most Guatemalans are peace-loving people, but many are so poor and uneducated and have no way of making a living. Kidnapping is a problem here for the same reason."

"Roderick cautioned me that the crime rate here is on the rise."

"He is correct. More murders and more drugs. Certain departments—you can think of our *departmentos* like your states—are safe, but drug cartels from Mexico have moved into the northern departments where the jungles can hide their drug operations. And the Mayan population there is defenseless against them."

"From my reading, I'm getting the picture that women aren't treated too well here, either, much like Africa. One article said you've had over four thousand unsolved femicides here in the last few years—so many they've coined a new word for them. What's your take on that?"

Remembering her conversation with Roderick about these murders and recalling how the customs agent had made her feel in the airport last night made Caroline squirm in her seat. She wanted to know what Reyna knew about this subject.

"What you read is true, and the more frightening aspect is we have no idea how many other disappearances are never reported. Not that any murder is typical, but these femicides, as you say, are unusually gruesome." Reyna adjusted her glasses. "To answer your question, I think it is a combination of drugs, alcohol, and the *machismo* element in this culture—male domination of women. Even as a pediatrician, I see far too many young girls in their teens who have been brutalized and sexually abused."

Caroline realized that Lydia's interest in anthropology had initiated her research before this trip, but talking about brutal murders at the breakfast table was not her idea of how to start the day. She shuddered thinking of Ernesto's bloody beating of Gretchen and Bella last October. "Ladies, ladies, let's talk about something more pleasant. I'm getting squeamish."

"Forgive me. Don't guess you have to think too much about these kinds of things in . . . in . . . where is it you live?" Lydia set her coffee cup down.

"Moss Point, Georgia. And you're right. It's a small community of mostly family and friends, and we don't often hear of such violence."

"You live in a cocoon, and once you start this work, you'll get a taste of how the majority of women are treated in this world. But you have a dream for helping these beautiful people help themselves. Let these children sing their songs and tell their stories all over the world. But for now, let's talk about something else." Lydia shifted her attention to Reyna. "I've been reading about the Mayans, anticipating my trip here. I'm anxious to see some of the ruins and to visit some museums. I think Caroline built in a day or two to do that."

"Yes, that will be on our way back to the city once we have finished our business in Xela. Enough talk about thieves, kidnappers, and murderers. Our driver will be here in about half an hour to take us to the university. I need to go back to the room and come up with a short program for this morning. I'll meet you in the lobby at nine thirty."

"And I'll go put on something that makes me look like the founder of the Ugandan Children's Choir."

Caroline quickly signed the ticket and gave it to the waiter before the three women headed for the courtyard.

Reyna had said nothing last night or this morning, but she was not comfortable with the report Caroline had given her last night about her treatment at the airport. Too many questions and too much corruption. Earlier, Reyna had noticed a pony-tailed man in a shiny dark-green suit at the table behind them. She was aware of him now as he followed the three of them to the hallway where Caroline took a left turn to go to her suite.

Chapter 13

Misgivings and Markets

Later on Saturday morning

Standing a proud five feet five inches tall in front of the passenger's door of the van, their driver wore dark pants, a short-sleeved white shirt, and a narrow blue-striped tie. His size, his brown skin, and thick, dark hair smoothed to his head all suggested he was of Mayan descent. He stood even straighter when the three women approached. "*Buenos días*. My name is Paco Alvarez. I am your driver." He pointed to his watch and tapped three times. "I am Guatemalan, but when I drive you, my watch is on Anglo time." His humor brought laughter as they climbed into his small white van, as clean as if they were its first passengers and smelling of plumeria. "I take you to the university first."

Between Paco and Reyna, something of interest on every street corner was pointed out during the fifteen-minute drive to the university. He drove them to the front door of the building where they were to meet the professors. "I park the van there." He pointed to a space under the shade of a large tree near the perimeter of the parking lot. "I read magazines in English and wait for you." He proudly pointed to a stack of year-old People magazines in English.

Two hours later, they were on their way to lunch with the senator.

Lydia sat in the front passenger's seat. "Paco, you remind me of my driver in Uganda, always having to dodge holes in the road." She turned to Caroline. "Your playing was exquisite this morning, and I can see why Mr. Adair is quite taken with you."

"Why, thank you, Lydia."

"As his wife, you'll probably have folks stumbling all over themselves to attend to your needs. Don't let it spoil you."

In just this morning, Paco's incessant attentiveness had already reminded Caroline of how life might be from now on as Roderick's wife. Acer would drive them and pilot the jet and Lilah would take care of the house. "Oh, Lydia, if you only knew what my life is really like, you'd know I'm completely unspoilable."

"No one is unspoilable, my friend."

After a successful lunch with the senator and a couple of stops at music stores, Paco dropped them at the hotel's entrance late in the afternoon and asked for instructions for Sunday morning's pickup. They agreed on nine o'clock, which would get them to Xela before dark unless it rained.

Without slowing or even turning her head as she entered the hotel, Lydia said, "I'll meet you two in the restaurant at six thirty for dinner."

"See you then." Caroline saluted the back of Lydia's head as Lydia walked away and then turned to Reyna. "She never follows anyone, and she's always on a mission, isn't she?"

"Yes. But that is why she gets things done."

They waved goodbye to Paco, walked together into the

hotel lobby, and stopped to admire the table in the entrance, its hand-carved, wooden legs almost as delicate as the bowl of lilies and orchids they supported.

"You're right, Reyna. But did you get the idea that underneath all that striking African garb, she still has on her cargo shorts?"

Reyna laughed. "You surprise me sometimes, Caroline."

"Don't mean to. I think I'm ready to push the Off button and take a break." The look of bewilderment on Reyna's face caught Caroline's attention. "Really, am I that surprising?" Then she realized Reyna was staring at something behind her and turned to see. "What's so interesting?"

"Shhh, do not look now." Reyna's natural smile turned plastic and insincere, like smiling was only what she was supposed to do. "That man, the one in the green suit pouring himself a cup of coffee at the hospitality table . . . I've seen him twice today."

Caroline casually looked in that direction as they walked through the lobby. "Yeah, so did I. I think he's the one who was having breakfast at the table next to us this morning."

"He was, but he was also in the music store this afternoon. What is the chance of that?"

"Maybe he's a musician."

"Maybe so." She didn't sound convinced. "We should get ready for dinner." She took Caroline's arm and led her toward the courtyard. The smell of jasmine was intoxicating, and hummingbirds flitted and darted from one bottlebrush to the next, sucking nectar from the red blooms. They paused to watch the birds before crossing the covered bridge connecting the two buildings and spanning the pond underneath. The man in the shiny green suit followed a few steps behind.

Reyna jerked Caroline's arm and pulled her to the

bridge's railing and stopped. "Look, look at the fish." A tropical garden surrounded the waterfalls and natural pool below, its waters swirling with foot-long koi, sensing human shadows and waiting for breadcrumbs.

The green-suited man walked past them and entered a hallway. When he was no longer in sight, Reyna dropped her grip on Caroline's arm, and they continued their walk to their suites. "I don't like that man. Make sure you know who's at your door before answering it."

Caroline forced a smile. "No opening the door."

They parted at Reyna's door, and Caroline walked down the hall alone to her room. She took a few minutes before dinner to call her parents and Sam and Angel, giving them a report of a productive day, but mostly letting them know she was safe.

She was more than satisfied with her day. The university professors had agreed to supply her with culturally appropriate music for the children but encouraged her to compose her own after they heard her play the *Rockwater Suite*.

Lydia had been most convincing in her eloquent explanation of how this cultural exchange could be so advantageous to a developing country. The senator, a former president's daughter, pledged her support and promised to help with provisions of passports and visas as the orphans began to travel.

Caroline knew she was on speakerphone so Sam and Angel could both hear about her visit to two music stores and the array of available indigenous instruments. The shopkeeper had convinced her that marimbas must be a part of this program since Guatemala was the birthplace of that instrument. Her hopes of the storeowner offering to give the instruments to them, or to at least give a considerable discount, had vanished as he pressed her for payment.

Caroline stopped short of telling Sam and Angel how

Reyna shook her head when the shopkeeper demanded payment in order to close the deal. She told them Reyna had stepped in and explained they would phone him from Xela next week. Half the money would be wired when the order was placed, and the other half would be wired once it was safely delivered in Xela.

Even with all the activity of the day, there had still been time to stop at the Museo Nacional de Historia, which she described in great detail to Sam and Angel, stopping again before telling them how Reyna had discouraged Lydia's request to visit the Mercado Central, describing it as another haven for pickpockets and thieves.

She refreshed herself before joining Lydia and Reyna in the restaurant. More chicken, rice, and beans for dinner, and a strong cup of coffee accompanied flan and more conversation about the day. Reyna affirmed that the pledges made by the university professors and the senator were as much as anyone could hope for. Their commitments would not only undergird Caroline's work, but Caroline's choir would bring international awareness to the university and a certain clout to the senator's position. Plans were made to meet for breakfast and then the drive to Xela, stopping at Lake Atitlán on the way.

Sunday morning

Pacaya was shrouded in low-hanging clouds, and the air was thick with moisture, putting a blanket of heavy mist over the city.

Lydia, in her safari outfit again, had already claimed her front seat in the van when Caroline stepped through the doors and stuffed the hotel receipts into her bag. "*Buenos días,* Paco." She handed him her backpack. "Careful, it has my laptop in it." She crawled into the van seat behind the driver. "Sorry, I'm running late. Roderick called as I was walking out of my room. Have you seen Reyna?"

"Not since breakfast." Lydia sat in the passenger's seat next to Paco, both feet on the floor, her arms crossed, and looking straight ahead, obviously ready to go. "You might want to shake that expensive ring on your finger now that we're leaving the city. From the article I read in the paper this morning, a thief wouldn't think twice of using his machete to cut your finger off for it."

"*Buenos días,* Dr. Morris." Paco rushed to meet Reyna as she came through the hotel door. "Where are your luggage?"

"In my room. I need to speak with Miss Carlyle."

Paco opened the van door, and Reyna stuck her head in. "I am so sorry, Caroline. My mother just called. You remember, she is keeping my children while I travel with you. Enrique is very ill with high fever and congestion. With his disabilities, this condition can get serious very quickly. I am so sorry, but I must stay here and get back to my home."

"Of course you must." Caroline leaned to take Reyna's hand as it rested on the van seat.

"I really am sorry. I was looking forward to being with you and Dr. Pipkin, and of course I wanted to see Sister Gabriela and the children at the orphanage."

"I know you did, but your place is here with your son."

"Thank you for understanding. I pray he will get better, and maybe I can join you in a couple of days."

Lydia turned around in her seat. "And if you don't, will I see you again?"

"Of course. If I cannot get to the Highlands, I will see you when you return to the city next week." She turned to Paco. "Paco, I know we talked of driving by Lake Atitlán today, but I do not think it a good day to do that. The air is heavy, and visibility will not be good. Please take them by Antigua. Today is a good market day. If the air clears, they might like to see the cross that overlooks the Old City." She shook her head in disappointment and turned to Caroline. "I feel like I am abandoning you."

"Oh no, we will miss you. You could explain to Lydia so much about the country and culture I have forgotten, but we'll just hope you can join us for the trip back."

Holding the van door open, Paco stood next to Dr. Morris. His wide smile exposed yellow teeth that looked like kernels of corn, and just as straight. "Dr. Morris, I take good care of them. I lead many groups in Antigua. I show them everything. They will have wonderful time and buy many things from the market."

Reyna patted Paco's shoulder. "Thank you, Paco."

Caroline wrote on her notepad, tore off the piece of paper, and handed it to Reyna. "Look Reyna, you need to get back home to take care of your son. Here is my cell phone number, and I have yours right here. We'll stay in touch, and I certainly hope little Enrique is feeling better by the time you get home." They squeezed hands, and Paco closed the door.

Caroline watched Reyna follow Paco to the front of the van. She spoke in rapid Spanish, pointing and gesturing as though giving last-minute safety instructions. He climbed into the van, cranked it, and adjusted his rearview mirror.

Paco drove the small white van under the hotel's porte cochere. They waved at Reyna as the van bounced over the cobblestones and they rode slowly through the stucco arches and down the lane to the highway.

Reyna walked briskly back to the hotel entrance. She flinched at a clanging noise and turned to see a man's hands up in the air as he jumped away from a vehicle. The heavy metal top had slammed shut, covering the bed of the small blue pickup. He stepped back to the truck and adjusted the padlock, locking in whatever was in the truck bed or locking out unwanted attention. Worn jeans and an undersized T-shirt had replaced the shiny green suit. Nonetheless, he was familiar—brown, short and stocky, a thinly sculpted moustache suggesting vanity, and greasy, long dark hair pulled tightly into a ponytail at the nape of his stubby neck. He hopped in, started the engine, and quickly caught up with the white van.

She grabbed her luggage and checked out of the hotel. Once in her car, she searched her purse for Paco's card and placed a call. She wanted to alert him without frightening Caroline. But Paco reported no sign of the truck and driver.

Relieved her friends were well out of the city and that no such vehicle was in sight, Reyna drove home to take care of Enrique.

Even for a Sunday, the city streets were crowded, and the air, already heavy with moisture, allowed no escape for the gas fumes. Caroline sat quietly in the back, the van floor vibrating under her feet. She saw Lydia reach for her jacket in the back seat and wrap it around her bare legs to stay warm. Lydia insisted on using the air conditioner until they were out of the heaviest traffic.

"So sorry. The air is no good." Paco pushed several buttons on the dashboard until cool air flowed. Caroline guessed the air conditioner was rarely used.

"No kidding. They really ought to do something about this."

"Too many cars. Too many crazy drivers." He adjusted the vents. "Macadamia nuts."

"It's nuts all right." Caroline chimed in.

Paco's head tilted back as his laughter rumbled around in the van. "Not nuts like *loco*, crazy," he explained in thickly accented English. "Real macadamia nuts. Big project in Antigua. Government give away many trees to farmers to make better living. Better than coffee plantations. They use branches for firewoods, sell nuts for to make candy and oil. Good idea, yeah? Trees make the air good, too, and they use the wood and shells to make top for the road. Good, big project, yeah?"

"Brilliant. Replacing catalytic converters with macadamia trees. Just brilliant." Lydia pulled a small tablet from one of her vest pockets and a stubby pencil that looked like it had been sharpened with a pocketknife and made a note.

"You want to eat at the tree station today? They make pancakes from macadamia *masa*. No, not *masa*. How you say in *inglés*? Flour?"

"They make flour too?"

"*Sí*, and butter, good butter, better than peanut butter. You want to eat there?"

"We already had breakfast, Paco," Caroline answered as she thumbed through her guidebook of Antigua.

Lydia continued writing in her tablet and mumbled her list as she wrote. "Environment, economics, food source, check on climate and sources." She returned her pad and pencil to her vest pocket. "Yes, I want pancakes."

Caroline was not about to disagree with Lydia. She would eat pancakes too.

"Good choice. They serve pancakes all day. You like. I promise. You not like? I pay."

"Can't beat that deal with a drum mallet. So how far is it and what else can you tell me about where we're going?" She removed her jacket from around her legs, turned off the air conditioner, and opened her window. They were out of traffic and into the countryside.

"It is ancient city, less than one hour from Guate. Big place for tourists, and many peoples come here to learn Spanish." He pronounced it "Espanish." "Many, many schools. New York got Central Park. Antigua got Parque Central, beautiful flowers and a big, big, fountain. You can sit there and see all the peoples. Beautiful."

"What about the market?" Lydia asked. "My guidebook says it's open on Sunday."

"Sí, many, many peoples there today. Tourists and locals. And I take you to Cerro de la Cruz, the Hill of the Cross. You can see the city, and if no clouds, you can see the Volcán de Agua."

"A water volcano? Interesting. Can I climb it?"

"Sí, a water volcano. Long time ago, it bury the city in hot water and mud. Not good idea to climb. Too many bandits."

"Bandit and smog. Crap. These people are killing themselves by not taking care of those problems. Bandits rob their own when they're robbing tourists."

"I take you to the market first. I help you shop. Good prices for you. Then we eat pancakes before we go to Cerro de la Cruz. I walk with you there. It is dangerous. More bandits."

Caroline would warn Lydia at the first stop that the drivers and tour guides often got kickbacks or commissions from bringing tourists to certain places of business. She imagined it was no different in Africa. "If there's time, Paco, I'd like to stop at the jade factory." Caroline turned to Lydia. "You must see the marimba made of jade. Amazingly beautiful, all mined right here in Guatemala. I'd like to buy cufflinks for Roderick."

"Oh, sí, I take you there. I get good price for you."

It was obvious Paco's favorite clients were women with money to spend.

In spite of the damp weather, the park was filled with people. The locals wore their colorful native dress and attempted to sell their trinkets to anyone who did not look like them. Paco pointed to a young woman carrying her wares in a large basket perfectly balanced atop her head. "She wears her *huipil.* She make it on a loom and she sew the flowers and birds on it. The flowers and birds mean what village is hers."

With her was another young woman from the same village, nursing a baby as they worked the crowd. The *huipil's* design was obviously as practical as it was beautiful.

Lydia reached into her vest pocket for a few quetzals and handed them to Paco. "Would you give her these and ask if I can take a few photos?

"*Sí, señora.*"

Lydia watched him approach the women. When he returned with a big smile and a thumbs-up, she asked, "Now, if they marry outside their village, do they wear the *huipil*?" Lydia pulled her camera from one of the larger pockets on her vest and snapped away.

"No. She must make a new *huipil* for husband's village."

"What a shame! If they move, they lose their identity. Like the African tribes."

El Mercado was busier that the Parque Central, its narrow aisles a flourish of colorful hand-loomed fabrics, like the plumes of the tropical birds found in the jungle. Lydia was not surprised to find that most of the shopkeepers spoke some English, at least enough to push their bags and blankets and embroidered pieces that would surely fetch a large sum if sold in the States.

"Look at this. Can you imagine how long this piece must have taken?" Lydia held the tapestry of hand-embroidered birds close to her face. "Smells like smoke."

"That's not unusual of the pieces you buy here. The women sit around the campfires at night and sew. I have some pieces that still smell of smoke after several years."

Lydia was bartering for a *huipil* when she caught sight of the ponytailed man. She saw him more than once as they snaked their way through the maze of shopkeepers.

She pointed to a table filled with hand-woven fabrics. "African fabrics are more earthy in their colors, and their patterns are so harsh and geometric, nothing like these vibrant primary colors and floral designs."

She and Caroline had practically chosen the costumes for the children's choir before they were ready to leave.

They tried to avoid the area of the market where they were selling the meats, mostly plucked chickens hanging like garments on a clothesline. But Paco insisted. They walked briskly by the meat counter, holding their breaths until they reached the produce market.

Caroline stopped to look at the bins. "Now you see where they come up with their flair for color. Look at all those fruits and flowers."

Paco approached them from behind with a tag of small red bananas and three mangoes. "This I buy for you. Sweet bananas. You like."

"Thank you, Paco. I'm certain I will."

Lydia, normally out front, stepped back to where Caroline was buying fried lima beans. She waited for Caroline to zip her purse and then took her arm, practically pushing her forward and motioned for Paco at the same time. "Let's get out of here. Didn't I hear you say you wanted to buy some cufflinks?" She looked behind them as they crossed the courtyard. No pony-tailed man in sight.

The trip to the jade store cost Caroline all the money she made in one week of teaching piano lessons, but as she explained to Lydia, the cufflinks would be a wedding gift to Roderick. Lydia quickly approved and admired the jade marimba before leading them back to the van.

After a plate of three macadamia-nut pancakes slathered in macadamia-nut butter and drenched in local honey, Lydia wanted another cup of coffee. Still, during her meal and her conversation with the shopkeeper about the particulars of the macadamia tree project, she kept vigilance, scanning everyone who entered the restaurant. "Okay, Paco, what do you say we walk the Hill of the Cross?"

Paco pushed back from the table and patted his round belly, the buttons on his white shirt pulling at the buttonholes. "Not good, not good," he drawled, his accent even stronger. "Too many bandits."

Caroline laughed. "I think too many pancakes."

"I drive you there. Policeman will walk with us. That is his job. If we do not let him, he might lose his job." He flashed his yellow teeth again.

The midday sun had pulled some of the moisture from the air, leaving only inflated, bottom-heavy white clouds off in the distance. Lydia cautioned. "A steep ascent, jagged rocks and flip-flops are a combination for pain. You got hiking shoes?"

"No hiking shoes, but some better for climbing." Caroline retrieved her walking shoes from her bag before they started the ten-minute climb to the summit.

Lydia led the pack with Caroline behind her, stepping

cautiously to avoid a fall. A misstep in these rocks would mean an injured hand, not something she wanted to deal with ever, let alone in Guatemala.

Paco and the policeman, armed with a machine gun, followed close behind, talking secretively in Spanish and snickering. Lydia had kept her Spanish-speaking abilities from Paco, not by design originally, but for now there was no need for him to know she understood everything he said. She was not offended that these two brown men, clearly six inches shorter and ten times less tightly wound than she was, found her odd. They were not the first persons to observe her eccentricities. Neither did she find it strange that these two had never seen a woman so beautiful as Caroline, fair skinned and blue eyed with hair the color of glistening onyx.

Halfway up the hill, Lydia asked Caroline, "How did you find your driver?"

"Paco?"

"Yes."

"Actually I didn't find him. Roderick's assistant made all the arrangements for the trip. She found him."

"Did he give you a business card?"

"No. I saw him give Reyna one yesterday morning. Why would he give me his business card?"

"No reason. Just wondering."

Drier air and the altitude made for excellent visibility. The vista was worth the climb, with the water volcano in the distance on the south side of the city and the air clear enough to see the grid of perpendicular cobblestone streets in the old city below. The view was much like the one from their hotel in Guate with Pacaya in the background, only Guate was a modern city with garbage-strewn streets and rooftops of slums that looked like Monopoly houses.

The sun's angle created a shadow of the cross over the ancient ruins. Lydia unzipped her vest pocket, removed her camera, and motioned for Caroline to stand still. "Move two steps to your left. That'll get you out of the shadow. That's it. Stand right there. On three."

Paco rushed to Lydia's side. "I take your photo, Dr. Pipkin. Stand next to Miss Carlyle."

"No, thanks, Paco. I'm doing just fine. Step back, I want your picture." Lydia raised the camera and snapped a picture of Paco. "Stay right there, Caroline. I need one more." She turned back toward Caroline, zoomed in, and refocused her camera to capture a close-up of the ponytailed man, his muscle-bound, tattooed arms folded tightly at his chest as he stood next to a group of Japanese tourists at the edge of the summit. *Click.* "Got it. Now let's go."

Chapter 14

Gut Feelings

Monday morning in Moss Point

Sam poured his second cup of coffee and went to the door of the back porch where Angel was watering her begonias. "My sweet Angel, I'll be in the library making some calls for the next little while."

She blew him a kiss and kept watering.

His walking cane, hand-carved walnut from a tree on Meadows property and used by his favorite uncle, tapped across the wooden floor and echoed down the hallway as he walked. He entered the library and bypassed his lounge chair in front of the fireplace, propped his walking cane next to his desk, and sat down in the leather chair that had been in his courthouse office for nearly forty years. He'd brought it home when he retired sixteen years ago because it suited him. He picked up the phone and dialed a local number and without identifying himself asked to speak to Tom Ellison.

"Good morning, Judge Meadows. Mr. Ellison is in, and I know he'd be just delighted to talk to you this morning. Just a minute, hon."

Sam had been called many things in his time, but no one ever called him "hon." He chuckled at how the secretary caught herself, just shy of calling him "honey."

Tom answered, "What's up, Judge?"

Sam cleared his throat. "Well, we have a problem this morning, Tom."

"Hope it's nothing to do with Mrs. Silva and Bella."

"No. You did a mighty fine job of getting her divorced from that scoundrel of a husband of hers and getting her the money she deserved. She and Bella are in North Carolina at Duke University doing just fine now. Little Bella's being educated, and Gretchen's getting ready to open a bakery. Caroline's future sister-in-law, Sarah, is quite a help to them. She's on staff at Duke."

"That's wonderful news, and I'm glad to hear it. But something must not be so mighty fine for you to be my first call on this Monday morning. What can I do for you, Judge?"

"Well, I'm about to disclose to you a very carefully guarded secret this morning because I need your help. You know the Pendergrass twins?"

"Sure. Everybody in town knows of those two. Why, if it weren't for Bo Blossom, those two would take first place for being the town characters."

"I suppose they do come up a close second. Well, you know them, and you know every year for the last fifteen or so years some of our most deserving graduates get full four-year scholarships to a state school?"

"Yeah, I know about that too."

"Well, Ned and Fred Pendergrass are responsible for those scholarships." He could just imagine the look on Tom's normal, lawyer-poker face.

"Shut your mouth." Tom coughed. "Excuse me, Judge. Man, you talk about a surprise. I always thought you gave those scholarships."

"No. I've educated some kids in my time, but my money's tied up in a trust at the university."

"Where in the world did those two fellows get a fortune like that? You can't make that kind of money doing odd jobs and mowing grass."

"Their daddy bought some Coca-Cola stock when those boys were just crawling around over sixty years ago. And when he had a little extra money, he'd buy some more. He put it all in his sons' names, but they didn't know it until after their daddy died. With what he bought and all the stock splits, they have about six and half million dollars' worth of stock. But you got to stay quiet. Only the twins, Ed Brooks over at the bank, and I know about this. At least that was until a few weeks ago."

"Six and a half million? None of that sounds like a problem to me."

"The problem is that it appears GiGi Nelson found out they're wealthy. We think she overheard Ned talking to me at the ribbon cutting for the new park, and now she's in hot pursuit of old Fred, the tight-lipped one." Sam could hear Tom trying to control his laughter. "I hear you, Tom, but this is no laughing matter. Ned wants things fixed in a hurry. He knows Fred understands just about as much about their wealth as he understands about women."

"I'm getting the picture."

"Neither of those men have a will, and Ned's worried to death that his brother's being taken in by that orange-haired floozy. We got to protect those boys, Tom."

"I understand. What would you like me to do?"

"I'll be picking up some financial information from the bank later this morning, and I want you to be thinking about the best way to get all this secured so that Miss Hot Pants can't get her hands on those boys' money. You got time to see me this afternoon?"

"Yes, sir. What time would you like to come in?"

"I'll see you at three o'clock." Sam hung up the phone and dialed the banker.

Monday morning in the Guatemalan Highlands

Paco picked up three sack lunches and a six-pack of water bottles from the hotel café and met Caroline in the lobby. "*Buenos días,* Miss Carlyle." He held up the sacks and water. "Lunch for you and water for the day. Water here no good for you."

"Wonderful. Thank you. Have you seen Dr. Pipkin this morning?"

Paco shook his head and glanced at the staircase.

"I'll wait a few minutes, and if she doesn't come down, I'll call her room." It had been so late when they got in Sunday night there had been no chance for her to see if any changes had been made in the hotel lobby since her last visit. She had warned Lydia about the accommodations here.

The rooms in this hotel, unlike the luxurious suites at the hotel in Guate, were basic—stone floors, a small wooden desk and chair, a bed so low to the floor that Caroline had trouble reaching the lamp switch on the bedside table, and ratty curtains covering a narrow slit for a window. The three-foot-wide closet had shelves, but Caroline had learned years ago never to unpack her clothes in this hotel. Leaving them packed in the gallon zip-lock bags protected them from moisture and from near microscopic bugs that caused red rashes.

The bathroom was basically an over-sized shower stall with a commode and a small, stained sink with a rubber stopper on a chain and a drain in the middle of the floor. Caroline was glad they had arrived when they did last night because all the water was cut off at ten o'clock and didn't come back on until six o'clock this morning.

The lobby was an improvement over the guest rooms. Morning light revealed the same coral-colored stucco walls, a warm backdrop for the unusual embroidered fabric pieces hung at random around the rather small area. On previous trips, she had heard tourists offer to buy the pieces, but the hotel owner had refused, stating that his wife had designed and sewn them.

Caroline walked to the corner of the lobby to a rather large cage, home to several colorful birds chirping away. Singing birds always made her think of Bella and the nightingale Roderick had given her for Christmas. A light blanket in primary-colored stripes, folded and lying on a small table next to the cage, was likely used to drape the wire enclosure at night to keep the birds quiet. Earth-colored Saltillo square tiles were laid in diagonal patterns across the floor.

There was no elevator, only six flights of mosaic-tiled stairs to her third-floor room. Dark wood trim on the staircase, no doubt handmade, matched the woodwork encasing the doors and windows. The only house phone in the lobby was at the front desk, which was basically an opening in the wall and a counter where the clerk checked in guests, answered the phone, and did the accounting on an adding machine that could have been purchased in an antique store back home. Behind the clerk was a wall of numbered boxes that held room keys and messages for guests.

She approached the counter and handed the clerk her room key, a rather large metal one on a key chain attached to a wooden block with her room number etched and burned into the wood. Five more minutes and she would call Lydia.

—•—

Lydia sat at the small desk with her laptop open. She took a bite out of her granola bar and talked to herself as she waited for her computer to boot up. "They turn off the water at night. I can sit on the toilet and take a shower at the same time. I can't get the news because there's no cable. No room service, not even morning coffee. I can only make local calls on the rotary dial phone. But they have wireless internet connection. Thank God for modern technology."

She connected her camera to her laptop, downloaded the photos she'd taken in Antigua, and began clicking through them. For three of the photos, she deleted their identifying numbers and renamed them. She then disconnected her camera and drafted an email to her assistant.

G'morning, Jess,

In Xela at the Bonifaz Hotel. All is well. We visit the orphanage today. I need you to start doing research on the Guatemala Macadamia Tree Initiative. I'll explain later. I've attached three pictures and be sure to keep them in a safe place. If things don't go just as planned, they may become useful. One photo is of Caroline Carlyle, my host. The second one, the man in white shirt and tie, is our driver, allegedly named Paco Alvarez. The third man in the t-shirt is unidentified, but he seems to show up wherever we are. Don't worry. I'm just being cautious. Call if you need me. LP.

She hit the Send button and got up, grabbed her travel vest from the back of her chair, and put the camera back in one of the pockets. Her travel clock on the bedside table read ten after nine. "Oh, crap. I'm late." The email was taking longer than usual, no doubt the photos and a slow connection. She finished putting her gear for the day together while her computer hummed. When all was done, she gathered her things and walked out. "Oh, crap again. The key. I need the key to lock the crappy door, then I have to leave it at the crappy front desk." She retrieved the key, locked the door, and took the stairs two at a time down six flights.

Monday morning in London

Roderick walked out of the office building and dialed the number again. Still no answer. He entered the cab waiting for him at the curb. London cabs, actually built for passengers with accommodating doors and room for bags, helped him understand his father's appreciation for British practicality.

Acer sat in the back seat with their luggage in front of him on the floorboard. "Deal done?" He closed the book he was reading.

"Deal's done. Ink's dry. Funds will be transferred this afternoon, and I'm ready for the trout stream at Rockwater. Will we make the early flight?"

"I think so, and the jet's ready when we touch down in New York. You'll be up to copiloting by the time we land?"

"I'll be ready, but I'd be more ready if I could reach Caroline. I haven't been able to reach her since she left Guatemala City Sunday morning."

"Did you try her hotel?"

"No, just the phone Liz got for the trip. I don't have her

itinerary with me since I assumed I could reach her by phone anytime, anywhere. I'll just try her again before we take off."

"Maybe she's traveling in some remote areas."

"Maybe. Guatemala's one place I've never been. I know when she left the city, she was going to what they call the Highlands, somewhere west."

"But her satellite phone should work even in the remote areas. Countries like Guatemala have towers everywhere. Cheaper to build towers than to lay underground cable over that terrain. Maybe she just doesn't have it on."

"No, she would keep it on. We discussed that. I'll just keep trying."

Guatemala Highlands

Caroline was at the front desk dialing Lydia's room number when she heard Lydia's voice in the lobby. She turned to see the imposing woman in her daily uniform of khaki safari clothes, her untamed gray hair poking out from under her hat and her backpack slung over her left shoulder. "Oh, good, you're okay. Sleep well?"

"Until 5:00 a.m. when all the fireworks started. What in the crap was all that?"

"Oh, it's customary. Someone's celebrating a birthday, and they shoot off fireworks in the plaza."

"Scared the crap out of me. You hear that in some places of the world, and you take cover. Sorry I'm late. Internet was a bit slower than I expected this morning, but I'm ready." She tried to catch her breath. "Wow, must be the altitude."

"Or the six flights of steps."

"And on top of that, no coffee this morning." She took another deep breath. "I thought we were going to the orphanage to see the girls. Why are you wearing a skirt?"

Caroline saw Paco disappear from the lobby. "Just habit, I suppose. I've always worn long skirts around the nuns. Paco's getting your coffee and a bag of sweet rolls for your breakfast, unless you prefer some fresh fruit."

"Sweet rolls are fine." Lydia looked down at herself and back at Caroline. "Well, it's either this or African garb. What do you think? I don't want to upset anybody. Should I go change?"

"No, you're fine. You'll be comfortable, and besides the sisters and the children will think you *are* wearing African garb."

Paco returned with an extra-tall paper cup and handed it to Dr. Pipkin. "Coffee. The best in the world. You like milk and sugar?"

"Thank you, Paco. Yes, some kind of powdered milk will be fine and three sugars for a cup this tall." She walked toward Caroline. "Are you ready to go?"

"All ready. It'll take us about forty-five minutes to get there. It's not really that far. It's just that once we leave the main road, it's fairly rugged driving. I hope Paco's vehicle is up to it."

Paco returned with a small pitcher of warm milk and a sugar bowl and spoon. "No powder. *Leche*. I know the way. My van is good. No problem. No problem."

Lydia stirred her coffee and started out the door, "Okay, let's ride." The van was out front, and Lydia took her passenger's seat and held on to her coffee and a bag of sweet potato-stuffed empanadas.

Narrow, cobblestoned passages snaked the steep hills of the town. No traffic lights or stop signs. Rustic old buildings, housing families and businesses, lined the maze of one-way streets. Caroline flinched at the horns blowing at every intersection and was certain the imprint of her fingers would be permanent on the vehicle's armrest. All the while, Lydia drank her coffee and ate the empanadas seemingly oblivious to the close calls.

Once out of town and on the two-lane road leading to Salcajá, the village nearest the orphanage, the sky was bluer than blue and speckled with tall, white, gray-bottomed clouds that appear daily in a land sandwiched between the Gulf of Mexico and the Pacific. The clouds would most likely bring quick showers later in the day, and possibly thunderous downpours, but they usually passed quickly.

They had ridden a few miles on the paved road out of town when Paco turned onto a deeply rutted dirt road with high embankments on each side, appearing to head into miles of hills and cornfields. "You come here before, Miss Carlyle?"

"Yes, but it's been about four years ago." Preferring country lanes to the roads in Xela, Caroline relaxed and loosed her death grip on the armrest.

"This is the way, right?" His accented words sounded unsure.

Lydia's head swiveled quickly from looking out the side window at the close wall of the blackest dirt she had probably ever seen to staring at Paco. "Why are you asking her? You're the driver. You don't know the way? Where are you taking us?"

"It's okay, Lydia. This is the way. The orphanage is only a few more miles. Almost everyone's first reaction is the same when we leave the highway. From here on, you'll see mostly cornfields with an occasional one-room shack surrounded by dried cornstalk fences."

Paco blew his horn as he rounded the hairpin turns.

"But what if we meet someone?"

Caroline snickered. "That's why he blew his horn. Just like in town."

"Yeah, but there are no intersections out here, and nowhere to go if we meet a vehicle."

"Don't worry, drivers around here know what to do. One vehicle just has to back up. Maybe you didn't notice, but at each turn, there is space for two vehicles. Besides, once we zigzag a few more times, we'll be on the mountain crest, and the road will be flat through the fields."

Paco jerked the steering wheel trying to miss a mudhole and practically brushed the embankment on the passenger's side.

"Holy crap. That was close. And how many times do we have to make this trip?"

Caroline giggled softly. *An anthropologist whose favorite word is "crap."* She thought it odd for a woman of such credentials and distinction, but nonetheless amusing. "Yeah, that was a bit close. We only have to make this trip maybe three more times this week. You're strapped in. Just sit back and enjoy the scenery."

Another twenty minutes and right in the midst of the cornfields a white structure surrounded by a wall of light-colored stacked stone appeared atop the mountain like a giant pearl on green velvet. "There it is. There's the orphanage. Blow your horn, Paco. Let Sister Gabriela know we're coming."

As they neared the gate, they could see the children running into the front yard. One small brown boy and a larger, even darker brown boy unlocked and opened wide the gate from the inside, allowing their entrance.

Paco stopped the vehicle once inside the stone walls, and Caroline did not wait for him to open her door. She bounced out of the van at the first sight of Sister Gabriela coming through the double wooden doors of the home.

Running to each other, they embraced like sophomores who had not seen each other since the end of the last school term. "I'm so glad to see you, Sister. Where's Blanca? Is she here?"

"Greetings, my dear friend. Blanca is in school, but she will be here this afternoon."

They embraced again. Caroline turned to wave for Dr. Pipkin and Paco to come forward. They were surrounded by children, chattering like a bunch of biddies and all vying for the closest position to their visitors.

Sister Gabriela stepped aside and in Quiché said, "Wait, Hector, do not close the gate. I think someone else needs to come in. Maybe they are with our guests." She then repeated her message in English.

Paco, Lydia, and Caroline turned to see a dark-blue pickup with two men inside cruise slowly on down the lane in front of the orphanage.

"They're not with us. Maybe local farmers." Caroline took the sister's arm, and they walked together through the heavy, wooden doors.

Chapter 15

Desperation

Monday morning at the orphanage outside Xela

Caroline sat next to Sister Gabby and across from Lydia at the primitive wooden table in the sisters' humble dining area. She savored the last drop of hibiscus tea as they wrapped up their conversation.

Sister Gabby was slight of frame, fair skinned with dimpled, rosy cheeks, and looked at the world through penetrating, small, near-black eyes with perfectly arched brows. She could have been a cherub as a child, although a slight one. Where she walked, she left a scent of grace and peace and true beauty. Anyone who walked through the doors of Hogar Luis Amigo could see Gabby's soulprint in the children, in the monastic but immaculate rooms, and even in the courtyard and gardens.

A spectator most of the day, Caroline asked a few questions and took notes of the questions and answers volleyed across the table between the sister and Lydia. She marveled at how Gabby maintained her gentle demeanor all day even when Lydia was all business and pressed her hard with instructions and questions.

As the western sun peeked through the dining-room window, Lydia leaned forward and propped her gangly arms on the table. "It's late in the day, and we're finishing up, but let me say this one more time because it's very important. I've done this in Africa, starting a choir with one orphanage. But you must understand something: the children from Hogar Luis Amigo do not represent Hogar Luis Amigo; they will represent all the orphans of Guatemala."

Humbly, Gabby replied, "Yes, Dr. Pipkin, I do understand. It is our honor that you start with the children in our home. I will explain to the children about the responsibility that comes with so great a privilege."

Caroline looked at her watch. Too late to call the music store in Guate and place the order for the list of musical instruments they'd decided on today. "Enough, ladies. We've been at it all day, and I can't take any more notes. I think we've made progress, don't you?"

Sister Gabby sat erect with her hands cupped in her lap and nodded quietly in agreement.

Lydia leaned back in her chair, rapped her fists on the table, and said, "Certainly we have. Why would we waste precious time if we weren't making progress?"

Sister Gabby rose from her chair. "Would you stay and eat with the children?"

Caroline stood and gathered her papers. "That is so kind of you, but I think we should be getting back to our hotel. It'll be dark before long, and I'm the one who'll be dealing with all these notes tonight." She put her notebook in her bag.

Lydia stood and pushed her chair to its place at the table. "And I don't want to think about making those hairpin turns to get back to the highway in the dark, especially after the rains we've had this afternoon." She stretched her long arms high above her head, almost touching the ceiling, and then reached down to touch her toes before grabbing her backpack.

"Thanks for allowing us return to spend tomorrow morning with the children. That's another thing I need to do tonight. Prepare some musical things to do with them." Caroline led them out of the dining room into the courtyard. An aerial view of the building would have revealed a large rectangular, two-story structure surrounding an open courtyard such that every room opened into the gardens of roses, hibiscus, zinnias, and lush, unbelievably green grass. A covered walkway sheltered the sisters and the children from either sun or showers as they moved from room to room throughout the day.

When they reached the front door, they stopped to enjoy the late-afternoon coral sky now void of heavy-bottomed clouds. Caroline wanted to say goodbye to the children, but they were in their quarters studying before their evening meal. They would be in bed by eight so they could rise at four thirty for prayers, chores, and breakfast.

Sister Gabby picked up a small brass bell from a shelf next to the wooden double doors and rang it gently. The sound reverberated around the building in an almost ethereal way. In less than a minute, the two boys who opened the gates this morning were standing beside the sister. "Josue and Hector will open the gate for you." The boys ran ahead, and Gabby kissed both Caroline and Lydia goodbye. "We'll be happy to see you in the morning."

Paco leaned against the van as he talked on the phone. Lydia approached and climbed into her front seat and grumbled as Caroline followed. "Let's get out of here before the darkness sets in."

Monday evening at Rockwater

The jet had barely come to a stop when Roderick started removing his headgear, loosening his seatbelt, and reaching for his cell phone. "Take over, Acer. I'll see you on the ground." He had been Acer's copilot on this trip since the FAA regulations required one, but he was tired. He stepped into the passenger area of the plane. Hank, the mechanic who worked at the private airstrip, was there to help with the steps when Roderick opened the door to the plane. He waved at Hank and was already dialing Caroline's number as he descended the steps to the ground. No answer. He tried again. Still no answer.

He walked toward the hangar area, and Acer joined him with the bags. "Did you reach her?"

"No. No answer." He looked at his watch. "Liz could be still at the office. I'll call her and get her to check into this."

"Good idea." Acer, bags in hand, asked Hank to secure the plane. "I'll be back tomorrow to finish up the paperwork."

Roderick had already called Liz. "What do you mean her phone isn't a satellite phone? I told you to get her an international satellite phone."

"I just decided to get her a regular cell phone with international calling."

He disliked her dismissive tone and her explanation. "I don't pay you to decide anything. I pay you to do what I tell you to do. Now, I'm telling you to order Caroline a satellite phone and overnight it to her wherever she is. It had better be there in the morning. I'll be home in forty-five minutes. I want her detailed itinerary on my desk."

"You'll have it. How did the meetings go? Did you close the deal?"

He couldn't believe she was nervy enough to ask about business at a time like this. "I don't want to talk about the damn London deal. You just do what I told you to do before I get there. And put a note in the overnight package and tell Caroline to call me as soon as she gets the phone."

Acer put their bags in the trunk as Roderick took off his jacket. He knew Acer had rarely heard this tone of voice from him, especially on the telephone, but he had not been able to restrain his frustration with his assistant. "Hand me the keys. I'm driving. Can't do anything else right now. Might as well drive."

Monday evening in the Highlands

Paco put his cell phone away, made sure Caroline and Lydia were secured in their seats, and waved an energetic goodbye to Josue, Hector, and Sister Gabby as he drove through the gate. Rich soil mixed with the powdery volcanic ash and afternoon rains made for a slippery drive once they were outside the orphanage walls. Paco's cheerfulness seemed contrived, perhaps to ease their fears about the roads after the storm; but Caroline noticed he gripped the steering wheel as though his tight grasp would hold the vehicle in the ruts.

She looked out across the mountains, a rolling patchwork quilt of damp, green hues colored by swatches of wild, yellow-blooming mustard. The sound of Lydia's voice recapping the day grew fainter as images of a rainstorm and a mudslide and David on a mountainous jungle road hovered around Caroline like the shroud of mist covering the peak of the San Pedro volcano in the distance. They were rounding the second hairpin turn when Paco hit the brake and a series of expletives escaped his mouth. A blue pickup was stalled just ahead. Neither the van's slow speed nor brakes could prevent it from skidding and swerving in the slick ruts, stopping just a couple of feet from the rear bumper of the truck.

As the van jolted to a stop, two men, their heads covered in white hoods, each carrying a baseball bat, jumped out of the blue truck and approached the van. Caroline and Lydia were too startled to heed Paco's warning to lock the doors. Paco was struggling to put the van in reverse as the first hooded man opened the door on the driver's side, pulled Paco from the van, and pushed him into the waist-high patch of mustard several yards from the road. Even with her very limited Spanish, Caroline understood Paco was begging the hooded men not to hurt the women.

"Do as they tell you to do, Caroline. Do as they tell you!" Lydia voiced loudly as the taller hooded man opened her door, pulled her from the vehicle, and wedged her body between him and the van. Then she became silent.

Caroline was able to lock her door and cram her phone into her inside jacket pocket while watching the hooded man taking Paco into the brush. She closed her eyes and screamed as the man swung the bat and Paco crumpled to the ground, hidden in the lush foliage and yellow blooms.

It took the assailant only seconds to return and shatter the window with the bat to get to her. He reached in to unlock the door, his fuming Spanish needing no translation. Although he was only a couple of inches taller than Caroline, he was stocky and solid, his stubby fingers digging into her arm as he pulled her from the van. She screamed and attempted to escape his grasp as he pinned her against the vehicle with his body and one arm while he reached into his pocket.

"Caroline. Do not fight and do not scream. You'll only

get hurt if you resist." Lydia's voice remained calm.

The thug turned Caroline's rigid body to face the van and pulled her arms behind her. Pressed against the vehicle, she felt the shattered glass gouging into her flesh as ropes tightened around her wrists. She could see Lydia standing resolute on the other side of the van, her hands bound and a stained kerchief pulled tight across her open mouth.

Caroline gagged from the rancid odor of the soiled rag now being stretched between her lips. The man's breathing was raucous and fast as he tied the ends of the rag at the nape of her neck. It was only the look in Lydia's eyes that kept Caroline from utter panic.

No way to escape. Nowhere to go. No one within shouting distance. Paco rendered helpless, lying in the mud. Pray and do as Lydia says.

The hooded man clenched her arm tightly and reached into the van for her backpack. The other man did the same with Lydia. In total silence, they led their prey to the back of the blue pickup, where the tailgate of the covered truck bed was open. The men pushed Caroline and Lydia through the slit under the cover and onto the grimy floor. They lay back to back, unable to communicate as the kidnappers shoved the backpacks in beside them. Just before the tailgate was slammed shut, Caroline saw Paco's face grimacing in pain as he tried to lift his body above the brush. Metal clanged against metal. Then darkness, total darkness under the makeshift sheet of metal just inches above them. No way to escape and no way for anyone to see them.

Five minutes earlier, she had been in a sanctuary, a safe and peaceful place with Sister Gabby, where the smell of flowers and hibiscus tea floated through the room and the sounds of a tinkling bell echoed through the sacred halls. Now, in the bowels of a vehicle with the stench of the filthy rag in her mouth and her wrists rubbed raw from a rope of hemp, she was being transported to place more than likely worse than the bed of this pickup.

The truck sped along the rutted road, slowing only for the hairpin turns. There was no way to brace herself from the constant jarring as her body bounced and rolled across the mucky truck floor. If only her hands were free or she could sit up. If she could just get to her backpack, it would provide some cushion.

Once on the highway, the ride was smoother. Caroline could hear herself crying even over the snarling engine, but Lydia was silent and still. She shifted and maneuvered until she could feel Lydia. When her hand brushed Lydia's, Lydia grasped her fingers. She felt Lydia's hand twisting the pink pearl ring on her ring finger. She wished she had listened to Lydia about removing the ring, but the best she could do now was to twist it until the pearls and diamonds were cradled in her palm and only a narrow gold band was visible on the top of her hand.

For what seemed like hours, they recoiled in silence, back to back, each holding the other's fingers as if that human touch was their only grasp on staying alive. Caroline's arm burned from the small cuts made by the shattered glass.

The vehicle left the highway again. More jarring and jolting up a steep climb until the truck slowed to a stop. Voices, clanging metal, splinters of light, then rough hands pulling at her feet and legs. The truck bed almost seemed like a safe place compared to the unknown of what was coming.

Hooded captors spoke softly to each other as they pulled Caroline and Lydia from the truck bed. The night air was moist and cold with lambent lights in the distance. With only one of the kidnappers using a flashlight to light the footpath, it was difficult to get a good look at the where they were headed. Surrounded by midnight darkness, they walked single file for several yards on the damp floor of the jungle until they came to a small structure, possibly cinderblock, with a makeshift lean-to on one end. While the short one held the flashlight, the man in the rear pulled keys from his pocket and opened the padlock on the wooden door.

They pushed Caroline and Lydia through the door of the boarded up lean-to. The tall one pulled a knife from its sheath on his belt and cut the ropes, freeing their hands. The short one shined the flashlight to one corner. There on bare ground was a stack of blankets next to a cardboard box of bottled water and an empty bucket. "*Baño y agua.*" Even with limited Spanish, Caroline understood they had drinking water and a toilet. The men backed out the door and secured the padlock.

Her shaking uncontrollable, Caroline worked to remove the gag from her face before falling to her knees. She gasped for fresh air. "Lydia, what—"

As if in one motion, Lydia yanked the gag from her mouth and moved to the door. "Shhh."

Streaks of light coming through cracks in the wooden structure allowed Caroline to see Lydia's shape. Caroline joined her. Through a crack between the slats in the door, they watched the men walk a few steps away, the flashlight revealing their path. An unseen door opened and closed.

Caroline remembered her cell phone and reached inside her jacket. When she flipped it open, it provided enough light to see Lydia's face. "What's happening to us, Lydia? What will they do to us?"

Lydia remained silent.

Caroline fell to her knees and cried, not the whimpering cry of a child, but the desperate cry of a anguished woman facing acts worse than death. "What are we going to do? We have to get out of here. They're going to kill us."

At that, Lydia turned and knelt in front of Caroline, holding her trembling body as a mother would hold a frightened child. "Okay, enough of this. I'll tell you what we're going to do. We're going to use our heads. That's what we're going to do. Now get up and hand me your phone." No signal, but she used it like a flashlight to look at Caroline as they rose to their feet. "Are you hurt?"

Between heaving sobs, Caroline answered, "I'm okay. Some cuts in my arm from the glass, but nothing serious." She tried to brush any remaining slivers of glass from her jacket. "What about you?"

"I'm fine." Lydia paused. "No, I'm not. I'm sore as hell from that bumpy ride." Lydia turned and directed the light from the phone and walked carefully toward the corner. "It's too dark to check out where we are. We'll wait for daylight. Here, take these." She handed Caroline some blankets. "Spread these on the ground and sit."

"They're wet, but they're better than mud." Caroline spread out three of the blankets.

"Never did like mud. That's why I moved to Africa." Lydia grabbed more blankets and a couple of bottles of water. She sat down on one of the blankets Caroline had spread and wrapped a drier one around her shoulders. "Here, take this one, it's not as wet. If that rapscallion hadn't taken my backpack, I'd have weapons."

"What kind of weapons?"

"Keys and a ballpoint pen. You have to be close, but they'll hurt somebody. And we'd have food. I learned in Africa never to travel without food. Granola bars, mostly. But these guys have to feed us. But we have to be careful what we eat."

Caroline's shuddering breaths slowed as she sat down and took the blanket Lydia offered. "I haven't known you long, Lydia, but I don't get it. We've been gagged and bound and abducted. We have no idea where we are or what will happen to us. God only knows what they'll do to us, and you're talking about keys and granola bars?" Caroline started to cry again.

"Yeah, I prefer talking about that instead of the obvious, and I'd really prefer it if God had decided this wasn't going to happen to us. But it has, and you're right. There are some things we don't know, but I didn't take you for the kind of woman who's going to whine about what you don't know. Me? I prefer to think about what we do know and see how we can make that work for us."

"What do you mean?"

"We know these guys have been planning this because they made preparations. That means this is not the end of their plan. We know they didn't hurt us, not bad anyway, and apparently they intend to keep us here for a while. They know the drinking water would make us sick. That's why they gave us bottled water. We'll be okay."

They both sat in silence for a few moments before Lydia spoke again. "More than likely they've kidnapped us for a ransom, and we're no good to them dead. They're not too dumb to know that no one pays a ransom without proof of life."

"Yes, but we also know they're brutes. Look what they did to Paco."

"True. But Paco was of no value to them." Lydia took a swallow of water. "Caroline, I know it was dark even when we got out of the truck, but you've been here before. Do you have any sense of where we are?"

"What? You think just because I've been to Guatemala a few times I can figure out where we are? I didn't see anything after they put us in the truck." She rubbed her wrists, now raw from the rope.

"Okay, my guess is we rode for about three hours. Picture this. We took a right turn onto the highway from the dirt road to the orphanage. So, I think that means we were heading east. We were on that highway without turning for at least a couple of hours. And there was traffic, significant traffic with busses or large trucks passing us."

"How can you know all that?" Caroline was gaining respect for Lydia.

"I know it because I made a choice to pay attention. Are you with me?"

"Yes, we made a right turn headed east on a highway."

"Good. Reyna and Paco told us there are only a couple of major highways connecting Xela back to Guatemala City? Do you think we're near the city?"

"No, we didn't ride long enough, and the night sky's too dark for us to be near the city." Caroline was beginning to understand Lydia's line of thinking.

"Okay. So, we're not near the city. I'm fairly certain we left that highway onto another road that veered off to the right, and that's when we started descending. That's when I could see some lights through the cracks in the metal covering. We must have passed through a couple of villages or a small town, and in one of those places we made several turns, and the street was rough like cobblestone. That's when we started ascending again."

"That's it. We must be near Panajachel. I think we're near Lake Atitlán." Caroline got up and moved toward the cracks of light in the door. "Come here, Lydia, look. See those lights way in the distance, the ones up on the mountain. And look lower, see those clumps of light? That could be the shoreline. Lots of small villages along the shore."

Lydia put her arm around Caroline's shoulder. "See what we know?"

"We know we're locked in this muddy hovel and no way to get out."

"Yet. We don't know it yet. Just think, Caroline. We know possibly where we are." Lydia stood silent. "We must think this through. I've seen stark fear in the eyes of women and children for the last thirty years. These brutes will not see that from me, and they won't see it from you. Do you hear?"

"I hear you."

"Do you have a place to hide that ring on your finger?"

"Only in my jeans pocket."

"Then you have no place. Give it to me. I have a secret pocket in the waistband of my shorts where I keep mine. They're not about to take off an old lady's shorts."

Caroline handed her the ring.

Lydia was fumbling with her waistband when she heard a door open. She pulled her shirt and vest down. "Quick, hide the phone. Sit down."

Moments later, the padlock rattled and the door opened. Now there were three.

The pain in Paco's knees was sharp, unrelenting, and radiating now through his thighs and calves. His legs were as useless as the legs of the marionettes he played with as a child. He lay motionless until the blue pickup was out of sight, and when he attempted to move, he passed out from the tortuous pain. When he came to, the night sky was black. He didn't know how much time had passed, but he had to get help, and he had to let someone know about Miss Carlyle and Dr. Pipkin.

Paco tried moving again. His hands became bloody

from pulling his full body weight through the rocks and mud to get to the vehicle. Dragging his battered legs across the uneven ground sent painful shocks all the way up his spine. The thug had left the van door open on the driver's side. If he could just get to the van, he had a chance of getting help. The frightened look on Miss Carlyle's face before the kidnappers closed the tailgate was enough to motivate him to crawl another yard.

He gripped the floorboard and pushed up as hard as he could to get within reach of the steering wheel. Maybe he could pull himself up. With both legs broken, he had no leverage. The horn was less than a foot away, but it might as well have been across the road. The orphanage was near, and surely they'd hear the horn the way sound traveled through these mountains. One last push. The heel of his right hand brushed the horn. Its blast penetrated the night's silence for no more than a second before his body gave way to the pain and he slipped back into the mud. Not enough to get anyone's attention. Not this time of night.

He lay there, crying for relief and praying for help to come soon. He thought of his cell phone. It had been in his hand when his assailant attacked him. Why didn't he think of that before he crawled to the truck? Even if he could crawl back through to where he was, the brush was thick, and finding the phone was a long shot. His hopes were fading into the night sky when he remembered the umbrella behind the driver's seat. If he could get to it, maybe he could use it for leverage or to pull himself up.

The darkness was thick and heavy, and he had to feel his way. He placed the palms of his hands on the floorboard and pushed, holding himself up with his left hand and straining to reach the umbrella with his right. The space between the back of the seat and the door opening was so narrow he was barely able to pull the umbrella through. This flimsy contraption, purchased at a roadside market, would never withstand his body weight, but maybe he could lodge it between the seat and the steering wheel.

He fell on his first attempt but got up to try again. It was his only chance. He pulled himself up and pushed the handle of the umbrella against the horn on the steering wheel and the pointed end against the cushioned seat of the van. If the umbrella had been one inch shorter, his plan would have failed. The horn blared without stopping.

Paco slid back to the ground beside the van.

Sometime later, he realized two young boys now knelt beside him. One picked up his head while the other tried to turn his body over in the mud. He groaned. “My legs, my legs.”

The smaller boy sat in the mud and held Paco’s head in his lap while the other continued positioning Paco’s body.

Paco screamed in pain when the boy moved his twisted legs, covered now in bloody trousers. He grabbed the boy’s hand and in broken Quiché said, “Get help. Please get help. Go to the orphanage. Bring Sister Gabby. Bring the sister.” Paco’s voiced trailed as he lost consciousness.

He woke when Sister Gabby lifted his head, still lying in the young boy’s lap, and caressed his brow.

“Oh, Paco, you’re badly hurt. Help is coming. Where are they? Where are Caroline and Dr. Pipkin?”

He whispered from weakness and from sheer dread of telling her. “Two men, bad men, took them.”

Chapter 16

Word Gets Around

Late Monday evening at Rockwater

Roderick picked up Caroline's printed itinerary from his desk. Liz had left the information as he instructed and vacated the office before he got home, no doubt to avoid a confrontation. He ran his finger down the page. *Monday night through Sunday night at the Bonifaz Hotel in Xela*. No telephone number. Liz had not made this easy.

A few computer clicks and he retrieved the number. He looked at the clock. Eleven seventeen. He dialed the number.

"El Bonifaz." A young male answered.

"My name is Roderick Adair, and I'm calling from the United States."

"*No inglés. No inglés.*"

Roderick twisted the telephone cord tightly. "Does anyone there speak English?"

"*Un minuto, por favor.*"

Roderick waited several minutes and was about to hang up when the sleepy voice of an older man answered. "This is

Jorge Bonifaz."

"Good evening, Mr. Bonifaz. I'm calling from the United States for a guest in your hotel. Her name is Caroline Carlyle."

"Ah, yes. Miss Carlyle is a guest here. I know beautiful Miss Carlyle. She stay here many times when she visit the orphanage. My family has most beautiful hotel in Xela."

"May I please speak with her?" Roderick paced behind his desk, stretching the telephone cord to its maximum.

"Miss Carlyle is not here."

"What do you mean she's not there?" Roderick sat down in his desk chair.

"She checked in yesterday, and she stay overnight. She and Dr. Pipkin go to orphanage early this morning. They no return."

"But shouldn't they be back by now? It's almost eleven thirty."

"Maybe they stay at orphanage. Big rainstorm this afternoon. Bad roads."

"Could you please leave a message for her to call me as soon as she returns to the hotel?" Roderick spelled his name and gave him the number and had him repeat it for accuracy.

"Oh, yes. I leave a message with her key. She be fine, Mr. Adair. *Buenas noches.*"

Roderick put the phone down. This was no *buenas noches*. He searched the itinerary for the orphanage number. *Hogar Luis Amigo*. But again, no number. An internet search for the orphanage provided nothing. But help from an overseas operator, and the phone was ringing. Four rings, no answer, a strange white noise, and then . . . disconnected. He redialed. Nothing. Maybe the rainstorms had knocked down the lines.

A familiar fear rose through his gut and into his throat.

Images of his mother's battered body and blood washed away by raindrops. Something was wrong. He felt it. He knew it. Caroline would find a way to call him if she were safe. Rainstorms. Bad roads. A mudslide? He prayed Mr. Bonifaz was right and that Caroline was resting peacefully at the orphanage. He'd try again in the morning.

Predawn Tuesday in Xela

Neighbors had helped Sister Gabby get Paco to the clinic in Salcajá, but the doctor quickly determined Paco's injuries required surgery and made arrangements to transport him by ambulance forty-five minutes away to Xela, where a surgeon would be waiting.

Paco had only been able to tell Sister Gabby that two men in white hoods and driving a small pickup had abducted the women. She had stayed behind to talk to police in Salcajá before driving Paco's van to the hospital in Xela. Local officers seemed more irritated by the middle-of-the-night interruption than concerned about the kidnapping.

Her rosary sliding familiarly through her nimble fingers, Sister Gabby sat in the hospital waiting room in Xela, praying for Paco and anticipating the arrival of local Xela police. She had called them as she drove to the hospital. She hoped they would be better trained and more helpful—at least more interested in pursuing the kidnappers.

Two officers in green uniforms approached her. "Sister Gabriela?"

Gabby rose quickly. "Yes, officers, I am Sister Gabby."

"Please sit down, Sister. I am Officer Ramiro Cantu." He pulled up a metal folding chair in front of her. "You're reporting a kidnapping?"

"Yes, a kidnapping and a beating." Gabby described how Paco's legs had been broken and how the hooded abductors had driven away in a pickup with Caroline Carlyle and Dr. Lydia Pipkin.

Officer Cantu asked several questions about the nature of the women's visit to the orphanage, who knew why they were there, what time this happened, and if she had reported this to the locals in Salcajá.

Gabby answered his questions as best she could.

"Not much to go on. We deal with a few kidnappings, but most of the kidnappings for ransom are in Guatemala City, not out here in the Highlands. Someone had to learn about these travelers in the city and make plans from there."

Gabby continued to run the beads through her fingers as he spoke. "Yes. You must be right, but what can be done?"

"Not much until someone hears from the men who took her. That usually takes at least twenty-four to forty-eight hours. They like for the families to be scared and desperate before they make a call. Meantime, at daylight in a couple of hours, we'll ride out and take a look at the crime scene to see if any evidence was left behind."

The doctor, still in scrubs, walked through the double doors and approached them.

Sister Gabby rose to meet him. "How is Paco?"

"He's resting. I reset the legs and cleaned away as much of the bone fragments as I could. He will walk again, but only after months of rehabilitation. The danger now is infection. The compound fracture opened the skin, and the exposure in that environment is dangerous. I'd advise you to get some rest. He'll be sleeping for several hours, and then we'll have to manage his pain." The doctor took Gabby's hand and patted it before leaving.

"Thank you, Doctor. I will be here when Paco awakes." She closed her eyes in silent prayer before turning back to the officer. "We were talking about the kidnappers making contact. Will they contact me?"

Officer Cantu shrugged his shoulders. "I do not know. It depends on how much they know about the women and where they got this information. But they have a plan. They always have a plan." He pulled the pad from his shirt pocket. "Do you know any family members of either of the victims?"

Gabby paused. "No, but I know a doctor in the city who would know about Miss Carlyle's family. I will contact her." Gabby pulled her cell phone from her skirt pocket. "Here. Her name is Dr. Reyna Perez-Morris. Here's her number." She held the phone for the officer to write down the information.

The hooded men stepped into the lean-to, the tall one having to duck as he came through the door. The short one held the flashlight, shining it in Caroline's face. The one in front spoke in heavily accented English. "Ah, ladies. Welcome to our home. I hope you are comfortable."

Caroline and Lydia remained silent.

"I search your bags. No cell phone. Why?"

His guttural sneer sent a chill down Caroline's spine, but she remained silent, not moving a muscle.

"I think you have cell phone. Now, which one give it to me?" Sensing her fear, he stepped toward Caroline.

"You, Miss Carlyle?" He knelt in front of her and fingered her hair. "I like looking for your phone, Miss Carlyle, and . . ." He nodded his head toward the tall one. "And my friend? He like hurting you because you no give it to me."

Still looking straight ahead, Lydia said, "Give him the phone, Caroline. It doesn't work out here anyway."

Caroline trembled. She brushed his arm away from her face, reached inside her jacket pocket for the phone, and dropped it into his waiting palm.

"Good girl, Miss Caroline Carlyle." He got up and motioned for the other two to step outside. He followed them.

Caroline surprised herself. "Please, please don't take the phone. It's our only light. We can't make calls on it. There is no signal. See?"

He checked the phone. "Ah, you are correct. No signal, but I keep it anyway." He nudged the short one. "Give Miss Carlyle your flashlight. The princess wants light."

The short one approached her and dangled the flashlight above her before dropping it into her lap.

Caroline grabbed it and turned it on as the men walked out. White hoods, but one had a ponytail. She waited, listening to them mumble as they padlocked the door and walked away. "What will they do with us, Lydia?"

"I'm hoping they'll make some money and let us go. Kidnapping is likely their business, and killing their prey hurts business. Folks don't pay ransoms for murdered captives."

"Dying is not what's worrying me. It's what they might do to us before they let us go."

"Can't answer that. This was a carefully hatched plan. The ponytailed fellow has been with us since Guate. He was at the hotel, again at the music store, and in Antigua."

"I didn't see him in Antigua. Reyna and I saw him at the hotel and the music store, but he looked different."

"Yeah, a green suit. I took his picture in Antigua. Emailed it to my secretary yesterday morning before we left the Bonifaz."

Caroline shined the light in Lydia's face. "You what?"

"My gut told me this guy was up to no good. So when we walked up the mountain in Antigua to see the cross, I made sure he was in a couple of the pictures I took. I emailed the photos to Jess and told her if anything happened, the pictures of the man with the greasy ponytail just might be helpful. I thought we lost him in Xela, but that could have been him in the truck after we entered the gates of the orphanage this morning."

Caroline shivered from the damp chill in the air. "Something tells me this started with the immigration officers at the airport. They thought I had money. But it's good that you sent the photo." She was quiet for a moment. "That's good.

"It is what it is, Caroline, maybe good, maybe not. But we're still alive and well this moment." Lydia paused. "Look, I don't like the thought of suffering any more than you do, so we do our best to figure out what we can do about it, and we remember that we're not alone in this."

"I know, but sometimes I feel alone. Seven years I have felt alone, and just when I was beginning to live again after David's death . . . why now? Why did David have to die like he did when he was out doing good? Why are there orphans in Guatemala? And now I've involved you. It makes no sense. We're just trying to do something good."

"Yeah, I know the questions. Asked them myself when I first smelled the stench of death and stared suffering in the face in a village in Uganda many years ago. I was really looking at the faces of hollow-eyed children with swollen bellies and deep trenches between their ribs. And when I turned around, there were the grieving mothers too physically weak to weep for their children. Husbands dead, no work, no food, no hope."

"What are you saying, Lydia? That I should be grateful

that I'm not one of them right now?"

"No, not at all. Just letting you know that we're not immune from suffering. I saw so much agony that I got angry and calloused from trying to figure out why. Finally came to me in the middle of a restless night in a tent on the plains of Uganda: Sometimes God allows bad things to happen. Sometimes we bring suffering on ourselves. And when we do, usually some other folks suffer—like those Ugandan men bringing home AIDS to their wives and children. And then sometimes bad things just happen."

"So that was your answer?"

"Don't know if I'd classify it as an answer, but that kind of thinking brought some resolution for me. Made me understand I am not God, and that I can sit in my comfortable Miami high-rise and waste my life asking unanswerable questions, or I could get up and do what I can to relieve some suffering and give folks some hope. You can't live without hope and purpose."

"Where were you seven years ago when I needed those words?"

"I was where I needed to be, giving other folks some hope. Perhaps you weren't ready to hear those words then."

"Maybe I am now. And right now my hopes of staying alive and seeing Roderick again give me purpose. We have to get out of this alive, and then I'll spend the rest of my life making it up to you that I got you into this mess."

Lydia put her arm around Caroline. "No need for that. You and I, well, we made our choices, and we made them for the right reason. But our ponytailed friend made his choice too."

"I guess he did, didn't he?"

Tuesday morning, daybreak in Guatemala City

Reyna was giving Enrique his six o'clock meds when the phone rang. Early-morning phone calls were not unusual when she was on call, but she was not on call. She had scheduled to be away from the hospital, planning to be in Xela for the week before Enrique got sick.

"*Hola.*"

"Dr. Morris, this is Sister Gabby."

"Good morning, Sister. You're up early."

"Yes, it is early. I hope not too early for you."

"No, I was up giving Enrique his medicine. Is something wrong?"

"Yes. I do not like to tell you bad news, but you must know. Late yesterday afternoon, Caroline and Dr. Pipkin were abducted just a couple of miles from the orphanage."

Reyna put the medicine bottle on the counter and steadied herself. "What do you mean a couple of miles from the orphanage?"

"They were with us all day. Late in the afternoon, after the rains, they left to return to their hotel."

"Yes."

"Hours later, I learned the driver had been beaten and left on the road, and Caroline and Dr. Pipkin had been abducted by two men in a pickup truck."

"And did you report this to the police, and have you heard from the abductors?" Reyna frantically asked.

"Yes, I have reported to the police in Salcajá and in Xela. They will be out to look at where this took place later this morning, looking for any sign to help them. And no, I have heard nothing from the kidnappers. The police officer said it would be at least twenty-four, maybe forty-eight hours, before they make contact."

Reyna ran through a mental list. "Who do you think

they will contact?"

"The police think someone in Guate planned the abduction, and we have no idea what the kidnappers know about Caroline or Dr. Pipkin."

"Wait. Wait a minute. Was it a blue pickup?"

"I do not know the color. Both Paco's legs were broken, and he's been in surgery most of the night. I got very little information from him, and it will be hours before he awakes." Sister Gabby had mental flashes of a blue pickup outside the orphanage walls just after Caroline's arrival. "Why do you ask?"

"Just a hunch. There was a suspicious looking man staying at the hotel here, the Quinta Real. He seemed to show up everywhere we were, the restaurant, the music store. There was something about him that gave me goose flesh. And then Sunday morning, he was in the hotel parking lot when Caroline left. The truck had a metal covering, and I saw him put something in the back and slam the lid shut. He was following the van when they left. The man was stocky and had a ponytail."

Nodding as her memory strengthened, Sister Gabby told Reyna about the blue pickup she had seen that morning just after Caroline's arrival at the orphanage. The driver had had a ponytail.

"You must give the police this information. Meantime, while we wait, I must get in touch with Caroline's parents. She told me she's engaged to a man, but I have no idea how to reach him. But Caroline's parents will know."

"Yes. This is a good plan."

"And Sister, we must pray. Surely God would not take the lives of two others who are only out to do good, especially for the people of our country."

"Prayers have been on my lips since I learned of this. And Reyna, if they do not return to us, it is not God who has taken them. It is the act of two men with darkness in their hearts."

"Yes, Sister. Call me if you hear anything. And please give the police this new information. It could be helpful." Reyna hung up the phone and sat down on the stool at the counter. This felt all too familiar—the hours she had waited for Josh to return, only to learn days later that pieces of his truck had been found at the bottom of the mountain. Neither his body nor that of David Summers, Caroline's fiancé, were ever found.

She went to her desk for her address book. *J. Rogers and Martha Carlyle.* She looked at her watch. It was early, but she had no choice. Caroline's parents needed to know. She thought of what she might say to let them know their daughter had been abducted. No way to make preparation for a call like that.

Tuesday morning early, somewhere near Lake Atitlán

Caroline sat huddled next to Lydia. The voices of two men approaching the door roused her from light sleep. She could make out a few words—more food, money, tomorrow.

The ponytailed man came through the door and shoved the phone in her face. He turned to the bearded older man and said something she couldn't understand. They locked the door behind them.

"Lydia, wake up. We have the phone. They gave it back."

"I am awake. They got the information they need from your phone. They're about to make their calls."

"But who will they call?"

"I would suspect they'll call the numbers you called

using the phone. Who did you call?"

Caroline had that sick feeling that comes with sheer dread. She felt it in the pit of her stomach. "Sam and Angel, my parents, and Roderick." Her mind raced as she pictured those she loved getting this news. But Roderick would know what to do.

"My guess is that all three will be getting calls shortly."

Caroline heard the truck engine. "Did you hear that? I think you're right. They're leaving. We could be here, wherever here is, alone."

"Not alone, remember."

Chapter 17

Calls

Rockwater

Roderick lay in his bed awake, his mind darting as he made plans and backup plans.

The phone rang.

No need for his plans. He could breathe now. Only Caroline would be calling this early. "Good morning, Miss Blue Eyes."

He didn't expect the guttural voice on the other end speaking in broken English with an accent. "Do you know Caroline Carlyle?" The chilling sound of the voice catapulted Roderick straight out of bed.

"Yes, yes, I do. Is she all right?" Roderick felt lightheaded as the blood drained from his face. His gut told him this was bad. Very bad.

The voice returned. "How you know her?"

"Who is this? And why are you asking me how I know her?"

The caller repeated himself, this time more agitated. "I say, how you know her?"

Roderick realized the caller had the upper hand here. "She is my fiancée."

"What that mean, 'fiancée'?"

"It means she's going to be my wife. Is Caroline safe?"

"For now. I have her."

"But who are you? What do you want?"

"What you want? You want her back like she is? Or you want her back in little pieces?"

"Let me talk to her." Roderick panicked. He stood up as he yelled into the phone. "Let me talk to her, I said."

"You talk to her when I get what I want."

"But what is it you want? How much? Name your price." Roderick had plenty more he wanted to say to the caller, but he'd have to wait for that.

"Twenty-five thousand dollars. You have today to get money. I call tomorrow with instructions. Do not call police." The caller hung up.

Roderick looked at the clock. Six thirty-seven. He paced the floor like a caged animal, imagining where Caroline was and how afraid she must be. And what about Dr. Pipkin? The caller had said nothing about Dr. Pipkin. The kidnapper was obviously an amateur or he would have asked him for millions. Twenty-five thousand was nothing for a ransom, not in Roderick's circles. Dealing with a desperate amateur could prove to be more dangerous than dealing with seasoned, professional kidnappers.

He had to get a hold of himself. *If I'm in Guatemala, someone has to stay here to answer my phone. I have to get to the bank for cash. Do I call Caroline's parents and Sam and Angel, or should I wait until I know more? What else do I need to do?*

Roderick called Leo Bradford, his chief of security, gave him the information, and told him what he wanted: one hundred thousand dollars in cash, phones and computers, a security team at Rockwater within two hours, and Leo ready to fly to Guatemala.

He grabbed his bag, stuffing clothes in it like it was a punching bag, and dialed Acer. "Acer, get the plane ready. We're flying to Guatemala."

"Roderick, what? What's going on?"

"Caroline's been kidnapped." He grabbed the papers on his desk and stuck them in the bag too.

"Oh, God, no." Acer paused. "But we can't fly your plane out of the country."

"Well, find one we can. Leo's going with us, and see if there's an airport in Xela. Call me when you get things set up." Roderick put the phone down and went to the bathroom to clean up. He stood under the showerhead and let the warm water drench his body. The reality was settling in. He closed his eyes and sank to the shower floor on his knees. "No, no, this cannot be happening." He wept. "God, not now, just when we've found each other. Please, God, I've never asked you for much, but please, please take care of Caroline and bring her back to me. Help me know what to do."

He wished his prayers were backed by more than panic.

By the time he had finished getting ready, Acer called. He had secured a plane and a pilot familiar with Guatemala and the airport in Xela. There was only a private landing strip in Xela, but they could land there. They could leave by ten o'clock.

Roderick opened the safe for his passport and called Lilah. Outside of Acer and Leo, she was the only one he could trust. He explained what he knew and told her what would be going on with the security team at Rockwater in his absence. She promised to come and stay at the house until he returned with Caroline.

"And Lilah, I'm leaving for the airport in the next five

minutes. When Liz comes in this morning, you tell her she has been fired for insubordination and she is to leave immediately. Do not tell her why. If she asks, you tell her I'll be calling her, and if she gives you any trouble, get one of the security guys to escort her off the property. She is to take nothing with her from her office." He knew Lilah would gladly give that message to Liz. "And Lilah, you mustn't tell anyone about this, no one, do you understand? No one needs to know Caroline has been kidnapped. Leo's going with me, but his security team will be here within the hour. Please take care of them. I'll be in touch."

Early Tuesday morning in Moss Point

Angel was standing in front of the kitchen window pouring Sam a cup of coffee when the phone rang. She shuffled across the kitchen floor and handed Sam his coffee before answering the wall phone next to the breakfast table. "Hello." No response. "Hel-lo-oh."

The gravelly voice was unfamiliar. "Do you know Caroline Carlyle?"

Angel was caught completely off guard. "Of course, I know her. She's like my daughter. Who is this?"

"I have her."

"What? Who is this?"

"I am the man who has Caroline Carlyle, and if you want to see her again, you will do what I say."

"Roderick? Is that you? Don't be playing that kind of joke on me this early in the morning?"

"This no joke. I have her and her old lady friend."

"Oh, God!" Angel's desperate whisper reverberated through the Twin Oaks mansion. She handed Sam the phone and slumped to her chair.

Sam barked. "Who is this? What did you say to my wife?"

"I have Caroline Carlyle. I want twenty-five thousand dollars. I call you tomorrow with instructions. Do not contact police. I call back tomorrow." The caller hung up.

Sam lowered his head, unable to look at Angel. "Oh, Angel, somebody has Caroline. He wants money, and he's calling back tomorrow. Did you hear me?" He looked across the table at his wife.

Angel's eyes were shut tight, and she shook her head from side to side. "No, no, no."

"I had a bad feeling about this from the start. I told you I did. Now Caroline's in a bad way." Sam's lips quivered as he talked. Not Caroline. Not this caller. He couldn't bear to think what he was picturing. "I have to call Roderick. He needs to know. Get me his number, Angel."

Early Tuesday morning in Ferngrove

By the time Reyna Morris made the call to Caroline's parents, they had already received the call from the abductor and had called James and Thomas. As an attorney, they'd assumed James would know what to do. He lived only a few blocks away and came immediately to be with his parents. Thomas was on his way.

Martha and J. sat speechless in their chairs in the sunroom while James took Reyna's call. He was able to fill her in about the calls Roderick and the Meadows had received from the kidnapper earlier this morning.

Reyna gave James a detailed report of Sister Gabby's conversation and how she had involved the local police.

James responded. "I'll make sure Roderick has this information. He's leaving within the hour and will be there by early afternoon. He's flying into Xela in a private jet."

"I'm in Guatemala City, but I can meet him in Xela. I'll do whatever is needed of me."

"Thank you, Reyna. We're still in shock, and we don't understand what is needed at this point. But we'll stay in touch. Roderick thinks the kidnappers are amateur and don't have any idea who he is or what he's worth. Maybe that's good news, and maybe it's not. No way to tell this early, and we've both agreed there's no need to contact officials here yet."

He stepped out of the room to continue the conversation. "Tell me, Reyna, you live there and hear about these kidnappings all the time. What usually happens in situations like this?" His eyes were intent as he listened.

Reyna responded calmly. "Usually, they ask for cash, and once they receive it, they release their victim."

"That's good news. Roderick's bringing cash but expects they'll want it wired. Either way, he's prepared. He's called in his own security team to be at his house for the next call. He also has experts attempting to trace the call that came in this morning."

"Get somebody to check to see if Caroline's phone has a tracking device. If it has one, it's possible to find her that way." Reyna's good thinking gave him some hope.

"Great idea. I'll call Roderick before he leaves. Maybe his experts here can do the research to see if that kind of locating device was on Caroline's phone. I'll give him your contact information and Sister Gabby's. I know he'll want to talk to her."

Early Tuesday morning in Raleigh-Durham

Sarah was blow-drying her hair and didn't hear the phone ring.

George entered the bathroom with his hand cupped over the phone so the caller couldn't hear what he was saying. "Sarah, it's Gretchen, and she sounds upset."

She put the blow dryer down and took the phone. "Good morning, Gretchen. Is everything all right?"

"Oh, Sarah, I'm sorry to call so early, but I didn't know what else to do. Something is not right with Bella, and I am afraid. I have never seen her like this, not even on the worst days with Ernesto."

"Okay, I'll help you. But tell me, is she ill or in pain?"

"She is not sick, no fever or pain. She has been playing the piano since early evening yesterday. She played all night, the same thing over and over. She will not stop. Karina is frustrated with her, but we cannot get her to stop."

"Has anything happened to make her this way? Did she get upset about something?"

"No, no. We were finishing our evening meal, and she became strangely quiet. Then she got up and started playing the *Rockwater Suite*, the loud section that sounds like a storm, and she hasn't stopped. If we try to stop her, she screams and her body becomes very rigid. She calms down if we release her to play the piano. And the neighbors . . . They have called many times."

"I get the picture. I'll be there in a few minutes. Just let her play until I get there. And don't worry, all this change is probably catching up with her and she's just overly stimulated. She will be fine. I'm on my way."

Sarah called to George as she hung up the phone. "George, would you please fix me a cup of coffee and find my cell phone? No time for breakfast. I need to get to

Gretchen's—a problem with Bella this morning." She hurriedly dried her hair and slipped on a skirt and blouse.

Like a butler, George was standing at the front door with her coffee, her cell phone, her purse, and her keys. "Anything else you need, Sister Sarah, the one always coming to someone's rescue?"

She stood on her tiptoes to kiss him. "How could I possibly need anything else when I have you?"

He handed her the items. "I have no classes today, but I have an eleven o'clock department meeting, so don't count on me for lunch."

"That's good. I don't know what I'm getting into with Bella. I may need to medicate her if we can't get her calmed down. I'll give you a call later. Love you."

George kissed her cheek and opened the front door. "Love you too. Try to get home before midafternoon. Thunderstorms headed our way. Just heard the weather report."

She waved as she got into her vehicle. The distance to Gretchen's was so short that she would have walked if Gretchen had not sounded so frantic. She was parking in front of the apartment when her cell phone rang. She switched the car off and answered, "Hi, Gretchen, I've just parked, and I'm getting ready to walk in."

"Hey, sis, it's not Gretchen."

"Well, good morning, little brother. We're both stirring early this morning. I just parked in front of Gretchen's. Seems Bella's uncontrollably agitated, and she's been playing the *Rockwater Suite* literally for the last fourteen hours and will not stop. I'm here to help. What's up with you this morning?"

"It's not good, Sarah. I got a call a couple of hours ago from an unidentified man who claims to have kidnapped Caroline. We don't know about Dr. Pipkin."

Sarah felt like someone had a choke hold on her neck. "Oh, God, no, Rod. Tell me this isn't happening. What else? Tell me what you know."

"Seems the same caller phoned Sam and Angel and Caroline's parents within minutes of calling me. He told each of us he would call again and tell us how to deliver twenty-five thousand dollars and he would let her go."

"What about proof of life? Are you sure he has her?"

"No proof of life, but she either gave him the telephone numbers or he had to get the numbers from her cell phone. I spoke with the hotel manager in Xela late last night, and I know Caroline and Dr. Pipkin didn't make it back to their hotel. I'm on my way now to the airport. Leo has set up security at the house. Acer has secured a plane and a pilot, and the four of us are flying out within a couple of hours. Seems this pilot has a lot of experience flying into this airstrip. Something about teams that go down to build wells. I'll know more when I get there."

Sarah found it difficult to take a deep breath. "How could she know?"

"What? What are you talking about?"

"Wait a minute, Roderick. When was Caroline abducted?"

"Sometime late yesterday afternoon, the best we can tell."

"She knows."

"Sarah, who knows? What are you talking about?"

"Bella. I think Bella knows something is wrong with Caroline. Gretchen said she got unusually quiet at the dinner table last night, then got up and went to the piano. She's been playing the storm scene movement of the *Rockwater Suite* since then."

"That's nonsense, Sarah. Bella couldn't know."

"I know it doesn't make sense, but I am not going to tell

you that Bella doesn't know. I can't tell you what makes her brain work the way it does. But I know she has a connection to Caroline." Sarah hesitated. "Roderick, let me take care of Bella, and then I'll join you. Have Liz send me the details, and I'll catch a flight today."

"Liz will be fired upon her arrival this morning. She did not follow my instructions in assisting Caroline with this trip. If she had ordered the satellite phone like I instructed, then we would know exactly where Caroline is this minute."

"Not necessarily, Rod. You'd only know where the phone is."

"That's more than I know now, but I do know Caroline needs me, and I have to believe that I'll find her."

"Just tell me where you're going. I'll get the rest of the information from Lilah."

"No, you stay where you are. Besides, it sounds like Bella and Gretchen need you. I will have Leo and Acer, and Caroline's brothers are making plans to fly down later. I'll stay in touch. You can always call Lilah. She'll have the latest information."

"But, Roderick . . ." Sarah had always been there when her brother needed her.

"No buts. I'm going to get Caroline. Love you, sis." He was gone.

Sarah sat in the car seat, gripping her phone in one hand and squeezing the steering wheel with the other. *This is too much for Roderick. His heart recovered from Mother's death only when Caroline appeared, and now she's gone.*

Sarah called George, gave him the news, and asked him to cancel his eleven o'clock meeting.

As Sarah walked toward the dark-green door, she heard the piano. No gentle melodic phrases, only the rhythmic roar of the storm Caroline had painted with her music. She rang the bell. Gretchen answered, her peaceful expression gone and replaced by tiredness and tension.

"Let's sit down, Gretchen."

"But don't you want to talk to Bella first?"

"No, Gretchen, I have some news for you."

Fear and curiosity supplanted the weariness in Gretchen's eyes. "News? This cannot be good."

"No, it isn't. I just had a call from Roderick. I don't know how else to say this, Gretchen. Caroline and Dr. Pipkin have been kidnapped and are being held for ransom. Roderick got the call this morning, and he's on his way to Guatemala."

Gretchen's eyes filled with tears.

Bella's music stopped.

"Oh, no. This cannot be. Not my beautiful friend with the kindest of hearts. Oh, no." Gretchen sobbed and her body rocked in the same rhythm as it did when she had tried to calm Bella through the years.

"Roderick will take care of things. He will bring her home. But . . . I think Bella knows."

Gretchen stopped rocking. "What? Bella? How could she know?"

"Listen. The music stopped. Look at her, she is frozen still. I don't know how she knows—and maybe she doesn't, but what else can explain her behavior? It started at the time Caroline was taken, and it has only stopped this minute."

Sarah left Gretchen sitting on the sofa, her arms folded and almost doubled over as if in intense pain. She gently approached Bella and sat down on the piano bench beside her. "Bella, it's Sarah. Look at me."

Bella moved not one muscle.

"Please, look at me, Bella. Everything will be all right."

"Caroline. Not home. No music." Bella stood upright and robotically walked to her room without making a sound.

Sarah heard the bedroom door shut.

Near Lake Atitlán

Daylight crept through the cracks of the shed. Lydia stirred from her nap to pull the blanket over her shoulders. Caroline sat as she had all night, hugging her knees, her body rocking back and forth as she prayed the same prayer over and over. Her mind had darted back and forth for hours—speculating on what the men would do to them, wondering if anyone back home knew by now, remembering the helpless look in Paco's eyes, and trying to figure out how to get away.

The sound of the lock startled them both. At first, Caroline could only see the silhouette of the hooded man against the morning sky as he opened the door. She smelled cinnamon when he handed her the bag.

Caroline despised the sound of the padlock clanging against the metal bracket, but she was glad he was gone.

By the time the door was locked, Lydia was sitting up beside her. "What did he bring?"

Caroline opened the bag. "Fresh empanadas. They must have gotten them in the village when they left this morning. Do you think they made the call?"

"Makes sense that they returned your phone earlier because they got what they needed and left to make the call. I think it's their way of letting you know. They're amateurs." Lydia took a bite out of the fresh empanada. "Here, you'd better eat something. We have to stay well. Did you sleep?"

Caroline put her head in her hands and cried again. "No, I'm too scared to sleep. All I could do was to think and pray."

"Praying's good. But I'm not going to sit here on hell's

doorstep waiting for your prayers to be answered. I never have done much sitting around waiting on anything. What we need is a plan."

Caroline wiped her eyes on her shirt sleeve, took a piece of bread from the basket, and looked at Lydia. "Well, while I was praying, I came up with one."

Chapter 18

On the Way

Tuesday midday, somewhere in the skies over the Gulf of Mexico

The morning's timing and takeoff ran smoothly in light of the chaos that one phone call had generated at dawn. Roderick completed his conversation with Sam and dialed Caroline's father. "I apologize for not calling you before takeoff, but time was precious. Lilah said you called. Call her anytime."

"Thank you, Roderick. You and my boys must find my daughter."

He could hear the angst in J.'s voice. "Sorry, I just moved so quickly, I couldn't wait for Thomas and James. Certainly, I'm grateful to have them join us. Just give them my contact information and tell them to call me when they get here."

"Will do. The boys have all of Reyna's contact information if you need that.

"You and the Meadowses and I all got the call within five minutes of each other this morning. The conversation was the same—twenty five thousand." Roderick reached quickly to grab the pencil about to roll off the tray table in front of him.

The red light flashed in the cabin. Acer's voice interrupted. "Make sure you're strapped in. Rough air ahead."

Roderick checked his seatbelt. "I must go now, Mr. Carlyle, but I will not leave Guatemala without Caroline. I'll be in touch. As I said, you may call Lilah at any time. She'll have the latest information." He said his goodbyes, put his phone in his briefcase, and secured it in the seat next to him.

Leo had been at the rear of the plane on his own phone but approached the seat across from Roderick after Acer's warning. He put his phone into his shirt pocket, sat down, and reached for his seatbelt. "Well, that was good news. Carl located the papers about the cell phone Liz ordered for Miss Carlyle. It is not a satellite phone like you wanted, but it has a device that might be of some help. I just have to coordinate a few things once we get to Guatemala."

The furrows in Roderick's brow relaxed. "That's a relief. What you're saying is that we can locate her?"

"No, Mr. Adair. That's not exactly what I'm saying. We have the capability of locating the phone, but we cannot be sure the phone is with Miss Carlyle. The kidnappers could have tossed it or trashed it, but it's a step. And when we locate it, that'll be another piece of information. Carl's on it, and we will be, too, at touchdown."

The airplane dipped, and Roderick looked out the window to thick, layered gray clouds in the distance. He turned back to Leo. "Spoke with Caroline's parents and with the Meadowses. They are the older couple in Moss Point where Caroline lives. They're like a second set of parents to her. Apparently, they all got the same call I did, with the same voice and message. Sounds like the kidnapper made all three calls right between six thirty and seven this morning."

"What do we know about the doctor Miss Carlyle was meeting? Has anyone heard from her?"

Roderick shuffled the papers in the folder and pulled out the itinerary. "Caroline was meeting Dr. Lydia Pipkin in Guatemala City. Dr. Pipkin has done this same kind of project with orphans in Africa and agreed to help Caroline." His eyes scanned the paper. "Says here they were joining Dr. Reyna Perez-Morris at the hotel in Guatemala City, and they were to leave the city for the Highlands altogether on Sunday morning." Roderick shook his head and looked away from the paper.

"What is it?"

"Something's odd. I'm remembering something Caroline's father told me. Dr. Morris had just called them. She had learned about the kidnapping from Sister Gabby, the nun at the orphanage, very early this morning. So that means that Dr. Morris is not with them. And I'm almost certain Dr. Morris told James that Dr. Pipkin was kidnapped too. Guess we'll get the details when we get to Xela. Dr. Morris is still in Guatemala City. Either way, James and Thomas know how to reach her, and I'll get to her."

"Okay, so what about Dr. Pipkin? Any information on her?"

"No, the caller didn't say a word about Dr. Pipkin to any of us. Only about Caroline."

"Interesting."

Roderick didn't like the feeling in the pit of his stomach. "What does 'interesting' mean?"

"Just that. Interesting. It could mean the kidnappers are making contact with Dr. Pipkin's family separately." He pulled out his pad again and reached for his pencil. "Know how to reach her family?"

"No. I know very little about her." He fumbled with the papers in the folder. "Here's her assistant's contact information. Name's Jess. We'll call her when we land. Maybe she knows something. When I talked to the hotel manager, he said that neither Caroline nor Dr. Pipkin returned to the hotel."

Tuesday midday at the Atlanta airport

James and Thomas locked the car doors and walked toward the entrance to the airport. "Wait, James, I left my jacket in the trunk."

"Forget it, Thomas. If we miss this flight, we won't get to Guatemala until tomorrow. I don't plan on spending the night in Atlanta. Got your passport?"

Thomas was accustomed to his older brother checking up on him. James was just built that way and had been doing it for over thirty years. Thomas checked his vest pocket and stepped up the pace. "Got it. Come on, James, keep up."

They were traveling light, only Ferngrove High gym bags stuffed to their nylon limit and a backpack each. Thomas had gone by his sporting-goods store earlier this morning to pick up lightweight packs along with a few other items he hoped would make it past security without a hitch. When they were settled at their gate, James called Reyna again, letting her know their flight would be on time. She agreed to pick them up at the airport and drive them to Xela. They would be there before midnight. With any luck, Roderick would have news.

"James, you know if anything happens to Caroline, it'll kill Mom and Dad, don't you?"

"Yeah, I know." James removed his windbreaker and stuffed it into the last bit of space in the top of his backpack.

"We just won't let that happen now, will we, little brother?"

"Well, we wouldn't if I had a couple of my buddies and the right ammunition."

"I know what you mean. Don't think it would set too well for the kidnapper whose head appeared in my crosshairs right now. Guess we can be grateful Roderick's a man of means and he's resourceful. We're not having to deal with this by ourselves, especially not in Guatemala."

"What do you mean by that?"

"It's a long way from Ferngrove to Guatemala, Thomas. They don't do their business down there like we do ours, and we don't have the time to learn."

"Maybe we don't need time to learn. Might turn out better if we just do things our way." Thomas rechecked the contents of the zippered pockets of his duffle bag.

Tuesday afternoon in the Guatemalan Jungle

Rain pounded the tin roof of the hovel. The water, coming down in sheets, seeped and gushed underneath the makeshift wall and created widening ruts across the mud floor until it flowed out the backside. This muddy lean-to was barely attached to the building, and the ground's slope toward the back wall was getting steeper with every hour of rain. Thoughts of a different rainstorm and a mudslide invaded Caroline's thoughts. She could only hope that David never saw what was coming and that it happened quickly. Damp with sweat and mud spattered, she continued digging the trench wider and deeper. "Look, Lydia."

On alert, Lydia stood at the door with a couple of blankets ready to cover the trench should one of the kidnappers approach the door. "That's great progress."

Caroline's hope returned, and she was beginning to see a way out of this mess. "Thank you, Father, for sending this flood. Thank you for every drop of water running across this mud floor and for making it softer to dig." She almost felt like humming while she scooped away the gray sludge.

"What? What did you say? I didn't understand you. You want me to dig for a while."

"No, Lydia. I wasn't talking to you."

Lydia turned toward Caroline. "Then pray tell, who were you talking to? I'm the only one in here."

"No, you're not. I was talking to God. I do believe God sent us this rain to help us dig our way out of here and get us out of this hellhole. We need to thank Him."

"Yeah, and while you're at it, thank Him for that Swiss Army knife I had in my vest pocket that made a fine plastic scoop out of your water bottle. Otherwise those pretty little fingers of yours would be close to mincemeat by now."

"I've already thanked him for that and the fact that you didn't have on your fine African garb when we were kidnapped. That vest of yours and your khaki shorts, full of secret compartments, have proven valuable. Make sure you keep my engagement ring safe. I intend to wear it the rest of my life."

The rain subsided, but Caroline kept digging.

"Shh, here he comes." Lydia tossed Caroline another blanket. "Quick, cover the hole and yourself."

Caroline went into action doing exactly what she and Lydia had planned. She filled the hole with the extra blankets, spread the cleanest one on top and lay down on it, pretending to be asleep but whispering, "Oh, please God, don't let them take us from this hut. Please."

Lydia took her place at the upper end of the hut where the towels and water bottles were stacked. Neither of them roused until the abductor had opened the door. He was carrying a tray.

"Too much rain." He moved closer and dropped a small box of plastic garbage bags near Lydia's feet. "Put on floor. No more wet." Lydia sat up and grabbed the box before it sank in the mud.

"*Tortillas, huevos, y frijoles. Más agua.*" The short stocky man took a couple of steps closer extended the tray to her. "*Denme las mantas.*"

Lydia, still keeping her knowledge of Spanish to herself, held the tray and did not adhere to his command. He waited and then snatched the blanket covering her and moved toward the stack of remaining blankets in the corner.

"Oh, crap, he wants the blankets. Quick, throw him yours, Caroline."

Caroline complied, tossing the soggy blanket toward the man, trying to hide the stack of blankets filling the trench underneath her body.

"*Paulino.*" The voice came from the next room where the abductors had been holding out. "*Paulino, donde está tu telefono*?"

The short one holding the muddy blankets ran out the hovel door and quickly secured the padlock. "*No digas mi nombre! Estás loco*?"

The voice from the room continued. "*No hay problema, hermano. Ellas no comprenden.*" The door to the next room slammed.

Lydia balanced the food tray on her knees. "Guess we can also be grateful at least two of our kidnappers speak Spanish and they think we don't understand. And we wouldn't understand if they only spoke Quiché. Now we know one of them is named Paulino. Put that in your memory bank for when we get out of here."

Caroline joined her, trying to wipe some of the mud from her hands, cleaning them enough to eat. "Why did he want the blankets?"

"Don't know. My guess is they're not planning on bringing us fresh towels and linens, though. Maybe they need them for something else."

"Oh, I hope they're not planning to put them in the truck and move us because of the rain."

"Possible." Lydia looked at her watch. "We can be glad they didn't take my watch too. It's around four o'clock. Let's eat. At least these fellows can cook beans and eggs. We can use the protein. We should eat, then we should try to take a nap. We need to get some rest if we're going through with your plan."

"Do you think they'll be back in here before morning?"

"Hard to say. He may come back to get the tray. But if they start drinking and playing cards like they did last night, they might forget about us until morning. Is the trench big enough yet?"

"Maybe." Caroline took a second tortilla, spooned the beans and egg on top, and rolled it up.

"Just say it. What you mean is that you can get out, little one, but I can't."

Caroline swiped her shirtsleeve across her mouth. "But if we could just remove that one bottom board, then there'd be no question."

"We can't take that chance in the daylight in case they come back in, and even in the dark it might make too much noise."

"It might be worth the try. It's on the back wall, and maybe they wouldn't notice. Or maybe we could cover it up if they come back."

"You're right, but we don't know what's on the backside of that wall. Could be the jungle, the edge of a cliff, or it could be a larger mudhole."

Thunder boomed, rolled, and echoed around the heavens. "Thank you, God, for thunder." Caroline jumped up. She went back to the trench, sat on the blankets, leaned back on her elbows, securing them in the mud, and put her feet against the bottom board. She was poised to push. "Come help me, Lydia. We can do this. We have to see what's on the other side."

Lydia set the tray on the cardboard box in the corner and moved toward Caroline.

Caroline motioned for her to sit on the blanket next to her. "Come on. We can do this. We'll wait until it thunders again so they can't hear us, and we'll push hard."

"What if it doesn't thunder?"

"It will thunder. And if my plan works, we'll know what's behind this wall."

"And if it doesn't work?"

"It will, Lydia. It has to."

"And if they hear us and catch us?"

"Then I'll grab the board and prop it in place, and they'll go away wondering what they heard. It's our only chance. You have to help me."

Lydia hugged Caroline before she sat down. "What's become of you, my delicate friend?"

"It's what you said this morning. I don't like sitting on the edge of hell. I want to go home. I'm praying like God is going to reach down and pick us both up out of this muddy mess and take us home, and I'm going to kick this board like my life depended on it."

Thunder bellowed so loud it vibrated the earth beneath them. "See Lydia, now. Kick hard."

Late Tuesday afternoon at Twin Oaks

Sam was on the phone. "Go ahead, Tom, have her bring over the first draft on her way home, but I don't know when I'll get around to reading it."

"Are you under the weather, Judge?"

Sam sat at the breakfast table, rubbing his brow back and forth as if to conjure up some new idea. "No, no. I'm not sick. Just something else going on." Sam heard a knock on the screen porch door. "Just a minute, Tom."

Sam covered the telephone receiver with the palm of his hand and called to Angel. "Angel, somebody's banging on the porch door, and I'm on the phone with Tom." He continued his conversation and watched Angel scuffle through the kitchen toward the back porch. "I know I said you needed to get this done as quickly as possible, but something's come up." Sam paused. The lump that had continually appeared and reappeared in his throat since their early-morning telephone call rose again. "Tom, I just can't think about this right now. Caroline's somewhere in Guatemala, and she's been kidnapped. We just found out this morning when her kidnapper called here."

Angel entered the kitchen with Ned behind her. Sam raised his head just in time to see Ned's ruddy face turn pale.

"I need to go, Tom. Keep the news of Caroline's kidnapping all to yourself. We don't want it getting out yet. I'll call you back later." Sam put the phone down. One look at Ned's face and he knew he would have to explain. "Sit down, Ned. I know you just heard what I said to Tom Ellison about Caroline."

Ned did not speak and stood as still and stone cold as one of Angel's garden statues.

Angel took Ned's arm and guided him to the chair at

the end of the breakfast table. "Have a seat, Ned. Let me get you a cup of coffee."

Ned sat down and remained quiet and still, except for the constant twisting and curling of his John Deere ball cap.

Sam waited for Ned to speak. Angel returned with the coffee and sat down next to Sam. "Say something, Ned. Would you like cream and sugar?"

Ned stood up. "No, ma'am. I'm sorry to trouble you about the coffee, Miss Angel. I . . . I can't drink it right now. This news done give me the jimjams." Ned paced from the kitchen door, in front of the breakfast table, and across to the pantry.

"I know what you mean, Ned. But sit down, and let me tell you what we know. I'm sorry you heard it like you did. I aimed to keep it to myself until Caroline's back home, safe and sound, and could tell the story herself."

"Mr. Sam, you don't know iffen she's ever goin' to come home. They's some bad folks in this world, and it would take a real bad one to hurt Miss Caroline. Why, that young lady ain't got even one dram of badness in her, but she's got more'n her share of pertinacity." Ned lumbered back and forth across the kitchen floor.

"Yeah, I had a bad feeling about this trip from the get-go, but she was determined."

Ned stopped his pacing long enough to look Sam in the eye. "How'd you find out she's been snatched, Mr. Sam?"

"We got a call from a man early this morning, asking if we knew Caroline. Then he told us he had her and he would call again to tell us where to send the money."

"I got money. You just tell me what to do and where to send it."

"We appreciate that, Ned, and if we needed it, I'd be asking you. The kidnapper called Caroline's parents and Roderick and asked for twenty-five thousand dollars from each us."

"Me and Fred seen this happen on TV a bunch of times, and sometimes it ends up all right and sometimes it don't. But they always ask for a lot more money than that."

"For sure. Roderick thinks they're amateurs or else they'd be asking for more."

Angel put her hand on top of Sam's. "They may be amateurs, and if they are, they're probably scared and desperate. That could make them even more dangerous and unpredictable."

"My gut tells me Roderick's more desperate than they are. That's another thing, Ned. Roderick and his security guy flew out late morning, and Caroline's brothers are flying down there to meet him. Roderick is probably already there. We have to trust with God's help, those men will take care of things and find Caroline. And meantime, we just keep praying Caroline's not hurt and that God will bring her home."

"Ain't that something? Just a quid of a thing . . . Caroline losing the man she was going to marry when he went to Guatemala, and now she's in big trouble down there. That's just wrong ever' which way you look at it, Mr. Sam."

They commiserated a while longer, and Sam told him that Tom Ellison had finished the draft of the will that would protect Ned and Fred's fortune from GiGi Nelson.

"I'll be keeping all this to myself 'til you tell me I don't have to. And right now, Mr. Sam, I don't give one whit about that fortune, but I don't want you worryin' yourself about legal papers right now. I ain't about to let Fred do somethin' stupid with that orange-haired floozy." He looked Sam straight in the eyes. "But I'd give ever' last penny of it as a ransom for one more of Miss Caroline's songs."

Tuesday afternoon in the Guatemalan Highlands

As they descended, Roderick studied the landscape from the plane window, the rolling mountains a patchwork of lush green dotted by small scraps of fallow brown earth. Tall, heavy-bottomed clouds shrouded the peaks and promised rain. *Caroline's down there somewhere, but which mountain, which valley, under which roof?* The plane seemed to float through a dense layer of gray as if a thick curtain had been dropped. Suddenly he could see nothing. *She's here, but where? God, don't let my fear paralyze me like it did with Mother. Help me. I don't know where to start.*

An abrupt jolt of the plane and a dip in altitude startled him. He only hoped this pilot had experience.

Acer's voice came through the speaker. "More bumpy air until we land in a couple of minutes. Check your seatbelt." Roderick heard Acer's voice trail off before he turned off the microphone. "I've never seen clouds this thick. Never flown through anything like this."

The wind shear between the mountains caused the plane to bob and bounce as though it were tied to an elastic string attached to the ceiling of clouds. Roderick, who had never known a minute of fear while flying, found himself gripping the armrests and straining to see any sight of ground through the window.

"Leo, I'll be calling Reyna Morris as soon as I can get a signal. If I'm on the phone, tell Acer to get us a driver. He and the pilot can secure the plane and join us later, but you and I need to get to the Bonifaz as quickly as we can."

"Yes, sir. Will do."

The wheels touched down. The speed at which the plane braked indicated a short runway. Whipping wind, the speed, the water on the runway all caused the plane to swerve as it came to a hurried stop. They sat. No one appeared to help with the door or the stairs. The pilot came through the cockpit door and began to prepare the cabin himself.

"Where's the ground crew" Roderick gathered his papers.

"Ground crew in Xela? Probably siesta. Nobody coming out to help during this downpour." The pilot tried to shield himself from the rain as he shoved open the door. "Maybe we could wait until this passes. It won't be long. Never is this time of year." He closed the door.

"Sounds like you're familiar with this weather."

"Yes, sir, I am. I've piloted this plane many times into this makeshift airport. I fly lots of do-gooders down to work on clean water projects."

"You speak Spanish?"

"Yes, sir, I can get by."

"Then we may need your help. Could you get us a cab to take us to the Bonifaz? I have the address right here."

The pilot smiled and shook his head. "Oh yes, sir, I know where the Bonifaz is. It's about a half an hour from here, but we won't find a cab at this airport. I'll need to pay somebody around here for the use of their vehicle, then I'll drive you there."

"What's your name?" Roderick asked.

"Name's Goodluck, sir. Goodluck Gibbons. You can call me Goodluck or Gib."

Hearing the man's name was the only thing that had brought a hint of lightness since Roderick's call from the kidnapper early morning. "I think I'd like to call you Goodluck."

Roderick quizzed him about the area, the people, and how the law worked here. Leo and all his technology would help, but somehow Goodluck might be more valuable. Roderick cut a deal to get him to stay.

"Yes, sir. I'm with you. I need to make a few phone calls, but I'll be here as long as you need me. I'll have to hire someone I trust to stay with the plane though."

Roderick handed him a roll of hundred-dollar bills. "Here, take care of that and getting us a car. There's more money if you need it."

Goodluck handed him the wad of bills back. "Can't use hundreds down here, sir." He pulled out a sleeve of crisp, new twenty-dollar bills from an inside pocket in his flight jacket. "This will get you more than your hundreds will. In these parts, folks understand twenties."

Roderick nodded his head and returned the cash to his pocket.

"I'll get you to the bank when we need to. Think the rain has stopped enough for me to get out now and take care of things. I'll be back for you in a few minutes. Just sit tight."

Roderick pulled out his phone and his notepad and watched Goodluck through the window as he dodged the widest puddles on his way to the hangar. The thick moist air invaded the cabin and brought with it a chill. Leo put on his jacket and went to the back of the cabin to get his bag and computer. He sat down and called Carl back at Rockwater.

Acer entered the cabin from the cockpit and sat down across from Roderick, trying to learn what he could from Roderick's end of the conversation.

"Dr. Morris, this is Roderick Adair, Caroline's fiancé. We just landed in Xela. James gave me your contact information, and I wanted to speak with you."

"I'm grateful to hear from you, but I'm so sorry it is like this. I am waiting in the city for James and Thomas. They will be landing in a couple of hours, and I will pick them up and drive them to Xela."

Nervously, Roderick asked, "How long will it take for

you to get here?"

"It make take five hours or longer depending on weather, but we'll be in later this evening and will see you at the Bonifaz."

"That's good. Do you know how to reach Sister Gabriela?"

"Yes, she is with Paco, the driver at the San Rafael Hospital. Someone at the Bonifaz can give you the address and directions. He's had surgery but may be awake enough now to speak with you. I will do everything I can to help find Caroline."

"Thank you. We'll get settled at the Bonifaz, and then we'll get to the hospital. I need to go, Dr. Morris. You and Thomas and James get here safely and as fast as you can." Roderick ended the call and turned to Acer. "We need to get checked in and get to the hospital to find out everything this driver knows."

"Did Dr. Morris say anything about the police involvement?" Acer asked.

"No." Roderick put his phone away. "Oh, and that pilot you found. He's staying. He's familiar with the area, has flown lots of missions down here, and he speaks Spanish."

"Yeah, I filled him in on our mission and got his story during the flight. Guess we got lucky."

"Got a feeling Caroline would call it something else." Roderick looked out the window again. He stuffed the files into his briefcase and grabbed his jacket. "Come, on Leo. We have things to do. Here comes Goodluck."

Chapter 19

Hard Kicks

Late Tuesday afternoon in a hovel in the Highlands

In concert with the rolling thunder, Caroline and Lydia, sitting side by side in the mud, kicked and pushed hard against the board. The nails gave way on Lydia's end, the snapping timber giving way and sending her farther down and underneath the wall. The more she tried to raise herself back up on her elbows, the more she slid. No chance of getting traction in this muck.

Caroline rolled over and grabbed her and pulled her to the edge of the trench until they could sit up to see the results of their efforts. The bottom board had broken and splintered only a couple of feet from the post it was nailed to, but it gave them an additional ten inches of crawl space above the trench Caroline had already dug.

"Quick, grab the plank in case we need it, Caroline."

Caroline crawled across the sludge to grab the board and pull it into the hut. Rain still pounded.

"Can you see? All I can see from here is more mud and jungle. What's on the other side?" Lydia asked. Caroline knew the older woman was accustomed to the hardships of primitive life but unacquainted with these relentless downpours and slick soil and jungle life.

Caroline lay on her side, her head level with the ground. "Oh, thank God. There is no other room, just jungle floor, and not much of that. I think we're on the edge of something."

"We need to get out of here before this whole hut washes away." Lydia rolled on her side and struggled to her knees. "Look, Caroline!" She pointed toward the door. Water and mud were oozing through the cracks around the makeshift entrance. "That's the high side, and we have no idea what's building up out there. This lean-to has no foundation and could wash away at any minute. Then we go with it, and not on our terms. Come on, hurry!"

Lydia got to her knees and reached around for what few blankets they had left. "Here, Caroline. Wrap one around yourself and tie it. Try to make some kind of sack out of it like the Guatemalan mothers do." Lydia did the same and grabbed the box with the plastic bags. "Take one of these and stuff it with as many of the blankets as you can."

Caroline secured the knot on her shoulder and adjusted the sack she made. She rolled three blankets, put them in the doubled plastic bags, and secured them with a fist-sized knot. "Are you sure this is the best plan? Can't we wait until after dark when the men won't come back?"

"No. I have a feeling about this, and we cannot wait." Lydia grabbed water bottles, tucking them into her vest pockets and into the sack she had created with the blanket tied around her. "Here, take some of these." She tossed the plastic bottles to Caroline. "Those men are the least of our worries right now. I have not survived the deserts of Africa, dehydration from the heat, and snakebite to get buried in a mudslide in Guatema—" She stopped, obviously remembering Caroline's story about David. "Oh, crap. I'm so sorry, Caroline. Didn't mean to be so insensitive. It's just that we have to get out of here." She looked around for any other supplies or food to take with them. "Got your phone and my Swiss Army knife?"

"Right here in my hand." Caroline held up her right arm.

Lydia pulled another plastic bag from the box and stuck the box back into the sack. "Here, wrap this plastic bag around the phone to keep it as dry as we can, and hand those items to me. I'll put them in my pocket. Hurry! We have a chance to make some tracks while it's still raining. They won't come back out here in this storm."

Soaked and mud streaked, each wrapped in a Guatemala blanket stuffed with other blankets, a few bottles of water, a couple of soggy tortillas and cold scrambled eggs, they faced each other in the dim light. Lydia was seasoned and tough, but Caroline had spent her entire existence in a safe cocoon. Yet here she stood, adrenalin pumping, ready to crawl out of a muddy hut to only God knows what for her survival.

"Caroline, we're going to make it. We're getting out of this hellhole. Follow me."

"No, Lydia, let me go first. That might make it easier for you."

"Okay, then start crawling."

Caroline dropped to her all fours and lay down on her belly in the trench. She pushed the bag of blankets out in front her hoping for some protection.

"You're going headfirst?"

"Why would I go any other way? I want to see where I'm headed." Caroline wondered if it might be best to go feet first and look later.

"Then go, and make haste." She glanced back toward the door. More sludge, more water, more pressure, and the planks were beginning to bulge to the inside. "Hurry, Caroline, hurry."

Caroline inched her body through the trough and through the opening at the bottom of the wall. Rain pelted her face and upper body as she moved to where she could see. Jungle. Thick, muddy jungle. The back of her calf caught a protruding nail from the board above as she pulled her legs through the trench. She felt flesh rip and the stinging of an open wound, but she never slowed or made a sound. When she was safely outside the hovel, she took Lydia's arm and began to pull her through with one hand and push the mud away with the other.

Lydia grimaced as she pushed herself through the tight space. Finally, she was on the outside. Caroline watched the woman's chest rise and fall as she lay there, her breath ragged from fear and exertion.

"Come on, Lydia, stand up. We need to go. Which way?"

She watched as Lydia surveyed the landscape as best she could with the rain beating down and the ground seeming to move underneath them. To the right sat the cinder block house attached to the lean-to. To the left the jungle, too thick to see more than a few yards. They were near the top of a ridge, and there was another one in the distance in front of them. That meant a valley between. And in the valley below, possibly there was a river leading to the lake or maybe to a village within walking distance.

Caroline looked behind them. Slivers of bright sky pierced the clouds across the horizon above the peak. Maybe the rain would stop soon, but for now, it was constant.

Lydia pointed straight ahead, adjusted her sack and supplies and motioned for Caroline to follow her.

Unaware of passing time, they slogged along the ridge without talking, just clinging to the ground like mountain goats and zigzagging their way to a lower elevation, but periodically glancing behind them to see if anyone was following. They had to get as far away from the hut as they could and make their way down this mountain at the same time. Giant philodendron leaves swiped them as they pushed and pulled their way forward. The jungle was so thick they quickly lost sight of the shack they'd left on the ridge. They used their bare hands and the rain to wash the mud from their hair, faces, and arms as they slogged through the dense foliage.

As though tired of being squeezed, the clouds quit giving up their moisture, and the rain finally slowed to a foggy drizzle. Caroline stumbled and slowed briefly to look at her leg. There was still a trickle of blood oozing, but she could not stop now, and even if she could, she had nothing to stop the bleeding. They kept trudging through mud and jungle for what seemed like a long time.

Something echoed behind them. Thunder? No, but a low rumble. She turned her ear toward the sound. There was no wind or heavy rain to make that sound, but a crackling noise and a low, guttural, grinding roar reverberated all around as if some long-buried, underground creature had been aroused underneath her. Caroline walked faster toward Lydia. "What is that sound? It's getting louder."

Lydia looked back to the top of the ridge behind them as the sound became thunderous. "Oh, God, Caroline, run, just run!"

Late Tuesday afternoon at the Bonifaz Hotel in Xela

"Does this rain ever stop?" Roderick held fast to the armrest as the rattletrap truck bounced over the cobblestone streets, barely wide enough for the truck to get past the parked cars. Leo sat in the middle, both arms wrapped tightly around his computer case.

Goodluck held on to the steering wheel as though the street was trying to take it away from him. "Sir, you're in the land of Eternal Spring, and that means rain. It'll stop in another couple of months. You're here during their winter, but that just means it's the rainy season."

"No wonder everything is so green." Leo had grown up in Arizona.

"Always hated flying down here during these months. The showers come every day, but there'll be a break later this afternoon, and the mud will dry quickly, almost to a powder."

"How so?" Roderick had never been to Central America, and its climate and culture were more than foreign to him.

"Volcanic ash in the soil, sir." Goodluck slammed on breaks at the intersection. No sign, no stoplight, and a fenderless small car taking ownership of the street. "Yes, sir, more volcanoes in Guatemala than in any other country in the world. Climbed one a few years ago on one of my trips down here."

The more Goodluck talked, the more Roderick realized having Goodluck Gibbons around was a stroke of more than just good luck. Perhaps God's providence. "Ever seen one erupt?"

"No, sir, I've seen one huffing and puffing in the distance. You may see that, too, but eruptions are rare. In all my years of flying missions down here, I only know of one, and that was Pacaya, about eighteen miles from Guatemala City. Shut the city down for nine days, no flying in or out because of the ash. Covered everything, and the rain washed it down the sewer and clogged up their system for weeks. Ash fell for days. Saw folks shoveling it off their porches and verandas. Brooms wouldn't sweep it."

Roderick heard all he wanted to hear about ash and rain and stared at his phone as though willing it to ring. When would the kidnapper call? He looked at his watch. Almost ten hours since the call had come this morning. His images of Caroline included her in a pink gown at the piano or a navy skirt and blazer at a press conference or a soft blue sweater and jeans in the library at Rockwater, but not here, not in this land of jungles and volcanoes and corruption.

"When we get to the hotel, Goodluck, could you secure us a driver and a vehicle that'll carry eight?"

"Eight, sir?

"Yes, for the four of us who came in this morning, for Caroline's two brothers joining us tonight, and for . . ." Roderick paused.

Goodluck voiced his hope. "And for Miss Carlyle and Dr. Pipkin. Yes sir, that'll mean a van."

"Then get a van. We'll follow you back to the airport and pick up Acer. Maybe he's finished with the plane by now, but I want that plane prepared to fly back out of here before we leave the airport."

"Yes, sir. Anything else?"

Roderick pulled the piece of paper from his shirt pocket and reached around Leo to hand it to Goodluck. "Here's the name of the hospital where Sister Gabriela and the driver are. Could you get directions or make sure the driver can get us there?"

"Yes, sir."

"And one more thing, could you please just dispense with the 'sir'? No need for it. Just call me Rod. We're here together to get one job done and get out of here."

"Yes, sir. Excuse me, Rod. Just habit from my military days. Consider it all done."

Roderick felt safe with Goodluck. When his father had

coaxed him into the waters of the deep blue spring at Rockwater to teach him how to swim, he'd told Roderick he was there with him. He'd also told him to always be careful in life about the folks he jumped into things with, whether it was friends or business associates. *"Don't choose the kind of folks who'd pull you under,"* his father had cautioned. *"Choose the kind you'd go under to save if they were struggling."* Roderick's discernment about Goodluck told him Goodluck was that kind of people. They were now in deep water together, and Caroline was already under, but Roderick was certain Goodluck would help him keep his head above water until they rescued Caroline and all got safely to shore.

They were quiet until Goodluck pointed up the one-lane street. "We're here." The Bonifaz sat at the top of a steep hill just one block off the plaza. "The only place to park is up the hill and in the back. There's a guarded, walled entrance."

Leo released the stronghold he had on his computer bag. "Oh, good. Security. I feel safer already."

Their pickup truck pulled hard up the steep hill, turned a sharp corner, and stopped at the solid-metal brown gate with spray-painted white letters reading *Bonifaz*. Goodluck rolled down his window a few inches and said something in Spanish. The guard unlocked the gate and pushed it only wide enough for the truck to pass through, and closed it again. Goodluck parked in a row of expensive-looking vehicles underneath a tin shelter. He pointed to a veranda surrounded by potted bougainvillea. "We'll go through there and work our way down four floors to the lobby. You can leave your bags here, and I'll get some help and come back for them."

"No can do." Leo slid across the seat to get out of the vehicle. "Let's just get it all now. There's not that much, and it's not anything I want out of my sight."

"I understand." Goodluck untied the tarp covering the luggage, protecting it from the rain. Roderick and Leo grabbed their bags and headed for the veranda. Goodluck quickly secured the tarp and caught up with them before they got to the door. He grabbed a bag from Roderick and another from Leo.

"Where's your bag?" Leo asked.

"Don't have one. Didn't come prepared to stay."

"I forgot about that. Maybe you should pick up what you need before we head out." Roderick reached for the wad of hundred dollar bills again.

Goodluck took the money. "Best to keep your money out of sight, Boss. There's a market down on the plaza. I don't need much. I'll run get a shirt and jeans and a jacket, and maybe some rain gear. You guys need some rain gear? I'll get it while I'm out. We're going to complete this mission quickly and head home, but we'll likely be wet when we do."

Goodluck led them down several flights of Saltillo-tiled steps until they reached the lobby.

"Just get whatever you think we need." Roderick remembered James and Thomas. "And get extra for Caroline's two brothers if you would."

"Yes, sir, and I'll get this money changed down at the bank. Remember, we'll do better with twenties and *quetzals*."

"You know best, Goodluck. I'm counting on you." Somehow, Roderick knew he could.

"Sir, I'll tell you what I told my captain in Iraq. I'll give you my very best, and when you need something better, I'll do my best to find it. Now I'll be on my way to get this business done and get us a driver and vehicle."

"We'll get our rooms and meet you in the lobby in an hour." Roderick almost expected Goodluck to salute. He was a man who understood chain of command. But Roderick did not want to be the boss or the captain. He only wanted to be and do whatever it took to find Caroline. The only place he knew to start was with the driver who was with her when she was taken.

Roderick and Leo approached the desk. Leo had assigned one of his security team back home to call and make reservations. A young Guatemalan male in black pants, white shirt, and a colorful, striped bibbed apron stood behind the wooden counter, waiting to greet them. Roderick knew that Leo might be standing casually at the front desk but his eyes would peruse that area like a video camera, taking note of everything from the window placements to the doors to the number of room keys hanging on the wall behind the counter.

Leo pulled the slip of paper from his shirt pocket. "We're here to check in. We have reservations. Do you speak English?"

At the sound of Leo's voice, a silver-haired, bronze-skinned man in a gray pinstriped suit stepped from the back office and approached the counter. "*Señor* Adair? I am Javier Bonifaz. We spoke last night."

Leo quickly retorted. "My name's Leo. This is Mr. Adair."

Mr. Bonifaz turned like a ballroom dancer toward Roderick. "You are Mr. Adair?"

"Yes, and you are Mr. Bonifaz?"

"*Sí, señor.* I am most sorry about Miss Carlyle. I see her a few times in past years. She is so beautiful and kind."

"Yes, she is. What do you know?"

The hotel owner gamely continued in accented English. "You call last night, and Miss Carlyle no return. Something wrong. Your man call this morning for reservations. Two cops here asking questions this afternoon. They say she taken by two men in a blue truck. They call you for money yet?"

"Yes, they called this morning. They called me, Caroline's parents, and the couple Caroline lives with in Georgia."

"Come sit down. We talk." Javier led Roderick over to a couple of wicker chairs. "You know Mr. Summers, the man Miss Carlyle was planning to marry?"

"No, I never met David."

"He do much good for our country, so I give him his room all the times he come to Xela. So sad he got killed in the mudslide. I no see Miss Carlyle for two years, then she come for the baby for her friend. Now she here to do more good, and this terrible thing happen. I say goodbye to her when she go yesterday morning. I am so sorry, so sorry." Javier hung his head and shook it back and forth.

"Thank you, Mr. Bonifaz. Now we just have to find her."

"You give them the money, you get her back. That happened my wife. I have hotel and other business. Kidnappers think I am rich. They take her from my house in the daylight. Call me next day ask me for three hundred thousand quetzals. Too much money, but I pay everything for my wife. She come home in two days okay, but never the same. Always scared. Miss Carlyle okay too. Just pay the money."

"I pray you are right. Do you have internet access here?"

"Oh, yes, *señor*. For you and your friends, it cost nothing, and we leave on water and electricity in your room all the time. No cut off at ten o'clock tonight."

"Thank you." Roderick saw Leo approaching with two keys attached to four-inch blocks of golden-colored wood carved in the shape of Guatemala. The room numbers were burned into one side of the wood and the word *Bonifaz* burned into the other. "Javier, could I please get Miss Carlyle's room key? I need to look around and see what she left here."

"Oh, yes, yes, *Señor* Adair." Javier waltzed across the tile floor in his light-colored shoes and back through the swinging doors.

Leo handed Roderick his room key. "We're just down this hall, right off the lobby."

"Is that good? Should we be nearer the back entrance up the hill?"

"No, this is better. No elevator in this place, and our driver will be picking us up out front. They'll have us a case of water in our rooms in a few minutes, and they're preparing food for us, something safe for us to eat. There's a guard at the front door every night after eight o'clock. He'll be informed that we are allowed to come and go freely."

Javier returned with the key. "The room for Miss Carlyle is on floor three."

"Thank you very much." Roderick took the key, turned, and followed Leo down the hallway.

"What about the food, not that I'm even hungry?"

"Have to be careful here. Don't eat anything that hasn't been cooked, and don't drink anything that hasn't been boiled, and no ice. Only drink bottled water."

"How do you know these things, Leo?"

"Too much foreign travel in places I don't want to return to." Leo stopped at the door to his room. "You're next door. And keep your eyes closed when you take a shower. Water's got bacteria you can't handle, and it can enter your body through your eyes."

Roderick unlocked his room and stood at the door. "I need to make a couple of calls, then I'm going up to Caroline's room and have a look around. I'll be back down in time to meet you and Goodluck."

"I'll make my calls and go upstairs with you."

"Thank you, but no. I'd rather do this by myself." Roderick closed his room door. He called Lilah and gave her a report of events since his last call at the airport in Lexington. Still no more word from the kidnappers. Liz's firing had not been without a high-pitched, high-volume response. Roderick knew Lilah would take pleasure in telling him all about it, but he didn't want to think about Liz right now and postponed the detailed account. He instructed Lilah to call the Carlyles and the Meadowses to see if they had any more word from the abductors. He would call her back within half an hour.

Roderick picked up the key to Caroline's room and took the six flights of stairs to the third floor. When he reached the third floor landing, hand-painted room numbers and arrows that looked like bird feathers directed him to the right hallway and to Room 316. Unexpectedly, his urgency to see her room halted when he approached the door. He inserted the oversized, ornate key into the lock and had to jiggle it before it would fit perfectly enough to turn. He walked slowly in and closed the heavy, wooden door, turning the inside lock and securing the safety chain. He wanted to be alone.

The room was much like his, small with monastic furnishings. Tired, dingy beige curtains hung on each side of the window overlooking the cobblestone street down to the plaza. The drab stucco walls rose from an earth-colored Saltillo-tile floor and were in need of fresh paint. Only the reds, yellows, and blues in the striped blanket on the bed brought any color to the room. The damp chill in the stale air sent a shiver through him. The room was so hushed and so still, like the inside of a tomb where there was nothing to break the silence. So unlike Caroline, who brought music and life to him.

The bathroom was immediately to the right. Hanging

on the towel rack was the travel bag holding her toiletries. The wooden handle of her hairbrush poked through the side. Her shampoo bottle was in the shower. He reached for it, unscrewed the cap and breathed in its fragrance. Caroline. It smelled like her hair—her soft, curly, long ebony hair. He closed his eyes and thought of the October night he'd buried his face in her curls on the patio of an Atlanta hotel. He remembered holding her close and looking up at the biggest, roundest, fullest moon he had ever seen. It was a blue moon, perfect and complete, like his life would be with Caroline. That was the night he knew he did not want to live without her.

His eyes brimmed with tears. Now, he couldn't live without her.

He closed the cap on the shampoo bottle and walked into the other room.

It was no surprise to him that Caroline's things were left tidy and orderly. Her travel folder was neatly aligned on her desk. He opened it to find her penciled notes from the music store in Guatemala City and some information about the African Children's Choir, apparently given to her by Dr. Pipkin. He looked around. She must have taken her computer with her.

Caroline's large suitcase sat on a chair in the corner on the other side of the bed. The wooden floor creaked as he stepped around the bed, very low to the floor and sagging in the middle. He stood in front of the suitcase. She had put the lid to the suitcase down but had not zipped it shut. He opened it. Her clothes, packed in zip-lock bags, lay as perfectly in the suitcase as her travel folder lay on the desk. Underneath the chair sat her sandals, side by side as though deliberately lined up. He sat down on the side of the bed and picked up her shoe, so small, thin soled, with narrow straps, almost like a child's. He held the shoe to his chest and wept.

How could I do it? I knew better. How could I let my love come here without me while I'm away doing business? So fragile, and so beautiful. I never should have let her come here alone. Just like I never should have let Mother ride her horse that day, knowing it might rain. Oh, God, I'm useless. The only two women I've ever truly loved, and I didn't protect either of them.

The deep ache in his chest spread to his arms, and he cried like he hadn't cried since his father died, like he would have imploded without the release of his tears. When he could no longer cry, he put her shoe back on the floor just as it was.

On the bedside table lay a small green paper bag, its top neatly folded, hiding its contents. He picked it up, unfolded the creases, and pulled a small box from the inside. It was covered in a deep green satin and was the size of a ring box. He opened it and removed the carefully placed velvet covering. A pair of jade cufflinks.

What was she doing with cufflinks, and why did she leave them here out in the open? That's like Caroline, trusting.

There was a knock at the door. "Roderick, you still in there? The driver's here. We need to go."

"Yes, I'm coming. I need to call Lilah first to see if there's any news. I'll be down shortly. Go back to the front desk and tell them I want all of Caroline's things moved to my room right away."

He cleared his voice and called Lilah. No news. He began to secure Caroline's personal belongings. These things were all he had of her, and he wanted them close. Stuffing the small box back into the green bag, he put it in his jacket pocket and headed toward the door. He stopped before he opened it to wipe his eyes and take one last look at this room.

You were here, Caroline. I feel you. I sense you. Please come back to me.

Chapter 20

Hospital and Hope

Late Tuesday afternoon, somewhere in the jungle

"Turn around, and run, Girl. Run the other way." Lydia lumbered around Caroline and took her hand, pulling her along. The low-pitched, thunderous sound was steady, punctuated by the crackling sound of trees toppling to the jungle floor.

Caroline and Lydia ran with abandon, slapping at foliage, rarely looking at where their feet might land, figuring nothing in their path could be more deadly than the earth moving behind them. The peak of the ridge from where they escaped had given way to torrents of water and wind, and the loose earth rumbled and slid down the mountain, taking with it anything in its path. They were no longer on their original zigzag pattern down the mountain to get to the valley below but on a lateral course midway across the ridge, attempting to stay out of the unpredictable path of the mudslide.

The foliage was so thick that Caroline only got momentary glimpses of the top of the ridge above them. She found it harder and harder to breathe from running at this altitude and from trying to inhale the thick, damp air. Behind them, it appeared the worst was over, but she knew the ground could shift at any time. There was no safe place. Climbing to the crest provided no assurance, and descending to the valley could mean a muddy burial. They could only trust their instincts, and their instincts said, "Just run away from the sound."

Running for her life, Caroline thought of David. Countless moments in her grief, she had tried to imagine what David must have experienced on the road from El Tablón seven years ago as his vehicle was washed down the mountain. She had prayed that whatever happened, happened fast. Tasting her own fear now, she wondered if he'd heard the warning sounds or if he and Josh saw what was coming in time to attempt an escape.

Sounds of the rumbling earth were fading and seemed below them now, but Lydia continued to run and pull Caroline behind her. When they came to a narrow ravine, Lydia's long legs enabled her to jump safely in stride to the other side.

It happened so fast. Caroline's foot was caught by a vine-like root running atop the ground, her hand slipped from Lydia's, and she fell hard, almost bringing Lydia down into the hidden gully with her. The soggy blankets she carried provided little cushion against the tangled roots and protruding rock. Face down in a bed of mud and rotting leaves and too breathless to cry out in pain, she grabbed at anything to steady herself.

Lydia turned, fell to her knees and grabbed Caroline's arm to keep her from sliding further down the rift in the mountainside. "Hang on, Caroline. I have you. Don't fight. Be still. I have you." Lydia regained her own position and got a better grip on Caroline's right arm.

As Lydia pulled, a sharp stabbing pain in Caroline's left shoulder took what little breath she had away. "Wait, Lydia, I can't."

Lydia stopped and surveyed the ground below. "Okay, Caroline, okay, you're safe. You won't slide. Just keep holding my hand." Careful not to move Caroline, Lydia held tightly to her wrist and maneuvered her own body around to Caroline's side. "Here now, I'm letting go of you." She let go of Caroline's hand and climbed over her until she was kneeling on the ground, wedging herself between Caroline and the descending ravine. "See, you're not going anywhere. I have you now. Can you turn over?"

"I, I think so." Caroline, still face down, raised her head and felt the earth beneath the palms of her hands. When she attempted to push herself up, her left shoulder gave way. "Oh, God, the pain."

"Where, where's the pain?"

"My shoulder." Caroline's face fell back into the decaying leaves.

"Okay, I'll help you. We have plenty of time."

"But what about the mudslide?"

"Listen. Just listen." The rain had stopped, the tropical forest was silent and still, no rustling foliage and no birds. "We've weathered the storm, Caroline. We're going to be fine."

"Oh, thank you, God." She turned her face toward Lydia. "But, my arm?"

"I'll get you turned over and take a look." Lydia slid one arm underneath Caroline's body, preparing to turn her. "Can you put your right arm down by your side?"

Caroline moved her arm into position. The slightest movement caused pain across her upper chest.

"Good. Now try to hold it there. I'll hold your left arm just where it is and turn you over on your back." Lydia's careful tactic worked. Caroline lay flat, holding her left arm across her abdomen.

"Now it's time to check you out. I call myself an anthropologist, but I've done my share of doctoring at times in places where I've been. I have to untie this blanket and get your jacket off. It may hurt like hell, but I need to see your shoulder. You ready?"

Caroline moaned, feeling the color draining from her cheeks. "I'm ready. Slowly, please."

Lydia untied the blanket and removed the items it carried. "Good that you had this thing around you. All these wet blankets cushioned your fall."

"Tell my shoulder that." Caroline's voice was weak.

"Okay, now the jacket. I have to move your arm."

She moaned louder as Lydia tried to slide her arm from the jacket sleeve. "Wait, Lydia. The pain . . ."

"I'm so sorry." Lydia stopped, reached into the inner pocket of her vest, and pulled out the Swiss Army knife. "There's another way, Caroline. Here, I'm going to just cut your jacket and you won't have to move. Don't think you'll want to wear this one again anyway."

Lydia lifted the jacket and sliced it from the buttonhole across to the sleeve, pulling it away to reveal Caroline's shoulder. An awkward bulge protruded from the blood soaked area of her white blouse.

"Why is it so hard to breathe?" Caroline's voice trailed into unconsciousness.

The Bonifaz in Xela

Roderick stood in the lobby of the Bonifaz and looked through the glass-front door at the people scuttling unhurried across the plaza in the rain, adults in business suits, teenagers in jeans, and Mayan women in their native dress. He turned when he heard footsteps. Leo was finishing a phone conversation as he approached Roderick.

"Any news?"

"No word. Nothing." Leo put his phone in his pocket.

"What about tracing the phone the kidnapper used?"

"It wasn't Caroline's. Some kind of prepaid, disposable phone. No way to trace it."

"That's no good. Maybe this waiting is some kind of psychological tactic they're using, and it's working."

"Maybe. I don't think they're that sophisticated. Regardless, the team at Rockwater is ready when the call does come in. And it will."

"Sophisticated enough not to use Caroline's phone."

Goodluck and the young man from the front desk joined them. "Sir, Rolando is having all of Miss Carlyle's things brought downstairs to your room, and I went ahead and had Dr. Pipkin's things taken to your room, Leo. I hope that's okay."

"Sure. I already took a look around in her room. Nothing there. If she had a computer or a phone, she took it with her. Probably nothing to help us anyway."

Goodluck pushed the heavy door against the blowing rain. "Van's here." He motioned for Roderick and Leo to join him. "Watch your step. These cobblestone streets are good for slipping and sliding in this mess." He led Roderick and Leo to the gray van parked just outside the Bonifaz. When they were secured in their seats, Goodluck manually closed the doors, climbed into his front seat, and spoke to the driver. *"Primera parada. Calle Novena. Hospital San Rafael, por favor."*

"How long will it take us to get there?" Roderick adjusted his seatbelt.

"Not long. The hospital's in the same zone as the hotel and just a few blocks away. But I'll warn you, sometimes with these narrow one-way streets, it takes longer to go a few blocks. We might have walked if it weren't raining."

"Let's get going. The clock's ticking."

"Sir, I've booked the driver a room at the hotel, and he understands he is to be available twenty-four seven."

"That works. Let me know how much you need. I want him compensated well."

"Yes, sir. Will do. Need to ask you about something else."

"Just ask, Goodluck."

"Thank you, sir. I told you I can get by with my Spanish, but it's not real good, and neither of you speak Spanish."

Leo patted his computer case. "Got it right here. Several ways to translate on my computer."

"I understand, but that's assuming the people we're talking to can read. Sir, I think we need a translator. What we're dealing with is heavy stuff. Time and clear, accurate communication are important. We can't afford any mistakes or miscommunications."

"Hire one."

"Thank you, sir. Actually, I already did. She's meeting us at the hospital. Remember, I told you I brought teams down here to work on water projects?"

"Sure."

"Well, I called the company here and asked for Maricela. She used to translate for our teams. I told her about Miss Carlyle, what she's doing here and what happened to her. Maricela volunteered to help us out. We need her at least until Dr. Morris gets in tonight and maybe longer. She's good, sir, and she lives here in Xela and understands the culture."

"Good thinking. Pay her well too."

"Don't think that'll be necessary. The company gave her the time off. She came out of an orphanage, and she's glad to help find Miss Carlyle, somebody down here just trying to help the orphan children."

"But find a way to pay her anyway."

They rode in silence. Roderick watched the unhurried pedestrians whose faces showed no discontent in having to wade in ankle-deep water to cross streets. He remembered the rainstorm at Rockwater on the afternoon of Caroline's first concert there last summer. She had taken a walk down to the stream and an afternoon storm came up before she returned. He had hopped into the truck with dry towels and found her sitting underneath a tree, her wet sable curls framing her face like they had been painted there. She was beautiful even then and was quite contented to sit there waiting out the rain. He opened the truck door, and she climbed in. He had just met her two days before, and yet he had an urge to embrace her as he draped the towel around her shoulders. Somehow he had known to be more cautious with her.

"We're here, sir." Goodluck's voice pulled him back to narrow streets of Xela in front of a small white building with bars on the windows.

"Good." Roderick unfastened his seatbelt. "Let's see if we can find Sister Gabriela. She knows we're coming."

Hospital San Rafael looked like no hospital Roderick had ever seen, not outside nor in the lobby. They were folding up their umbrellas when they were approached by a slight-framed woman dressed in a gray skirt, white blouse, and a brown sweater. Something more akin to a white scarf replaced the normal veil worn by a nun and allowed short brown curls to escape around her hairline. Her cheeks were rosy, shining as though they had been polished, and her narrow, pale forehead forced her small brown eyes to rest near the tapered bridge of her nose. Only two steps away from them, her eyes met Roderick's as she extended her hand, which had been holding the crucifix she wore around her neck. "You are the man who has won Caroline's heart."

He shook her hand. *How did she know? Did Caroline show her a photograph or does she just have an otherworldly sense about her?* He hoped for the latter and that she could help him find Caroline. "And you must be Sister Gabriela."

Her voice was as gentle as her countenance. "I am. Please come with me." Sister Gabriela led them across the lobby. The sounds of their steps on the stone floor echoed through the plastered walls of the hallway. She opened a door and held it, motioning for them to come inside.

"This is the hospital chapel. I think we can talk best here."

The chapel was wasn't much larger than a jail cell and had the colorless hue of Caroline's room at the Bonifaz. A short center aisle, flanked by four rows of backless wooden pews on each side, led to an altar table covered in candles with handpicked flowers lying between them. A garish crucifix hung on the wall above the table.

Why is she bringing us to the chapel? Maybe she already knows something. Fear gripped Roderick.

"Please sit. The hospital does not have a meeting room, and this will give us a quiet, peaceful place to talk."

Following her lead, Roderick sat at the end of a pew facing the aisle and took a quick survey of the stark room. Leo took the end of the pew behind Roderick, and Goodluck sat across from Leo. Sister Gabriela stood in front of Roderick. "I am so very sorry for what has happened to Caroline, but God is with her, and my lips have not been without prayers since I found Paco. I am praying for her safety and that of Dr. Pipkin. Our God takes care of His children, and I am trusting He will bring them both back to us."

She doesn't know anything. Roderick's grasp on the pew in front of him relaxed. "Thank you, Sister, for your prayers. Is there anything you can tell us?"

"Yes, I will tell you all I know. But first, which of you is *Señor* Goodluck?"

Goodluck stood up and put his arms behind him and bowed his head. "Just Goodluck, ma'am, I mean Sister. Just Goodluck."

"Your friend, Maricela, is in with Paco. She arrived about half an hour ago. Paco is recovering from surgery he had last night. He will tell us what he knows, but he is still sleepy with medication."

"Sister, do you think he might have been involved in this kidnapping?"

She turned to Leo. "And you are, *señor*?"

"Leo, Mr. Adair's chief of security."

"No, Leo. Paco had nothing to do with this. The two men who took Caroline and Dr. Pipkin planned this. They dragged Paco from the van and crushed his legs with a bat and left him in the middle of a cornfield. He will have a long recovery and will never walk normally again. No, he had no part of this."

Thoughts of the same men who could crush a man's legs with a bat touching Caroline sickened Roderick. "Were you able to talk to him and get any information? How many men, color of the vehicle, anything?"

"Yes, I will tell you." Sister Gabriela told them about the two men, one short and muscular with a ponytail, the other taller and heavier, and the blue pickup truck.

"That's something to go on."

"Yes, and the police here are working with the officers in Salcajá. That is the village where we live. It is thirty minutes away. Ours is a poor village, and our officers do not have knowledge of kidnapping. They can only look for blue trucks. They will work hard to help. They know Miss Carlyle is here to help the children."

Leo quizzed her about what time Caroline had left the orphanage and what time Paco was found.

She answered him and explained how Paco used the horn of the van to attract the attention of a family who lived nearby.

Sister Gabriela placed her hand on Roderick's shoulder. "Let us pray now, and then we will talk to Paco." The sister prayed fervently for the safety of Caroline and Lydia, and for the souls of the men who had taken them, for God's blessing on the people who were searching for them, and for God's comfort for Roderick and all the family.

Roderick thought her prayer was intimate, like the request of a daughter to her father, and like the prayer he had heard Caroline pray on the boulder at Rockwater. He wanted to be able to pray like that.

Sister Gabriela led them out of the chapel and down several hallways to get to Paco's room. Goodluck greeted Maricela while Roderick went immediately to Paco's bedside. Paco's small frame was covered in a sheet and a stained blanket. Both Paco's legs were in casts and were bent and propped in a fixed position underneath the cover. Sweat, either from the humidity in the dank room or from intense pain, ran from his brow. Roderick wondered how people with serious injuries could ever get better in these conditions.

He spoke Paco's name, trying to rouse him. Paco labored to open his eyes before closing them again.

"*Señor* Adair, I am Maricela Lopez. I am so sorry about Miss Carlyle, but maybe I can help you."

"Thank you, Miss Lopez. I'll take any help. We must

get Caroline and Dr. Pipkin to safety."

"I have been talking with Paco, and he gave me much information." Maricela gave the same description Sister Gabriela had given of the two men and the truck.

Roderick listened and Leo wrote in his small, black tablet.

"Paco saw the man with the ponytail at the Quinta Real in Guatemala City and again at the market in Antigua. He thinks the man was following them. Also, he heard the man speak to his partner in Quiché."

"'Quiché'? What is that?"

"It is a Mayan dialect spoken by the people who live in certain places in the Highlands, usually in the lake area. Not many people in Guate speak this anymore."

"Could Paco understand what they were saying?"

"A little, *señor*. Paco is from the city. He heard the word 'Atitlán.'"

"Do you recognize that word?"

"Oh, yes, *señor*. That is the lake, the big lake. Maybe they take her there."

"Is it close to here? Can we go there?"

"It is three hours from here, *señor*, and it is a very big lake, surrounded by volcanoes. There are many mountains, and much jungle, but different than the jungle on the coast." She hesitated. "It will be very difficult to find her there."

"I understand, but if that's where she is, then that's where I'm going. We have to start somewhere. We can look for the truck. Where can we get a map of the area?"

"*Señor*, we have very good maps in our office. Many of these roads in the area are not on the tourist maps because they are made by the villagers who live nearby. We do clean water projects around the lake, and we do not even know all the roads."

Roderick was beginning to get a sense of things—primitive living, tribal dialects, centuries of footpaths connecting villages. And jungle. And unrelenting rain.

Leo's phone rang. "Excuse me." He stepped outside to the hallway.

Goodluck edged nearer to Paco's bed. "Your offices still in the same place, Maricela?"

"Yes, they are. Nothing much changes around here. I will go there tonight and get copies of the maps. You can talk with police tonight or in the morning and see what information they have. Then we can start out for the lake midmorning. That will give us time to get there before the afternoon rains come."

Leo stepped back into the room and motioned for Roderick and Goodluck to join him. "We have news."

Roderick could feel the pulse in his temples. "Did he call back? Did they get a trace?"

"No, no call. But it seems that Paco wasn't the only one who noticed the ponytailed man." Leo reached into his bag for his computer and walked toward the end of the hall. "Our Dr. Pipkin must have a keen eye for trouble. One of our men just talked with her assistant down in Miami. Name's Jess. Seems early yesterday morning, Dr. Pipkin sent a strange email to her with a picture attached. She's forwarding it to me right now." He propped his computer on the windowsill and powered it up.

"What you mean is that we have a photograph of the kidnapper?" Goodluck spun around on his toes, snapping his fingers before he caught himself. "Excuse me, sir. Couldn't help myself. That's good news."

Roderick remained silent for a moment before asking, "Why hasn't this Jess contacted someone if the email and photograph were so strange?"

Leo balanced the computer between his knee and the

windowsill. "My man asked the same question. Seems it's not unusual for Jess not to hear from Dr. Pipkin for days. Said the doctor is a bit on the eccentric side. She also said the doctor spoke Spanish."

"Spanish won't do her any good if the kidnappers speak Quiché." Roderick paced.

Maricela interrupted. "Sir, people often speak both languages here. The villagers speak it in their homes with their family, but most of them speak Spanish in the towns and cities."

Leo's fingers wouldn't move fast enough across the keyboard. He read Dr. Pipkin's email aloud to them.

> *In Xela at the Bonifaz Hotel. All is well . . . I've attached three pictures and be sure to keep them in a safe place. If things don't go just as planned, they may become useful. One photo is of Caroline Carlyle, my host. The second one, the man in white shirt and tie, is our driver, allegedly named Paco Alvarez. The third man in the t-shirt is unidentified, but he seems to show up wherever we are. Don't worry. I'm just being cautious. Call if you need me. LP.*

Roderick stepped closer. "Let's see. Let's see this unidentified man."

Leo pulled the photo up to full screen. Roderick stepped even closer. The man with the ponytail, the one who took Caroline. "Goodluck, any idea where this was taken?"

"Yes, sir. That's the Cerro de la Cruz in Antigua." Goodluck pointed to the photograph. "There's the water volcano in the background. Been there many times. Not a safe place to go alone, not even for a foot soldier like me."

"Leo, let me see the one of Caroline, please." There she was, his Caroline, in front of the cross with the volcano against a blue sky. Her ball cap did not hide the brilliant smile on her face. His eyes were fixed. *What if this is the last photo I'll ever have of her?*

"Look, Rod. Look closer." Leo pointed over Caroline's right shoulder. There was the muscular man with the greasy ponytail just steps behind her, his arms folded and his eyes peering at Caroline. Leo pulled the picture tight. "We got his face and his tattoo." He tapped the screen with his pen.

With the photograph pulled up, Roderick stared into the blue eyes that had seen into his soul months ago. He would give all he owned to ransom her and to see her eyes again.

Chapter 21

Come, Morning, Come

Tuesday night, deep in the jungle

Lydia unbuttoned Caroline's blouse to see where she was bleeding. An odd bulge appeared over her clavicle, and blood was beginning to clot around a gash on the front of her shoulder. *Oh crap, she's broken her collarbone. Could have some broken ribs too. At least no bone's protruding through the skin. Must have hit a rock when she fell so hard. Not that much blood. Probably would have already stopped bleeding if it weren't for all this rain and this hellish jungle. She's having trouble breathing. Must get her comfortable.*

She smoothed the moisture from Caroline's brow. "Caroline, I need to move you. Caroline?" No response.

Lydia knew that broken ribs could puncture a lung and that Caroline would have to be moved with care. "Come on, Caroline, I need to set you up a bit." If she could get her turned, the ravine formed the perfect shape for holding Caroline's body in a safer position. She reached for the extra blankets and padded the ground, stuffing the woven blankets around the sharper rocks. "Caroline?"

Caroline opened her eyes.

"That's right. Wake up, Caroline, and help me. I need to move you. Just don't move your left shoulder." *Thank God her breathing is better.*

"I don't think I could if I wanted to."

"Don't think you'd want to right now. I'm fairly certain you've broken your collarbone. I've seen these kinds of breaks before. And you might have cracked some ribs—nothing serious, but you'll have some pain, and it'll hurt like hell when we move you. I know because I cracked some ribs a few years ago when I was thrown out of a jeep." Lydia kept smoothing the blankets.

"Are you hurt, Lydia?"

"What? Me hurt? Wouldn't think of it. Don't want to hurt you either, but let's do it. Let's get you over on those blankets where you can sit up a bit. I think you'll be more comfortable that way." Lydia pulled Caroline's jacket to cover her bloody blouse. "I'll help with your legs if you can ease over this way." Lydia had seen the face and pallor of pain before. "Not too fast. Let's just take it slow."

"Why would I want to prolong the pain? Let's just get it over with." Caroline pushed herself with her good arm and crumpled into the blanketed crevice. She groaned louder, "Oh, that really hurts."

"I'm so sorry, Caroline. But you did it. This is perfect, just like a baby's cradle. You'll be fine." She adjusted the folded blanket underneath Caroline's head. Perhaps she had been wrong about this blue-eyed, delicate-looking girl. *She might just have it in her after all, and she's never been put to the test.* Lydia took a bottle of water from the makeshift pouch around her. "Here, you need to drink a sip of this. Slowly."

Caroline drank, got strangled and coughed. She groaned again.

Lydia remembered how it hurt to cough for months after she broke her ribs. "Careful, careful, girl." Lydia removed the blanket tied around herself and started stacking the water bottles next to the large stone near Caroline's head. "Oh, yes, plastic bags. What did we ever do without them? Don't think Paulino knew how handy they'd be when he tossed them to us this afternoon. Look, we have three dry blankets."

"Um-huh." Caroline almost whimpered. "I'll rest for just a bit, but we have to keep going."

"Who said we have to keep going?" Lydia pulled a couple of the large trash bags off the roll in the box and continued to organize and protect their supplies.

"But the men . . ." Caroline's voice trailed off.

"What men? We're in charge now. Don't give the men another thought." Lydia knew the kidnappers were the least of their worries now. Darkness was setting in, and Caroline's pain would increase.

"But they could find us." Caroline tried to raise her head to look around.

"Not likely. I'm thinking that shack might be buried under about twenty feet of mud at the bottom of this mountain, and my guess is they were in it."

"But what if they weren't?"

"Well, then, they're probably somewhere getting drunk, thinking they've just lost their ticket to a life on Easy Street. We're gone, and they have nothing. No proof of life? No ransom."

"I hope—" Caroline coughed again and grabbed her side. "I hope you're right."

"I was moving fast, but the last time I could see, part of that structure was gone. If it was the part Paulino and his buddies were in, they had a quick burial without a funeral. If they escaped, then they're sitting at some local bar, telling about their close call and thinking we're buried at the bottom of this mountain. The way I figure, they don't know we got out of there before the mudslide."

"You really think it's safe to stay here?"

"Safer than trying to make our way through this jungle tonight. I don't like snakes. I've been bitten once. I'm sitting right here and keeping both my eyes open."

There was still just enough light for Lydia to see the slight grin on Caroline's face. "You're in luck, Lydia. No snakes at this altitude. So you can close at least one eye."

"Thank you for that news. Sounds almost comfortable to me. The rain's stopped, and we'll nestle in right here and wait for daylight." Lydia sat on the bed of wet leaves next to Caroline. She wasn't so concerned about things she could see but worried more about microscopic organisms in this environment that could wreak havoc after an injury like Caroline's. Lydia perused their surroundings in the last light of dusk before the darkness cloaked them.

Late night at the Bonifaz

James, Thomas, and Reyna entered the front door at the Bonifaz. "Wait here, please. I'll get our rooms." Reyna left Caroline's brothers standing near the door, looking at their surroundings, unfamiliar in every way to them. She returned with two keys in hand. "Your future brother-in-law took care of everything. Here's your room key, and all our rooms are right down this hall." She pointed to the left corridor just beyond the entrance to the small dining room. "The night clerk is calling Roderick now. He wanted to speak with us tonight."

"Okay, we'll wait here." James held on tightly to his

duffle bag as though the unfamiliar would rip it from his hands. He could not rid himself of the relentless thoughts ricocheting through his mind—thoughts of Caroline and this Dr. Pipkin traveling alone in what he had seen of this country since his plane touched down in Guatemala City. For a man who'd grown up in the South where men took care of their women, he thought this no place for two ladies, especially since one of them was his baby sister.

He looked at his younger brother. They were both weary from travel, but James recognized the look on Thomas's face. It was that same look he'd had in the huddle of the last high school football game they'd played together. It was a championship game with only seconds to go, and they were eight yards away from their last chance for a winning score. The coach called the play—a quarterback sneak. Thomas was the quarterback, and the outcome was up to him. He was eager and ready, like a racehorse waiting for the gun to be fired and the gate to open. Thomas knew the moves of his teammates who would clear the way for him, and he knew how much they wanted to win. His careful footing and sheer determination to cross that goal line won the game.

James knew Thomas was anxious, but this time, neither of them knew their teammates nor the play. They only knew the goal was to get their sister back safely to home soil.

James heard the echoing footsteps and saw Roderick's silhouette coming down the corridor. The two met and shook hands. When Roderick extended his hand to Thomas, Thomas embraced him like a real brother, like the way he and James had grown up.

"I'm glad you're here. Let's go over here and sit down." Roderick pointed them to the only two sofas in the lobby. They were alone.

"So sorry we couldn't get here any earlier. Hope we

didn't wake you up." James finally released his duffle bag and sat down.

"Oh, no. There'll be no sleep for me until I know Caroline is safe." He turned to Reyna. "And you must be Dr. Morris."

"Yes, but please just call me Reyna. Any news?"

"Not yet. The only lead we have is that the abductors may have taken her to the lake area. I think Leo spoke with you about that." Roderick sat down on the small sofa next to Thomas.

"Yes, that's one reason we're running later than expected. After I spoke with Leo, I had to stop in an area where I had a good signal to make a couple of calls back to the city."

"Anything come of that?"

"We probably won't know until morning. I called *Señor* Saldivar, the international marketing director of the Quinta Real, and told him of the kidnapping and that we have reason to believe the kidnapper was a guest at the hotel on the two nights we were there. *Señor* Saldivar will check guest and vehicle registrations."

James twiddled with his wedding ring. "If we can assume this guy wasn't giving false information, the fact that he appears to be Guatemalan and drives a small blue pickup should narrow the field of suspects even though we don't have a license number."

"That's true. We may be able to get a name." Roderick lowered his voice. "This man was seen at the hotel in Guate, and we know he was seen in Antigua, and a vehicle of the same description was seen on the road outside the orphanage early Monday morning. No doubt he's the one, but finding him won't be easy."

Reyna spoke quietly. "Leo said something about Lake Atitlán."

"Yes, Paco heard one of the men say Atitlán, but the man spoke in Quiché, and Paco couldn't understand him."

James asked, "You mean we're looking for a guy who is not Guatemalan?"

Reyna responded quickly. "No, no. He is Guatemalan. He's probably from Sololá. Lake Atitlán is in the department of Sololá. That area of our country is rich with indigenous traditions, and that is why so many tourists go there from all over the world. The Quichés and the Cakchiquels are ethnic groups living in that area, and they speak the native languages. Most of them also speak Spanish, but Spanish would be their second language. All that is to say, if you did not grow up in that area, more than likely you would not speak Quiché."

"I see." James sat back in his chair. "What about this lake?"

"As I said, the lake attracts tourists because of the indigenous people living around it and because of the sheer beauty of the area. Some say it's like Lake Como in Italy, but even more scenic, surrounded by volcanoes and native villages. Geologists come to study the volcanic formations, and it's also a popular vacationing spot for wealthy Guatemalans."

"The lake is large?"

"Yes, I'd say roughly fifty square miles. But we're not talking about the lake, we're talking hundreds of square miles of mountainous area surrounding it."

A chill went down James' spine. He knew a lake that size would be a perfect place to dispose of two bodies that you never wanted found.

Roderick stood up. "As far as I'm concerned, the lake gives us a place to start. I can't just sit here waiting for a call. I have men back at Rockwater managing that. My plans are to head out in the morning about ten."

Thomas stood next to Roderick. "We'll be ready."

"I haven't told you about Goodluck."

It was the first time James had smiled all day. "Sounds like we could use some of that."

"That's true, but the Goodluck I'm talking about is a person, former military and knows the area. Seems Acer lucked out this morning in securing this plane and pilot. Name's Goodluck Gibbons, and he's flown into Xela on several missions, bringing in teams and executives who are working on water projects in the area. He has agreed to stay and help us."

"Great. From what I hear, we need all the help we can get." Thomas reached down to pick up his duffle bag. "There'll be six of us with Acer and Leo?" He looked at Reyna. "Seven if Dr. Morris can stay?"

"Actually, we have a driver and a translator. Goodluck hired a translator from the company he used to fly teams in here for. She knows the area, the culture, and she knows a bit of Quiché. She's also bringing us the most up-to-date maps from her company." Roderick looked at Reyna. "We'd love to have you stay, Reyna, but we know you have responsibilities back in the city, and we know you have a sick boy."

"Thank you, Roderick. My son is better, and I'm here. You may need me."

James did not like the sound of that. Doctors were only needed when someone was very sick or injured. "Thank you, Reyna. Caroline spoke always kindly of you. I know she would like to know you're here with us."

"Then I'll stay. I must tell you that Caroline is stronger than you think, and Dr. Pipkin seems to know her way around and can speak a little Spanish. She strikes me as being of afraid of nothing. She challenged me when I told her it was not safe to climb the volcano near the city. She practically had on her hiking boots."

"I'd say she's fairly savvy. She provided us a perfect photo of her kidnapper." James nudged Thomas. "Come on, little brother, let's get to our room. I need to call my wife. She'll get word to our parents that we're here and what our plan is. Too late to call Sam and Angel. I'll call them in the morning."

Roderick stopped them. "Thank you both for coming. I am so sorry. I should never have let Caroline come alone. This is all my fault. If she didn't have the money to start the choir, she wouldn't be here." Roderick's eyes welled with tears, and his body tensed with trying to prevent the shaking.

Thomas tried to sooth him. "But you didn't give her the money."

Roderick looked at Thomas. "I was responsible."

Thomas was about to say something when James gave him the you've-said-enough look and spoke. "Roderick, you are not responsible. We know our sister. She might look helpless, but she's as stubborn as they come. You couldn't have kept her from this. We don't blame you, and we know you're hurting just like we are."

"You don't have to blame me. I blame myself."

"Look, Roderick. We're nearly brothers now, and we have several things to go on. We'll start with everything we know and build from there. You've brought in your resources. Reyna's helping, and the good Lord brought us Goodluck. We'll bring Caroline back. We have to."

Roderick nodded in agreement but said nothing.

Reyna picked up her bag. "Gentlemen, let's get some rest. We have work, serious work, ahead of us."

—•—

In the rainforest late at night

The jungle was still and silent and darker than any night Lydia had ever spent in Africa. At least on the plains, she could see the sky from horizon to horizon and every star in between. But here, trees with unusually slick bark stood around them like armed guards, some standing straight, others leaning like tired soldiers. A canopy of leaves spread out above them and only allowed an occasional glimmer of a star. The hyena's howl and the chatter of monkeys were familiar visitors, but this jungle silence was a stranger. She wanted to know what time it was but hesitated to use the light on the phone to see her watch. An unusual glow might invite even more strangers, and she wanted to conserve battery.

Lydia had spread another blanket on the ground just above the fissure cradling Caroline. She had only to stretch her arm to touch the girl's brow. Caroline's breathing was shallow, interrupted by an occasional cough or groan. Lydia had drifted off when a voice awoke her.

"Lydia."

She brushed her damp hair from her face. "Yes, Caroline. What is it?"

"I need some water, please. I need water."

Lydia raised herself up, stretched carefully across Caroline to reach for a bottle of water. She had memorized where everything was before the darkness came. She knelt beside the crevice and lifted Caroline's head. *Oh, God, no. She's burning up. How did infection set in so quickly? That area was clean, no mud, no nothing but blood.* "Here, Caroline. Take a few sips. Slowly, you hear?"

Caroline did as she was told, coughed, winced, and whispered, "Thank you."

Crap, crap, crap. If only they hadn't taken my backpack,

we'd have meds, painkillers, bandages and antiseptic. But now what do I have? Some bottled water, day-old tortillas, wet blankets, and a few plastic bags.

"Are you in pain?"

Caroline's voice was weak from fever and dehydration. "Only when I breathe, but not too bad. Mostly my leg."

"Your leg? What about your leg? When did it start hurting?"

Caroline whispered something unintelligible.

Lydia crawled down the side of the ravine to get to Caroline's legs. She took the phone from her vest pocket. So much light from one small phone in a dark jungle. She raised Caroline's right leg and pushed up her pants. Nothing. She ran her hand down her thigh to check for any swelling. Nothing. Caroline showed no sign of pain.

Lydia maneuvered around until she could reach the left leg and lifted it. Caroline moaned and shivered. Lydia repositioned the phone to get a better look. *Oh, God, more blood on the back of her pants leg.* She'd only slid the moist fabric a few inches before she saw the mud and blood-encrusted gash in Caroline's calf. *Why didn't she say something about her leg? No telling what kind of crap entered that wound. Too late to clean it now, and besides with what? Got to do something about the fever.*

Lydia found the box of plastic bags and pulled out two. She gently removed the blankets covering Caroline and replaced them with the unfolded plastic bags. When Caroline's body was wrapped in the black plastic, Lydia replaced the blankets and crawled back to her spot just above Caroline. The digital time on the phone read two thirty-seven. Lydia lay down, turned off the phone, but kept it in her grip. She put her other hand on Caroline's brow and left it there. *We need some help here, Miss Blue Eyes. You can't travel, and I can't leave you here alone in the dark.*

Ransom for a Song

Things always seem better in the morning, but it's going to be a long night.

—•—

The hotel in Xela

Roderick lay on his back staring at the shadows on the ceiling. The plaza was finally quiet. He thought of Caroline. He prayed. He begged God just like he had when his mother lay bleeding on the stones on the bank of the running stream at Rockwater. Praying didn't seem to help. Was Dr. Pipkin with Caroline or was she alone? Was she awake or asleep? Was she afraid? Had they hurt her? He rolled over and looked at the clock. Two forty-one. He wondered if the morning would ever come.

Chapter 22

Unfamiliar Paths

Wednesday morning in Moss Point

Angel sat in her rocking chair in the library. Ordinarily, her oak rocker would have creaked in rhythm to the pendulum clock on the mantel, but she had no energy for movement this morning. Besides, she had a need for stillness. The sultry air of a July morning and the tightness in her chest made normal breathing difficult. "Sam, would you hang up the phone?"

Sam was across the room at his desk in conversation with Caroline's mother. "Yes, Martha. I know she's your baby girl. She feels like our baby girl too. I'll call you the minute I hear a word, and you do the same. We need to get off the phone. Goodbye."

Angel's face felt flushed and her breath was short. "How can the kidnapper call if you're on the phone? Have J. and Martha heard anything?"

"Not a word from Roderick or the kidnappers." Sam rose from his desk, hobbled over to his lounge chair, and set his mug on the table next to his seat. "James and Thomas landed yesterday afternoon, and Dr. Morris drove them to Xela. I hope James will call in regularly. Martha and J. are worried sick with all three of their kids down there in that hellhole."

As he sat down, his walking cane slipped from his hand and bounced on the hardwood floor. Angel jumped at the thud. "Sam, could you be just a bit more careful today? I can't take too many more surprises. I just crave a thimbleful of peace and quiet."

"I'm sorry, my Angel. I'll try to do better." Sam took a sip of coffee. "Let me tell you what I know."

Angel fanned her face with the morning newspaper as she turned her head to look at him. "Please tell me it's good news."

"Well, it's news. James called and said he and Thomas made it to Xela last night and met with Roderick. Said Roderick is in gear but is suffering, thinking this is all his fault. Some good news. Seems now they have a picture of the kidnapper, and they have an idea of the general area where he might be hiding Caroline and her doctor friend."

"Roderick must have more resources than I imagined."

"Wasn't Roderick's doings. Apparently, this Dr. Pipkin was suspicious of a fellow who kept showing up everywhere she and Caroline went and took his photo without his knowing it. Then she sent it to her assistant with a note. This assistant's been in touch with Roderick's security team. Yesterday, Roderick met with Paco—he's the driver who was beaten up pretty bad when the kidnappers took Caroline. Well, Paco verified the identity of the assailant when Roderick showed him the photo, and he told Roderick he heard the abductors say something about a lake."

"Not much to go on, but I guess it's something."

"It's plenty to go on. The kidnapper's been following them around. He stayed at the same hotel in Guatemala

City, and they have a description of his vehicle. Cases have been solved with less information."

"Well, that's fine and dandy, but as for me, I'd just as soon get the call from the kidnapper, wire our twenty-five thousand, and have him drop Caroline off at a place where Roderick can pick her up." She removed a tissue from her pocket and wiped the perspiration from her top lip. "It's Wednesday and more than twenty-four hours. Why haven't we heard back from the kidnapper?"

"Can't answer that. Could be he's wanting us to sweat, and making us wait is a surefire way to do that."

"But tell me again. I need to hear it. Didn't Roderick say that the kidnappers usually don't harm their victims?"

"That's what he said. I guess if they murdered them, families would learn not to pay the ransoms. These criminals just grab somebody, ask for a little money, hold 'em until the money's delivered, and then let 'em go and move on to grab somebody else."

"Maybe they're not such bad people. Maybe they're just poor and feel hopeless and look at ransom money as a way of making a living, and they're not really criminals after all."

Sam leaned over in his chair to pick up his walking cane. "Yeah, that's why they left the driver with two bashed-up legs in a cornfield. They are brutal, and they're criminals, Angel, and they have Caroline. No use in sugar-coatin' what's happened. We just have to face it."

"Have they been able to track her phone like Roderick said?"

"Not yet. Said it was possible, but there's been no signal to trace. Don't know what that means, but they're still working on it." Sam stood up and steadied himself with his cane. "Now, I know you said you couldn't handle any more surprises, but there's just one more little one."

Angel leaned forward in her rocker. "If it's just one, then tell me."

"Well, Roderick's sending one of his men to be here for a few days. Should be here within the hour. And one's headed down to be with Martha and J. That way these experts can monitor any communication that comes in here or down in Ferngrove and get that information unfiltered by us back to Rockwater. That's Command Central."

"Why, that's just great news." Angel stood up and took Sam's arm and headed toward the kitchen. "I'll call Hattie to get herself on over here. Cooking for this fellow will give us something to do, and we'll have the latest information right here at the kitchen table. We'll have our own Command Central."

"Just like my Angel to look on the bright side of things, thinking criminals are just poor and misguided and everything can be fixed with a fine meal. But it's early. Why don't you let Hattie be for another hour?" Sam leaned to kiss Angel's cheek. "Oh, I forgot. Ned will be by this morning to pick up the papers. We got him and Fred protected now from GiGi. That ought to make him sleep better tonight."

"And what irony is that? Fred doesn't even know he needs protection, yet you and Ned are taking care of him." Angel thought again about what she said. "And then, there's Caroline off in another country trying to do some good and help somebody, with not one thought she was in danger or in need of protection herself."

"Um-huh, but she knows she needs help now."

"But just like you're protecting Fred when he didn't know he needed it, somebody's protecting Caroline, don't you think?"

Sam smiled and continued his way to the kitchen.

Wednesday daybreak in the jungle

An unusual sound woke Lydia from her light sleep. The sky was still dark. She lay quietly, listening for the sound again, and moved her hand across Caroline's brow. It was wet like everything else—their clothes, their hair, the leaves, the blankets, everything wet. Her hopes that the dampness on Caroline's forehead was from sweating off a fever were short lived. She guessed Caroline's temperature was at least a hundred and one or maybe two. Not a good thing to be in a dark jungle crawling with only God knows what and without medicine or antibiotics. She had to get help.

Caroline woke from her touch. "Mama?"

"No, Caroline, it's Lydia. I'm right here. How's your pain?"

"Oh, Lydia, it's you?" Her voice was weak. "About the same. Could I have some water?"

"Certainly." As Lydia reached for the water bottle, the strange sound fractured the thick air again. "Caroline, did you hear that?"

"Umm."

"Is it what I think it is?" Lydia unscrewed the cap, raised Caroline's head, and put the water bottle to her lips.

Caroline sipped the water. "A rooster?"

"Yeah, a rooster. But it can't be. It's still dark." She let Caroline drink as much as she wanted but was careful not to waste one drop. Their three bottles might have to last for another few days.

A rooster was a domestic bird, and surely if one was crowing in the middle of the night, there must be a village near. Lydia knew from experiences on the plains in Africa that animals had an extra sense about weather and natural disasters. She could only hope that the rooster had escaped and the village and its residents weren't buried under eight layers of mud and debris.

"Maybe morning's coming soon." Caroline opened her eyes to look at the sky. Only darkness.

"Morning would be a welcome sight." She put Caroline's head back down. "Just maybe, somebody's looking out for us, Caroline. Roosters can fly, but the good news is they can't fly far."

"Why are you talking about roosters?"

"Because they make such a beautiful sound. They make such a beautiful sound." Lydia lay back down and hatched her plan. Caroline drifted off back to sleep or semiconsciousness.

At first signs of light, Lydia began to stir. She ate a half a tortilla and drank a few swallows of water. When she removed the blankets and plastic bags that had covered Caroline during the night, the sick girl lay motionless. Lydia pulled the jacket gently away from Caroline's chest. The swelling had increased across her collarbone and shoulder. *Still with fever, but thank God, no more bleeding.* Lydia took her Swiss Army knife and sliced off a corner of one of the blankets to make a small rag. She couldn't waste the drinking water, so she found a few large leaves that had cupped enough rainwater to wet the makeshift bath cloth.

She bathed Caroline's face and then moved to her injured leg. The knife sliced precisely through Caroline's pants leg so that Lydia could see the wound. She cleaned the area as best she could with the wet rag. The lesion, oozing bloody pus, appeared to be deep and about four inches long. The flesh around it was red and swollen with an angry streak creeping up the leg.

With Caroline repositioned and covered again, Lydia searched for more leaves holding rainwater. She was able to almost fill one of the empty water bottles. It would have to do when their bottled water gave out, but only as a last resort. It was probably clean enough but could still contain some bacteria or pathogen that could make either of them sick. Neither of them needed what that might bring.

When she had secured the site and had the water and what food was left at Caroline's fingertips, Lydia tried to wake her. "Caroline, can you wake up? We need to talk. Caroline?"

Caroline opened her eyes. "I'm so thirsty."

Lydia gave her another drink. "Caroline, can you eat? Would you try to eat this tortilla?"

"I don't think so."

"But you need to eat something."

"I'll try."

Lydia moved around behind Caroline. "Okay, I have to lift you up a bit so you won't get choked. I'll be as careful as I can." Again, she remembered the pain of broken ribs.

Caroline groaned loudly as Lydia held her up. "Oh, it really hurts to breathe." She used her right arm to move her torso, obviously trying to adjust to a less painful position. But when she took the tortilla from Lydia's hand and looked at it, she shook her head. "Lydia, I can't . . ." Caroline dropped the tortilla on the wet blanket as she wretched, spitting up the water she had just drunk. She grabbed her bad shoulder with her good hand.

Lydia tried to support her as her body convulsed. The nausea could be coming from infection, from pain, from only God knew what. She had to get help and fast.

Caroline coughed up the last bit of phlegm. "Back down, please. Just put me back down."

Lydia gently laid her back on the wet blankets. At least they were warm from Caroline's body temperature. "Stay with me, Caroline."

Lydia knew what had to be done.

The morning sun peeked through the limbs and leaves sheltering her. Caroline opened her eyes. "I won't leave you, Lydia."

"I know you won't leave me, but I must leave you and go for help. The rooster crowed until sunup, so there must be a village near here. I'll find someone and bring help. Do you understand me? This is the only way, Caroline."

Caroline nodded.

"Look. Look, Caroline."

Caroline opened her eyes again, trying to make sense of her surroundings. She felt Lydia moving around her.

"Here is an extra bottle of water right next to your hand. Drink it when you get thirsty, but try to make it last the day." She paused. "Caroline, stay with me. I have to take the phone. It's no good to you anyway. I know we came a long way to get to where we are and the mudslide changed things, but I plan to be back before dark. Hopefully, I'll find a place where I can get signal. But here's the bottle of water." Lydia placed the bottle in Caroline's hand and wrapped her fingers around it. "I want you to hold this in your hand until I get back, do you hear me?"

Caroline's voice was weak. "Until the rooster crows in the morning?"

"No, no. I'll do my best to be back before the rooster crows."

"I'll not stop praying until you return, Lydia."

"You do that." Lydia stood up, picked up the torn pieces of blanket and plastic, stuffed them into her vest pockets, and looked again at Caroline. "I'll mark my path, and I'll bring help. Sleep, my young friend, until I return."

Caroline closed her eyes. She didn't know how much

time had passed, but when she tried to lift her head, she saw Lydia in the distance, climbing muddy rocks, grasping at low-hanging limbs, trudging on until she was out of sight. She lowered her head, closed her eyes, and prayed.

Roderick's worry had turned to impatience. Briefcase in hand, he stood at the door to the gray van, ready to climb in. The young Guatemalan carting bags from the front door of the hotel spoke to him. "*Señor*, what you like me do with Miss Carlyle's bags?"

"Put them in the van, please."

Goodluck approached. "Sir, we don't really need to take them. The manager said he would store the bags."

"We're not storing any bags. Put them all on the van. Caroline and Dr. Pipkin will need their things when we find them."

"But, sir, we have to come back to Xela for the plane anyway."

"No, Goodluck, you and Acer have to come back for the plane. I'm taking Caroline from the lake directly to the city, and you can meet us there for the flight home."

"Yes, sir. I understand."

"I thought you would. Can you tell the others we're ready to go?" Roderick opened the door to the van and climbed into the seat behind the driver. He left the front passenger's seat for Goodluck.

Everyone had traveled light and tossed their bags in the back of the van as they passed by. Goodluck ushered Dr. Morris and Acer to the very back seat and James and Thomas to the seat behind Roderick and Leo before climbing into the passenger's seat. He spoke quickly to the driver and then got out, leaving his van door open.

Leo leaned forward. "Where's he going? *Donde*?"

"*Agua, señor. Un minuto.*"

Leo turned to the passengers. "He's gone back for water."

Goodluck returned to the van with two cases of water, put them in the floorboard at his feet, climbed in, and shut the door. "Let's go. We'll pick up Maricela on the way." He opened the case of water and started passing out the bottles. "Here, keep one of these on you. At this altitude, drinking water keeps you from getting altitude sickness. We have work to do. No time for headaches and nausea."

Roderick took the bottle of water without even looking at Goodluck. They were moving now, and he knew the others were talking, but he had no idea what they were saying. Strategic thinking had always been his long suit, but it was useless now. He had been doing deals long enough to know that plans and deals change on a dime, sometimes for unimaginable and unforeseen reasons. *Something's changed. These guys are amateurs. Should be anxious to get their money. Why haven't they called? What does that mean? Something's changed. Something's happened that altered their plans.*

After nearly a half hour's driving the narrow streets, the driver made a quick stop to pick up Maricela. She entered the van with a small backpack and a large roll of maps under her arm and looked at Leo. "*Señor*, may I sit next to you? I need to speak with Goodluck and the driver."

"Of course, but wait a minute. You take this seat. I'll be on the phone anyway. Better if I sit in the back." Leo's phone rang as he was making the move.

It wasn't the stop that broke Roderick's trance. It was the sound of Leo's phone that brought him back to the loathsome reality that was now his. *News. Something's happening.* He sat rigid, his heart pounding in his ears and every muscle in his body tense. His fists were clenched, holding on to his last strand of hope. He hardly breathed, waiting for any sign from Leo, a word or a change in expression.

No one spoke while Leo was on the phone. The air was tense with anticipation that the kidnappers had made contact. They rode the cobblestone streets through Xela in silence and had reached the main highway to Sololá when Leo finished his conversation. "No news. No calls from the abductors. I've sent one man to Ferngrove to be with the Carlyles and another to Moss Point to be the Meadows couple. If they hear anything, it'll be patched through to Rockwater, and we'll know immediately."

Thomas turned around in his seat to look at Leo. "What about Caroline's phone? Any ping? Any activity?"

"Nope, nothing."

James spoke to Roderick, "Caroline said she would have a satellite phone. How can there be no signal on a satellite phone?"

Roderick didn't move a muscle but answered resolutely, "There is no signal on her phone because my assistant—that is, my *former* assistant—Liz Bevins, did not order a satellite phone as I instructed. She only got a cell phone for Caroline's use in Guatemala."

Leo's voice carried all the way to the front of the van. "Not to worry, guys. We'll get it. It's just a matter of time."

Roderick knew that Leo prided himself in managing the impossible, and he had wondered more than a time or two if Leo had a thing for Liz. If he did, he'd have to look for her back in Louisville now.

Again, they rode in mostly silence. Roderick could hear James and Thomas whispering at times, and occasionally Goodluck spoke something in broken Spanish to the driver. Maricela studied the maps and passed them back and forth to Goodluck When a phone rang, seven people reached for cell phones.

Dr. Morris spoke briefly to her caller, and then announced what she had learned. "Okay, my friends, we have news. That was my contact in Guatemala City. We have a name. They showed the photo of the man with the ponytail to the clerk at the Quinta Real. He checked into the hotel with the name Duarte Chavarria and registered a blue pickup. They are working now to verify the license plate. Officer Alcocer will call again soon."

Roderick turned in his seat to look at her. "What about an address? Do we know where this Chavarria lives?"

"Officer Alcocer is trying to confirm that. They cannot be certain this Chavarria registered under his real name and gave truthful information, but they are checking phone records. They are checking everything."

Thomas chimed in, "Yeah, just how stupid would that be? Register your real name and address at a hotel you're staking out for a kidnapping?"

Leo retorted, "Can't be too smart or he would have asked for a lot more money."

Roderick was quiet and detached. He heard conversations, but he wasn't listening. His thoughts were of Caroline and what would happen to this Duarte Chavarria if he found him.

It was near noon when they made a stop at a roadside park for a quick bathroom break before starting their descent to Panajachel, the town that would be their headquarters. Lined up like magpies on a telephone line, Mayan women with their babies tied to their backs displayed their wares on blankets covering the ground and on homemade tables. As the passengers got out of the van, the local peddlers stormed them with their trinkets hanging from the hands and arms, all chanting, "I give you good price," which were probably the only English words they knew. Maricela and Dr. Morris tried to shoo the women and children away.

While the guys found their way to the primitive cinderblock bathrooms with no doors, Roderick stood at the edge of the mountain and gazed toward the south. With crystal-blue deep water, Lake Atitlán appeared like a jewel in the distance, edged by mountains rising from the shoreline. Bottom-heavy clouds shrouded some of the peaks flanking the water's edge.

Maricela approached Roderick. "*Señor*?"

"The water. It's the color of her eyes."

"Pardon me, *señor*. It is beautiful, no?"

Wistfully, he answered, "Yes, it is beautiful. My love, my life is out there somewhere."

"We will find her, *señor*. We will find her." Maricela pointed to the east of where Roderick was gazing. "Look. There is Volcán Atitlán, and over there is Volcán Tomilán. And that one? That is Volcán San Pedro, all named for the apostles. The clouds, they cover the top this morning."

A beautiful young woman dressed in her Mayan *huipil* approached them. The dress she held billowed in the hillside breeze. The white fabric bodice was embroidered in bright yellow, red, blue, and teal flowers that matched the border of flowers and green leaves around the hem. Roderick looked at her and the dress she held. He imagined that Caroline would give life to such a dress.

"*Señor, para su esposa. Es bonita.*"

Roderick looked into the woman's brown eyes and then at the dress. "What does she want, Maricela?"

"She wants you to buy the dress for your wife because it is beautiful."

Roderick reached for his wallet. "How much is the dress?" It sounded like Maricela was bartering with the young woman. He pulled three hundred dollar bills out of his wallet and flashed them at Maricela. "Is this enough?"

"Oh, *señor*, she will take twenty-five dollars."

Roderick handed the woman a hundred-dollar bill and said, "Gracias. My wife will be more than beautiful in this dress."

The young woman's brown eyes got even larger. She hurriedly stuffed the crisp white dress into a worn plastic bag, tossed it to Roderick, and skipped off giggling and calling to her friends.

Maricela practically shoved Roderick into the van. "Quickly, *señor*, they will all come to sell you something. Hurry."

The others coming from the facilities had to wade through a mob of the peddling women and begging children to get to the van doors. Goodluck kept the women busy looking at their jewelry and buying leather belts while the others got into the van.

As they drove away, no one asked Roderick what he had purchased. He sat erect, his feet flat on the floorboard, and his eyes closed.

I will see you in this dress, Caroline. I will see you.

Chapter 23

Feeling Alone

Wednesday afternoon at Moss Point

Angel stopped in front of Sam's chair and looked at him as he slept. The muscles in his face were relaxed, and the chiseled lines of worry that had creased his brow for the last day and a half were smooth. She hated to wake him to the reality of Caroline's abduction again. She leaned and pressed her cheek to his temple and whispered, "Sam, time to wake up. Mr. Handley's here."

Sam woke quickly, almost startled, from his deep sleep and sat up. "Okay, he's here. Let's get this show on the road."

"Just sit for a minute. He came in here looking like an FBI agent, driving up in his black sedan and dressed in his gray suit and sunglasses. No telling what the neighbors will think."

"Why didn't you wake me up?" Sam moved forward in his chair and reached for his cane.

"Don't get up just yet. We've handled everything. Mr. Handley's setting up his computer in the sunroom. Hattie helped him get the card table. He's planning to sleep out there in the daybed and stay next to his computer and phone. That way, he's near the kitchen and the bathroom, and he'll have everything he needs. But what he needs now is a half an hour to set up his equipment." Angel sat down in her rocker.

"That setup will keep him isolated in case anybody stops by. Nobody needs to know he's here."

"On another subject, I talked to Gretchen again while you were asleep, so now we're expecting more guests. She is so worried and frightened, and she wants to come here."

Sam sat back in his chair. "Of course, she does. We should have thought of that earlier. It'll be good to see her, but what about Bella and Karina? Aren't they in school?"

"No. Karina's staying in Durham, but there's nothing to keep Bella from coming, and Sarah's coming too. She can stay here with us, and Gretchen and Bella can stay down in Caroline's studio. Gretchen says Bella's extremely agitated, and Sarah thinks Bella has some kind of unexplainable connection to Caroline that's causing her to be so upset. She won't eat, and she plays the second movement of the *Rockwater Suite* constantly until she is so tired she falls asleep. This has been going on since Monday night about the time Caroline was abducted. Sounds like Gretchen's growing weary from dealing with Bella and worrying about Caroline."

"My heavens above. That Bella's a complete mystery to me, but we'll just all worry and fret together."

Angel saw the crease in Sam's forehead deepen. "I'm just praying we won't have to worry much longer."

"Just long enough for Caroline to be safely back at home." Sam strummed his fingers along the leather armrest of his chair. "Angel, I don't know how we're going to keep this secret much longer. We have a black sedan parked in the driveway, and now a group coming in from North Carolina. You know how folks around this town have eagle eyes and flapping tongues."

For the first time in two days, the hint of a smile curled Angel's lips. "Sure do, and Hattie and I have it all figured out. Nobody knows about Caroline except you, Tom, Ned, Hattie, and me. Tom's bound to keep quiet as an attorney, and Ned would cut his own tongue out before he'd say a word about this. So, Hattie's going to tell her kids that I'm a bit under the weather and she's just moving in for a few days to take care of me. Once Gretchen and Sarah and the girls get here, they won't be getting out and about. Even if they do, we can just say they're back for a visit. And if we need anything, Hattie's here to go get it."

"Yes, but what about all these cars parked in the driveway? You know the neighbors will be calling, and Delia Mullins is always smelling a story to put in the paper."

"Already took care of that. Ned and Fred are coming by to get our car. That way, there'll be room in the garage for Mr. Handley's car and Gretchen's. Ned said he'd keep our car in his barn until we're ready for it. Nobody will see anything unusual."

"I do believe if I had stayed asleep thirty more minutes, you might have arranged to get Caroline home." Sam stood. "Let me go meet this Mr. Handley."

Angel leaned forward in her chair, put her elbows on her knees, and buried her face in her hands. Her voice broke as she tried to speak. "Oh, dear Jesus, how I wish I could make it so."

Sam stroked the back of her neck. "I know you do, my Angel. We're both praying it will be so."

Angel stood and nestled herself against his shoulder. "I'd trade my life for that girl's, you know. I've lived my life, and she's just beginning hers. It's just not fair, Sam. It's just not fair."

"I know. Life's not fair. Never has been. And life's certainly brought Caroline more trouble than her share. But she's in God's hands, and there's no better place to be." He squeezed her. "Come on, now, let's go see if Mr. Handley is ready for business."

"You're always right, Sam. I just want Caroline to be here where I can touch her with my own hands." She chose to keep her deepest thoughts silent as they walked out of the room. *If Caroline's truly in God's hands, she's with her first love, David, and she's happy. If that's not where she is, then Roderick has to find her and bring her home. Either way, Caroline will be fine, but I won't be until she's here.*

Wednesday afternoon at the Hotel Atitlán in Panajachel

The van pulled into the Hotel Atitlán's entrance. Roderick sat quietly as Goodluck hopped out and opened the side door for Dr. Morris.

She was getting her phone and papers out of her bag. "I will return in a few moments. I made the reservations, but I want to make certain the accommodations are what I requested."

Goodluck assisted her out of the van. "I'll get the bags out and ready for check-in." He stacked everything at the rear of the van and left the group to walk over to an emergency vehicle parked alongside the building and to a small group of men who looked like paramedics.

Roderick and the others were out of the van when Dr. Morris returned with room keys. "All is good. Not many guests in the middle of the week, especially in the rainy season. They gave us a wing to ourselves." She looked at the hotel registration paper and began to distribute the keys. "Maricela, you and I will share a room, and so will you, James and Thomas. The rest of you have private rooms with phones and internet connections."

Dr. Morris led the group toward the Spanish-colonial entrance and pointed them to the left hallway as they entered the lobby. "All our rooms are down this way. The restaurant is lakeside and is open if anyone is hungry. What would you like us to do now, Roderick?"

"Why don't we get settled and then get together." He looked at his watch. "Let's say half an hour. Do we have a suite where we can assemble, or is there a conference room?"

"Yes, Leo is in the suite at the end of the hall."

"Then, let's meet there at four o'clock."

Roderick was about to pick up his bag when Goodluck returned.

"Sorry, sir. Just talking to the guys over there. Seems like they've had so much rain here in the last few days, they had a huge landslide not too far from here."

Dr. Morris stepped forward. "That is not uncommon here. The soil is made up of volcanic ash and is not so solid in the mountains. Did they speak of damages and loss of life?"

"No. They don't know anything yet. They're still trying to get there. Apparently, it took out some of the roads on the backside of a ridge."

Maricela pulled out her maps. "It will take many days to have information. I know of mudslides in this area that wiped out villages and hundreds of people. Do the men have good maps?"

"Didn't think to ask about the maps. Maybe we should go back and talk to them." Goodluck stepped nearer to Maricela and took her bag. "Come on, I have your bag. You'll get more info. We're in the Quiché region, right?"

"Yes. That is why we came here. Paco heard the men speak in Quiché, and he heard them speak of the lake."

Roderick walked with purpose, leading them to the vehicle. "Then let's go talk to these guys. If they've been driving up and down these mountain roads looking for survivors of a mudslide, they might have seen a blue truck."

Maricela struggled to keep up with him. "Did they say when the mudslide was?"

"Some time yesterday."

Roderick knocked on the window of the vehicle and pointed to Maricela. The medics got out and listened to Maricela's story about Caroline and Dr. Pipkin. Maricela unrolled the maps, and the driver pointed out the general area where the mudslide had occurred and assured them anyone in its direct path had had little warning and would have been buried alive. Before driving away, they agreed to look for any blue pickup as they made another trek to the other side of the ridge.

Goodluck gave them his contact information and explained they'd be staying at the hotel. He helped Maricela roll up the map. "How long will it take to search that area?"

"Not very long once they get there. They will only make a quick scan for survivors."

Roderick asked, "But what about the casualties and recovering the bodies?"

Maricela shook her head. "No. In Guatemala, it is our custom to bury our dead as soon as possible so they have a quick passage to heaven. The tribal people out this way would also bury the dead with their treasured items so their spirits will not return to haunt them."

Goodluck glanced at the mountains against the horizon. "Guess that makes sense. Not like in America where we spend fortunes to give folks fancy funerals."

"Not here. Here, people would think the mudslide

caused the deaths and burials to come quickly, and they were buried with the things they treasured. No reason to uncover their bodies for another burial."

Roderick stood in silence, wanting to run and never stop, his gut wrenching at the thought of his beautiful Caroline lost and buried and with nothing or no one she loved.

Wednesday afternoon in the jungle

Lydia's legs were beginning to cramp from the constant climbing. She found a spot where the sun peeked through the canopy of leaves, sat down, and looked at her watch. Her father had worn this watch his entire adult life, resisting the traditional fob and pocket watch used by his university colleagues. At his death fourteen years ago, Lydia had inherited the timepiece, had a band designed to fit it and her bony wrist, and had worn it every day since. The crystal was so foggy with moisture that she could see the gold hands just enough to know they were in the same position they had been hours ago. The watch had stopped, but her feet told her she had been walking for hours. Without her compass that had been in her backpack, she wondered if she'd been walking in circles.

Although most of her time in Guatemala had been spent inside a hotel or locked in a dark shack, she knew that daylight came early and so did darkness. The sun's rays, when she could see them, slanted through the thick foliage. Not many daylight hours left and no more time for rest. She took a sip of water, secured the bottle in her vest, and tied another piece of the blanket to a limb where it could easily be seen before she started climbing again.

Her original plan to descend to the bottom of the mountain had changed as she neared the area of the mudslide. Surging mud had cut a swath at least a hundred and twenty yards wide through the jungle and taken down trees and anything else in its path. She had no idea what was left in that direction. The destruction reminded her that even though Caroline lay alone in the jungle with a broken collarbone, their escaping alive bordered on the miraculous. A mass of mud and debris could have buried them. Treetops poked through the mounds of wet earth where they had walked only twenty-four hours ago. Africa had shown Lydia plenty of devastation from drought and wind, but never the force of moving earth and gushing water like this. Finding help below seemed a long shot in spite of a crowing rooster, but she knew there was civilization on the other side of this mountain.

Descending had wasted valuable daylight and was no longer a sensible option. Lydia began climbing back toward what she thought was the site of the lean-to, knowing there was a road leading to a village from there. She followed the edge of the mudslide, tying colorful strips of the shredded blanket tied to low-hanging limbs. These strips would mark her way back to Caroline when she found help.

The jungle was silent now except for the birds, which she never saw, and an occasional roll of distant thunder. The blue butterflies that had flickered around her earlier had disappeared. At times, there had been so many she thought she could hear the flutter of their wings.

As she climbed, she found it more and more difficult to breathe in the heavy, moist air and altitude and wondered if she'd ever make it to the top. Traveling in Africa, the horizon was always in view, and her guides were often impressed with her sense of direction and distance, but this mountainous rainforest was foreign to her. She thought she couldn't be that far from where they'd started, but everything looked different and disorienting. To see the horizon, she had to climb. Besides, if she could get to the top, she might be able to find the road the abductors had taken from the village below to the shack. She remembered lying in the back of that pickup when it left the main highway and descended for quite a while until they reached an area with lights and sounds of a busy street market. Then they'd started their ascent on a road that had left her back bruised from the constant jarring over bumps and the jolting of hairpin turns. The road was there. She had to find it. It would lead to help.

A path parallel to the mudslide seemed the most prudent since it would get her back to the hovel or to where the hovel was. As she climbed, she noticed wooden planks protruding from the mud. They had to be from a wooden structure since she had seen no other structures during their escape. The signs were good and eased her fears of running into their abductors. Paulino and his ponytailed friend were either buried under the mud or had fled the scene assuming their kidnapped prey was dead. She kept climbing until the trees no longer hid the sky.

Finally—light. But the red glow of the sun was low in the heavens. Once it touched the horizon, it would melt quickly out of sight. She knew she wouldn't make it to get help and back to Caroline before dark. Not one to second guess herself, Lydia began to doubt her decision to leave Caroline alone.

She clambered farther to the top, but even with this vantage point, it was difficult to get her bearings, just looking down on a sea of green foliage and muck.

Stepping carefully across the mud that had already dried, she could see no building or vehicle of any kind, only the river of sludge below that looked like lava topped with a trail of cinderblocks. The hut where their abductors had stayed was made of concrete blocks. And the wooden planks below were probably from the wooden lean-to where she and Caroline had been captives. This had to be its location.

The earth had moved and carried with it what could have been her burial ground. The hovel was demolished, gone. What was once this ridge was now strewn down the side of the mountain, and she could only hope that it had not taken a section of the road to the cabin with it.

In the last light of the day, Lydia paced, searching for any sign of the road, a path, any trail that would lead her to a village below this ridge. There, twenty yards ahead—ruts. Fresh ruts made since the mudslide.

Late afternoon at the Hotel Atitlán

With the phone in his hand, Roderick paced in front of the window overlooking manicured rose gardens like the ones back at Rockwater. His gut was in knots being here in this hotel, looking out on such beauty and feeling that Caroline was somewhere near, either buried or in the hands of brutes. His weakened ability to concentrate made it difficult to listen to his sister. He paced, holding the phone tightly in his grip. "I'm glad you and Gretchen are with the Meadowses now. They love Caroline like a daughter, and this cannot be good for them at their ages. Angel has a weak heart, and she doesn't need this stress."

"I think our being here helps. It gives Angel someone to take care of and Sam someone to talk to, and Bella's not as agitated. I can't explain it, but I think Bella has some kind of connection to Caroline, Rod. I think she knew Caroline was in trouble. But she's quiet now. They're staying down in

Caroline's cottage, and Bella just sits on the piano bench with her head bowed. Her hands are touching the piano keys, but she doesn't play. She's completely still and calm."

"So, if this connection to Caroline is real, I hope this calmness means something good."

"Me, too, little brother, but what about you? How are you holding up?"

He stopped in front of the window and stared at the lake in the distance. "Not so good. Can't sleep, can't eat. I just feel like I'm moving around from one place to another, gathering little bits of information from this one and that one, and I can do nothing. Never have liked feeling helpless. If I just hadn't . . ." He stopped in midsentence.

"If you hadn't what, Roderick?"

"Nothing. I'm not making any sense. It's just that I look out across these mountains, and I know she's out there somewhere, and I don't know where to start."

"From everything you've told me, you're in the place to start, and you don't have to find her all by yourself, Rod. You have a name, a description of the vehicle, and you have the locals involved."

"Yeah, but Leo's getting no intel. Nothing." He looked at his watch. "Nearly thirty-six hours since any contact from the kidnappers and no activity from Caroline's phone. So here we sit waiting on information about this Chavarria. If we could just find out where he lives or if he has family in the area . . . Hell, we don't even know if that's his real name."

"You'll find him, Rod. And you'll find Caroline. They have no reason to harm her. They only want money. Remember that. They have nothing to gain by harming her."

Roderick's voice broke. "But I just can't bear to think they have her, Sarah, or what she must be going through and how scared she must be. She could be hurt . . . or worse. Why? Why did I let her come by herself? Why her and why now? Hasn't she been through enough?" He stopped when his voice cracked. "Guess this could be the perfect ending to her love story with David Summers—both dead in some godforsaken rainforest in Guatemala. And if she's gone, that's the end of me. I cannot go on without her, Sarah. My life's no good without her."

"Stop it right now. You must not think those thoughts. Caroline loves you with all that she is, and she's planning to spend the rest of her life with you. She's out there waiting for you, Roderick, for *you*. Now go find her, do you hear?"

"I hear you, sis."

"You need to be doing something. What can you do right now, right this minute?"

"What I'd like to do is to get my bare hands on Chavarria. But what can I do? Nothing. I can't do anything except wait and pray. It's getting dark and too late to start the search, and we're waiting to hear from the locals." He paused. "I can't talk any longer, Sarah. I really need to go."

Roderick put the phone on the bedside table and paced in front of the window and fought the urge to scream or wail. Instead he picked up the hand-carved wooden figure from the bedside table and threw it across the room.

Late afternoon in Moss Point

Gretchen sat in Caroline's favorite chintz chair, thinking and praying, looking through the window into the garden where she had spent so many hours with Caroline. Her memories of sipping tea and sharing rich conversation were no solace. They only reminded her of what she might never have again. All she could do was to pray, asking God to preserve Caroline's life and thanking him that Bella was calm.

There came a gentle knock at the kitchen door. She rose to answer. "Come in, Sarah." Gretchen led her to the great room near Bella and the piano. "I'm glad you're here. Bella's calm, and I've been sitting here praying while she just sits quietly at the piano. Sometimes she just whispers something that I cannot make out."

"I think God's answering your prayers. I just came down to give you the latest news. They think they know who took Caroline, and they're near where they think she might be. Roderick has help, and he has many of the locals involved."

"That news is good?"

"I'm praying it's good. It still leaves us hope that she is alive and will return to us."

Bella stood from the piano and walked to Caroline's desk. Gretchen and Sarah sat in silence, watching her. Bella picked up the mosaic piece from the desk, took it to the window, and held it in the late-afternoon light.

Sarah asked, "What do you think she's doing?"

"I do not know. That is the piece Bella made for Caroline. Once, when we were visiting, Caroline broke her favorite teapot. I asked her for the shards because I knew what Bella could do with them. She made the hand from plaster of paris, and then the heart, and glued the broken pieces to cover the mold and make such a beautiful work of art." Gretchen stood and began to move toward Bella.

"No, please don't disturb her. Let her experience whatever it is she's experiencing."

Gretchen sat back down. After several minutes, Sarah broke the silence with a whisper, "Oh, how I wish I knew what is in Bella's mind and heart right now."

When there was only a glow of light left in the sky, Bella

returned the piece to the desk and went to the piano and began to play and hum.

Gretchen and Sarah looked at each other. Sarah asked, "What is that beautiful piece she's playing?"

"I do not know. She has never played it before. But it is lovely."

Sarah smiled peacefully. "I guess Bella just answered my question—my question about knowing what's in her heart and mind. I'm glad it's beautiful."

Sundown in the jungle

Furled green leaves on low-hanging limbs created a natural awning above Caroline. Her body shivered from the chill of fever and the cool breeze that whispered through the foliage when the sun slipped behind the ridge.

Her mind drifted in dreams. There was Bella, beautiful Bella, with the late-afternoon light around her, making her hair golden. They were picking up acorns on the sidewalk in Moss Point, making up melodies to go with the rhythms of the acorns as they thumped against the bottom of their tin bucket. Then they were sitting on the grassy bank of the pond in the Meadows Park, watching the swans, and Bella's voice was violin-like as she hummed Saint-Saëns' "Le Cygne." Snow was falling and building drifts against the rock walls in the terraced garden at Rockwater. Bella's hair shone like spun silver in the moonlight reflecting off the snow. They began singing "Silent Night." Always with Bella, there was the music.

But there was the small child with dark-brown hair and sad, chocolate-colored eyes, her face smudged and her hands dirty. Her song was unfamiliar, but haunting and rising from a deep place. She closed her eyes, and her cello-like voice sang her story.

Then she was gone.

Bella took her place, standing in the sunlight with Bel Canto, the songbird Roderick had given her for Christmas, perched on her finger. They sang together . . . such an enchanting sound.

Water trickled from the curled fronds above Caroline's head, spattering softly against her face and waking her. She opened her eyes, slowly trying to focus them, and looked straight above her. The slivers of light that had earlier been a bright blue were now a dark bluish-gray, and the rainforest's bright greens were almost navy in the darkening sky. She had wakened from music and pleasant dreams to her waking nightmare. She was hurting and alone, except for a bird singing in the distance. The bottle of water Lydia had placed in her hand early this morning was now empty. Lydia had not come back. Her pain was all there was to keep her company.

She lay still, mesmerized by the butterflies swirling in circles above her, their wings trembling from brown to blue. She remembered the dream she'd had months ago—the dream where she was hanging on to the limb on the riverbank while surging water pulled at her body, dragging the life from her. Instinctively, she had clung to life and to the leafless limb until it grew strong and sprouted new leaves. And in her dream there had been a vortex of butterflies churning around her, as though their whirling wings were keeping her head above water.

In her dream she'd reached toward David, only to see him step away from her and into the light. But a voice had called to her from the other side of the stream. Roderick.

Roderick. He must be so worried. Maybe he could have found me if we had stayed put. Where's Lydia? She's not coming back now, not today. It's too late. Maybe tomorrow when the morning comes again. What do I smell and what's this sweet taste in my mouth? I should try to eat something and drink more water.

Trying to lift her body reminded her she was injured. Even breathing was difficult. She raised herself up with her good arm, but reaching for the second water bottle took more strength than she had. Bracing herself, she took in her surroundings. There was just enough light for her to see the carefully arranged slices of dragon fruit outlining her body and the blue butterflies feeding on their sweetness and swirling above her.

She remembered.

Was it another dream? The girl with the chocolate-brown eyes and the haunting song.

Chapter 24

Prayer Meetings

Vespers at Hogar Luis Amigo

Hector was first in the line of children picking up their trays from the counter and finding their places at the tables filling the dining hall. When Sister Gabriela became the orphanage director four years ago, she'd had the long rectangular tables in the dining hall removed and replaced with round ones. No one, not even she, would sit at the head of a table. Mealtime would feel like family time, with everyone having an equal place at the table. Every evening, there was a fresh flower on one table. The children seated at this table knew to leave one chair vacant for their special dinner guest, Christ.

On each plate boiled cabbage, potatoes, and carrots encircled a smear of refried beans and one boiled egg to be washed down by fresh lemonade. Dessert was fresh mango slices and one wafer cookie. Not one child picked up a fork until everyone was seated and Sister Gabriela stood in the center of the room.

She dried her hands on her apron as she stepped

through the kitchen door into the dining hall. The room was quiet with only the whispers of children and an occasional giggle. As she took her place, she smoothed her apron and adjusted the crucifix hanging around her neck. "Welcome to dinner. And where is our honored guest sitting this evening?"

The excited children from table seven raised their hands, pointed to the empty chair, and raised their voices, "He is here. He is here."

"Then let us welcome Him and be thankful for our food." She pressed her hand across the wooden crucifix and pressed it near her heart. "We are grateful, our Lord, for the food You have provided through our friends and neighbors in our community. Thank You for our family around these tables, and thank You for the sisters who labored to prepare our meal. And now, Lord, we welcome You as our honored guest. Amen."

The echo of "amen" reverberated around the painted stucco room.

"Children, before we eat this evening, I have something to tell you. Tonight is a special night. When we have finished our meal, you will have an extra hour of free time before vespers. You may play or study for that hour. And, our vespers service will not be in the chapel. It will be in the prayer garden this evening. Bring a jacket to stay warm. We'll gather at the front door when you hear the bell and walk down together." Sister Gabriela looked around the room for Adriana. "Adriana, let us see if you have been a good listener. Could you please tell the rest of the children what I just said?"

Adriana, eight-years old and their newest resident, recited Sister Gabby's announcement almost word for word.

"Thank you, Adriana. You are an excellent listener and speaker. Now, let's enjoy our mealtime together."

Sister Gabriela had prayed and planned for the vespers service all afternoon. Telling the children that Caroline and Dr. Pipkin had been kidnapped would raise so many questions and would also remind many of them of their own experiences of abandonment and their own pain. She finished her dinner quickly. Before excusing herself, she asked Sister Rosario to please ring the bell at seven o'clock and bring the children down to the prayer garden. She left the table and walked alone to her quarters.

Her cell-sized room was monastic with a single cot, a wooden straight chair, a desk that also served as a bedside table, and a rustic wooden armoire for her clothes. The walls were bare except for the unframed, frayed-edged drawing of a lily. No leaves, no grass, no sky, only a white background for the blossom, but the pale-yellow petals and mossy-green stem had been created with precise detail. The drawing had been a gift from a girl named Liliana who had grown up in the orphanage and was now a nurse. She drew the picture after Sister Gabriela had read to her the passage of Scripture reminding her that God took care of even the lilies.

Sister Gabriela stared at the drawing. She kept her questions hidden from everyone except God. The "why" questions that crept into her thinking when someone like little Adriana showed up at the orphanage, malnourished, bruised, weak, and sad. The questions that asked why the good suffered and why Caroline and Dr. Pipkin were snatched from them. The lily. God had taken care of Liliana through the orphanage, and Sister Gabriela trusted God to take care of Caroline and Dr. Pipkin too.

The one window in her quarters framed the mountains to the east. She was most often sitting in that chair praying at sunrise, waiting to greet the day. But now she stood in front of the window, letting go of the last light of day as she prayed, mostly for wisdom in talking to the children.

The tinkling bell arrested her from her prayers. She quickly grabbed her warmest shawl and left alone through the back door. If she walked briskly down the quarter-mile path bordering the corn patch, she would be there when the children arrived. The pebbles burrowing into her tender feet reminded her the soles of her shoes were growing thin.

The northeast corner of the property was a ruggedly steep slope, not good for growing vegetables. But over the years, the sisters and the children had created natural terraces by moving some of the rocks and planting flowers. Small boulders provided places to sit. The natural amphitheater had become their gathering place for prayer and for special plays and performances. The cornstalks and the mountains had joined their audience on many an evening or a Sunday afternoon.

The sun had disappeared behind the mountains to the west, and the full moon was rising over Volcán San Pedro to the east. Above her spread the perfect night sky. Sister Gabriela stood on the hillside and looked at the blanket of yellow-blossomed wild mustard covering the fields below—the same blossoms the injured Paco had crawled through Monday night to blow the horn of the van for help.

The children entered the garden area two by two and found places to sit. The older girls made certain all the sisters had places to sit first. Then they found their own places and held the smaller children in their laps. It had taken years of persistence and diligent patience to create an atmosphere where children behaved this way, respectful and putting others first. Life had taught them to snatch and grab and take care of themselves because no one else would. Now the older ones did as much teaching of the younger children as the sisters did.

When everyone was seated, Sister Gabriela began. "*Esta noche es especial . . .* This night is special because I have something to tell you. I want you to close your eyes and imagine this with me." She paused in silence before beginning, "There was once a large house on the top of a green hill, and in this house lived many beautiful, brown-eyed, happy-faced children. And one day, someone rang the bell at the front door. When the sister opened the door, there were two women. One was a friend whom the children had not seen for a while, and the other was a new friend."

Sister Gabriela heard low giggles and a whispered voice. "*Carolina y la médica de África.*"

"That is right. You are so smart. You already know my story. You see, our friends came to visit us because they need our help. Our friends knew of other houses in Guatemala where there were beautiful, brown-eyed children who had sad faces, not happy faces like ours. Carolina and Dr. Pipkin had an idea about how we could work together to put smiles on the sad-faced children. They wanted us to sing our songs and travel all around the world telling others the stories of the sad-faced children. Then, when people heard our music and our stories, they would join us to help give the sad children what they needed to make them smile."

Five-year old Luis, who was sitting in Analie's lap, started to clap his hands. Sister Gabriela had no desire to stop him, and in just a few seconds all the children joined him with applause echoing through the paths of the terraced garden.

Allow them to be joyful for just a few more moments before their faces become sad.

The last corals and lavenders were gone from the horizon, and the stars sparkled against the night sky. The pale moon grew brighter, almost like a halo around San Pedro's peak.

"I bring you to the prayer garden tonight because our friends need us to pray for them." Sister Gabby paused and swallowed. "On Monday evening when our friends left us to return to Xela, they were taken away by two men. These men injured our friend, Paco, the driver who brought Carolina and Dr. Pipkin to us. Paco is in the hospital with broken legs, and we do not know where Carolina and Dr. Pipkin are."

Most of the children sat in utter silence, but a few started to weep and moan as was their native custom upon hearing of one's death. It was not in Sister Gabby to tell them not to cry. She wanted to weep herself. She did not rush her silence nor their weeping.

"We are going to help our friends by having a special service of prayer for them this evening. I want to ask you something: why would I bring you out here tonight? It is cold and uncomfortable."

Analie spoke up. "Here we can pray and not see your tears in the darkness, Sister Gabby."

"Yours is a very good answer, Analie, and it is true. But there is more. Look at the sky, the beautiful night sky that goes on forever with the stars and the moon over San Pedro. Who sprinkled the stars in the heavens?"

All the children, young and old, responded, "God did."

"And who caused the sun to come up this morning?"

Again, the children answered, "God did."

"Who cares for the lilies growing in our garden, and who cares about Paco and Carolina and Dr. Pipkin?" She paused.

The answer was a harmony of children's voices, some saying, "God does," and others saying, "I do."

"Oh, you are so right, my sweet ones. God cares about our friends, and so do we. I wanted you to look into the night sky and see the heavens and remember the One who thought of the heavens and spoke them into existence. He cares so much about His children that He even provides light in the darkness. We want to ask Him to watch over Carolina, Dr. Pipkin, and Paco and bring them back safely to us. Every night at vespers, the other sisters and I say the prayers for you, but tonight is different. I want each of you to pray in your own way for our friends. You may say your words in your heart or you may say them out loud."

Some of the children sat with their eyes closed tightly, their lips moving in silence, and others of them fell to their knees, holding their heads in their hands and praying out loud. But the most beautiful of all were the young ones mimicking the older ones who knew how to pray. Sister Gabriela held her rosary and silently prayed for her friends in danger and for the children in her care and for the sad-faced children who might never smile.

"O God, hear the prayers of Your children. Wrap Carolina and Dr. Pipkin in Your strong arms and bring them back to us. Amen."

Wednesday night in Moss Point

Hattie had outdone herself with her pot roast and vegetables for dinner. Mr. Handley had refused to abandon his phone and computer to come to the dining room, so Angel set up trays for him and Sam in the sunroom. He came to the table only long enough to give the ladies the latest information from Guatemala, which had not changed since his midafternoon contact with Leo.

For now, the dishes were done, and Gretchen and Bella had returned to Caroline's cottage. To keep their minds off the clock and their silent worry, Hattie persuaded Angel and Sarah to join her in the library for one game of Scrabble before she went to bed. Sam lounged in his favorite chair across the room and pretended to read his latest Civil War book. Truth was he could not concentrate. He kept going over the conversation he'd had with James and Thomas this afternoon. Their descriptions of the terrain and what they had learned would keep him awake all night.

A rapping noise came from the kitchen. It stopped and started again. Angel stood up. "Sam, I think somebody's at the back door."

Sam looked at the clock on the mantle. Eight forty-five. "Who in the world? Oh, you just sit down, little lady. Old Sam'll get the door. Maybe Gretchen's back, bringing some more of those sweet treats she makes."

Angel sat back down. "Oh, my, like you need one more sweet treat today."

Hattie picked up four tiles and placed them on the board. "Looky, looky. I done run out of fingers, and I may have to take off my bedroom shoes to count up these points."

In just a few moments, Sam returned to the library with Brother Andy beside him. "Would you look who dropped by this evening?"

The ladies turned to see. Hattie immediately got up from the table. "Well, good evening, Brother Andy. Give me five minutes, and I'll have you a cup of coffee and a slice of my coconut cake."

"Thank you, and it sounds mighty tempting, Hattie, but I won't be staying that long."

Sam pointed to the game table with his walking cane. "Well, let me introduce you to Dr. Sarah McCollum. Sarah is Roderick's sister from North Carolina, and she came over with Gretchen and Bella for a visit."

Brother Andy stepped to the table and shook Sarah's hand. "It's my pleasure to meet you, Sarah."

"And Sarah, this is Brother Andy. He's the pastor of the

Methodist church here in town. That's where Caroline plays the piano."

Brother Andy turned to Sam. "Judge Meadows, we've been friends for a long time, but this is a pastoral call. I know about Caroline, and I know you must be hurting. Tell me what I can do."

Sam looked at Angel, a knowing glance that almost spoke out loud. "Well, Brother Andy. Have a seat, and tell me what you know."

The ladies remained at the game table. Sam sat down in his lounge chair, and the pastor chose the wing chair in front of the fireplace. "I was told that Caroline's been kidnapped in Guatemala and that Roderick and her brothers are already down there looking for her."

"If you don't mind, Reverend, would you tell me how you came by this information?"

"We were having our regular Wednesday-night prayer service tonight when GiGi Nelson interrupted everything, stood up, and told us all about it. Said that Caroline and this doctor who's with her were kidnapped when they left the orphanage Monday evening and that you got a ransom call. To tell you the truth—and forgive me Lord for saying it—I had a hard time believing this coming from GiGi, but she swore it to be true. Said that Fred Pendergrass told her all about it. I didn't even know Fred could talk."

Sam felt his face reddening. "She did, did she?"

"Yes, she did, and we believed her enough that we stopped everything and had a special hour of prayer just for Caroline. Tell me, did we waste our time?"

"For certain, nobody ever wasted a minute of time praying, and I do hate to tell you this more than you know, but everything you heard is true. We've been sitting here for two days waiting for another call or for any news from Guatemala."

Sam explained about Mr. Handley and why Sarah was here with Gretchen and Bella. "I had hoped to keep this quiet, Brother Andy, but I guess it's too late for that. We just don't want to complicate the matter. We're worried enough as it is. Roderick and Caroline's brothers are there, and Roderick's got a team of experts working on this. We have to give them time to take care of things."

"I understand. I'll do my best to keep a lid on things, but you know this news will be all over town before the courthouse clock strikes eleven tonight. I'll certainly be in continual prayer, but is there anything else I can do for you?"

Sam stared at the floor and then looked to Brother Andy. "As a matter of fact, there is. I'm in no mood or shape to be answering all these questions. Would you consider being our spokesman to keep the community informed?"

"Certainly, Judge. You just tell me what you want them to know, and that's what I'll deliver."

"Angel and I would be mighty grateful for that. It would be a relief now that the word is out, and if I know Delia Mullins, she's probably already hiding in the bushes and peeking in the windows to get her story for the paper."

"Well, don't you worry. I'll handle Delia." Brother Andy stood up to leave and said his goodnight to the ladies. Sam led him back through the kitchen to the back door, and Brother Andy shook his hand and walked across the porch to the screen door before turning back. "One other thing I don't quite understand, Judge, and I didn't want to say this in front of the ladies. I've lived here a long time, and I've never heard Fred Pendergrass utter a word, so do you think GiGi was telling the truth when she said Fred told her?"

"Unfortunately, yes. Ned was here when we got the call yesterday morning, and he must have told his brother. Seems like Gigi's trying to set her hook in Fred, and the old coot doesn't know how not to get reeled in. But Ned's doing his best to take care of his brother."

Brother Andy shook his head. "I guess stranger things have happened, but I don't know about them. Good night, Judge. I'll talk to you tomorrow, and if you're not answering your phone, I'll just drop by during the day to check on you."

"You do that, Reverend, and good night." Sam went back inside and was walking by the door to the sunroom when the phone rang. Mr. Handley called out, "Judge Meadows, caller ID says it's Delia Mullins. You want the call?"

"No. She's the editor of the local newspaper. Put the ring on silent, and just let it ring." Sam kept walking to the library.

Hattie and Sarah were putting away the Scrabble board. Angel met Sam as he walked into the library. "Well, it seems that GiGi bared more than her wrinkled cleavage tonight, and it seems you didn't get the Pendergrass Trust set up one day too soon."

"You're right, my Angel. We're into it now—Caroline's kidnapped and Fred's hoodwinked."

Late Wednesday night on the road to Panajachel

The rainforest was silent except for the slow shuffle of Lydia's shoes over the narrow, rocky path. She had no idea what time it was, but she was almost out of water and near exhaustion. Walking since early morning, she had stopped only to eat a tortilla and to periodically relieve herself. As dark as it was, she was glad to look up and see sky and stars instead of leaves and limbs. At times the full moon was visible, but even when it was not, it gave enough light to keep her from tripping over the stones protruding from the packed earth of this centuries-worn trail. She had walked this road since dusk, and she understood why her back was so sore and bruised from her bumpy ride up this path Monday night. The blue pickup had had no chance of avoiding these rocky bulges.

At every turn on this zigzag trail, she hoped to see lights below or to hear something indicating civilization. But nothing yet. She and Caroline had figured they were in the vicinity of the lake their first night in the hovel. Through the cracks around the door of the wooden shack, they had seen lights in the distance, flickering lights at high elevations and sprays of lights lining a possible shoreline across the lake. She stepped to the side of the road, leaned against a tree, and pulled the phone from her vest pocket. Barely enough battery to turn it on. No signal and too dark to see the time.

Fruit the size of small pears hung from the tree limb above her. She reached for one and plucked it easily from the tree. It had no smell, but the rough, dimpled skin felt familiar, and a gentle squeeze indented the fruit. An avocado. She didn't even search for the Swiss Army knife in her pocket, but instead used her thumbnail to peel the hard covering away from the soft flesh of the fruit. It was buttery in her mouth and had a nutty flavor. Lydia had never been a fan of avocadoes, but she picked two more, sat down under the tree, and finished her welcome feast.

Sitting made her more aware of the chill in the air. She pulled her knees up and wrapped her arms around them. *I'm so tired. I'll rest for just a few minutes. Then I must get going . . . back to Caroline.* She leaned against the smooth trunk and drifted off to sleep.

Late Wednesday evening, deep in the rainforest

Caroline winced in pain. Her dreams and reality blurred together like murky pond water after a heavy rain. Intense pain in her shoulder summoned her from her dream state. The sky was still dark. Slowly her thinking cleared enough for her to remember what had happened and how Lydia had left in the morning. But which morning?

She was warm—not hot with fever like before, just warm. She was thirsty and tried to lift her good arm to reach for the bottle of water, but her arm would not move. Something held it underneath the blanket. When she tried to move it again, she heard a whimper.

The whimper of a child.

Her eyes had grown accustomed to the darkness. As Caroline raised her head to look, she felt the softness of hair against her cheek and neck. Someone was next to her. All she could see was the top of a child's head and the form of the child's body cuddled next to her underneath the blanket. The girl with the chocolate-colored eyes was real.

Caroline's voice was weak. "*Niña, agua, por favor. Niña?*"

The little girl moved gently, reached for the water, and helped Caroline sit up enough to drink. She cried quietly as Caroline sipped the water.

"*Gracias, no más.*"

The child cried as she returned the bottle to its place and sat back down and pulled the blanket over them.

Caroline lay back down and whispered, "*Como te llamas?*"

"*Rosita.*"

"*Gracias, Rosita. Me llamo Carolina.*"

The child sobbed. *"Mi familia . . . Todos están muertos."*

"Oh, no . . . *Lo siento.*" Caroline's eyes filled with tears. *"Estoy aquí contigo, Rosita."*

Caroline put her arm around Rosita and pulled her near. She held the child close and felt Rosita's small hand on her cheek.

Dear God, her family was killed in the landslide, and she found me. She has been with me all day.

Chapter 25

Surprises

Thursday morning in Panajachel

Roderick answered the door. It was Goodluck. "Sir, I'm gathering the troops. Dr. Morris has news, and she says we leave in ten minutes."

"What news? Where is she?"

"Get what you need. She's at the van."

Roderick grabbed his jacket and briefcase. His heart raced as he practically sprinted down the hall. He stormed through the front door and out to the van. "What's the news?"

Reyna was putting on her jacket. "Moments ago, I received a call from the local police. They have someone who may be Chavarria in custody, and we need to get to police headquarters right away."

"But what about Caroline? Any news about her?" Roderick shuffled papers, cramming them into his black bag.

"They would tell me nothing. That is why we need to get there."

Leo climbed in the van. "Goodluck's getting the driver,

and everyone else is on the way."

In less than ten minutes, they were climbing in the van. The sky was still a dark gray with only a hint of yellow on the eastern horizon. As they took their seats, Maricela handed each of them a cup of coffee and a roll from the box she was carrying. Roderick declined.

Reyna took an extra roll and coffee from Maricela. "Roderick, we may have a long day of work ahead, you need to eat something."

He shook his head. "I'll eat later. Let's go. How far to the station?"

"Only a few minutes."

Reyna repeated again what she had been told by the official so that everyone could hear.

Thomas asked from the back of the van, "What does that mean? What about Caroline?"

"We do not know. We will find out when we get there and speak with the official."

The only voices heard after that were Goodluck talking to the driver and Leo calling the team in Kentucky to give them the latest report. "Yeah, that's all we know now, but do not call the Carlyles or the Meadowses yet. Wait until we know for certain they have Chavarria."

Roderick knew this could be the break they needed or it could be nothing, adding to the tension that was already palpable.

When Leo finished his phone conversation, Reyna spoke up. "The officer wants very much to help find Caroline. That is why he called so early. You may be present, but it would be best if you allow me to speak with him. Maricela will communicate to you what is being said, and then I will translate any questions you have for the official."

Thomas asked from the back of the van, "Can we see this Chavarria?"

"I do not know, but I will ask. First we must find out if this man is the abductor in the photo."

Roderick knew they would all be asking the same question: *If Chavarria is in jail, then where are Caroline and Dr. Pipkin?*

They rode in silence until the driver parked in front of a small, tan-painted stucco building with twelve-foot-high cinderblock walls extending from each side of the structure. The wall was topped with coils of barbed wire. No way to scale it without injury.

Roderick was first out of the van and waited for Reyna. They walked briskly to the entrance, and the rest followed in single file as they entered the police station and Reyna reminded them to allow her to do the talking. The walls were the same tan as the outside of the building, with small windows flanking the front entrance. On one side of the room, two wooden desks sitting perpendicular to each other guarded a heavy-metal door. A few wooden straight chairs lined the wall on the opposite side.

Roderick and Reyna approached the officer at the first desk, and Reyna explained who they were and why they were there. The officer said something and disappeared through the metal door. Reyna turned to the group. "He is getting Officer Valdez, who is with Chavarria right now."

Roderick's mind was racing; he was ahead by miles. He wheeled to Leo. "Turn on your computer and be ready with the photo."

Leo put his computer on the empty desk and turned it on. Goodluck, still drinking coffee, stood next to Maricela. Roderick moved from Reyna's side and stood with Thomas and James.

Thomas pounded his right fist into his left hand. "Five minutes with this guy, and we'd have truth or else."

Roderick watched as James put his arm around his

brother's shoulder and said, "Okay, we're going to do as Reyna said. We will stay calm and quiet. Here, we have no influence, and we don't need any extra trouble."

They all turned to look when the metal door opened. A short, stocky, brown-faced man dressed in a khaki uniform approached. "*Soy el official Valdez.*"

Reyna greeted him and introduced the group. They exchanged words, and Reyna turned to Leo. "Could you show him the photo?"

Officer Valdez took plastic-rimmed glasses from his shirt pocket and put them on. He leaned over to the computer to get a closer look at the photo of the ponytailed man standing on the hillside in Antigua. He stared, leaned even closer, and squinted his eyes to see. He nodded his head and spoke to Reyna.

Reyna turned to Leo. "It is Chavarria. Give the officer your computer. He wants to use it as he interrogates him."

Roderick, his stomach churning, stepped up quickly, "I want to go with him."

Reyna spoke with the official and turned back to the group, "Only one of us and a translator. I think it best if Leo and I go."

James stepped forward, "What about me? I'm an attorney. Wouldn't that carry some weight here?"

"Being an American attorney here would not help. I have told Officer Valdez that Leo is a security expert and an investigator. I'm hoping they assume he is with the federal government, and I will tell them no differently. Leo will be more helpful."

Officer Valdez, Reyna, and Leo disappeared through the metal door. Roderick stood alone just outside. He was stone-cold still and silent, but inside he raged with fear and anger and impatience.

After nearly an hour, Goodluck suggested they step

outside for some fresh air. Roderick and the group followed him. Again, Roderick stood alone near the door while the others paced the sidewalk and watched the town come alive. Today was a market day, and men and women dressed in their native clothing came down from the mountains with their goods—fruit, vegetables, fried lima beans, homemade candies and baked goods, and other items for the tourists. An older Mayan woman balancing a basket of fruit on her head walked past them.

Roderick heard Thomas ask Maricela, "What's that she's carrying? That large pink-looking potato with green scales like asparagus?"

"*Pitaya*, or dragon fruit. Would you like one?"

"No, just never saw one."

"They grow around here, but you do not see as many during the rainy season. They grow better in our summer. Inside, they can be white or pink, slightly sweet with little black seeds like a kiwi. They are good, and the natives also use them for medicine."

"Interesting. Dragon fruit, you say?" Thomas began pacing and looked at his watch. "They've been in there well over an hour."

As Thomas spoke, Leo came through the door with Reyna following him. "Get in the van. We'll tell you what we know."

Roderick was the first one in. When they were all seated, Leo spoke. "I'm sorry to say this is not such good news."

Roderick felt the blood rush from his head.

Leo continued. "The man is Chavarria. No doubt. He was at his home when they arrested him last night. He denied he had been anywhere but home for days and he denied any knowledge of a kidnapping. Even when we told him Paco was alive as a witness and we had hotel records of his stay in Guatemala City, he stayed quiet. But when we showed him his photo from Antigua, he changed his story."

"But what about Caroline?" Roderick's voice sounded weak and breathless to his ears.

"Yeah, where is my sister?" Thomas asked from the back.

"All we know is what Chavarria said. We have to check things out to verify if it's the truth. He confessed to the kidnapping and said that he and a man named Paulino had taken Caroline and Dr. Pipkin to Paulino's place up in the mountains. But the rains came hard Tuesday afternoon. There was a mudslide. When it started, Paulino went to get the women out of the lean-to and Chavarria went to get the vehicle to get them off the ridge. He said it happened quickly. Chavarria barely got away but saw the building being pushed from the ridge by a wall of water and mud. His buddy, Paulino, didn't make it."

Roderick's eyes closed as though that could help him avoid the reality of what he was hearing. His face felt cold. "And Caroline?"

"Chavarria says there's no way they could have made it out alive."

"But has he been back to the ridge?" James asked from the back, still clinging to hope.

"No. Said he was scared to. Bad spirits."

Desperate, Roderick asked, "Do you believe him? Do you think he's telling the truth?"

Leo looked at Reyna. "Hard to tell, but that's why we have to check it out. He could have heard about the landslide and made up the story to protect Caroline's whereabouts. What do you think, Reyna?"

Reyna looked at Roderick as she spoke. "I cannot be sure, but I think he is telling the truth. He was afraid, and he gave the information about his friend Paulino. The officials will check that out."

Leo looked at his watch. "So, we're headed back to the hotel to wait for further news. Rod, you and James and Thomas, don't you be giving up hope, now. We don't have the whole story yet."

Roderick wrestled with his seat belt and reached for the door handle. "I have to get out of here." He got out, slammed the door shut, and went around behind the van. After a moment, James joined Roderick there. Reyna followed and stayed beside the vehicle out of sight. Roderick leaned against the van, burying his face in his folded arms.

James touched Roderick's shoulder, "Come on, Roderick, we can't give up hope. We don't have all the facts yet."

"This is just so wrong. And facts? Here's a fact. I gave Caroline the money, at least the biggest part of it. I gave a large sum to my philanthropist friend because I knew it was something Caroline wanted. If I hadn't given her the money, she wouldn't have come here. This is all my fault."

"Roderick, what you did, you did out of love because you knew this was Caroline's dream."

Roderick turned to James. "But Caroline's gone now, and I'm to blame."

"Roderick, no one is to blame but the men who took her. Caroline's my sister, and I know how stubborn she is. She would have found another way to do this. No one blames you. Don't go down this guilt road, brother. It leads to nowhere good. Come on, nothing's for sure yet. Let's get back to the hotel."

"You said 'is.' How stubborn she 'is.' What you meant is how stubborn she 'was.' Everything's 'was' now. No present, no future, only past. She's gone, buried, and we'll never really know what happened. God, this is so wrong." Roderick doubled over in pain, the kind that comes from a deep, hollow place.

Reyna ran around to the back of the van. "We must go.

Someone just called Leo. There has been a ping on Caroline's phone. We need to get back to the hotel."

—•—

Thursday morning in the rainforest

Caroline woke with Rosita lying next to her asleep. She needed to move but hated to wake the child. With her good arm, she pulled away the blanket and her jacket to look at her chest. The swelling was still there, and the bruising was bright, reddish purple. She was peeling her blouse away from the dried blood on her shoulder when Rosita stirred.

"*Buenos días, Rosita,*" Caroline whispered.

Rosita sat up and rubbed her eyes. She said nothing but stared into Caroline's face and then looked at the bloody blouse.

This was the first time Caroline had really seen Rosita, except in her dreams and in the moonlight last night. Petite, with broad cheekbones underneath caramel-colored skin and thick, dark-brown hair falling below her shoulders, she was probably older than her tiny body suggested. Her *huipil* and wraparound skirt, though mud spattered, indicated she was Mayan and probably lived in a village somewhere on this mountain or just below.

Caroline pulled her blouse back over her injury. "*Agua*?"

Rosita looked for the water. Only half the bottle left, but she helped Caroline to drink a few sips. Rosita looked into Caroline's face and pointed two fingers at Caroline's eyes. "*Sus ojos son azules.*"

Caroline understood enough to know that Rosita was talking about her eyes and that possibly Rosita had never seen anyone with blue eyes. "I know my eyes are blue, but *tus ojos son del color del chocolate.*" She used her good arm to take hold of Rosita's shoulder, trying to pull herself into a sitting position.

Rosita got on her knees and gently helped Caroline sit up. Caroline drew her right leg up and pulled her pants leg away and tried to look at the wound behind her knee. The pain. It hurt to move. It hurt to breathe. She groaned.

"*Espere.*"

Caroline did not understand, and her puzzled look must have communicated her confusion.

"*Espere, Carolina.*" Rosita placed her hand on Caroline's good arm to stop her from moving and then knelt to look at Caroline's leg. She quickly got to her knees. "*Acuéstese.*" She gently guided Caroline back to her reclining position and then stood up. She started picking up the pieces of fruit outlining Caroline's body and tossing them into the jungle. "*Iré y conseguiré la medicina y la comida. Entiende?*"

Caroline thought she understood *medicine* and *food*, but nothing else. "*No, no comprendo.*"

Rosita pointed to herself and then turned and pointed down below in the jungle. Then she pointed to herself again and raised her fingers to her mouth as though she were eating.

Caroline nodded in understanding.

Then Rosita pointed to Caroline's shoulder and her injured leg. "*Medicina.*" Then she ran away, her brown hair flying.

"No, don't go. *Por favor, Rosita.*" Where was she going? Her family was dead and anything down below had been destroyed. How was she going to find food and medicine? Caroline raised her head and watched Rosita until the girl was out of sight. Out of breath and strength, she lay back down, hoping and praying that Rosita would bring help, someone who could carry her to safety.

Caroline must have drifted off because she woke to the

sound of Rosita's voice. She had no idea how much time had passed.

Rosita held a bouquet of flowers in her left hand. "*Esta es la medicina.*"

Caroline understood. She recognized the tiny white flowers and the lacy, fernlike leaves. It was yarrow. Angel always kept some in her garden. "*En inglés, la medicina es* yarrow. Yarrow."

Rosita tried to say the English word. Then she dropped the hem of her skirt that she held in her right hand and something that looked like pink artichokes spilled out onto the ground. Rosita pointed. "*Esta es la pitaya, la fruta dulce.*"

Caroline smiled. She understood it was for them to eat, although she had never seen a more exotic-looking fruit. That was the sweet smell and the sweet taste in her mouth. Rosita must have tried to feed her earlier.

Rosita picked up one of the pitayas, pounded it against a nearby tree trunk, and broke it open with her tiny hands. "*Esta es para usted y las mariposas azules.*"

She knew the word *mariposas.* Butterflies were favorites of the orphans. "For me and the blue butterflies?" Caroline remembered the butterflies swirling all around her yesterday. Maybe they were real after all and not just in her dream.

Rosita peeled the fruit as best she could and bit into it to show Caroline how to eat it. "*Es dulce.*"

Caroline took the wedge with her right hand and put it to her mouth. "*Es dulce.* It is sweet like kiwi or melon."

Rosita smiled. "*Sí, melón.*"

They ate two of the *pitayas.* Then Rosita sat down on the rock above Caroline's head. She crisscrossed her legs, straightened her skirt, and reached for the bouquet of flowers next to the rock. Plucking the feathery leaves from the yarrow plants, she dropped them into her lap as she peeled them away. Then she took some of the leaves, put them in her mouth, and chewed them. Rather than swallow, she spat the macerated leaves into her right hand and lifted her skirt to reveal a small wound on her ankle. She took the paste she made of the yarrow leaves and put them on the wound. Then she pointed to Caroline. "*La medicina para usted.*" She pointed to Caroline's shoulder and her leg and handed Caroline a handful of the leaves to chew.

When Caroline had chewed them enough to make a paste, Rosita carefully pulled back Caroline's jacket and blouse and helped her put the paste on her shoulder. "*Más, más.*"

"Okay, I'll do more." Exhausted and weak, Caroline chewed more of the bitter leaves and gave them to Rosita. When Caroline's shoulder and the back of her leg were covered in the green paste, Rosita got up and started pounding more pitayas against the tree.

Caroline was beginning to drift back into her dream world.

After Rosita had cracked the fruits and pulled them into sections, she carefully outlined Caroline's body with the pieces and then sat beside her. "*Ahora, esperamos las mariposas azules.*"

"Now we wait for the blue butterflies," Caroline whispered before losing consciousness.

On the road through the rainforest

The sound of birds woke Lydia. She had not moved from her position underneath the avocado tree since she fell asleep sometime before dawn. She stretched her long legs and arms and crawled to a standing position. Her first thoughts were of Caroline and how to get help. In her own way, she lifted her eyes to the morning sky and prayed.

Finally, the sky lightened enough that she could clearly see the road lined with tall trees and thick foliage. Vegetation here was different than at the higher altitudes. She must be getting closer to the base of the mountain.

Lydia stepped out of sight of the road to relieve herself and returned to the tree for a breakfast of two avocados. When she finished eating, she sat down to remove her shoes and socks and massaged her feet. She put them back on and ran her fingers through her damp hair, the humidity making it more uncontrollable than usual. She missed her hat that had been lost in the scuffle when she was abducted. She stood up and started her trek down a path she could now see.

She walked for a while, always looking and listening for any sign of life that didn't have large green leaves. Rounding a curve, she finally caught sight of the lake. The water glistened far in the distance, but it gave her a sense that she was at least two-thirds of the way down this mountain. This gave her a new energy. She had to hurry. Caroline needed help. The hours she'd spent walking were far more than Lydia had planned, but at least she was moving and on a mission. Caroline was alone and sick.

She rounded another hairpin turn and saw the apex of a tower. A cell phone tower. *I can get signal!* Quickly she pulled out the phone and turned it on. Only a hint of battery left but . . . a full signal. Lydia wanted to do the dance her African friends did when their prayers were answered, but her back was too sore.

She dialed the prefix for the United States and the only number she knew: Jess's. She waited for the sound indicating the call had gone through. It was ringing. Even with tired feet, she paced the well-worn road. "Please answer, Jess. Please. If you've ever come to work early, please let it be today."

"Good morning, this is Jess, Dr. Pipkin's—"

Lydia interrupted her. "Jess, it's me, Lydia."

"Dr. Pipkin, are you all right?

"Yes and no. I've been kidnapped, and I'm somewhere in the jungle."

"We know. The ones looking for you think you're near Lake Atitlán. Mr. Adair and his whole team are there now."

"Just shut up and listen. This battery could go out any second. I'm on a dirt road in the jungle, coming down the mountain from where our kidnappers were hiding us up on the ridge. We escaped, but there was a mudslide. I think I am getting closer to the lake. Maybe getting near a village called Panajachel. Not sure."

"Is Miss Carlyle with you?"

"No, she's—"

The phone went dead.

"Jess? Are you there?"

Nothing.

Lydia looked at the phone and shook it as though she might revive the battery. *At least she knows I'm alive. Maybe she can get help.*

Hotel Atitlán

The group walked down the hall toward Leo's suite. "Roderick, I'll give the guys another call right now. Maybe they have more information about this ping on Caroline's phone."

Goodluck was the last one through the door. Reyna and Maricela sat down on the love seat at the far end of the room. Thomas and James took the sofa across from them. Leo went to the desk, and Roderick stood at the end of the desk by the window and looked out on the lake. Thoughts ricocheted through his mind—one second he had hope, the next only despair.

Leo dialed. "Hank, it's Leo. Find out any more about the ping?" Pause. "Okay." He hung up.

Roderick stepped toward the desk. "What, what's okay? Why'd you hang up?"

"He needs to call me back. He's on the line with Dr. Pipkin's assistant, Jess."

Roderick pounded his fist on the desk. "Call him. Call him back. Get him on the phone now. He can talk to this Jess person later."

"But Jess just got a call from Dr. Pipkin. He'll call me as soon as he gets off the phone with her."

A roar of relief rippled from one end of the room to the other. James stood. "Thank God, they're alive. I'm going to call our parents right now and let them know."

Leo stopped him. "Why don't you just wait a few more minutes? We'll have more information."

Thomas pulled a quarter from his pocket. This is how he and his brother had settled disputes most of their lives. "Hey, big brother, I'll flip you for it. I want to make that call."

Leo's phone rang. He answered and then turned to the group. "It's Hank."

Roderick stepped closer to Leo. "Put him on speaker."

Leo pressed a button on his phone. "Hank, we're all here. I'm putting you on speakerphone so everyone can get the report from you."

"Yes, sir. This is what I know: Dr. Pipkin called Jess about a half an hour ago. That had to be from Miss Carlyle's cell phone. Dr. Pipkin was on a dirt road coming down a mountain toward Panajachel she thought, but she wasn't sure. They escaped from their kidnappers, but there was a mudslide."

Roderick interrupted. "Hank, this is Roderick. What about Caroline?"

"Sir, Dr. Pipkin was alone, and the phone went dead before she could explain. I have my guys pinpointing a location for that call right now."

Roderick went back to the window. *Dr. Pipkin is alone. That means Caroline is too.* That hollow feeling inside returned. He felt utterly numb as he forced himself to consider the possible outcome.

She might truly be dead.

Chapter 26

Search and Rescue

Caroline's cottage in Moss Point

Bella was playing a beautiful melody on the piano, and every few phrases, she would sing. Sarah watched her for a few moments and then turned to Caroline's desk. She looked at the clock. Caroline had told her on an earlier visit that it was handmade by her father and one of her treasures.

Gretchen came from the kitchen with two steaming cups of tea. "Shall we sit at the table on the patio?"

"Sounds good." Sarah's fingers traced the graceful form of a girl's hand holding a heart. "This piece is just as beautiful and rare as Bella. And to think she made it." She placed it back on the desk and took the cup of tea from Gretchen.

"You are so kind, Sarah. Yes, Caroline served me tea from this pot, her favorite because it was her grandmother's. When we had tea, she told me that pansies were symbols of friendship. When Caroline broke it, I could not bear to think of the broken pieces being wasted. I knew that Bella could make it into something beautiful. It is no longer a teapot, but it is . . ."

Sarah saw Gretchen's eyes welling with tears. "An exquisite work of art like the music she's playing."

"I am pleased she is not continually playing Caroline's storm scene anymore. It was so fierce, but now she seems to be making her own gentle melodies and lyrics about butterflies. Shall we have our tea in the garden?"

"Strange connection she has with Caroline." Sarah followed Gretchen to the patio. They had only just taken their seats when Sarah's phone rang. "Morning, Roderick, I'm sitting on Caroline's patio with Gretchen."

"Good. I'm glad you're not alone."

She heard the crack in his voice. "Thank you, brother. I wish I were there with you."

"I have a bit of news. One of the kidnappers has been identified and is in custody, but he no longer has Caroline. He reported there was a mudslide where they were holding Caroline and Dr. Pipkin. He made it out to safety, but his partner didn't. But we have reason to hope that Dr. Pipkin is still alive. She placed a call to her assistant this morning, but the signal was gone before . . . before she . . ." His voice grew faint.

"Then she escaped her abductors and the mudslide. You'll find her."

"She's our only hope, Sarah. Our only hope.

"There is still hope, Rod. When you find Dr. Pipkin, you'll find Caroline. If I held the phone to the window, you could hear Bella playing Caroline's piano, and she's singing her new song about butterflies. I think maybe that's a good sign. Do not give up hope. I love you, little brother, and we'll stop to pray right now."

Sarah put the phone on the table and reported all that Roderick had told her—the news about Chavarria, the mudslide, and Dr. Pipkin's call to her secretary. "But

Caroline was not with Dr. Pipkin. So, we don't know yet."

Gretchen wiped her tears away again. "Does Mr. Handley have this news, and will he tell Sam and Angel, or should we go and tell them?"

"Mr. Handley may know what's going, but he won't tell the Meadowses, and Roderick asked me not to break the news to them either—at least not until we know something more consequential. I told him we would pray."

"I do not think I have stopped praying since I learned Caroline was kidnapped."

Sara took Gretchen's hand across the table and held her delicate fingers. "I know. I just can't stop thinking about her and what she must be going through. Now that I know what it's like to have a sister, I can't imagine our lives without her. She has to be all right."

They bowed their heads in silence for several moments, each murmuring silent prayers. Sarah opened her eyes and looked through the picture window. The early-morning sun's rays dancing off the windowpane, allowed her to see only Bella's silhouette, but she could hear the girl's lilting voice.

Flowers with wings you are, how does it feel to fly?
Silent angels you are, please don't fly too high.
You have no song, so I will sing. You can fly, be my wings.

Midday on Thursday at the Hotel Atitlán

"Come on, let me in!"

Everyone in the room paused when they heard Goodluck pounding on the door. He was almost breathless when Thomas opened it, his eyes wild, his drink sloshing out of his paper cup.

"Goodluck, you still drinking coffee? Maybe you should slow down on that stuff."

"Forget the coffee. Dr. Pipkin's here."

Roderick put his phone in his pocket and raced toward the door. "What? Here?"

"Yes, sir. She's here now. Remember the emergency vehicle and the first responders we met in the parking lot yesterday. They found her this morning on their way up to the area of the mudslide and brought her here. They thought she might be one of the women we were looking for." Goodluck turned and motioned for them to follow him. "Come on. They'll be bringing her into the lobby any minute."

The entire group followed Goodluck and Roderick down the long hallway. Images of Dr. Lydia Pipkin being brought in on a stretcher flashed through Roderick's mind. He turned to Reyna. "If she was injured, surely they'd have taken her to a hospital. They wouldn't bring her here, would they?"

"Possibly. You just haven't met Dr. Pipkin." Reyna rushed to keep up with him.

The group entered the lobby just as Dr. Pipkin bolted through the double doors of the hotel entrance with the two first responders following. She was exactly as Caroline had described her on the phone—tall, lanky, with a mane of unruly, sandy gray hair. Her khaki travel vest and shorts showed the wear of three days of jungle life, and the hat Caroline had described was nowhere to be seen. Her leathery brown face was creased with deep wrinkles, and her cheeks and eyelids sagged not from age but from weariness.

Roderick approached her. "Dr. Pipkin?" He wanted to extend his hand, but his father had taught him to follow a woman's lead where handshakes were concerned.

Dr. Pipkin did not lift her hand but stood still with an intense, penetrating look. "And you must be Roderick."

"Yes."

"I know you have questions, and the first one must be about Caroline."

Roderick felt lightheaded and wanted to sit, but he couldn't move. "Yes. Tell me, is she alive?"

"To be honest, I don't know. When I left her just after daybreak yesterday, she was alive, but barely. I had to leave her alone to get help. There was no other way."

Reyna moved to Roderick's side. "Dr. Pipkin, I am so glad to see you. Can you fill us in and then let me check you?"

"No time. The only reason I'm here and not in the jungle with the medics looking for Caroline is that they told me Americans looking for two women were at this hotel, and I knew it had to be you. No medical care needed for me. I am tired and thirsty, but I'm fine. We have to get back to Caroline. She is the one who needs medical care if she made it through the night."

Roderick, still stunned, saw Goodluck lean over to Maricela and whisper. They both left the group.

Roderick knew Caroline's injuries had to be life threatening for Dr. Pipkin to have left her alone in the jungle. "How bad was she?"

"Broken collarbone and a deep gash in her shoulder. Couldn't tell for sure, but she either has some broken or cracked ribs. She can get over that, but I'm worried about a punctured lung and the cut in her leg. She lost a good bit of blood, and she had fever. A high fever. We have to get back to her."

Reyna asked, "What about her heart rate and her breathing?"

"Heart rate high, breathing shallow. And by now she's

in real need of water. It took me longer than I thought to get across and up the mountain and down the other side. I'd still be walking if the men in that truck hadn't found me this morning." She turned to face Roderick. "Told me they met a group yesterday looking for a woman like me and brought me here. I surmised it was you. From the way Caroline talked, I didn't figure you for the kind of man who'd still be sitting in Kentucky."

"You figured right, ma'am." Roderick turned to Acer. "Could you check the front desk and get Dr. Pipkin a room?"

"A room? I don't have time for a room. We don't have but a few hours of daylight left. Caroline and I spent two nights on the edge of hell in that jungle, and she spent another night alone. It's time we go get her."

Reyna interrupted. "Wouldn't it be better if you told us how to get there and you stay here? I can give you something that would help you rest."

"No. I left markers along the way, but you need me, and I'll not rest until we find Caroline."

Goodluck and Maricela returned. Goodluck handed Dr. Pipkin a glass of water. "Look, I just ordered the supplies we need. They'll be here within half an hour. If it took you more than twenty-four hours to walk out, it'll take us several hours to go in, and we need to prepare."

"Thank you, Goodluck." Roderick approached Lydia. "Look, at least let Dr. Morris take a look at you while we talk with the guys who found you. We have maps, and they can help us. Besides, we'll have to make arrangements to airlift Caroline out."

Thomas stepped forward. "Sounds like a lot of jungle to cover, and we may need to divide up."

Lydia turned to look down at Thomas. He barely measured up to her shoulder. "No need to divide up. And who are you?"

"I'm Thomas, Caroline's brother." He pointed to James. "And the tall one over there, that's James, our older brother."

"Yeah, you both look like her. No need to split up the group."

"But we can cover more ground that way."

"Don't need to cover more ground. Why would I leave Caroline alone in the jungle without a way to find her?"

Thomas had hunted in deep forests and knew how easy it was to get lost. "Yes, ma'am, I understand. But from what I've seen of this place, it all looks the same after a while."

"Damn right it does." Lydia pulled the cut-up strands of blanket from her shorts pocket. "That's why I used these."

Thomas shook his head and grinned. "You marked the path. You're a genius."

"Been called lots of things in my life, young man, but never a genius." Lydia had the hint of a smile on her face. "Who's running this show?"

Roderick stepped forward. "I am, but I'll follow your lead."

"Now that's real genius. Let's be ready to go in thirty minutes. You're right, you'll need to arrange to airlift her out of there. She can't walk, and it's too rugged a climb to carry her. You'll need a satellite phone. There's only phone signal just for few miles up the road, then no more."

"We have satellite phones."

"Good. And you'll need plenty of water, and a blanket for each of us, and rain gear. And Reyna, Caroline's bound to be dehydrated by now. I left her with a high fever and only two bottles of water. You'll need an IV and antibiotics. There was a nasty red streak running up her leg."

She turned to Thomas. "What size shoe do you wear?"

"I wear a size nine."

"Good. I wear a woman's ten. Give me your shoes and go buy you some more. I'm done wearing these damn wet boots. And while you're buying shoes, get me some clean, dry socks."

She looked at Goodluck. "And what's your name? Goodluck? Is that what I heard?"

"Yes, ma'am. I'm Goodluck."

"I hope you can live up to your name. If you're in charge of supplies, we need a stash of protein bars and bottled water. I'm serious about the blankets. It's cold on that mountain at night. Keep it light, because each will carry his own."

It was not in Roderick's take-charge nature to allow someone else to call the shots, but he had a growing respect for this Dr. Lydia Pipkin. After all, she had been there, she had risked her life to save Caroline's, and she was willing to return to the edge of hell to get her. "We'll be ready when you are. Count on it."

Lydia stepped closer to Roderick. "Give me thirty minutes. And if you're a wise man, Roderick, you'll enlist the help of those first responders standing there. They know things."

"It's done."

"And I need a clean shirt, and I'm just guessing you have one or two. And I'd like a hamburger with French fries." She started to walk away but turned around. "Oh, and a large cup of coffee with lots of cream and two sugars."

"It'll be waiting for you when you want it, and anything else I have. But your things are here. We brought them with us when we left Xela. They're in my room, and they'll be in your room when you get out of the shower." He paused and looked at her as intensely as she had looked at him when they met only minutes ago. "Dr. Pipkin, I don't even know how to begin to thank you for taking care of Caroline."

"Later, I'll help you think of a way, but not right now. We have a mountain of jungle to cross." She turned to Reyna. "Can you come with me? You can check some bruises on my back." Lydia walked off with Reyna.

Roderick gathered the group. It was agreed that Leo would stay at the hotel to coordinate and manage communications. Goodluck, with Maricela's help, would pack the supplies they needed and would stay behind to secure air transportation for Caroline. James, Thomas, Acer, Reyna and Roderick would go with Dr. Pipkin back to the rainforest.

Roderick asked James and Thomas, "What do you think about calling your parents and the Meadowses?"

Thomas spoke first. "Hey, brother, I'll flip you for it. I've been waiting to do this all day. We have real hope now. We know where sis is."

James looked at Roderick. "I'm not so sure. What do you think?"

"I'm not so sure either. I know what this is doing to me—one minute thinking she's gone, the next thinking she isn't, only to be let down again. I hate to think of them having to experience this."

Thomas blurted out, "Come on, guys. We're going to find her."

"I know we'll find our sister, Thomas, and I know there's still a chance we'll find her alive. But for the next few hours, wouldn't mom and dad have more hope and peace thinking she's in the hands of a kidnapper rather than thinking she's spent the last thirty hours lying in the jungle bleeding, with broken bones, a possible punctured lung, and maybe blood poisoning?"

"I get it. Maybe we'll have good news in just a few hours. Let's save them from the stress."

Roderick agreed. No calls home just yet.

James and Thomas left for the market next door to buy shoes and socks. Acer and Roderick walked back down the hall to Roderick's room. "God, there's no way of telling what Caroline's been exposed to in that jungle. Cold, rain, who knows what kind of bacterial infection has invaded her open wounds? What do you make of all this, Acer?"

"I'm thinking you're afraid, my friend, but I'm thinking Caroline has everything in the world to live for, and she's strong. Dr. Pipkin will lead us to her."

"I just hope she's strong enough. I need to be alone for a bit. Will you take Dr. Pipkin's luggage to her room, please?"

"Sure, is this all?" Acer picked up the canvas duffle bag and the leather backpack.

"Wait." Roderick pulled a light-blue, long-sleeved shirt from his suitcase. "Here, take her this."

"But I have her things right here. She won't need your shirt."

"Just take it. It's the only thing she's asked me for, except for a hamburger."

"Okay, boss. Anything else?"

"Yes, if you could get the burgers she asked for. That's all. I just need a few minutes to myself." Acer picked up the bags and left. Roderick closed his door. Images of Caroline alone in the jungle overwhelmed him.

The crumpled plastic bag lay on the seat of the chair where he'd put it when they checked in. He picked it up, sat down in the chair, and removed the embroidered white dress he had purchased for Caroline just yesterday. It had given him hope and something to hold on to. He held the dress, but more than anything, he wanted to hold Caroline. He felt as if all he had been holding was his breath since Tuesday morning when he'd received Chavarria's call. But he had to hold it only a few more hours. Then he'd know if he could ever breathe again.

—•—

Midday Thursday, returning to the rainforest

Roderick, Acer, and Leo waited at the front door for Lydia and Reyna. James and Thomas were helping Goodluck and Maricela load the van with the supplies.

Lydia entered the lobby like she might be headed to the Nile to wrestle crocodiles. She was dressed in her mud-spattered khaki safari clothes and Roderick's blue shirt, and she wore Thomas's athletic shoes with no socks. She had shirts of her own in her bag, but she wore his because he'd sent it to her room. She walked straight up to Roderick. "Your shirt looks good on me." She looked at the bag in his hand. "My hamburger and fries?"

"Your hamburgers and a double order of fries. I'll hold on to your coffee 'til you're in the van."

"Thank you. Then let's go."

Leo stepped toward her as she opened the door. "Dr. Pipkin, I'm Leo Bradford. I'm pleased to meet you, and I'm grateful for all you're doing. I'm head of Mr. Adair's security team, and I'll be managing everything from here."

She didn't have to look up or down, and her eyes penetrated his. "You sure have a lot of *I*'s in your sentences, don't you, Mr. Bradford? Pardon my manners, which I seemed to have left or perhaps lost somewhere. My pleasure to meet you, Leo, but I don't suppose you'll be managing everything since you won't be crawling through a jungle so thick it doesn't see the light of day. Guess you'll be relaying information."

"Whatever is needed, ma'am. Whatever is needed."

Forty-eight hours ago, Lydia had had no idea if she'd ever eat a hamburger again, but Roderick had located one in the land of tortillas and beans. She opened the bag and turned back to Leo. "Then stay close to your phone."

"Yes, ma'am," Leo said as she walked away with the first bite of burger already in her mouth. Before she passed through the door, she heard him speak to Roderick. "That one's a case study."

"I don't care what she is if she can lead us to Caroline."

They loaded their van with Lydia taking the passenger's seat up front and followed the first responders in their vehicle for more than half an hour up the rugged dirt road to the top of the ridge. While Lydia ate, Roderick filled her in on Chavarria and how her photo of him had sealed the case, causing him to come clean with the truth. "Chavarria said his partner died in the mudslide. You believe him?"

Stiffly, Lydia turned around to look at him. "If he was trying to get us out of the shed, then it's possible. Things on that ridge happened fast. The shed went down the mountain only minutes after our escape." She held to the armrest to brace herself against the continual bumps and winced in pain. "Crap."

Roderick leaned forward, "Are you okay?"

"Just sore. Last trip up this mountain in a vehicle left my backside looking like I was somebody's discarded punching bag." She began giving them details of the abduction and how they'd been tied and thrown into the back of the pickup and then bounced around for the four-hour trip from Xela to the top of the ridge. She described the hovel and how they'd planned and prepared for their escape. "We thought we were home free after we kicked the boards down and crawled out. Now I've run for my life in Africa a couple of times, even when I could have turned around and pulled the trigger, but I've never been in a spot where I was running from moving earth. You have no idea which way to turn. When I think about it, I don't know how we managed not to get buried." She looked out the van window and turned to the driver. "Stop. Blow your horn."

The van driver slammed on brakes and blew his horn to get the attention of those in the emergency vehicle. Both stopped. Lydia got out of the van, and the others, even the first responders, followed to hear her description of what had happened.

"Here. Here is where the shack was." She pointed down the mountain. "You'll see the cinder blocks strewn along for thirty or so yards, and the boards from the lean-to. That's where we were kept—dirt floor and wood slats for walls. That greasy, ponytailed man never figured us for a couple of women who would kick a wall down, but we did." She stopped talking, turned around, and looked at the group. Their faces showed their shock at the scene. "Thomas, you got my socks?"

Thomas fumbled in the shopping bag he was holding and pulled out three pairs. "Your choice, ma'am."

Lydia chose the thick white ones. "Like your shoes, and the new ones on your feet. You come with me."

"Yes, ma'am. You lead and I'll follow."

"Okay, everyone, get your stuff and let's go. We have only about five to six hours of daylight left. We need to get to Caroline before dark."

Lydia and Thomas led with Roderick following closely behind. Acer and James were there to assist Reyna when the descent was steep and the ground and rocks were uncertain. They generally followed the path of the mudslide down the mountain, veering and zigzagging when they needed to, and always following the colorful markers Lydia had tied to the limbs.

They walked for a couple of hours before Lydia stopped. "Okay, time to stop. Rest a few minutes and drink some water."

Thomas stayed near Lydia. "I can't imagine you and

Caroline finding your way through this jungle, trying to outrun a landslide."

"You do what you have to do to stay alive. We were just trying to get to what we thought would be a safe place, away from our kidnappers and away from rushing water and mud. We dug our way out of the hut and made haste before the mudslide, then we literally had to run to avoid the trees falling and the earth moving. That's when she fell, but your sister said nothing about the injury to her leg until that night." Lydia opened her water bottle and took a long drink. "Time to go. We're burning daylight."

They walked on mostly in silence for another hour, swatting at low-hanging limbs and wiping sweat from their brows, no one daring to call out Caroline's name for fear she would not answer.

"Stop." Lydia pointed to the deep gulch. "There. I think this is where Caroline tripped. We were running hard, and I had no trouble crossing, but she couldn't. I tried to pull her across, but her foot got caught under a root." She looked puzzled. "I don't remember seeing this when I walked this way yesterday."

Roderick stepped closer. "Maybe it's because you were going the other direction."

"Maybe. I could have been walking in circles." Lydia was confused.

Roderick squatted to get a better look at where Caroline had fallen. There, on the jagged rock only a yard away, was blood, Caroline's blood. The dampness in the jungle had kept it from drying. The sight sickened him. But before he could do anything other than look at it, Lydia stopped suddenly and gasped. "My God, look!" She pointed about twenty yards below them. The foliage obstructed their views, but Roderick hoped from Lydia's response that she was looking at Caroline.

En masse, they scrambled down to get a better look. The descent was steep, and they tried to avoid tripping over the roots and vines running like arteries and nerves along the floor of the jungle. Finally, a clearing.

Neither Roderick nor the others could have been prepared for what they saw. The late-afternoon sun's rays shone on the crevice where Caroline's body lay as though it had been staged. No one moved or broke the silence but stood together in a group taking in the scene. Roderick felt like his heart had stopped.

Below him, Caroline lay in the cradle of the green, mossy crevice, her form surrounded by flowers and sweet-smelling fruit that wafted through the philodendron leaves. She was covered in a Mayan blanket with a halo of white blossoms around her head as though her body had been prepared. There beside Caroline sat a small girl child who seemed not to notice them. The Mayan child, mesmerized by her own haunting song and the thousands of blue iridescent butterflies whirling around them, waved her arms as if she were conducting the whir of their wings to accompany her melody.

Lydia turned to Roderick and whispered. "Go to her. Go to Caroline." She looked at the group. "The rest of you, stay."

Roderick descended alone the last few yards down to where Caroline lay. He was breathless out of fear and anticipation. But he walked without hesitation into the swirling butterflies and knelt beside her. She had never been more beautiful, her black curls framing her face, her eyelashes almost sweeping her cheeks, and the flush of color on her lips. He closed his eyes with one last prayer and reached to touch her face. Her cheek was warm against the palm of his hand.

Thank God. She was still alive.

He could restrain himself no longer and reached to embrace her, careful not to move her shoulder. "Caroline, Caroline. I'm here."

She opened her eyes. "Roderick? You're here? You found me?"

"Yes, yes. I found you, and I've come to take you home." He kissed her then looked at the child whose chocolate-colored eyes were open now.

Lydia and the group stood in tranquil silence above the scene. They had watched the child open her eyes at the sound of Roderick's voice. Without saying anything, the child stopped her humming and movement and placed her hands palms up in her lap. The moment she was still, the butterflies swirled above them in a spiral flurry, climbing higher and higher until they were out of sight in the golden sunlight of the late afternoon. In all her years of travel and study as an anthropologist, Lydia had never seen anything so magnificent.

But more important, she could now see clearly that Roderick held Caroline and she was alive.

The rest of the group quietly descended, all sensing they had been witness to a mystical moment. When they reached the ground around the crevice, Reyna stepped forward, knelt beside Roderick and put her hand on Caroline's brow. "CC?"

Caroline opened her eyes again. "Reyna, are you real?"

"Yes, my friend, I am real, and so are Lydia and your brothers and Acer. Look behind me."

Lydia and the others acknowledged Caroline with their smiles and their tears.

Reyna looked across Caroline's body at the child seated on the edge of the crevice and asked her name. "*Como se llama, niña*?"

The child moved not one muscle of her body, only her lips as she answered, "*Soy Rosita.*"

"*Gracias, mi niña y sus mariposas, por guardar la vida de Carolina.*"

Lydia heard the words, but how could the girl child and her butterflies have saved Caroline's life? She did not know, but perhaps somewhere deep in her soul in that unexplainable place of knowing, she knew more than she understood.

Chapter 27

Dual Realities

Thursday night in the jungle

Darkness shrouded the jungle like a black fog. The group sat quietly on the folded blankets that each had brought in his or her stash of supplies. They listened nervously to Reyna's conversation as though they could understand her Spanish.

Reyna said goodbye and handed the satellite phone back to Roderick, who had been sitting in silence for the last hour. "All is well. They made it to the clinic, and Dr. Avalos, my friend, is there with her now. He is a fine doctor and will take good care of her. Leo, Goodluck, and Maricela are there with her too. Maricela's taking care of Rosita."

Roderick noticed that Dr. Pipkin was quieter than usual and turned to her. "I am sorry there was not a way to get us on that helicopter. You need rest, Lydia, but with the pilot, copilot, Goodluck, two medics, and a nurse, there was only room for Rosita and Caroline."

Lydia was almost somber. "Oh, why would I give up the opportunity to spend another night in the jungle, especially now that I am in such good company? I am just grateful Caroline is safe."

Thomas pulled protein bars from his backpack. "Anyone need nourishment?" No one answered. "Dr. Pipkin, I need to tell you how sorry I am you've had to suffer this kidnapping and this whole experience with my sister. But I can tell you, my family is more grateful to you than we can say, first of all that you came with Caroline to Guatemala, and that you stood by her, took care of her, and saved her life. I just can't thank you enough. Why, my brother and I will carry you all the way back up this mountain when it's daylight. I don't want you to have to walk another step."

"No need to carry me. I rather like your shoes. And you're welcome, Thomas. As hard as it was, all I endured was worth it just to witness what I saw today. How many people in a lifetime get to see what took place in this rainforest today? In just a few days, this mountain and your sister and I have become close friends. She fooled me with that magnolia-blossom look of hers, but she has grit. She stayed with us. And I suppose we should all be grateful to the child."

Thomas folded up the wrapper of his protein bar and put it in his backpack. "Yes, little Rosita. I'm just glad there was room on the gurney for her. I don't think we could have pried her away from Caroline. Guess Goodluck got a big surprise when he reeled the gurney into that chopper and there sat a little girl holding our sis's head."

Roderick broke his silence. "I'll be forever grateful to you, too, Dr. Pipkin. But what I'm wondering is, now that we know Caroline is safe, what actually happened here today?"

Lydia cleared her throat. "I'm wondering the same thing. I've studied primitive tribes—their religions, their myths, their medicine—and I've heard and read stories, but never have I seen anything like what we witnessed today." She turned to Reyna. "Reyna, what do you make of this?"

"It was more certainly more beautiful than anything I have ever seen. I have no explanation other than what I know of the Mayan beliefs." She sat on her blanket and pulled her jacket tighter around her. "What I got from the child is that she was in the rainforest chasing blue morphos when the mudslide buried her entire village, including her family. Chasing those morphos and being out of the path of the landslide saved her life."

Roderick shifted his weight and wrapped his arms around his knees. "Blue morphos? Those were the butterflies?"

"Yes, blue morphos live here in the rainforest. When Rosita could not find her village or her family, she followed the butterflies through the jungle and found Caroline. She thought Caroline, the woman with blue eyes, was sent to her so she wouldn't be alone, and she believed she could keep Caroline alive by keeping the butterflies near her."

The others sat in silence, allowing Roderick to ask their questions. "Now, tell me how that works."

"I did not say it works, but to Rosita, with her customs and beliefs, it was critical to keep Caroline alive. That is why she surrounded Caroline with the fruit and flowers—to keep the butterflies near her. The Tz'utujil Mayans live in this area. Or at least what is left of them after the civil war massacres several years ago. Rosita probably belongs to that tribe. I know it's difficult for you to understand when you don't live like these people, but the Mayans believe in a dual reality—the world of dreams and the world of work. Now this is where the blue morphos come in. Mayans look at these twin realities like the two wings of a butterfly, always moving simultaneously, our dreams and our conscious world. But here is what is most interesting. They believe life is like the butterfly's heart, and its heart is kept alive by the movement of its twin wings. Rosita probably thought the fluttering of the butterflies' wings would keep Caroline alive."

Lydia lay back on her blanket. "That's beautiful, Reyna. Sort of like our dreams and purpose give us heart and keep us alive."

"Yes, I suppose they do."

Roderick sat quietly on the floor of jungle, feeling the warmth of a Mayan blanket around his shoulders. The full moon winked at him through the canopy of limbs and leaves. He remembered other moonlit nights thinking of Caroline, but this one was different.

He could breathe again.

Friday afternoon in the clinic in Panajachel

Afternoon sun streamed through the windows of the modest clinic. Caroline slept peacefully while Roderick spoke with Sarah on the phone. "Yeah, sis, she's resting. I'm not letting her out of my sight. Reyna says she'll be fine. Fever gone, the infection is taken care of, and her arm is in a sling. She will need to take it easy for a while. She has a couple of cracked ribs, and she may need to do some therapy with the shoulder once we get her home, but it shouldn't affect her playing."

"We're so grateful, and it sounds as though God answered our prayers and made all the provisions necessary."

"Indeed. He provided the child and the butterflies. I'll tell you all about that when I get home." He returned to the details of Caroline's rescue. "And then Goodluck was able to secure a helicopter to lift her and the child out of the jungle, and the rest of us had to wait until daylight to walk back up the mountain to the road. I can't tell you how I felt when I saw Caroline being hoisted through all those treetops to the helicopter on that gurney in the dark."

"I can only imagine what your reunion was like after all you've both been through."

"I can't even begin to describe it. My heart has never been so full."

"When can she leave the hospital?"

"Caroline's good to travel in the morning. Dr. Morris is making the arrangements for us to go to the orphanage tomorrow. Sister Gabriela will take Rosita, the Mayan child who possibly saved Caroline's life. Look I need to go, sis. We'll give you all the details when we get home."

"We're planning a welcome-home party for all of you, and be sure to invite them all to Rockwater for the wedding."

"All right, Sarah, I will. I'll invite them all to the wedding. You don't want to miss meeting these characters. I'll see you in Moss Point."

Caroline woke as he hung up and smiled at him. "Where is everyone? They're not here yet?"

"They're still at the hotel. I think they're giving us some time alone. They'll be here later. I hope I didn't wake you, but I am glad to see your blue eyes." He kissed her fingers and held her palm next to his cheek.

"Well, you really do squeeze hard and talk loud when you're excited."

"Then I'm surprised you have a hand left. I don't recall ever having been so excited. We're together, and I'm holding your hand. It's going to take us a whole lifetime to process the last five days."

"The last I heard, we do have a whole lifetime, my love."

"Wait a minute. Speaking of hands . . ." Roderick

reached into his jacket pocket and pulled out a box and held it for her to see. "Recognize this?"

"Of course, I do. I wasn't so sure I'd live to give them to you. The jade cufflinks were to be your wedding present. What are you doing with them?"

"When we left the Bonifaz in Xela, I had them gather your things and Dr. Pipkin's bags and brought them with us here." He opened the box. "I wasn't really thinking of the cufflinks, but I was thinking of this." He pulled something else from the box and stood up. "I'll be careful." Cautious not to move her arm in the sling, he lifted her left hand. "I believe this belongs on your finger, not in a box."

"My ring. But Lydia had it. How did it get in the box?"

"Lydia kept the ring with her and gave it to me last night. Maybe I should ask you to marry me again. That's what I did the last time I gave it to you." He gently slid the ring on her finger. "Miss Blue Eyes, would you please marry me before you take another trip?"

"I would marry you right this minute if we could."

Roderick leaned over and kissed her long, then carefully climbed into the bed beside her and held her. "Caroline, I cannot tell you how afraid I was that I would never hold you again. I've never been so grateful in my life. When I think about all that's happened . . . And yet you had Dr. Pipkin and you got out of that shack just in time, and Goodluck was our pilot and helped fly you to safety through the jungle, and the first responders found Dr. Pipkin, and Paco is down the hall getting better every day, and Reyna was here to take care of you, and Rosita made green goop that probably saved your life . . . I'll be spending the rest of my life thanking these people."

"Yes, and there's one more 'and'—the One who made all those provisions."

"Him too!" Roderick held her close and ran his fingers

up and down her arm. "Seems there were lots of folks praying for you. Sister Gabriela told Reyna that the sisters and the orphans held a special vespers service just for you in their prayer garden on Wednesday evening. And you'll love this: Sam wanted you to know somebody named GiGi had told the whole town about your kidnapping. But at least all of Moss Point was praying for you."

"I guess even GiGi's good for something. Perhaps their prayers brought Rosita to me. Where is she?"

"She's with Reyna, but I can tell you she did not want to leave you."

"My thinking is so foggy. I was so ill and in and out of sleep or unconsciousness. I don't know what was a dream or what was real. I think she was with me during the night and the day, and she was humming, and there were butterflies. Were there butterflies, Roderick?"

His eyes filled with tears, and he laid his head on her shoulder and pulled her closer. "Yes, Rosita was humming, and there were mystical, beautiful butterflies, thousands of them as blue as your eyes. I'll tell you all about that when I have the words. Right now, I just want to hold you close."

"That's good. Sounds like you have everything worked out for tomorrow. Thank you, Roderick. I couldn't leave without going back to the orphanage."

"It worked out perfectly. We're not going back to the city. The plane's in Xela, and Goodluck will have it ready to fly home when we get to the airport."

"Oh, home sounds good. Sounds like you've talked to Sarah and my family, and to Sam and Angel, but what about Gretchen?"

"You bet. I've talked to everyone I know to tell them I'm bringing you home. I told them that your abductors did not hurt you, but they're anxious to see you and hear about everything that's happened. Gretchen and Sarah and Bella are in Moss Point with Sam and Angel. You'll see them when I get you home"

"That sounds so good. I feared I'd never see them again."

"Seems like you have a special connection to a little brown-haired girl and your silver-haired savant."

"What do you mean?"

"Sarah's all excited about Bella. She thinks Bella has some unexplainable connection with you. Seems Bella was uncontrollably agitated for a couple of days, just constantly playing the storm scene from the *Rockwater Suite*. Wouldn't eat and couldn't sleep. Best I can put things together, she seemed to settle down about the same time little Rosita showed up at your side."

"Umm. That's interesting. But I'm where I belong now, next to you, and I think I'd like to go back to sleep."

Roderick held her and listened to the sweet sounds she made when she breathed.

Early Saturday morning at Hogar Luis Amigo

The group was loaded into the van and ready to leave. Roderick and Caroline were saying their last goodbyes to the children and the sisters. "Sister Gabby, thank you so much for today. Hearing the children sing and hearing of their excitement about the choir and the future, it was all like the best dose of medicine. I'm so grateful for your prayers and the prayers of the children. They sustained me during long, frightening hours."

"I will tell you someday what I told the children, but for now, it is enough to say you are greatly loved, my sweet friend. We are so grateful for all your work, and we are so sorry for what happened. But our God delivered you, and He did it for a reason."

Caroline swallowed and tried to bridle her tears. "I sensed Him in the darkness. I know He was there."

"He was, my friend, and He's with you in the light of today."

"He brought Rosita to me, and now I bring her to you. Please take good care of her, and if she needs anything, I mean anything . . ."

"I will. I will let you know. I will take care of her. She is a very special child, close to the heart of God."

"Yes, yes, she is, and to my heart too."

Sister Gabby kissed both of Caroline's cheeks and hugged Roderick.

Caroline turned to Reyna, whose eyes were already glassy with tears. "Thank you, my friend, for all you did to help them find me and then to take care of me. How can I ever thank you?"

"By returning to finish what you started, Caroline. These children need you. I need you in my life." Reyna put her arm around Caroline and pulled her away from the group. "Caroline, we lost Josh and David in a mudslide, and I knew in my heart of hearts that I wouldn't lose you the same way."

Caroline turned to face Reyna. "I suppose I've always wondered what actually happened to David and Josh. I've had so many questions. Do you ever wonder about that?"

"Early on I did, but at some point there came an acceptance that I'd most likely never know for sure. I'll tell you, though, there were moments in the last few days when painful memories returned, and then it was like I almost sensed Josh's presence and realized I had a job to do. Guatemala is my home, and I know about these things. I think I've always known that whatever happened to Josh and David did so quickly, and I know they died doing what they were meant to do. I'm just grateful you're still here."

"I'm glad you had peace and acceptance like that. I didn't. It was odd, but I had a dream a few months ago. I was hanging onto a limb, grasping for life in muddy floodwaters. In my dream, David appeared on dry land and pulled me to safety and told me he was where he was supposed to be, and that I must go on. I've had a sense of peace since that dream, and now somehow this whole experience is bringing more closure for me."

"And in your dream, David told you what to do. You must go, on as I have. Roderick is a gift to you, and he cherishes you more than he does his own life. Help him, Caroline. He blames himself for what happened."

"I will. I'll do exactly as you say. I love you, my friend, and I will return to do what I started. And I ask that you stay in touch with Sister Gabby and check on Rosita."

"You can count on me for that. Seems she's waiting to speak with you. Do you need my help with translation?"

"Yes, please.

Reyna led Caroline over to the garden and stood behind her. Caroline knelt on the grass in the flowers and called Rosita from the group of children standing in front of the orphanage. Reyna helped her to say what she wanted to say to Rosita, but she repeated the words to the child herself. She held Rosita close, expressing her love and her promise to return. "*Te quiero, Rosita. Y volveré a verte.*"

Rosita raised her hand to Caroline's cheek. "*Hasta que vuelva, me recordaré sus ojos azules. Te quiero, Carolina. Vaya con Dios y recuerde las mariposas azules.*"

Reyna whispered Rosita's words for Caroline. Caroline hugged Rosita and released her to take her place in line with the children.

Roderick helped Caroline to her feet and walked slowly

with her to the van. "Let's go, Goodluck."

"Yes, sir." Goodluck drove slowly through the gate.

They waved through the windows until the children were no longer in sight. Roderick kissed Caroline's cheek, damp with her tears. He whispered, "What did you say to Rosita?"

"I told her I loved her and I would return to see her." She turned her face to Roderick. "Rosita said until I returned, she would remember my blue eyes. Then she told me to go with God and to always remember the blue butterflies."

Saturday midday at Hartsfield International Airport in Atlanta

Goodluck shouted from the cockpit. "Buckle, up, folks. We're cleared for landing, but we'll only have about fifteen minutes on the ground when we get there."

Caroline looked at Dr. Pipkin. "Lydia, we came home early, so you still have a few days before you return to Africa. Are you certain we can't persuade you to come to Moss Point with us?"

Lydia, dressed in clean safari clothes, a Guatemalan belt, a new hat, and a Mayan blanket draped across one shoulder, sat across the aisle from Caroline. "Most certain, young lady. Sounds like a lovely town, but a little too civilized for me. Besides, that guy of yours has made all the travel arrangements for me to get back to Miami this afternoon."

"Well, I'm sorry our trip turned out as it did and had to be cut short, but I think we got a head start, and I can follow up here." Caroline grabbed her ribs when the plane touched down. The noise from the runway drowned out any further conversation.

When the plane came to a stop, Goodluck barked again, "Now's the time to stretch your legs. It'll take a few minutes to refuel, and we'll be on our way. Only one off is the doctor. Acer will get your bags, ma'am. Since I'll be staying in the cockpit, Dr. Pipkin, it's been real. Can't say that I've ever met anyone quite like you. Hope to see you around sometime, maybe on another trip to Guatemala. They still got a few volcanoes you didn't climb."

Lydia laughed out loud. "Somehow I don't believe him, except the volcanoes part." She turned in her seat to face Caroline across the aisle and put her hand on Caroline's. Her laughter was replaced by a serious but tender look. "Goodluck's right, Caroline. It has been real, some of the realest moments of my life, out there in that jungle with you, wondering if we'd get out alive. I've been doing this kind of work for a long time, you know, this business of taking care of suffering children. And sometimes I get weary and numb. But what we're doing matters, and we're to stay at it. I'll be in touch." She leaned to kiss Caroline's cheek.

As she tried to stand in the plane, her hat fell off. She stooped to pick it up. "Oh, crap, about to lose my new hat." She stood as tall as she could but had to lean as she walked toward the front of the plane.

Caroline watched Roderick follow Lydia to the door and shake her hand. "Thank you again, Dr. Pipkin. You'll find a generous contribution to your organization when you get to Miami."

"That's kind of you, Roderick. Just take care of Caroline. She's a good one."

Lydia turned to Thomas, James, and Leo in the back of the plane and waved. "Goodbye, boys. When you decide to take another adventure, please give me a call. I'd like to join you." She threw her head back for a belly laugh, grabbed her hat before it toppled off her head again, and stepped out the door of the plane.

Caroline leaned against the window, watching Dr. Pipkin pick up her duffle bag and sling her backpack over the Mayan blanket on her right shoulder and walk toward the concourse. She heard Thomas cackling from the back of the plane. "Would you look at that, everybody?" Caroline turned to see them all looking out their windows. "That woman's still wearing my shoes."

Saturday evening in Moss Point

Sam picked them all up at the local airport and persuaded Acer, Leo, and Goodluck to join them for supper since they weren't flying out until Sunday morning anyway. Sitting next to him in the front seat, Caroline listened to his report of who was coming and what was going on to welcome them home.

"Why Twin Oaks hasn't hosted such a gathering since I was first elected judge in 1973. Your parents and your sisters-in law and all the kids are on the way. Angel's keeping Bella entertained while Sarah and Gretchen are in the kitchen helping Hattie prepare a feast for your homecoming. Even Mr. Handley decided to stay."

Caroline tried to take it all in. Three days ago, she hadn't known if she'd ever see Twin Oaks again, and now this old mansion was filled with happy and grateful people, sitting around the table, listening to her tell of her abduction and her time in the jungle. She fascinated them with tales of butterflies and yarrow poultices and a girl with chocolate-colored eyes.

Caroline's parents and brothers left not long after dinner for the three-hour drive home. Leo and Mr. Handley pulled the black sedan out of the garage and started the drive toward Rockwater. Goodluck and Acer grabbed their bags and followed Sam to his car.

A half an hour later after delivering Goodluck and Acer to the local motel, Sam's laughter entered the kitchen before he did. "You're not going to believe this. When I pulled out of the driveway, I nearly ran into Delia Mullins' truck parked on the street in the shadows. She had her telescopic camera lens out the window on the passenger's side. I can just imagine there'll be some murky photos of only Delia knows what in the Sunday edition of the *Moss Point Messenger* tomorrow."

Roderick and Caroline said their goodnights to Angel, Sarah, and Hattie. Gretchen and Bella had already moved their bags into the main house so that Caroline could spend her first night at home in the studio. Bella, who had barely left Caroline's side all evening, finally spoke. "Play the piano. Play Caroline's piano . . ."

Gretchen interrupted her. "No, not tonight, Bella. Caroline is very, very tired, and she needs to rest."

"No, no. I play the piano for Caroline."

Caroline winked at Gretchen. "Could she come and play one song? Just one?"

Gretchen smiled and took Bella's hand. "Bella, you may play one song. A sweet one. Maybe a lullaby for Caroline's sweet dreams."

Bella led the way, skipping down the moonlit stone path through the lilies and gardenias. Caroline watched her silently staring at the empty bird's nest in the hanging basket of Swedish ivy at the kitchen entrance of the studio while Roderick unlocked the door. She swished around them and rushed to the piano.

Roderick led Caroline into the studio. The lamp on her desk was the only light in the room, but it cast its warm glow for Caroline to see that everything was as she had left it just over a week ago. Everything except the crystal vase filled with fresh white irises and the card on the table next to her chair.

"Oh, my, the irises." She picked up the note. Beautifully penned letters, which filled up the front of the card, read, "You followed your heart, and welcome home. We missed you."

Caroline looked more carefully at the card—an intricate border of blue butterflies encircled the words almost like a hem of lace. Underneath were Gretchen's and Bella's signatures. "The card is so beautiful. Did you make it?" Caroline fingered the edge, feeling the indentation of the butterfly drawings.

"Yes. I did the calligraphy. That is a new hobby for me. And Bella stopped drawing the butterflies when there was no more room around the edge." Gretchen stepped behind Bella, who was already seated on the piano bench, and placed her hands on Bella's shoulder.

Caroline looked up at Roderick standing next to her. "Blue butterflies. It's beautiful. So very beautiful." Caroline went to Bella and kissed her silky hair. "Thank you, my sweet Bella. Now will you play for me?"

Bella had begun playing before Caroline could reach her favorite chintz-covered chair, the one that hugged her. Roderick helped her sit down and stood behind her.

"Bella, you are playing your new song." Gretchen moved away from the piano and knelt at Caroline's feet and whispered, "This is her composition. She started playing and singing it on Thursday. She plays it over and over. I think this is why she drew the blue butterflies."

Caroline rested her head on the back of her chair to listen. The melody was simple, delicate, and lingering, and for a moment, she thought she recognized it.

Then Bella, with a voice as clear as a crystal bell, began to sing.

Flowers with wings you are, how does it feel to fly?
Silent angels you are, please don't fly too high.
You have no song, so I will sing. You can fly, be my wings.

Caroline closed her eyes as her tears came. Remembering a velvety, darker voice humming the same melody as though it came from somewhere deep, Caroline's spirit floated with images of swirling butterflies and a small child with chocolate-colored eyes. She hummed with Bella.

Bella finished her song, rose from the piano, and took Gretchen's hand. They quietly closed the back door without disturbing Caroline.

Caroline hummed a moment longer before she realized Bella was no longer playing. She opened her eyes and turned to Roderick. "Where are they?"

"They left a moment ago. Come, my love, you need to rest."

She took the arm he extended and rose from her chair. She walked to the piano and fingered the melody and looked out across the shimmering surface of the pond in the garden.

Roderick spoke when Caroline stopped playing. "You already knew the tune, didn't you?"

Caroline moved toward him and nodded her head in silence.

He put one arm around her, cupped her quivering chin in the palm of his hand, and drew her close to him. "I could tell. You know I would have given all I have and even my life as a ransom for you and your song, don't you?"

One tear rolled down her cheek. She nodded in silence again and looked up at him. "Just as Bella sang, 'You have no song, so I will sing. You can fly, be my wings.'"

Roderick looked into deep blue eyes. "Forever and always."

Acknowledgments

As always, I begin by thanking you, the reader, for spending a few hours with my story. You bring it to life. I hope this book took you to new places and encouraged you to ask some questions. My desire, too, is that you learned a bit about the beautiful country of Guatemala and its culture. Thank you for your time in making the story leave its pages and live in your imagination for a while.

For all the friends, young and old, who have journeyed with me to Guatemala, I give thanks. Those shared experiences with you shaped my life and strengthened my faith.

Every writer longs for an editor like Leslie Peterson. She not only understands my "Southern," she also understands and corrects my broken Spanish. Whatever I write is always better because Leslie tends to it. Thank you, my friend.

Jordan Smith, with patience and encouragement, helped bring this book to you. He understands the jots and tittles and the beauty of the word on the page. How grateful I am for one who understands all the mechanics.

And just as I am always grateful for readers, I am grateful for my husband Bill. He is patient like Job, encouraging like John the Beloved, instructive like the Apostle Paul, and fearless like King David. He has led me to places where I would never have ventured and to adventures I would never have dreamed possible.

And to my Father, Master Creator and World-Maker, how grateful I am to You for eyes to see what You are doing and ears to hear You. Thank you for allowing me to tell your Truth, as best I understand it, through my stories and the characters You inspire me to create.

About the Author

Phyllis Clark Nichols's character-driven Southern fiction explores profound human questions using the imagined residents of small town communities you just know you've visited before. With a strong faith and a love for nature, art, music, and ordinary people, she tells redemptive tales of loss and recovery, estrangement and connection, longing and fulfillment … often through surprisingly serendipitous events.

Phyllis grew up in the deep shade of magnolia trees in South Georgia. Born during a hurricane, she is no stranger to the winds of change. In addition to her life as a novelist, Phyllis is a seminary graduate, concert pianist, and cofounder of a national cable network with health- and disability-related programming. Regardless of the role she's playing, Phyllis brings creativity and compelling storytelling.

She frequently performs half-hour musical monologues that express her faith, joy, and thoughts about life—all with the homespun humor and gentility of a true Southern woman.

Phyllis currently serves on a number of nonprofit boards. She lives in the Texas Hill Country with her portrait-artist, theologian husband.

Website: PhyllisClarkNichols.com

Facebook: facebook.com/Phyllis Clark Nichols

Twitter: twitter.com/PhyllisCNichols

CPSIA information can be obtained
at www.ICGtesting.com
Printed in the USA
LVHW021159130521
687331LV00008B/339